Christy Hadfield Publications

I0738267

Burnout

Christy Hadfield

Christy Hadfield Publications

Christy Hadfield Publications trade paperback edition 2022

Designed by Christina Hadfield

Text set in Baskerville Old Face

ISNB-13: 978-0-578-35175-9

ISBN-13: 978-0-578-35176-6 (Ebk)

This book is dedicated to my partner,

early days spent reading and editing this book together,

your hilarious comments inspired me to finish this.

Thank you.

Burnout

Part 1.

Florida & New Friends

1.

Two Pregnant Women Sitting On A Bench

"And you got there fine? No issues? And everything looks good with the reservations?"

"Yep, everything is fine, no problems at all," I stated, shifting my phone so I could pin it with my shoulder, fishing through the bag strapped to my waist. "I went out to the park yesterday, no issues. And I'm back again today."

"Well just let me know if you have any problems. I can't say we'd be much help, but we could probably catch a plane down to Florida tomorrow."

"I'll be fine, dad."

"I know. It's your mother I'm worried about."

And, as if on cue: "Natalie? Is that Natalie? Are you talking to Natalie on the phone, Bob?"

I zipped my bag shut and shifted my arms, so I was once again holding my phone in my hand.

"Yeah, I'm talking to Natalie. She says everything's fine."

"Give me the phone. I want to talk to her."

"Sorry, sweetheart, your mother—"

I heard commotion as my dad's phone traded hands over to my mother.

"Natalie? Oh thank goodness you're fine. You know, I was expecting a call yesterday and when I never got one..."

"Mom, I told you I wasn't going to call until later," I sighed. "I sent you the text when I landed so you'd know I wasn't dead. I figured that would cover until I got some more down time."

"Well a prompter call would have been nicer."

"I'm doing a lot of stuff, mom. Trying to make the most of my vacation. Is dad still there?"

"I'm just not so sure how I feel about you being in Florida all by yourself. I know you're at the park, but I just, the world isn't the nicest of places for young women—"

"I'm literally fine, mom. You sent me off to college for the past four years 'alone.' I don't see how this is any different. Just pretend I'm at school."

"—and frankly, you know I really wished you would have listened to me and gone down to the Caribbean with Lizzie. She's such a nice young lady, you know, and—"

"Mom, she's probably doing drugs right now. Lizzie is *not* the ideal role-model—"

"At least you wouldn't be alone!"

"I could have gone backpacking in Europe alone."

"Don't be sassy with me!"

"Look, mom," I stated, "I've got to go. I'm in line for a ride right now, and I'm about up to the single-rider cut-off point. If I don't go now, I'll be stuck here for an hour."

"I need more frequent updates from you. I think it's ridiculous that you went off galivanting just a few months before graduation and you don't even have a solid plan for your life."

"You just said you'd rather me be in the Caribbean!"

"Rather you not be alone, but also rather you put some effort into your future! You didn't apply to any grad schools, Natalie, and you've hardly even tried to find a job! You know, we aren't just going to support you while you sit at home and do nothing—"

"When did I say I was going to move back home and do nothing?"

"Well, your lack of planning tells me that's your only option."

I pulled my phone away from my ear, pressing it against my shirt, and let out a loud groan of frustration. Slowly, I raised my phone up to my ear again.

"Oh, what was that? I think we're breaking up, mom. Must be the building they house the ride in," I said.

"Don't you even try that with me, young lady! You say this every time we call—"

"*Ahh,* oh man, I can't even—what was that? Yeah, I can't hear you. Call you later."

I hung up on my mother and shoved my phone into my pack. Maybe part of the reason I chose to vacation alone was because I was so sick of my mother harking on me about my life choices twenty-four-seven! I shook my head and rolled my eyes. I noticed the couple in line in front of me kept stealing glances in my direction.

"Parents, right?" I stated. "I come from a family of seven. Just want some freedom for a while, you know?"

"Wow, seven, that's an awful lot."

"Totally," I agreed.

By then, the line had moved far enough forward that I could dash into the single-riders section of the line. That had to be the best thing about going to an amusement park by yourself. I could fly through ride lines much faster and in fact, on only my second day in the park, I had already been on every ride multiple times all thanks to that trick.

When I reached the loading docks of the ride, I had to stop at the gate for a moment. The worker manning the station made small talk, asking why I was riding alone.

"I'm here by myself," I answered. "I'm at college in Orlando and I got season tickets. My friends were busy this week, but I figured I might as well get my money's worth."

Before long, I was on the ride and already back off. I collapsed onto a bench outside, soaking in the hot spring Orlando sun. A man pushing a baby stroller wheeled over to me and sat beside me, messing around with a diaper bag.

"Gorgeous day, huh?" I questioned. "Having a fun family vacation?"

"Yeah, we thought the kids were getting old enough to come out and have some fun. I think it's spring break for a lot of colleges though. The park's packed."

"Yeah, I'm actually a college kid here on spring break," I stated with a laugh. "I'm an economics major, but I want to open my own amusement park someday, so I'm here doing research."

"That's pretty interesting."

The man looked away from me and I looked away from him. I realized that I was *really* bored. I was so bored, in fact, that I had resulted to lying to strangers, just making up fake backstories about myself. It was because I was embarrassed about my true reasons for being on vacation alone.

My phone started buzzing and I fished around in my bag to pull it out. I noticed I had a plethora of missed calls from my mother just in the short amount of time I was on the ride. Begrudgingly, I took out my phone and answered.

"Hey look, I'm off the ride and have cell reception again, crazy."

"Natalie, that's not funny," my mother declared. "Look, I'm going to email you some things, okay? Your aunt Deedee found a bunch of job postings that I think you might be really interested in."

"Mom, I'm on vacation!"

"And the world waits for no one. You know all your classmates and thousands of college seniors all over the nation are graduating and filling up all the jobs, so you need to be proactive. I still think you should go to grad school, but I'm okay with you taking a year off. But you have to work! Look at what I sent you; I think some of them are really promising."

"Mom, I went on this vacation so I could get away from school and work and all this stuff. It's only a week. I'll be fine."

"And make sure you get rid of that hideous hair color. Interviewers are not going to take kindly to your pink hair."

"I don't want to work for a place that's going to dictate how I look."

"Pink hair is childish, Natalie, and you're an adult now. You need a nice natural hair color. It will make you look more mature."

"My actions will make me look mature."

"Your actions? You mean like how you didn't apply to grad school, and you aren't applying to any jobs?"

"Oh geez, what was that? You're breaking up again... I gotta go."

"Natalie!"

"Bye!"

"*Natalie!*"

Click. I hung up. She was right; I didn't apply to grad school, and I hadn't been proactively applying to jobs. It was because I picked biology as my major, after my ER doctor mother pressured me into it, and now four years later I realized I didn't like biology that much. There was no way I was going to become a doctor—from my less than perfect grades alone—and I didn't want to do research work, which was essentially all graduate biology school was. My job options then, with only a bachelor's degree, were pretty much limited to lab technician work, and I hated doing lab work! But of course, I realized all this my last semester of undergrad when it was too late to change majors.

I was sick of all my college friends getting acceptance letters into other schools and landing jobs right after graduation when I had nothing to celebrate. I felt lonely, unmotivated, and left behind. So, when the option

12

to vacation alone in Florida arose—alone, without the constant reminder that I had picked a terrible major, hated all possible job prospects, and didn't know what I was going to do—I snatched it as quickly as I could and fled.

But now I was bored, which was why I had defaulted to making up lies about myself to share with various strangers. It was fun, for a while, to voice fantasies and pretend to be someone else. Now though, I was just sad those people weren't me. I needed something else to occupy my time. I'd already been on every ride, walked all over the park multiple times, and I still had six more days stuck at the park!

I started looping through one of my favorite rides, figuring it was more time efficient to just ride one ride over and over again as opposed to hiking all over the park in between. The ride ended in a giftshop, so afterwards I'd make the short trek back to the ride entrance, start over again, rinse and repeat.

On my seventh loop around, I passed by a bench with a pregnant woman sitting on it.

I didn't think much of this observation. I mean, yes, I noticed that she was pregnant, but it was more of a passing thought. Lots of women get pregnant every year. She was not the first pregnant woman I'd ever seen, and she wouldn't be the last.

While I was waiting a few minutes to board the ride again—waiting for the next cart to pull up and reload—I found myself reading the safety-warning sign out of boredom. *'Do not ride if you have a medical sensitivity to strobe effects. Do not ride if you have heart or back problems. Do not ride if you become motion sick, lightheaded, or are prone to fainting. Do not ride if you are pregnant. Do not ride if—'* Wait a minute. This was the same sign, verbatim, that was hanging up at all the rides. If someone was obviously pregnant, there was no way the workers would let them on any of the rides. Now the pregnant woman had me a bit curious. Was she stuck watching the bags while the rest of her family was off enjoying themselves? What a boring time... more boring even than my perpetual ride riding self-inflicted hell.

After that ride through, I was quoting the ride's story by memory. If I went through it one more time, I might actually lose my mind, which meant as inconvenient as it may be, it was time to find a different ride. As I headed out of the gift shop exit, I once again stumbled into the pregnant woman sitting on the bench.

She was, without a doubt, pregnant. Sometimes a woman can look pregnant without actually being pregnant, and then, when you ask when her due date is, she gets super offended—and rightfully so. That wasn't the case with this woman, however. I was convinced. She was stick thin everywhere except for her belly, which was protruding out a very noticeable amount. I slowed and considered my options.

I could continue doing what I had been doing for the past couple days, which was ride the same rides over and over again, or I could go out of my way to strike up a conversation with this random stranger. I went on this vacation to be alone... to remain alone by choice. Being polite to a friendly stranger was different than seeking out company with a stranger, which was the precise opposite of a lone adventure. But I was *so* bored.

I walked towards the woman, or rather towards the bench she was sitting on. She was petite and young, mid-twenties to low thirties if I had to guess—around my age, but probably a bit older. I noticed her hair color was similar to my own natural hair color: a mousey brown. She sat at one end of the bench, the other side unoccupied, so I sat down a good distance from her, still contemplating what I wanted to do.

If she noticed me, she made no mention of it. I tried to think of something to say to her, but I couldn't think of much. It was very unlikely we had anything in common, seeing as she was a mother-to-be and I was well... an idiot kid. I was bored though, and perhaps a bit curious, so I pushed my brain harder to think up a topic of discussion. Defaulting to basic white-people manners, I settled on bringing up the weather.

"Sure is a nice day," I stated, my voice coming out a bit louder and harsher than intended. I got the woman's attention though, as she turned and glanced at me. She nodded towards me politely but said nothing in return.

We sat in silence for a few moments more. I had nothing to offer, really, in terms of conversation, and she didn't seem entirely inclined to talk, so I considered leaving her be. I glanced down at my phone to check the time. It was barely 9:30 in the morning. I needed *something* to help pass the time, otherwise I was going to have a miserably boring and long day. Throwing caution to the wind, I turned back to the woman ready to give it my all.

"You've been sitting here awhile," I said. "I noticed because I've been walking past this bench all morning."

The woman glanced back at me, a peculiar sort of smirk on her face. I thought she was going to further ignore me, but then she cracked a full smile.

"I've noticed you too, actually," she answered. "Not very many people here have shoulder length, cotton-candy pink hair."

She had me there. I felt like the pink hair was almost part of my identity at that point. I thought about commenting on my appearance, explaining how it was my staple, but before I could, the woman continued.

"You're only ever going that direction though…" She pointed towards the entrance of the ride.

"Yes, well, that's because I've been riding that monstrosity all morning," I replied, gesturing to the building in front of us which housed the ride. "I have to walk from the gift shop where the ride ends back to the entrance over there to get back on."

"Wait, so you've just been riding one ride all morning?" she questioned.

"Yep."

"How?" she asked. "The wait time's an hour and a half." She narrowed her eyes at me suspiciously, and I found it a bit funny.

I took pity on her and explained my quick trick, which she agreed was ingenious. In doing so, however, I also had to explain that I was at the park alone, though I left out the details as to why.

"Anyway, are you here alone too?" I questioned innocently. I figured that she wasn't, but it wouldn't hurt to ask.

"No, actually, I'm here with some friends," she answered. "They dragged me off on a girls' getaway despite my current condition—" she gestured to her belly. "And anyway, they promised they wouldn't leave me alone, yet here I am, by myself."

"That's truly unfortunate," I said, shaking my head. "I'm alone by choice, but I have some spare time. I'll keep you company until your friends return."

"That's very considerate of you, but I'm actually not waiting alone. One of my friends is pregnant as well. We were waiting together but she's gone off to the bathroom."

Feeling comedic, I tipped my head down and jerked it back up as dramatically as I could, an over-the-top gasp escaping my lips. "You're pregnant!?" I gasped as ridiculously as I could.

The woman pursed her lips, but only for a second before a heavy laugh replaced her scowl. "You're kind of funny," she stated.

"Thank you," I replied. "I considered pursing comedy, but well, I chose biology instead."

"Are you a college student then?" she asked. I nodded. "That's pretty funny, actually," she continued, "because I just so happen to teach high school biology."

"Oh really?" I questioned with an impressed nod. "High school... that must be rough."

She gave me a skeptical look. "Yeah, and how far out of high school are you?"

"I'm actually in my last semester of undergrad," I answered honestly. "But even if I was younger, you have to admit that a high school senior is still far more tolerable than a high school freshman."

"I guess you have a point there."

"Do you teach freshmen by chance?" I followed up, feeling sympathetic if she did. I couldn't image dealing with me when I was fourteen, let alone a hundred other hormonal, emotional, dramatic teenagers.

"I mainly teach juniors," she answered. "My other pregnant friend, well she teaches public speaking to the freshmen. She says they're nightmares. You don't have to feel all bad for her though. She also teaches psychology to juniors and seniors... helps her maintain some of her sanity. I truly feel bad for our freshmen algebra teacher, though."

"Are you and your friend coworkers then, since you both teach?" I asked.

"Yes. We've been working together for several years now."

"That's pretty cool... being close to your coworker like that," I stated, thinking about working alongside my best friends. "Where do you work? Here in Florida?"

"No, Georgia," she replied. "We drove here for spring break."

"No way!" I laughed out loud. "I'm from South Carolina myself, but I'm going to school in Georgia! I'm at Georgia State!"

"*Ahh*, GSU," she said with a knowing smirk. "We teach a few miles from your campus."

"Shut up!" I exclaimed. "What a small world! Since we're basically neighbors, mind me asking your name?"

"Piper," the woman stated. "Ms. Kegan to my students."

I couldn't help but notice that she said 'Ms. Kegan' and not 'Mrs. Kegan.' My eyes instinctively fell to her hand, searching for a ring. I could have missed it, but I didn't spot any jewelry on her fingers. I kept my mouth shut though. It wasn't any of my business if she was or was not married.

"I'm Natalie," I answered, extending my hand for her to shake. "Ms. Natalie Benton to my teachers."

"So, you're a biology major. Great choice," she said with a wink, offering me a fist to bump.

Surprisingly enough, we had a fair bit in common, much more than I was expecting. We were from the same city, somehow, miraculously, and we even both liked biology. Having two things in common didn't mean we were going to be instant friends, but it was enough for a nice conversation. I was glad I hadn't made up a backstory for myself and just went with the truth for once. I was eager to keep talking to Piper, ask her for a funny school story or something, but before I could, we were interrupted.

Another woman approached the bench, her phone in her hand which she extended to Piper. The newcomer was tall. She was fit, muscular arms, not stick-like as Piper was. Her hair was long as well, a rich warm brown that complemented her tanned skin and dark eyes. Oh, and she was pregnant, even more so than Piper.

"Look at what Eleanor sent me! The imbecile!" the new woman hissed, shoving her phone at Piper.

Piper took the phone but pointed her attention towards me. "This is Natalie," Piper said with stressed syllables. "She's a senior at GSU, a biology major."

"Hi," I muttered a bit sheepishly.

Piper held the other woman's phone and was looking at it, reading a text as far as I could tell from my position. I looked over at the new woman, clearly Piper's friend and coworker, the one who taught public speaking and psychology. There was anger in her eyes, but she looked more hurt than anything. I considered excusing myself, thinking I was interrupting their rather personal conversation, but before I could, the newcomer spoke to me.

"Left alone waiting for your friends to get off a ride?" she questioned.

"Actually, I'm here by myself," I answered.

Piper finished reading the text message and passed the phone back to her friend. "You shouldn't take things to heart," Piper stated. "You know she says stupid, hurtful things when she's upset... things she doesn't actually mean."

Suddenly, the woman dropped down on the bench between Piper and me. She sighed heavily. "I hate her," she said sharply, but then she immediately buried her face in her hands. "I hate pregnancy hormones," she then grumbled a second later, promptly shaking as she began to cry. I raised my eyebrows in concerned confusion as Piper rubbed circles on her friend's back.

Piper leaned forward so she could speak to me around her wailing friend. "This is Karmen Caballero," Piper whispered to me.

"I should, um, get going," I muttered out, suddenly finding the situation very awkward and uncomfortable. "It was, um, nice meeting you both."

I jumped up from the bench and hurried away as fast as I could before either of the women could stop me, although I didn't figure they would try. It might have been a bit silly of me to just run away, but I didn't want to further impose myself. If I were Karmen, currently crying hysterically after some 'Eleanor' sent me an awful text, I wouldn't want a stranger sitting around and meddling. I decided that I absolutely did not want to continue walking past *that* bench, so I moved on to a different ride.

I spent my time meandering between park locations. On the one hand, a nice break from the stress of my life was welcomed. I didn't have to deal with a constantly nagging mother—when I kept my phone on silent—and I didn't have to laugh awkwardly and say, *"You know, I'm going to get a job and just save up some money,"* every time someone asked me what my plans were post-graduation. But on the other hand, being alone meant I was victim to my thoughts.

I just didn't really think I wanted to focus on biology for the rest of my life. But jumping ship meant I wasted the past four years of my life striving for a major I didn't even want. My mom was probably right. I should just suck it up and get a lab job somewhere. Maybe I'd enjoy it more than I thought. Natalie the Scientist... I didn't really like the sound of that, but I could have far worse titles. And either way, in exactly two months, one week, and two days I would be graduating with a degree, so I could at least use that to my advantage.

As of the present, however, I had a vacation to enjoy, and dammit, I was going to enjoy it. The weather was nice, I was responsibility free until I returned to school, and I had free time to just live and enjoy the freedom of life while I still could. I wanted to have an adventure, do something fun, and make some memories. I dashed off to another ride.

This ride was a simulation, housed in a big theater type building. The ride played a little video and the cart you sat in moved along with the video. However, it was making me a bit motion sick. The issue was the 3D glasses. I rode it twice without issue, then took a few minutes to compose myself, debating if I had it in me to go again. Back in the fresh air of the outside world, I felt mildly better and cockishly confident, so I headed back in.

I hopped back into line easily. Because the ride sat four to a row and I was a single rider, the worker at the top of the ride's stairway sent me to join the line behind a party of three. And, since it was a simulation, we had to wait outside until the previous group finished. I leaned against the railing of the upper-level deck, gazing out at the rest of the park from my vantage point.

"You're being a real jerk to her, don't you think?"

I glanced to the party in front of me out of the corner of my eyes. Trying not to intrude, I turned my back to them and acted overly interested in the paint job of the railing.

"It's not as if she doesn't deserve it."

"You both did horrid things. Stop acting like you're blameless."

"Well, I am! She's done far more horrid things to me!"

"You've both done equally horrid things to each other, and I'm sick of you acting like it's all her fault when you are *clearly* also at fault!"

I pursed my lips. I didn't want to be overhearing their conversation, but they were being kind of loud and they were the only other people in that section of the line with me. I cast another sideways glance at the trio. They were all women, in their twenties, maybe very early thirties.

The one being scrutinized by her friends—the one who was also, clearly, at fault—was a gorgeous black woman. She was rocking a fluffy, grown out afro, her dark eyes shining like daggers in her anger. She seemed quite unhappy.

The woman who had initially caught my attention, who shouted out the first thing I heard, was a tiny little thing, far shorter than me by a good foot or more. She was covered head to toe wearing jeans and a long-sleeved shirt. I wouldn't have been able to handle her outfit in this heat—I would have had a heat stroke—but I figured she was dressed that way for religious reasons if the hijab she wore was any indication.

The remaining woman, for the most part, had been avoiding the conversation. However, she was the one who got in the last comment, and she sounded utterly exhausted with the whole situation. This woman was basically my height, perhaps a bit shorter, and she contrasted the others with her pale skin and rounder face. He hair was a perfect platinum blonde, styled in a slight beach wave that hung down to her shoulders, just barely longer than my hair.

The blonde caught me staring and I turned away awkwardly.

"I think you should talk to her. As in, have an actual, civil conversation," the one in the hijab continued, ignoring the blonde's outburst.

"There's nothing to talk about," the irritated black woman huffed. "She got pregnant again, so it's 'end of discussion.'"

"Oh, because texting her rude insults is totally 'end of discussion,'" I heard the blonde remark, and I could almost hear her eye roll and air quotes.

"You know she loves kids," the other continued, but her friend lashed out again, causing her to shrink back a step.

"I told her it was over if she ever slept with him again, and now I come to find out she's been sleeping with him all along! How do you think that makes me feel!?"

"Shut up!" the blonde suddenly screamed over her friend. "You dragged me here for a 'week of fun,'" she mocked, "and now I have to put up with this crap! Shut up and enjoy this freaking ride or so help me I will—"

The door next to the blonde opened and a worker appeared beside her. "How many?" he asked with a fake smile plastered on his face. He could probably overhear all their shouting from just inside and was trying to hide his obvious irritation.

The blonde turned to the worker and tensed, but then she let out a breath and relaxed some. "Three," she said, glancing back at her friends, but then her eyes settled on me. "Oh, and that one too."

I cocked an eyebrow, surprised and a bit curious as to why she felt the need to mention me as part of their group. We hadn't even said anything to one another that would warrant such inclusion. The worker stepped aside, letting them in, and I meekly followed after the trio. We lined up on the waiting dock with several other groups of people where we were forced to stand through a legally required safety video.

A second passed before anyone spoke and when someone finally did, it was the blonde addressing not one of her friends, but *me*.

"I thought you'd like to ride with us," she stated.

I was going to be placed next to them whether I wanted to ride with them or not. Though, it was nice of her to consider me. "Thank you," I replied. "It's awfully considerate of you to adopt me."

"Not a problem," the blonde told me with a wink. Then she turned around to her friends and left me staring at her back like an utter fool.

She was *really* cute.

I shook my head slightly to clear my mind. Although my friends considered the only benefit of my solo vacation to be that I could hook up with cute girls without my friends cock-blocking me, that was absolutely not something I planned on doing. My last sort of relationship ended messily when I realized I couldn't juggle a girlfriend *and* the mess that was trying to figure out the rest of my life, and now, with the impending doom of graduation, I was pretty sure romance would only further complicate the problem. I was trying to take a relaxing break from people and life in general. It didn't matter if I thought this random woman was cute and oddly charming, albeit a bit hot-headed. That was all she was ever going to be to me: a cute woman that I saw once in passing. The end.

Pulling myself out of my thoughts, I realized the trio in front of me was now oddly quiet. The one woman was still fuming, her arms crossed tightly across her chest. I looked back to the one wearing the hijab and I couldn't help but think that she reminded me of a librarian. It was a major assumption on my behalf, of course, but she just seemed overly sweet and a bit nerdy, like a bookworm. And because I was observing her so closely, I realized that she looked like she was about to cry. The blonde seemed to come to the same conclusion, as she grabbed the librarian-like one, pulling her close, and promptly smacked her other friend on the arm.

"Apologize to Ellie 2.0 for yelling at her like that!" the blonde snapped. "Right now!"

"She was asking for it!" the grouch of the group huffed like a spoiled child. The blonde threatened to smack her again. "Fine, I'm sorry," she forced out. The librarian nodded but was still clearly upset.

A moment later and the ride opened up, allowing us to climb in. While we waited the short moment for everyone to get in and get situated, I found myself wondering about the name Ellie which the blonde had called out. It would be a hilariously odd coincidence if this Ellie was the Eleanor that Pregnant Karmen from the bench was so mad at. Although it would be funny, I couldn't picture the librarian harassing anyone to the point of Karmen's anger. It had to just be a coincidence. And besides, I had no plans of returning to said bench, so it would just have to remain a mystery.

After that round of the ride, I knew I couldn't handle another go around. My stomach was twisting, and I felt like I was having a hot flash, a high sign that if I didn't stop, vomit would soon be on its way. I decided to meander on to a different ride, taking my time so I could breathe in the fresh air and let my stomach settle. However, I wasn't paying that much attention to my path, and I suddenly realized, too late, that I had turned the wrong way and accidently ended up right back at the bench where Karmen and Piper were. And surprise, they hadn't moved. I considered sneaking past them, but before I could, Piper spotted me and waved. Since we locked eyes, I felt obligated to stop, so I walked towards them with fake excitement.

"Hey, guys," I stated. "It sure must suck not being able to ride anything. When are the kids due? We might be able to get you both back out here tomorrow for some fun!"

Piper grinned at my stupid humor attempt. Karmen scoffed, but she was clearly still feeling down, and my dumb joke wasn't about to alleviate all of that.

"I've got four more months," Piper answered me, "but she's got two."

"Nearly ready to pop!" I laughed towards Karmen, but as I mentioned, she really wasn't feeling it. She gave a sort of shrug in response.

I felt bad for Karmen. Well, I felt bad for them both, as their friends had clearly abandoned them and they were basically just sitting around, unable to enjoy the main part of an amusement park: the rides. Their friends were jerks for abandoning them, especially with Karmen working through some personal stuff.

I couldn't help but ask, "So, your friends are still not back, huh?"

"They were here just before you first came over," Piper explained. "We have a little... well drama in the friend group right now. There're some issues between Eleanor and Karmen, and they decided they weren't talking to each other. In the name of amnesty, the others took Eleanor off to ride some rides, let off some steam, while I stay here with Karmen."

"I'm sorry you guys are working through some beef," I said. "Friend group drama is literally the worst. I hope it all works out."

I was about to excuse myself again and leave the awkward mess that was none of my business, but I found my feet glued in place. Karmen was whimpering out the most pitiful sounds I've ever heard, and unfortunately, I was fiercely protective of women and *hated* when a girl cried. Call me empathetic or whatever, but I just wanted to help her feel better, even though I knew logically that I couldn't. I also found myself locked in place because I was overly curious if that trio I ran into was, by some miracle, their absent friends.

I hesitated further but felt my resolve break. "*Umm...* curious question...," I muttered. "You wouldn't happen to call this Eleanor 'Ellie' ever, would you?"

"No," Piper answered. "She absolutely hates it when we call her Ellie. Why do you ask?"

I felt a sense of calm flood over me. Of course the three strangers I ran into weren't their friends. That would be just too crazy. It was already hard enough to believe that they taught in the same city I went to college in. I couldn't hope for that many magical links in one day.

"Oh, I just, well it's kind of funny actually," I replied. "I was in line behind this group a few minutes ago and one of them was called Ellie. I just thought it would have been a hilarious coincidence if they were your friends. Of course, they aren't though. That would have been just too crazy."

Karmen looked up at me with puffy red eyes. "What did they look like?" she asked, perhaps a tinge of desperation to her words.

"Oh, well, um... let's see," I thought out loud. "There was a black gal rocking an afro... one wearing a hijab—I kind of think she looks like a librarian—and the other one was well... blonde."

"It probably was them, actually," Piper admitted.

"Yeah, those are definitely our friends," Karmen muttered out. She took an unsteady breath, shaking her head slightly.

"Wait, really?" I questioned, too shocked to really process.

"It would be near impossible that you ran into a different, equally diverse group of women that also had one called 'Ellie,'" Piper said all too logically. "Eleanor Taylor, she's the one with the afro. She teaches physics at our school. The blonde—a great way to describe her—her name's Amelia Lewis. She's our choir director. And lastly, the one you described as a librarian, her name is Eleanor as well, but we call her Ellie, Ms. Abdullah. She's not a librarian, but she does teach English, and that's basically the same thing, right?"

"Crazy," I muttered. I thought back to the trio and their spat I overheard. Eleanor... the grouchy one currently fighting with Karmen... that made a lot more sense. I looked back to Karmen, who continued to look miserable. "Look," I said, addressing Karmen. "I know it's none of my business, but Eleanor seemed really... vocally emotional about whatever is going on between you two. I don't mean to butt in, but maybe you two should talk."

"You're right," Karmen answered, and for half a second, I felt triumphant for my good suggestion. But then, she added harshly, "It *isn't* any of your business."

"Karmen, be nice, she's only trying to be helpful," Piper scolded. "You two *do* need to talk, and you know it. There's been enough of your fighting and playing petty. It's time to be real adults and have a civil conversation, and well, if you need a *college student* to tell you that, I welcome Natalie's input."

"I know we need to talk!" Karmen snapped. "I'm completely ready to sit down like adults and talk about things. It's Eleanor who keeps fighting me and being ridiculously childish! She's the one you should be convincing, not me!"

"Maybe you're right," I said, shrugging. "Maybe I could go find Eleanor again and convince her to come talk to you."

Piper looked at me like I was crazy, and to be honest, I was a bit surprised at the suggestion myself. Though I did want to ease Karmen's pain, I didn't want to butt into their personal problems. I had enough of my own personal problems to deal with without adding theirs on top. However, finding Eleanor and talking to her again meant that Amelia and Ellie would also be there... and I wasn't opposed to seeing that cute blonde again.

"Don't bother. She wouldn't listen to you anyway," Karmen huffed.

Karmen's denial only made me want to fight to prove myself. "Now give me a little more credit," I defended, hands on my hips. "I'm pretty good at sorting out problems, and in the very least, I'm good at listening. I mean, have you got a better idea on how to sort all this out?"

"Just ignore the problem until it goes away?" Karmen offered half-heartedly. Her answer was eerily familiar. That was exactly something I would do, would have always done. In fact, running away to Florida alone was basically me ignoring the impending doom of adulthood. But it's 'do as I say, not as I do,' right?

"No offense, but that's clearly not working out too well," I said. "I mean, I haven't got anything else I need to be doing. And it's not like I could make things worse; you two are already not talking to each other."

"Natalie, you don't have to, and you really shouldn't," Piper cut in. She sounded like a mother, or else a serious teacher, and I supposed both fit.

I fell down with a flop on the end of the bench next to Karmen. I didn't feel like exhausting myself arguing against them, but I now felt inclined to learn more about them. As I was thinking of something else to discuss, my eyes landed on a rather large ring on Karmen's ring finger, a fairly confident sign she was married. Curious about their lives, I asked, "So... what are the men up to?"

Piper grew reserved at my mention of this, which didn't entirely surprise me based on her current bare ring finger. I wasn't going to push. Karmen, surprisingly, let out a long sigh in response, and I wasn't sure how to interpret that.

"He's at home watching our two-year-old son," Karmen answered me.

"*Ahh,* so this isn't a first-time pregnancy for you," I concluded with a nod. "Got any pictures of your son?" I asked with the hope I could distract Karmen into a better mood. I was pretty confident all mothers carried around pictures of their kids at all times, and I never met a mother who was not excited to show off her kid.

As I suspected, Karmen did seem happy to oblige me. She pulled out her phone and handed it to me, showing a picture of a pretty cute toddler. His hair was brown, like his mother's, and it was shaggy, like he didn't have the patience to sit for a haircut.

I didn't really know what else to think. It was a kid. I realized I was more than old enough to be a mother. In fact, there were girls I went to high school with that had two kids by now! But I couldn't think of myself as old enough to have a child. I couldn't picture myself as a mother, not that I didn't want kids, but just that I still felt like a kid myself.

Speaking of feeling like an annoying, nosey kid, I was really tempted to open Karmen's messages and read the text Eleanor had sent her earlier. I refrained, luckily, because I didn't want to start any fights with my prying. I handed the phone back to Karmen before I could do anything regrettable, but as I did, I accidently hit the home button. The phone returned to its home screen revealing a picture of Eleanor. She looked happy in the picture, a vast contrast to the anger she wore when I last saw her. What confused me though was why Karmen had a picture of Eleanor as her phone's background image. I would have expected her son, or her husband, maybe a pet, or in the very least a beach, but not a coworker and friend she was currently feuding with.

As Karmen took her phone back, I asked what her son's name was.

"Michael," she answered.

I wasn't sure how to talk to Karmen about her motherhood, as I was very underexperienced in motherhood, but I tried to think of something reasonable to comment. I settled on, "*Aww,* that's an adorable name." I wasn't really sure if it was adorable or not. It was just a common boy's name to me. I continued, trying to sound relaxed. "Any significance as to why you named him that?"

"We named him after my abeulo," Karmen answered. "Michael is such a sweet boy... he reminds me of my abeulo sometimes, when the light is just right. But, well, he looks the most like his father. He's got his daddy's bright eyes, that's for sure."

"He's a real cutie."

"I just wish Eleanor would stop being such a jerk," Karmen nearly mumbled. "Why can't she see that her behavior is affecting more than just me? She's affecting Michael too, and Vanessa, and I just—"

"Hey, um, the offer still stands," I stated, bringing Karmen out of her thoughts. She gave me a distant look, so I puffed out my chest and sat up straighter. "No, I mean it," I declared more forcefully. "I will go find Eleanor and convince her to talk to you if you want me to. I'm serious."

"Natalie, I could never ask you to do that."

"You aren't asking. I'm offering."

"You know what, let her," Piper cut in. "What harm could it do? We aren't making any progress solving things on our own, and we're probably never going to run into another stranger so gung-ho about butting into your business. Just let her."

"I—fine," Karmen gave in.

"Perfect!" I exclaimed, a little too excitedly. I stilled myself a bit. I was excited to have a task to occupy my time with, a task that I felt confidence I could accomplish, and I was indeed excited at the possibility of getting to know Amelia more, but I didn't need to act so weird about it.

Piper gave me a quick run-down of the ride order the others claimed they were going on. I picked out the ride after the one I had first met them on, and then, with a smile, I bounded off. I had been gone a bit, probably long enough for them to move through the line and ride, so I decided to just wait for them outside the gift shop exit.

While I waited, I realized a few things. I knew their names now and was very excited to strike up another conversation with them, but none of them had any idea who I was or how I could possibly know them. That meant I would need to play it cool and not come on too strong. I also realized that in terms of my task, I had no idea how I was going to convince Eleanor to talk to Karmen. I didn't know anything about what happened between them. It could be something petty, or something super serious... it could be anything! I was smart though; I could generalize. I wasn't sure if a sob story would work on Eleanor, something along the lines of how miserable she was making poor Karmen, or if maybe something more logical would work.

As I tried desperately to construct a game plan, I climbed up on some fake rocks made of concrete to scan the top of the crowd. The ride let out, releasing a flood of people, and they swarmed out of the giftshop, huddled around a photobooth, laughing at their pictures from the ride.

I managed to spot Amelia first, not because I was purposefully looking for her specifically, but because her lighter complex stood out against the flood of typical brunette hair. Amelia grasped the trio's photo in her hands, skipping away from the others, laughing. Eleanor was chasing after Amelia, still furious, but clearly for a different reason now, as she was trying desperately to grab the picture away from Amelia.

"Give me that freaking picture, Amelia!" Eleanor shouted. The use of Amelia's name further confirmed they were indeed who I thought they were.

Poor little librarian-like Ellie looked after her friends meekly. She looked pale, a bit terrified, as if the ride had been too extreme for her liking. As the trio moved past me, I hopped down off my rock and followed.

Eleanor dove at Amelia and Amelia turned swiftly, swinging the picture up and out of Eleanor's reach. As she did this, I caught a glimpse of the picture. It was taken at one of the big drops in the ride. Amelia had both her hands straight up in the air, looking like she was having a blast. Ellie looked terrified. And then there was Eleanor, in perhaps the most unflattering pose to ever exist. I covered my mouth to suppress a laugh.

"Nope!" Amelia sung. "This is my prize! My souvenir!"

"I think I'm going to be sick," Ellie suddenly muttered from my immediate left.

I leapt to the side awkwardly, not realizing how close we got while I was busy looking at the picture. I hoped she didn't realize I was following them, but then again, she seemed a little preoccupied.

"Can we please stop for a minute?" the poor woman moaned. She looked green.

Amelia and Eleanor were going at it too hard to notice the distress Ellie was in, however. Amelia ducked around a few people and then leapt up onto a bench, holding the picture triumphantly high, out of Eleanor's reach. Taking what she could get, Ellie made her way to the bench and flopped down, holding her stomach, her eyes a bit glossy. Eleanor jumped after the picture, but Amelia easily deflected her away now that she had the higher ground. In that moment I came up with what was potentially a very dumb icebreaker, but it would work. I quickly jumped to their side.

"Excuse me," I stated, slipping into their view. Eleanor stopped jumping around and turned to face me. Amelia dropped her arm—and the picture—to her side.

"Hey, you're from that ride," Amelia recognized me.

"I am," I said with a nod. "Nice to see you again, my adopted family."

Amelia was momentarily distracted by my sudden appearance, giving Eleanor a window of opportunity to grab the picture from Amelia's hand. She snatched the ugly picture and jumped back from Amelia, cackling. Amelia let out a squeal of displeasure then lunged towards Eleanor. Frustrated at their lack of attention, I quickly jerked the picture out of Eleanor's hand as she dove back away from Amelia.

"Excuse you," Eleanor huffed.

"Look, I'm sorry to interrupt this," I stated, keeping the picture out of their reach for the time being. "It's just, well I'm in a real pickle, you see. I'm in desperate need of a physicist, an English expert, and a choir director. You guys wouldn't happen to know where I could find some of those, would you?"

Eleanor eyed me suspiciously. Ellie gagged towards a nearby trashcan—I felt sorry for her. Amelia simply stared at me. No one answered.

"Come on, I need help here," I pleaded, a fake pout on my lips. I lowered my arm—and the picture—as I let out a huff. "This is important!"

"Well... I'm a choir director," Amelia said, stepping down from the bench and towards me. "Eleanor here has a master's in physics and Ellie 2.0's an English major. It's not exact but well... we're high school teachers."

"She knows," Eleanor said, rolling her eyes, though I was hardly looking at her anymore now that Amelia was standing right in front of me. "Although, I want to know *how* she knows."

"She's probably one of your past students," Ellie muttered, sitting up from the trashcan only to collapse back against the bench. She looked perhaps a little better, but not by much.

Since my declaration, Amelia hadn't stopped staring at me. She stepped even closer towards me, resting her hand on my upper arm. "She isn't," Amelia practically purred in my face, "I would have remembered her." And then, before I could so much as think of a response—because I was having a lot of trouble thinking much of anything with Amelia so close—she ripped the picture out of my hand and jumped back with a shout of triumph. "Ha, take *that*, Eleanor!" Amelia squealed, jumping up and down. "This is mine forever now!"

"Stop acting like a maniac," Eleanor huffed. "Who is this pink-haired chick?"

"The name's Natalie," I stated. "I've been keeping these two pregnant gals company while their horrible friends are off having fun without them."

"You know Karmen and Piper?" Ellie questioned with genuine interest, most of the color returning to her face.

"I mean, I kind of just met them," I answered honestly. "But to be fair, they've been super nice. And once I found out you three were here with them, well, I wanted to come properly introduce myself."

"Are you here alone?" Amelia questioned.

"Yeah, actually," I replied with a shrug. "I thought it would be a nice, relaxing vacation, and it has been, but to be honest, I'm getting a little bored. That's why I offered to come talk to you guys."

"What do you mean 'offered?'" Eleanor questioned suspiciously.

"Look, you might not want to hear this," I said, turning to Eleanor, "but Karmen really wants to talk to you." As I said this, I could see the fight or flight response build in Eleanor.

"Thank god!" Amelia exclaimed. "Let's go and talk to Karmen and sort this whole mess out."

"No, I refuse!" Eleanor practically shouted.

"Stop being a baby!" Amelia yelled back. "You could fix all your issues if you'd just give her a chance to talk to you about it."

"We've tried to talk before," Eleanor continued. "That didn't do any good though, because she went and betrayed me!"

I cut in, trying to mediate. "I'm not trying to meddle here; it's your personal business. All I know is that you've got two pregnant friends sitting around being bored all day because you have this beef. And I don't know about you, but I don't think it's fair to leave Karmen bawling her eyes out all day, and likewise, I don't think it's healthy for you to be stewing angrily all the time. But you're never going to get past things and mend things unless you talk. And you need to fix things, right, because you guys work together, yeah? That means you can't avoid each other forever!"

"Yeah, easy for you to say, *Just talk it out.*' You don't have the slightest idea what even happened!" Eleanor snarled.

"You're right, I don't," I answered. "But trust me when I say that Karmen is really upset over all this, and she does still consider you to be her friend. And based on that alone, you *owe* her a civil conversation to try and save your friendship!"

"You don't even know the half of it!" Eleanor shouted. She pushed past Amelia to step closer to me, and suddenly I regretted pushing her. She looked past the point of being furious. I wasn't sure exactly what she was going to do, but I was about to get an earful. I braced myself as the yelling fit began. "I'll have you know that Karmen—"

Suddenly, Amelia jerked me back, stepping purposefully between Eleanor and me. She let go of me to turn and grab Eleanor tightly by both biceps, forcing eye contact. Then, in a forced whisper, Amelia stated, "We are at a family-friendly amusement park. This is not the place to be angrily yelling about your affair with another woman! There are *children!* Now calm down and come on." Amelia turned then, tugging Eleanor off along the path, and she snatched Ellie up in her other arm as she went.

I stared at their backs as they walked off, blinking in confusion, trying to process what I had just heard. And affair... with another *woman!?* I hadn't stopped to consider the potentially queer identities of any of the women I had just met, but I was happily surprised. I found myself selfishly more invested in their drama now that I knew it was queer. And I felt even more of a drive to one, get to know them better, and two, help them out. Quickly, I hurried after them, and, remembering the anger and tension, I tried to quell my excitement.

"Did you, um, say... an affair with another woman?" I questioned meekly after I cleared my throat.

"We are *not* discussing this here," Amelia snapped again. I fell silent.

I followed along behind them for a while. No one said anything. I was pretty sure Eleanor was further giving Amelia, and now me, the silent treatment, and Ellie seemed too meek to break the tension herself. Amelia seemed unhappy as well... fed up, perhaps, with the childish drama. However, quite suddenly, it seemed Eleanor realized we were heading back in the direction of one bench occupied by two pregnant women, and she got extremely vocal.

As if she had been struck by lightning, Eleanor reared up and kicked her way straight out of Amelia's arms. "No, don't you *dare* bring me to her!" Eleanor shouted. "I am not going to talk to her. She knows darn well that what she did was wrong, yet she did it to hurt me! I have nothing to say to her!"

"In the very least, you could listen to what she has to say," Ellie said.

"No, I've given her plenty of time to talk before," Eleanor huffed. "Give me my keycard. I'm going back to the hotel."

"Eleanor, stop it," Amelia chastised. "We're supposed to be here as a group of friends, yet we can't even all be together in the same place. I'm sick of it. We're going to all hang out and be civil, you and Karmen included, and we're going to have a good time. Now come on."

"No, give me my stuff," Eleanor said more forcefully, looking to Ellie. Ellie glanced between Amelia and Eleanor, questioning, before she slowly reached up and pulled the small backpack off her back.

"Ellie 2.0, don't you dare," Amelia warned.

"Amelia, come on. I can't keep her stuff from her, that's wrong," Ellie muttered. She was just starting to reach into the backpack when suddenly, Amelia grabbed the backpack out of her hands.

"No, Eleanor, you need to grow up!" Amelia shouted.

"Give me that!" Eleanor yelled, reaching for the backpack. "*You* need to grow up!"

Amelia jerked the backpack away, but she wasn't quite fast enough. Eleanor grabbed ahold of it, and they started a full-on tug-of-war struggle. Eleanor won, jerking the backpack out of Amelia's hands, stumbling back a step. She moved to reach inside and collect her things, but Amelia lunged at her again. And so, without much option, Eleanor just turned and ran, the backpack clasped tightly in her fist.

"Eleanor! Our room keys are in there! And all our money!" Amelia screamed after her. "Stop being a baby! Eleanor! Oh my god!"

"What are we going to do now?" Ellie practically wailed.

I was entirely shocked by Eleanor's behavior, but that wasn't the worry currently. It was clear this was a problem because Eleanor just took off with all of Amelia's and Ellie's things. It was a mess, and someone needed to stop Eleanor.

"I—I'll catch her," I stated with heroism I wasn't entirely confident of. "In the very least, I'll get your backpack, so you can get back into your hotel rooms." And then, before Amelia or Ellie could stop me, I took off in a sprint after Eleanor.

I began to question myself as I ran. What in the world was I doing? I just met those women, I didn't owe them anything, yet they had instantly roped me in. I blamed heteronormative culture for making me feel isolated, causing me to instantly latch on to anything even remotely queer, and consequently explaining my intense desire to get to know Eleanor and Karmen more. But I also blamed Amelia just because she was cute. No, I had to blame myself for that one. It was *my* fault I couldn't keep my thoughts on track. Running through the park though, I was committed. I was already giving them my 110% best effort. There wasn't any point in stopping now. I wasn't a quitter.

Eleanor was somewhere ahead of me. I saw her bobbing in and out of the crowd, but was still a bit behind her, unable to catch up. While my sights were focused on Eleanor, I failed to see the two men that came at me, and they grabbed my arm, flinging me off balance so that I fell straight to the ground.

Before I could even register what had just happened, the men were pulling me back up off the ground. They stood me upright and I took in their appearance, realizing they were park security officers.

"Where are you running off to?" the one questioned me.

"Where's the backpack? Did you stash it somewhere?" the other asked.

It took me a moment to regain my bearings, to which I replied, "What are you on about?"

"We got a call that some woman mugged another lady and stole her backpack, then ran off," the officer explained. "So, where's the backpack?"

Because I didn't figure Amelia or Ellie called park security on me, I pieced together that some bystander must have witnessed the exchange with Eleanor and just assumed it was an assault. Their physical description had to be off, as anyone with eyes could tell Eleanor and I were not the same person, but if they just said the mugger 'ran off,' well... I was running.

I quickly tried to rectify the situation. "No, no, it's all a misunderstanding. Our friend just ran off with the backpack because she's a freaking idiot. I guess... she wanted to get back to the hotel fast or something. I was just trying to catch up to her!"

"Yeah, likely story," the one officer muttered. He tugged on my arm, getting me to walk. "We're taking you back to the woman so she can identify you as her assailant. Then, you're going to show us where you stashed the backpack."

I just went along with them, figuring it was in my best interest to not protest. As we walked, I realized my elbow kind of hurt. I probably landed on it when I fell, and it was definitely going to bruise. I pursed my lips in mild annoyance.

This was just proof, physical evidence, of why you didn't let yourself get roped up into the drama of strangers right after you first met them. I should have just given up on them. It didn't matter if I had something in common with Eleanor and Karmen, and it didn't matter that I found Amelia attractive, because she was probably straight anyway.

The two security officers pulled me into a scene with Amelia and Ellie. The two women were seated at a bench with two different security officers questioning them.

"No, for the last time, I wasn't robbed, my *friend* simply took my backpack," Ellie exclaimed exasperatedly.

"But she... roughly took it from you against your will?" the one officer questioned.

"I mean... yes... but she's my friend! It's fine! Really, I just—"

"We caught her, but she dumped the backpack somewhere," one of the officers holding me cut Ellie off.

"I didn't dump the backpack. I didn't take it in the first place," I stated.

When Ellie heard me, she leapt up from the bench. "Oh golly! It's um... it's..." Her smile faltered when she realized she'd forgotten my name. That, or she was dry heaving into a trashcan when I introduced myself, I didn't quite remember. Either way, Amelia helped her out.

"It's Natalie," Amelia filled in. She grinned, her eyes locking with mine, and the intensity sent a wave of tingles straight down my spine.

To quote Ellie: *"Oh golly."*

"Is this the woman that stole your backpack?" one of the officers asked.

"No! Natalie was trying to help get my backpack *back*," Ellie corrected. "Really, this is all just a big misunderstanding! Please, everything is fine. We're perfectly okay."

"Yes, you can let Natalie go," Amelia said to the officers that were still holding me.

After another several minutes of the officers checking that Amelia and Ellie were absolutely, positively, sure that everything was okay, they finally released me and left us alone. I grumbled out an apology about not being able to catch Eleanor, but I was cut off by Amelia who immediately grabbed my wrist. She tugged me towards her and then, to my utter surprise, she started running her hands over me, lightly, inspecting for damage.

"*Umm...* what are you doing?" I coughed out awkwardly, feeling heat rise to my cheeks.

"I just wanted to make sure you were okay after you were manhandled by those security officers," Amelia answered, not slowing in her ministrations.

"Yeah, no, I'm totally fine," I stated, but when I said that, Amelia's hand brushed over my sore elbow, and I winced. Suspicious, Amelia flipped my arm over and found a bruise already forming.

"Natalie, this is hardly fine!" Amelia gasped. "We need to get you some ice."

My face flushed further. I could hardly focus with Amelia's close proximity. She smelled like vanilla, making my head spin. I didn't understand why she seemed so concerned with my health. It was just a little bruise. I'd be fine. It was hardly worth all the fuss.

I'm not sure what Amelia's next plan of action would have been, as Ellie cut her off. "I hate to be the bearer of bad news," she cut in, "but Eleanor took all our keycards, all our money, and our cell phones. How are we supposed to get ice, let alone find Karmen and Piper again?"

"We might just have to wait for them back at the hotel," Amelia sighed, releasing my arm. "Everyone's going to have to end up back there anyway."

I was worried their hotel was far away, so I asked, "What hotel are you staying at?" If it was far, I'd give them money for a cab just so they wouldn't have to walk.

"The Cabana," Amelia answered.

I nodded. The Cabana was one of the resort hotels located just off of park property, built close with the intention of allowing guests to just walk over to the parks. And, as a matter of fact, I was staying at the hotel right next to theirs.

"Well, come on, Amelia. Let's get going," Ellie stated, looping arms with Amelia to pull her forward. "We have plenty of time to enjoy the park tomorrow. And who knows, maybe we'll luck out and run into Eleanor back at the hotel."

"See you around, Natalie," Amelia said with a wink. Then she turned as Ellie pulled her forward.

I watched them go, biting my tongue. I wanted to follow them. I wanted to keep hanging out with them, get to know them better, spend more time in their company, but it wasn't my place to follow. And not only that, but it went entirely against my reasons for vacationing alone. I didn't need to be making new friends, especially friends with such drama. I needed to be detoxing from people and responsibility because I knew the second that I returned to school, I would be doomed. It was my last chance at complete and utter freedom. I couldn't waste it.

So, I turned on my heels and walked away in the opposite direction.

2.

The Guilt-Induced Return

I glanced down at my watch. It was around five, a good six hours since I was grabbed by park security, blamed with stealing Ellie's backpack. The park was open for several hours more, but all the screaming children really started getting to me, so I returned to my hotel room. I was on the trip to be alone, what did it matter if I was alone in the park or alone in my hotel room? Besides, my feet were really starting to hurt from all the walking.

I settled onto my hotel room bed, flicking on the TV as I massaged my aching feet. I got invested in some home improvement show, trying not to think about where I was going to be living over summer and what I was going to be doing.

Fifteen minutes into the show, I realized I wasn't focusing on it at all anymore, and was instead thinking about Amelia, Eleanor, Ellie, and two pregnant women. I wondered if Eleanor had willingly and civilly returned the backpack. I wondered if Karmen and Piper met back up with the others. I wondered if Eleanor and Karmen would ever make up. I wondered if Amelia and Ellie got back in their rooms. What if Amelia and Ellie had just been sitting in their hotel lobby all afternoon, no keys, no money, and no cell phones? I chewed at my lip guiltily. They wouldn't have been able to get any food for hours...

Ugh, I wasn't going to get any relaxation like that!

I hopped out of bed, trying to figure out something I could do to ease my mind. I was most worried about Amelia and Ellie. I didn't want them to be locked out of their rooms all evening just because they had no way to contact and find their friends. I decided my best bet was to just go over to their hotel and stroll around the lobby, see if I just happened to bump into them. Then, if I didn't run into them, I could conclude they had somehow reunited with their friends, and all was well. I could rest easily. I just needed to check.

I slipped into their hotel with ease, because hotel lobbies aren't really locked down. I got a bit sidetracked though, so my quick mission ran a bit longer than intended. Their hotel was nice, so I was having an enjoyable time strolling around and looking at the décor, taking in the atmosphere.

I strolled out into a cute garden, but when I went back inside, I ended up on a completely different side of the lobby I didn't know about. It was like a maze. I went through an archway I thought was going to take me back to the receptionist desk, but instead I tumbled headfirst into the hotel bar. It was pretty early for anyone to be turning up, so the place was completely desolate... desolate except for one woman at the end of the bar: a highly intoxicated physics teacher.

I hadn't planned on running into Eleanor, and I certainly didn't expect to find her wasted at the bar. In truth, Eleanor kind of annoyed me. I thought her behavior was overly childish, though I didn't know the entire backstory of her spat with Karmen, so I tried not to be overly judgmental.

Regardless, my goal was not to find Eleanor, but to find Amelia and Ellie, so I turned to leave. However, just as I started to turn on my heels, I saw *it*. Tucked up against the bar stool Eleanor sat on was Ellie's backpack. It was possible Amelia and Ellie had already found Eleanor and retrieved their things, but I didn't think they would have then left the backpack with Eleanor. That lead me to believe their things were still in that sack, untouched. I considered making a mental note and leaving to find the others, but I was worried Eleanor might leave. I concluded it would be safer to just take the backpack along with me on my hunt.

I walked up to Eleanor and sat on the stool next to her. She was currently chugging a beer, and the empty glasses around her told me she had been at it for a while. Tentatively I reached out, pushing the half-empty glass slowly down to the bar counter.

"Woah there, tiger, let's slow it down, alright?" I offered.

"Oh, it's you again," Eleanor slurred slightly, narrowing her eyes at me. "What was your name again? Jess? Teressa? Lily?"

"Natalie. You were pretty close," I answered sarcastically. "Listen, I'm not trying to interrupt... it's just that I noticed you still have Ellie's backpack and well, Amelia and Ellie need their stuff back."

"They can have it," Eleanor answered. "I don't want it. Tell them to take it! So long as I don't have to talk to Karmen."

"Okay, well that's just perfect," I replied with a nod. "I'm on my way to find Amelia and Ellie, as we speak, so just hand over the backpack and I'll be on my way."

I slid off the barstool, bending over to reach for the backpack. However, I then felt Eleanor shove at me. She pushed me slightly to the side, but she was far too intoxicated to be much of a threat.

"That's mine!" she practically shouted.

"Um, well, actually, it's not," I answered. "It's Ellie's. And like I said, I'm going to return this to her, alright?" I bent over again, that time successfully grabbing the backpack. Then, I quickly stepped out of Eleanor's reach.

"Give that back! Thief! I'm being robbed!"

I turned to bolt, thinking that would be the best solution, as I wasn't going to talk any logic into Eleanor's alcohol soggy brain. However, when I turned, I came face-to-face with the bartender, who demanded to know what was happening.

I groaned, trying to explain the situation.

As I explained, the bartender looked over my shoulder at Eleanor, seeming to contemplate if the trouble was worth more of an intervention or not. "You know what," he said, "fine. If she's your friend, then you can drag her back up to her room. I don't need anyone blacking out in my bar before the sun's even set." Then he turned and left, leaving me alone with Eleanor once more.

Eleanor seemed oddly quiet then, so I turned back to see what was happening. She was on the floor in a heap, leaning awkwardly against the bar, completely unconscious. I groaned audibly. I didn't want to deal with drunk Eleanor, not in the slightest, and I had half the mind to leave her there. The bartender didn't know me. I didn't owe him anything.

However, I found myself a bit worried about Eleanor's well-being, almost like a mother worrying about her child. I didn't want to just leave Eleanor there to possibly drink more. She was already passed out. So, choosing to be a good person, I let out a sigh and walked over to help Eleanor up.

Struggling, I adjusted Eleanor into a sitting position, balancing her so that she was no longer falling over. Then, I unzipped the backpack and rooted around inside until I found a keycard. The keycard was blank without a room number, not that it surprised me, but I realized I couldn't very well bring Eleanor upstairs without knowing her room number.

I shook Eleanor. "Come on, wake up!" I exclaimed. She groaned but remained mostly unconscious. I stood up then, looking for something to help, and spotted her half-empty beer on the counter. I grabbed it, turned back to Eleanor, and without pizazz, threw the drink right in her face. That woke her up.

Eleanor took in a large gasp, trying to immediately stand, but she only managed to whack her head on the underside of the bar. She fell back to the floor, cursing, rubbing at her head. I knelt back down next to her.

"Hey, Eleanor," I stated as calmly as I could. "Can you tell me what your room number is? Pretty please?"

I watched the gears turning in Eleanor's head as her foggy brain tried to recall basic information. "It's, um, 405," she answered miraculously. I nodded, happy she had been amenable, but before I was able to get her standing, her eyes rolled back into her head, and she slumped over again.

"Oh, for the love of—" I groaned loudly.

Fed up with struggling to get her to help, I just looped my arms under her shoulders. I turned, backing out of the bar, dragging Eleanor along with me. We got several weird looks from other guests, but I ignored them. Occasionally, Eleanor would stir slightly and mutter out something like: "Leave me alone!" – "Can I have another drink?" – "Is Karmen okay? I didn't mean to hurt her." But Eleanor always quickly drifted back into the land of unconsciousness.

Upstairs, I swiped the keycard on room 405, but realized it didn't work. I dug around in the backpack more, pulling out several other keycards, as it appeared the teachers all had their own room. I tried the other keycards and the third one I tried worked to open room 405.

I stuck my foot in the doorway to hold the door open as I reached back down and grabbed Eleanor's arm. With much effort, I jerked her over, looping my arms under hers once more. I pushed the hotel room door open fully with my butt as I backed in, dragging the slightly conscious Eleanor into the room. The second the door swung shut after us, I released Eleanor immediately. She fell to the floor with a *thud*, muttering out another expletive before drifting back off to dream land.

I turned around to see what I was dealing with—if dragging Eleanor up onto a bed was going to happen or not, or maybe see if I could get her a glass of water—but when I turned, I realized very abruptly that we were not alone. In fact, standing right in front of me was one very pregnant, gorgeous Latina psychology teacher who was wearing nothing more than a bra and underwear.

I covered my eyes immediately and quickly spun away just as Karmen questioned, "What... um... Eleanor? Is that Eleanor? What happened?"

My heart was pounding, mostly because Karmen had scared the daylights out of me. Clearly, this was Karmen's room, and evidently Eleanor's alcohol-soaked brain had wanted to see her again, as her room number was the one it remembered.

"Look, um..." I sputtered out, hands still over my eyes. "She's pretty drunk. I found her in the hotel bar. The bartender wanted me to take her up to her room, so that's what I did."

"This... isn't her room," Karmen stated the obvious.

"Yeah, but this is the room number she told me when I asked her," I answered. I held up the backpack to my side, my free hand still covering my eyes, my back still to Karmen. "Listen, um, Eleanor took Ellie's backpack, and I was just trying to return it to Ellie. Have you seen her around lately? Ellie or Amelia?"

"No, not since this morning. Piper and I got tired of waiting around, so we just came back to the hotel to relax," Karmen explained. "I... put on a shirt. You can turn back around if you'd like."

I slowly dropped my hand and turned, noting that Karmen now wore an oversized shirt. I relaxed a bit, although I still felt bad about the intrusion.

"Right, so I don't think Amelia or Ellie have their room key, or any of their belongings for that matter," I stated. I dug into the backpack again, pulling out all the contents, which I then unceremoniously dumped on the nearby bed. The keycards all came tumbling out, along with some money, three cellular devices, and various other items like gum, hairpins, and tampons.

"Those are their phones," Karmen confirmed with a nod. She reached forward and pulled one phone out of the mix. "This one is Eleanor's. I'll hold onto it for her. Would you... well would you be willing to find them? Amelia and Ellie 2.0, I mean, to give them their things back? I would, but my back is absolutely killing me and well, I have Eleanor now so—"

"I was planning on finding them," I answered, shoveling the items back into the backpack. "I tried to help them out earlier, but I failed and well, I was going to just relax in my own hotel, but I kept worrying about them not being able to get into their rooms or get any food."

"You came back to make sure they were okay?" Karmen questioned. There was a tone in her voice I couldn't quite place. It was a mix of surprise and accusation, though not necessarily distaste.

"Yeah, I um… well here, let me…" I looked down at Eleanor, swinging the backpack onto my back. Then, I bent down next to Eleanor and grabbed her under the arms again, pulling at her until I managed to prop her up against the bed. I knew Karmen would look after Eleanor, but in her pregnant state she wouldn't be sitting on the floor or dragging anyone around, so I wanted to get Eleanor as near to the bed as I could.

Once I was done, I stood up to find Karmen heading towards Eleanor with a glass of water in her hands. She walked over and sat down on the edge of the bed just next to the other woman. Slowly, she ran her fingers along the side of Eleanor's face, pushing a curl to the side.

"Alright, well, I'll see you around," I stated, heading for the door. I reached for the handle and turned it, pulling the door open slightly. "And um… well… sorry I saw you almost naked," I quickly added. "I didn't mean to barge in on you like that." Then I stepped into the hall, waiting as the door shut to make sure it locked behind me.

The last thing I saw before the door clicked shut was Karmen, already babying Eleanor, still playing with her hair. She leaned down slightly, as much as her protruding belly would allow, and whispered, "Eleanor, love, we've talked about this. Here, drink some water. You'll feel better."

Love.

Love meant all sort of things in different context and to different people, but love, to any degree, was still *love*. The way Karmen felt about Eleanor might only be platonic now, just a friend sort of love, but she still obviously greatly cared about Eleanor. Maybe I had done some good for them. Maybe Eleanor would wake, sober, in Karmen's arms, and they'd finally talk about their differences like real adults.

I didn't have time to dwell on the not-a-couple however, because I had two ladies to find.

I meandered back down to the lobby, not sure at all where to continue my search. I wandered around, still managing to find my way to new areas of the maze-like lobby. As I passed through a hall, I stumbled upon two workers, the one a fair bit more distressed than the other.

"Hey, do you know where Dave is? We've got two really troublesome guests out on the pool deck, and we need him to step in and make them leave. They won't listen to us."

"I'll page him. What's happening, exactly?"

"I don't know if they just lost their room keys, or if they snuck onto the property, but they keep trying to mooch food off people. Other guests are really starting to complain."

I turned, immediately following a sign towards the pool. It was a long shot, but it was possible those annoying guests were Amelia and Ellie.

I wasn't sure what I was expecting to run into, but it certainly wasn't what I found. I strolled out onto the terrace, the small backpack swung up over my shoulder. I scanned the crowd, trying to spot Amelia or Ellie, when suddenly there was a full-blow *scene* happening right in front of me. Stumbling across the pool deck was a short blonde physically trying to tackle what looked like an eighteen-year-old boy. He was trim and good looking, six pack and all, with a typical dude-bro haircut and mini hot pink swim trunks, contrasting nicely with his dark tanned skin.

The boy dodged away as Amelia made another leap at him. She exclaimed, "Just buy us a chili-dog, gosh dang it!"

"Hey, lady, geez! Chill out! You're freaking crazy!" the boy yelped. Amelia missed him and fell forwards, landing a tumbling smack right to the boy's left butt cheek.

All of the sudden, another woman joined the fray. She was older, so I assumed she was the boy's mother. She grabbed her son by the wrist and pulled him forward, away from Amelia. Then, she got between Amelia and her son and shouted right in Amelia's face, "Get your filthy whore mitts off my son, you disgusting excuse for a cougar!"

"Huh... filthy whore mitts," I muttered to myself. That was a new one.

"I'm not trying to make a move on your son!" Amelia backtracked, taking a step away from the woman once she regained her balance. "I just... well he's got his room key for the all you can eat snack shack, and all I wanted was one measly little chili-dog! I haven't had a single thing to eat since eight this morning! Please, can you just get—"

"What are you, some mooch who broke into this fine five-star resort to steal food?" the woman continued shouting. "How often are you in here trying these shenanigans? Well, it ends today. I'm calling security. Security!"

Figuring things were only going to keep escalating, I chose that moment to intervene.

I stepped between the furious woman and Amelia, holding up a keycard in front of Amelia's face. "I found it!" I exclaimed somewhat jubilantly. Amelia frowned at me in pure confusion, clearly not expecting to see me again, especially not with a keycard from Ellie's backpack. The woman, quickly piecing together what must have happened, graciously gave up and stormed off with a huff, leaving us in peace.

"Natalie?" Amelia questioned, still in shock.

"You know, I don't want to judge your skills or anything, but I think you're supposed to flirt with cute guys your age and mooch drinks off them... not target jailbait boys for chili-dogs," I said with a smirk.

Amelia, who up to that point had been staring at me with a dazed sort of look on her face, quickly grew serious, pursing out her lips. She snatched the keycard from my hand.

"I'll have you know that I am absolutely *starving* with no means of getting food! And Ellie 2.0 just wanted to sit around and wait for Eleanor to show up, but it was getting so late! I figured I could mooch some food off people, but Ellie 2.0 said I couldn't, so then I had to prove her wrong—"

"Prove her wrong!?" I scoffed. "I don't know what you were seeing, but from my perspective, you weren't being too successful!"

"I was working on it!" Amelia exclaimed.

She was standing really close to me. A whiff of her vanilla perfume sent my heart pounding, effectively shutting me up. We were standing close, too close almost, but yet I wanted to be closer to her, all the same. We were close enough that I could see the details of her face, like her smile lines when she talked and the faint creases around her eyes. I could also clearly see her eyes, illuminated by the slowly setting sun. Like Karmen's eyes, hers were brown, but they weren't quite so dark. There was something lighter, richer almost, about Amelia's eyes.

"Earth to Natalie," Amelia stated, snapping her fingers in front of my face. "Ellie 2.0, I think I broke her!"

I blinked a few times, realizing that Ellie had appeared at our sides. But then Amelia's words caught up to me...

"Wait, do you actually call her '*Ellie 2.0*?'" I questioned. After I thought about it though, I was pretty sure I had heard Karmen refer to Ellie as Ellie 2.0 as well.

"Well yeah, she's the second one after all," Amelia replied as if it were the stupidest comment she had ever heard.

"I—isn't that a bit insulting?" I asked with a frown.

Ellie, well Ellie 2.0, gave a shrug. "It doesn't really bother me," she answered.

"Eleanor gave her the nickname," Amelia continued to explain. "None of us had really talked to Ellie 2.0—aside from Piper—when she first started working at the school, but the second Eleanor found out they had the same first name, she ran straight to Ellie 2.0's classroom."

"She said I had to be Eleanor 2.0," Ellie 2.0 said with a bit of a chuckle. "So that's what they started calling me."

"But then we learned she actually likes to go by Ellie," Amelia added. "By then though, the number had stuck, and it's been Ellie 2.0 ever since."

"Exactly," Ellie 2.0 concluded. "But enough about that. How did you manage to get my backpack from Eleanor?"

Having almost entirely forgotten that I still had the woman's backpack slung over my shoulder, I quickly shed the bag and handed it over to Ellie 2.0. "I, well... I found Eleanor passed out in the hotel bar and she still had the backpack. Long story short, I dragged Eleanor up to her room, accidentally broke into Karmen's room, and left Eleanor with her. Then I came back down here to find you two."

"Thank god!" Amelia exclaimed, grabbing the backpack out of Ellie 2.0's arms. She rooted around inside until she pulled out her phone and some money. "We can finally eat! I am absolutely starving!"

"Thanks, Natalie," Ellie 2.0 said, nodding towards me, but then her brows tilted in confusion. "Wait, how did you run into Eleanor? You haven't been looking for her this entire time, have you?"

"Oh goodness, were you?" Amelia questioned, pausing in her musings momentarily to look up at me. She bore right into my eyes and there was almost a look as if she were seeing me for the first time, really *seeing* me. It made me uneasy.

"Um, no," I stuttered out. "I just, uh, happened to run into her."

"Oh, are you staying at this hotel too then?" Ellie 2.0 asked.

"No, um..." I paused. I could tell them the truth, the truth being that I couldn't stop thinking about them, worrying about them, and so I went in search of them, but that honestly sounded a bit creepy. Instead, I decided to lie and downplay my actions. "I'm actually staying at the hotel next door," I stated. "I heard this hotel was really well decorated though, so I came over here to walk around and take in the atmosphere."

"Well thank goodness you decided to go for a stroll. If it wasn't for you, we might have been locked out all night!" Amelia grinned at me.

I thought this was a bit dramatic on Amelia's behalf. Karmen was already back in her room, and I assumed Piper was as well. At any point they could have gone knocking on their friends' room doors. And yes, they wouldn't have gotten their stuff back until they found Eleanor, but I was confident Karmen and Piper wouldn't have let them just starve. I didn't feel like pointing this out though.

"No problem," I said, offering a small smile. "Glad I could help."

"Thanks again, Natalie," Ellie 2.0 answered, smiling in return.

"Yes, thank you," Amelia added. "Hopefully we'll see you around," she said with a wink.

Then suddenly, their presence was gone as they headed back inside, and I was left standing alone on the pool deck, surrounded by children's screams of glee.

3.

A Permanent Fixture

I didn't know if I would ever see the five high school teachers again. I mean, yes, I was pretty sure they were going to be around the park until the end of the week, as was I. And theoretically it was possible I could run into them again, as the park wasn't that big. But because my time had mostly been spent just whirling through ride lines, I didn't think it would be too difficult to never see them again.

Part of me was upset by this. I had somehow become a bit invested in Eleanor's and Karmen's relationship, especially after I saw how Karmen treated Eleanor in her intoxicated state. And I was maybe, just a little bit, possibly developing a teensy-tiny crush on one blonde choir director. That didn't matter though. Crushes were childish; they set in fast and hard, and then were gone just a fleeting blink later. I would survive and it would be fine.

Another part of me wasn't at all sad that I would never see them again. Yes, they seemed like a fun gang to hang with, but I didn't want to get roped into their drama. I had already been stopped by security once on their behalf and dealt with a drunk Eleanor. Neither of these things were top on my agenda when I came on this vacation alone under the intent to avoid people and all their issues. Based on my vacation plans, not seeing the five teachers again was exactly what should be happening.

The following morning, at 7:30 on the dot, I headed downstairs with a skip in my step, rejuvenated and ready to hit the park right as it opened for early access. The teachers were but a fleeting thought in the far back corner of my mind at that point. I was, however, suddenly brought to a halt when I ran into Amelia sitting in the lobby of my hotel. That... was definitely not something I pictured happening when contemplating things last night.

I slid to a stop in front of Amelia, who sat cross-legged, holding a cup of coffee in one hand. "Amelia?" I questioned, completely confused. She seemed pensive. "How long have you been here?" I asked. "And well, *why* are you here? Not that it isn't a pleasure seeing you again, I just—"

She cut me off. "I've been here for about an hour. I wanted to make sure I caught you before you headed out to the park."

"Is there a reason you wanted to catch me this morning?"

She patted the space on the chair beside her, so I sat down, not sure what else to do. I couldn't read her expression or body language. She seemed tired, which would explain the coffee, but also very caught up in her own head. Finally, after a moment she turned and looked at me.

"You lied to me," she stated. It was accusatory, but she didn't necessarily sound mad.

I was confused and caught off guard by her statement, so I muttered out exactly that: "What?"

"You lied to me yesterday," she continued, glancing down at her coffee cup, and I thought I almost heard a playful edge to her words. "You told me you went for a stroll and just *happened* to run into Eleanor... but Karmen told me that you said you were *worried* about us and went looking for us."

I colored slightly at being called out for my actions. "Yeah, well, what does it matter how I ran into Eleanor," I stated. "The point is I got your stuff back. That's the important part."

"It matters plenty, because you weren't just doing something nice out of convenience... you went out of your way to help us, and well, that means a whole lot more."

"Sounds like the same thing to me," I answered. "It's whatever, doesn't matter."

"It matters to me," Amelia then said, turning to look me in the eyes. I wanted to shy away from her gaze, but I held my head up, almost challenging her to argue further. "We just met each other yesterday... barely had a collective fifteen minutes of conversation between us, yet you chose to sacrifice your time to help us. And you took care of Eleanor... you *especially* didn't have to do that. I guess... well I just want to know why. Why did you go out of your way for us like that?"

I didn't know what to say. I nearly crumpled in on myself, whining about my hopeless future, escaping from reality to a theme park alone, and then my sudden and intense desire for human connection, but I absolutely couldn't confess such things to Amelia of all people. Instead, I started spitting out words, trying to fill the silence with something while I worked to think up an excuse for my actions. It didn't go well.

"I just care about people, I guess, I couldn't tell you why I did it. Something about seeing Eleanor so trashed in the bar just spurred me to help her, like when a person finds a stray kitten on the side of the road, that sort of thing. Like human compassion at its barest. And well, I know that doesn't explain why I went back out looking for you. What I said to Karmen was true, I *was* worried about you. I was worried you couldn't get back in the hotel, and you couldn't get food, and you couldn't find your friends... That alone isn't enough to spur someone to go seek out a stranger though, I guess, well, this is so stupid, I just... well I think you're cute. That's why I kept thinking about you and worrying about you and— this is so weird, I'm so sorry." I cleared my throat, my cheeks hot from my sudden and unplanned confession. Quickly, I jumped up. "I'm—I'm just gonna go," I muttered out, then I turned and ran straight out of the hotel and all the way to the park without looking back.

All morning I belittled myself. How could I have been so stupid? Why would I confess something like that to Amelia, especially in that way! Yes, I thought she was cute, but god! I had better game than that, could have flirted a little, anything other than say I couldn't stop thinking about her to the point I *stalked* after her, trying to *find* her! How creepy! She probably wasn't even gay, which made the whole situation even worse. Now she'd be weirded out by me, my crush, my sexuality, everything! I hoped I never saw her again! In fact, I would be better off never seeing any of the high school teachers again.

I sat down at a table for lunch, eating a hamburger. I was in a bitter mood, still mad at myself. And then, my day only seemed to get worse as I spotted, from my casual lunch-eating location, one particularly pregnant biology teacher. Piper was alone, from what I could tell, and I watched her navigate through the crowd before disappearing down a corridor to some bathrooms.

I shrugged off the sighting of Piper. My goal for vacation was a lone adventure, *alone*, which meant I needed to let them go. It was bothering me a bit, as I found them to be nice and fun ladies, but I couldn't face Amelia again after what I had confessed. Amelia and her friends were a package deal. It just... wasn't meant to be.

I finished off my lunch, just swallowing the last of my crumbs, when someone suddenly plopped down next to me—unannounced—and nearly gave me a heart attack. I turned in surprise, wiping a glob of ketchup from the corner of my mouth as I did, only to find Ellie 2.0 sitting beside me, surprisingly enough. She was hardly looking at me, and I was confused, especially as she hadn't said anything to me.

"*Umm*... hey," I stuttered out.

"I walked over here with Piper so she could go to the bathroom," Ellie 2.0 stated. "I was waiting alone, but then I saw you, so I thought I'd come say hi and sit with you for a minute. If you don't mind, that is."

I shrugged. "I mean... I haven't got anything else to do..."

Ellie 2.0 nodded at my response and then fell quiet. I contemplated saying something, but I was too occupied trying to figure out if Ellie 2.0 knew what I said to Amelia, and Amelia was totally grossed out by my sudden weird confession.

But then, without any prompting, Ellie 2.0 blurted out in a rush of words, "Amelia told me what you said to her." After she said that, she sighed in relief. "Oh, I'm so glad that's out in the open now," she muttered, rolling her shoulders, as if that 'secret' had been weighing an actual physical toil on her.

"What... exactly did she say I said...?" I questioned cautiously.

"*Hmm*, various things," Ellie 2.0 answered. "Things like, well, that you're a caring person at heart, oh, and you think she's cute."

I groaned, burying my face in my arms. Slowly I peeked up at Ellie 2.0. "How, um, how weirded out is she? Is she like, super grossed out?"

Ellie 2.0 just frowned at me. "No? Why would you assume that?"

"Because it was weird!" I exclaimed, sitting up fully. "Stalking after someone you think is cute is pretty weird and unwarranted, and I didn't mean for it to come off that way, but it's essentially the truth so I—"

"That is... not the impression I got from Amelia," Ellie 2.0 stated. "At least, that doesn't sound like how she took it."

It was at that moment that Piper came up behind me, startling me slightly when she rested a hand on my back. She moved to sit down on the other side of me, letting out a long sigh before she patted my back.

"Well, Natalie, like it or not, I think you've been adopted into our group," Piper stated.

I looked to her a bit quizzically, battling internally with how I felt about such information. Slowly though, I relaxed. I... liked them. Or in the very least I was drawn to them. We all sort of just hit it off, right off the bat, which was rare and hard to come by when making friends. Their acquaintance was something I should cherish, not actively fight against.

"I'm flattered you think that," I answered a bit too honestly. "You guys do seem like a fun crew. And I'm glad you feel like I'm part of the group now, because just a few minutes ago I was positive I had utterly weirded Amelia out and she'd never want to talk to me again." After I said this, I reached for my water bottle, taking a swig to wash down the rest of my lunch.

"Oh, Amelia's not weirded out," Piper confirmed what Ellie 2.0 had said with a dismissive wave of her hand. "She's pretty much flattered, smitten even."

I nearly chocked on my drink, spraying water across the table. "*Smitten*?" I coughed out.

Piper burst out laughing while I had a full-on coughing fit. Ellie 2.0, on the other hand, seemed contemplative of this information, as if she hadn't come to the same conclusion as Piper.

Once I collected myself, Piper continued. "I have known these ladies for quite some time, and I have found that if you know someone for many, many years, it becomes easy to notice subtle details about their mannerisms. Take Eleanor and Karmen, for instance."

"What are you talking about?" Ellie 2.0 questioned. "We already know Karmen and Eleanor are sleeping together. You guys think I'm so oblivious, but come on, even I know that!"

"I was referring to the fact that last night they mended something in their relationship. They're on speaking terms again," Piper corrected, and I filed that information away to bring up later. "But that wasn't my point. My point is regarding Amelia."

"What about Amelia?" Ellie 2.0 asked.

Piper turned towards me with a slight smug grin on her face. "We just so happen to run into a pink-haired girl at an amusement park, and suddenly Amelia's a fumbling mess."

"A fumbling mess?" I questioned skeptically.

"She's questioning her sexuality," Piper explained. "It's all a pattern. I noticed the same thing in both Eleanor and Karmen. Of course, their experimentation ended in a huge mess. Hopefully Amelia's exploration won't end in such a train wreck."

My head was reeling. The only semblance of sanity I could find in everything was that Amelia had to be straight and not interested in me. Even if I wanted to pursue things, I couldn't, because she wouldn't be interested. But now, with the possibility that she was very much indeed interested... I needed to know more immediately.

"How do you know Amelia's questioning her sexuality?" I asked. "Has she talked to you about it?"

Piper scoffed. "She doesn't have to say anything, I can just tell from her mannerisms. When someone hasn't been on a single date with a man in over a decade because they, *'Never really jived with guys—'*" she air-quoted— "her words, not mine, it's pretty obvious that ladies are more her thing. If you spend more time with her, you'll be able to tell too, just from the way she talks about women. Amelia's problem is that she's too scared to take that first step into lesbianism. Although, if she wants any pointers, I'm sure Eleanor would be glad to share."

"Or Karmen. Karmen sleeps with women. She could give Amelia pointers too," Ellie 2.0 added.

"Please, Eleanor is clearly the instigator," Piper argued.

I zoned out of their conversation, trying to do math in my head. A decade ago... late twenties... I tried to figure out how long it had been since Amelia last dated a guy. If she was, say, twenty-eight—potentially an incorrect estimation—that would mean she last dated someone at eighteen... senior year of high school or freshman year of college. I thought about my straight phase in high school, the hurried and inexperienced touches in the backseats of cars parked in lots late at night after dances. Then I thought about how much I changed in college, chasing after how I really felt, the burst of emotions at finally feeling at peace with myself in the arms of another woman, the continued romps and heart breaks...

I couldn't imagine going all of college having never hooked up with anyone ever.

I realized a bit too late that Piper's and Ellie 2.0's argument had died off. I should have seen it coming when Piper asked, "So, Natalie, are you single?"

"Yeah," I answered. "I've had... a few flings in college, that's what I'd call them. An official girlfriend once, I guess, but it didn't last. Everyone's always struggling in college, trying to figure out who they are and where they want to be in life, it's hard to really... commit to another person. At least, for me it is. And as of late, college has been pretty rough on me, so I'm just trying to keep my priorities straight."

"Girlfriend?" Ellie 2.0 questioned, not upset or offended, just slightly confused or perhaps shocked.

"Um, ex-girlfriend," I offered comedically, because that wasn't at all what Ellie 2.0 meant and I knew it.

"You don't have any gaydar," Piper stated to Ellie 2.0. "Natalie here is very obviously not straight, based on her appearance and attitude, but evidently also in how she acts around Amelia, according to Eleanor."

"I don't know what you're talking about," I muttered out, feeling my cheeks heat up.

"I'm only teasing," Piper offered.

"I know, I was just clarifying!" Ellie 2.0 huffed, finally defending herself. "I just try to not assume things about people, and yes, I know what Amelia said that Natalie said to her this morning, but words can be both said and taken in many different ways. I study literature quite extensively. It would be silly of me to not ascertain clarification."

"Well, I do very much only like women," I stated to clarify, "and I was truthful in everything I said to Amelia this morning—I was still half asleep and unable to filter my words. But I didn't just seek you guys out again because I was worried about Amelia... I was worried about all of you. And well, speaking of which, how's Eleanor doing today? She was very hammered last I saw her."

"She and Karmen are speaking again today," Piper explained. "So, although you probably didn't at all plan on helping them in *that* way, you accidently bringing Eleanor up to Karmen's room did do a lot of good for them."

"That was entirely Eleanor's fault," I corrected. "She was the one who told me that room number was hers. I had no reason to believe it was Karmen's room."

"*Hmm...*" Piper said contemplatively.

"Eleanor's getting on my nerves, actually," Ellie 2.0 grit out, crossing her arms defiantly. I looked to her, urging her to elaborate. "She just picks on people for no reason!" Ellie 2.0 continued effortlessly. "I know she lashes out at people when she's feeling insecure, but I'm tired of being at the receiving end of her wrath, and I think Amelia is too."

"She yelled at you guys?" I questioned. Piper seemed interested in this information too, as if she hadn't heard this extra bit of gossip.

"Amelia just kept going on and on about you," Ellie 2.0 stated, looking at me with a bored and drained expression. "And yes, you're cool and all, Natalie, but I'm talking *hours* of her going on and on. I finally needed to talk to someone else, so I went to seek out Karmen—to check up on Eleanor too, because you had mentioned her drunken state. Amelia followed me, of course—because she's like a puppy dog—but we walked in on Eleanor and Karmen being pretty snuggly. Eleanor was mostly sobered up by then and might have been a bit irritated that we interrupted her alone time with Karmen, but she just lashed out at us.

"She attacked me for not being independent enough to just go back to my room alone, and she said some kind of hurtful things about my family, but like—well it was really when she went after Amelia that I thought she was being unnecessarily brutal. She said some stuff about Amelia's personal life, and then she kept giving her trouble about her fixation on *you*—which I can kind of understand because like I said, Amelia would not stop talking about you last night. That's part of the reason I was so adamant she find you this morning, as she clearly wanted to spend more time with you and I couldn't guarantee we'd just run into you again. Of course, look, here we are—"

"I'm sorry," I interrupted. "I can't quite process all of this." I was really hung up on the fact that Amelia kept talking about me. And yes, I could see Eleanor teasing Amelia about this—my own friends probably would have done something similar—but to the point of it being cruel, bad enough that Ellie 2.0 thought she went too far?

"What all was Eleanor saying to Amelia?" Piper questioned, the hostility in her voice the only reason I caught her words at all.

Ellie 2.0 was about to answer, but I accidently cut her off. "Where are the others?" I questioned.

"Oh, well, um, Eleanor and Karmen, as Piper said, kind of made-up last night and are on speaking terms again," Ellie 2.0 answered. "And I know I said Eleanor and Amelia were really going at it last night, but today Amelia really wanted to ride roller coasters, and Eleanor's really the only one adventurous enough to go with her. That left Piper and me, and we just decided to hang out."

"Yes, and you're more than welcome to keep us company," Piper said to me.

"Sure," I answered with a soft smile. I decided I wanted to get to know them better, particularly if I was going to be a more permanent, though temporary, fixture in their group. "So, um, how long have you guys known each other? How long have you been teaching, since you all seem like good friends?"

"Piper and Karmen have been teaching together the longest," Ellie 2.0 answered.

"Yes, Karmen and I both started the same year. We've been teaching for nearly nine years now. Time certainly flies, especially when you start fresh out of college," Piper added. "Eleanor joined the school's team about a year after Karmen and I started. She's the same age as us but took a bit longer to get through school."

"It's only my first-year teaching," Ellie 2.0 cut in, clearly proud of her achievement. "I just got out of school. I'm only twenty-three. It's definitely difficult wrangling high schoolers when you're barely older than them, but I wouldn't trade my job for anything."

"Amelia started teaching at our school about two years after Eleanor did," Piper continued, "but she was teaching at a different school before we met her. We've known her for about, oh, four years?"

"Okay, wait, backtrack," I stated, pointing at Ellie 2.0. "First of all, you're only twenty-three? I'm barely a year younger than you."

Ellie 2.0 gave me a shrug. "You're in your last year of undergrad, right? That's all you need to become a teacher. I mean, we teach at a college preparatory school, so we technically need a masters to teach there, but they have a system in place where they'll hire you right after school and help pay for your masters. I just have to take night classes to finish off my degree."

"*Geez*," I muttered. "And so, wait, if my math is right, that means Eleanor and Karmen have known each other for what, eight years?"

"Probably," Piper replied.

"How long has that whole situation been going down then?" I questioned, and Piper easily pieced together that I was talking about their messy affairs.

"About five years," she answered.

"What... happened?" I asked a bit hesitantly. I wasn't sure if I wanted to know.

"Well do you mean in general, or why they've been mad at each other this week?" Piper tried to clarify. "Because it's been an issue in the first place since they decided to sleep together, but lately, they've been fighting because Karmen got pregnant."

"Wait, what?" I questioned.

Our conversation was cut off abruptly by several individuals yelling. I barely managed to comprehend the shouting, having yet to pull my attention away from Piper and Ellie 2.0.

"If I could just... wring his scrawny little neck!"

"Stop carrying on! Behave!"

Suddenly, Amelia plopped down across from me at the table, holding her head like she had a migraine. "Please, *please* let me hang out with you guys. Those two are driving me crazy!" she gasped.

I turned, realizing it was Eleanor and Karmen that I heard shouting, and they were heading towards us.

"What... happened?" Ellie 2.0 asked hesitantly.

I turned towards Amelia, our eyes meeting, and she seemed to startle slightly as if she had yet to notice my presence. I opened my mouth to say something to her, but I was cut off by Eleanor, who wiggled her way into a seat. I shifted slightly to allow Karmen to sit as well.

"Some kid was cat-calling Karmen," Eleanor stated. She was angry, that much I could tell.

"He and his buddies were standing behind us in line," Karmen added. She sounded... tired.

"It started off with just your regular, run of the mill cat-calling," Eleanor said. "We ignored them in the beginning. They were behind us, so they didn't know Karmen was pregnant. Karmen figured that if they knew, maybe they'd back off. However, when she turned and they saw her belly, they just started getting weirder... real predatory... lots of unnecessary slurs."

"I told them to mind their manners, there were children around," Karmen commented.

"Of course, they didn't," Eleanor continued. "I was pretty livid at that point, so I don't exactly remember the flow of conversation, but at some point, it came up that Karmen was with me."

"They were asking about 'my man,'" Karmen said with air quotes. "No need to start down that complicated road, so I just told them I was with Eleanor and wrapped my arm around her waist."

"Wrong thing to say to a couple of horn-dog boys," Eleanor practically growled. "One of the guys cracked a threesome joke, that was nearly inevitable. But *that kid*," Eleanor stressed out, "*that kid* said, 'stop wasting your time with this *nig—*"

"He slapped Karmen's ass," Amelia added as justification. "And then we were asked to leave the line because we were making too much of a scene."

"You were the one making the scene!" Eleanor shouted at Amelia. "You were yelling twice as loud!"

"You were the one who nearly punched him!" Amelia shot back. "If Karmen hadn't been holding onto you, we probably would have been kicked out of the park for assault!"

"Both of you were making a scene," Karmen snapped. She turned to Eleanor. "You need to just let it go. Yes, it was horrid what he said and did, and yes, his behavior should not be excused, but you can't go carrying on like that when there are children around." She then turned pointedly to Amelia. "You either."

"A very unfortunate occurrence," Piper cut in coolly. "I can't believe you two reacted as you did. I'm very disappointed."

I glanced towards Amelia, who was now fuming nearly as much as Eleanor was. I half expected her to snap at Piper, but instead she just let out a huff, crossed her arms, and turned her back on us. Eleanor, however, was not so silent.

"I didn't do anything!" she whined like a child. "I *could* have punched him, I *could* have snapped his scrawny little neck, but I didn't!"

Karmen squeezed Eleanor's arm harshly then, and the woman fell silent.

"Yes, well," Piper stated, "let's just be glad you have someone in your life to work impulse control, as you're clearly lacking in that department."

"Piper, don't be so harsh on them," Ellie 2.0 cut in meekly.

"I'm not being harsh, I'm being realistic."

I felt blindsided by the animosity at the table. Yes, I knew there was bad blood between Eleanor and Karmen, and yes, it seemed Eleanor was good at pushing people's buttons, but the cool hatred of disappointment laced in Piper's words? I hadn't expected that at all. Up to that point, Piper reminded me of Ellie 2.0, a little meek, trying to play peacemaker as much as possible. Now though... now she seemed like an overbearing mother. I mean, yes, it would have been bad if things escalated physically, but they hadn't, so why was Piper being so harsh with them?

Before more could be said, Karmen reached out to gain my attention. I turned, noticing she still had a tight grip on Eleanor's arm. She shook it slightly. When Eleanor didn't respond, Karmen elbowed her harshly in the ribs, and she let out a hiss.

"Eleanor has something to say to you, doesn't she?" Karmen stated in an amazing mother voice.

Eleanor cowered under Karmen's gaze. It was pretty evident that where yesterday, Eleanor had been so bent and determined to make Karmen miserable, she was now ashamed of how she acted. It was like she didn't want to further disappoint Karmen. There was still tension—drama from years on end wouldn't be solved in a night—but I felt as if I were witnessing a turning point.

"I'm, um, sorry about how I acted yesterday," Eleanor muttered sheepishly to me. "I'm sorry that you were caught by security when you tried to chase me. If I hadn't been so pig headed, none of that would have happened. And well, I'm sorry you ran into me when I was drunk... I'm sorry for anything I might have said or done that hurt you. I was very out of line yesterday. You're an oddly good person, Natalie. Thank you for helping all of us, even when it was a real headache for you. I'd like to make it up to you, if I could."

I smiled largely and reached forward, slapping Eleanor hard against her back. "Don't worry about it," I stated. "We can just start over from scratch and call everything good. How does that sound?"

"Sounds good," Eleanor answered with a smile.

Out of the corner of my eye, I caught Amelia watching our exchange. She still had her back to Piper but had angled herself just enough to watch us. She seemed intrigued, but contemplative. I wanted to talk to her... but I also wanted to help ease the tension surrounding the others.

"Hey, what do you guys say we do something fun?" I declared.

"Fun? Like what?" Karmen asked.

"Yeah, we're at an amusement park. Isn't everything supposed to be fun?" Eleanor added.

"Sure, but that doesn't mean we can't make things *more* fun," I said with a grin. "I was just thinking... we've got six people. That's two even teams of three..."

Amelia spun around fully, looking directly at me. "A competition?" she questioned with a smirk.

"Yeah, a competition," I answered.

There was much banter about what sort of competition we could have inside an amusement park without getting into trouble. I noticed a swarm of children around a worker dressed up as a superhero. All over the park there were workers dressed up as characters from various franchises, allowing for great photo opportunities. I grinned. That would work just perfectly.

"Pictures with characters," I declared, pointing towards the superhero to gain everyone's attention. "Let's give it... an hour. Whichever team can get the most pictures with characters in the park before time runs out, wins."

"What happens if there's a tie?" Eleanor questioned.

"*Umm...* first one back here wins?" I tried.

"I like it," Karmen agreed. "Adds an extra bit to the time management aspect."

Everyone nodded in agreement, but Amelia cut us off. "What's the prize?" she questioned.

"Bragging rights?" Ellie 2.0 offered.

"That's so boring," Amelia stated, rolling her eyes. "I want something actually good."

"Losers buy the winners ice-cream; how does that sound?" I suggested.

Amelia visibly lit up at the mention of ice-cream. I fought back my laughter. She looked positively radiant at the thought of a sweet reward. What a total goof.

"Ice-cream!?" Amelia swooned. "I'm *so* in! Though I have to warn you guys, theater kids are utterly notorious for their competitive nature."

"You're competitive? Have you *met* me?" Eleanor squared off against Amelia.

"Okay, okay, glad to see you guys have your head in the game," I laughed, "but we need some ground rules. Everyone has to be present in every picture, so no splitting up. And one pregnant gal per team, that's only fair."

"Team Karmen and Team Piper, go!" Eleanor frantically shouted. She jumped up from the table when she said this, looking to Karmen with a half shrug before she dove at Piper and grabbed the woman's hand.

Amelia took one look at her main competition—Eleanor—before she went and stood behind Karmen. Ellie 2.0 glanced around at everyone, contemplating, before she just slid closer to Piper, not one for jumping into action. I joined the remaining open space on Team Karmen, receiving a challenging glare from Amelia.

"You better not mess this up," she said to me, as if I would purposefully ruin our shot at getting ice-cream. I was a college kid. I lived for the words 'free food.'

"Yeah, well, you better not mess this up worrying about me messing this up," I retorted.

Karmen let out an audible sigh. "Have fun eating your ice-cream later, ladies," she said to Team Piper. "Looks like I've got two obstinate team members that will spend more time bickering than working."

"In your dreams!" Amelia declared with gusto.

"Okay, well, we'll meet back here in an hour, alright?" I questioned. Everyone nodded. "Alright. On your mark, get set, go!" I shouted.

The release of the race was very anticlimactic, considering the two pregnant team members prevented any mad dash away from the start. But both teams turned and headed off in opposite directions, so it was good enough.

Barely thirty seconds in, Amelia was delegating. She was a choir director; I shouldn't have expected anything less. I didn't have a problem with her being our team captain, I was just happy to be spending more time with her, even if she was being bossy. There was a chance for ice-cream, that was high stakes.

After we found our first character actor in the children's section of the park, Amelia had a brilliant idea. With every character were a couple of plain park workers, there to snap pictures for families. She asked them for a schedule of the times and locations of characters. The characters were workers after all, of course they had a schedule. And evidently that was pretty common knowledge, as the workers had a printout of that day's schedule. From there, we mapped out a path to hit every character out in the park during that hour, and after a lap we found ourselves back in the kiddie area with nearly twenty minutes to spare.

Amelia insisted we return to the finish line just in case Team Piper discovered the same loophole we had and there was going to be a tie. However, Karmen put her foot down, saying her back was killing her and she needed to sit down and rest for a few minutes. Amelia gave in, letting Karmen sit down, but I could tell she was anxious to get moving again. I looked around for a way to distract her and noticed a ride nearby. The entrance was right across from us, and a sign declared it had a zero-minute wait time. I turned to Amelia.

"Do you want to ride that with me?" I asked, pointing at the ride. "We have some time and there's no wait."

Amelia seemed hesitant, but Karmen waved us off. "Go on, have some fun and let me rest without you pestering me!" At that, Amelia cracked a smile and grabbed my hand, dragging me off to the ride's entrance like an excited child.

Despite the sign claiming there was no wait, we found a very short line just into the loading dock. Just a couple minutes though and we would be off. I noticed Amelia was practically vibrating, which made me laugh.

"What are you doing?" I questioned.

"I'm just really excited about this ice-cream!" she shot out with a squeal. I shook my head at her, though I was grinning. She was so, *so* ridiculous. Yet somehow, her intense excitement for ice-cream only made her more adorable.

"Asking for a character sheet was smart," I commented. "I think we have a pretty good chance at winning."

"I sure hope so."

The line moved forward, and we climbed into the cart, prepared for the 'interactive story' that was the ride. I found myself watching Amelia's movements. Despite my bitter mood earlier in the day, I found I was having a lot of fun. It was refreshing spending time with the high school teachers. They didn't have any expectations for me, nothing to nag me about or make me feel inferior with. They just... were fun. Despite everything though, I was still a bit worried about what I had said to Amelia that morning. I wanted to make sure things were okay between us. As the train moved out of the loading dock, I turned to Amelia.

"We never talked about this morning," I said. "I just... well I wanted to make sure you weren't weirded out."

Amelia turned and looked back at me. I felt her eyes tracing every inch of my face. It was a bit unnerving, the silence, and the intense stare was making my heartbeat pick up.

"You don't weird me out," she said after a moment. "You... intrigue me. You can be a bit annoying and foolish—I don't think I'll ever really understand why you darted off after Eleanor, or why you even agreed to try and convince Eleanor to talk to Karmen—but I don't know. You're nice and pretty fun, so I guess you're okay."

I scoffed. "Wow, flatter me so," I mocked.

Amelia dramatically turned away from me. "Shush, I'm trying to follow the story," she stated sassily, looking out at the animatronics we were passing.

Amelia... intrigued me too. I became hyper aware of her, no matter what I did, the ride was only a passing thought at that point. I could sense her breathing and smell her addictive vanilla perfume. The urge to reach out and touch her, rest my fingers on her soft skin, was almost unbearable to the point I was worried I might actually do it. I controlled myself, however, and turned away from her as much as I could, restrained by the ride's safety belt.

Once off the ride, Amelia and I ran straight back to Karmen. After a bit of pulling and pleading, we got Karmen up and started towards the finish line. I was starting to feel more playful around my new friends. I was comfortable enough to tease them a bit, especially Amelia, and an idea struck my mind.

"Hey, you're a choir director, right?" I asked Amelia.

"Um, yeah?" she answered, a bit of hesitancy in her voice.

"Well, you can sing then, right?" I continued.

"Yes..."

"Okay, perfect!" I grinned, a sinister glint in my eyes. "Sing me some good old '*Follow the Yellow Brick Road*.'" When I said that, I reached over and grabbed Amelia, looping our arms together. Before Amelia could react, I pulled her forward in a skip. She stumbled after me a few steps before she caught on and began skipping alongside me, no questions asked.

I loved her spontaneity, her willingness to do something so embarrassing with me without fuss. It was like she wasn't afraid of consequences but was just living in the moment. I felt free with her.

I expected, at best, maybe one line of the song followed by a laugh, skipping until I finally stopped, laughing too hard to continue on. What I hadn't expected was for Amelia to be so good at thinking on her toes. I wasn't used to theater nerds and choir directors, but I shouldn't have expected anything less, realizing she was probably well-versed in both acting and performing. But I also didn't expect for Amelia to sound as good as she did.

Amelia belted out a solid line of the song, no hesitation or self-consciousness. She skipped past me gracefully with the most sinful hip sway, tugging me forward, and my brain short circuited. I stumbled, finding my skipping off rhythm, and then I was down, smacking the pavement face first.

Half a second later I was suddenly staring up at the sky with Amelia hovering over me. She looked concerned. Everything felt cloudy, misty, my brain still focused on replaying the scene of Amelia singing. But then, quite abruptly, all my senses caught up to the current time. My face hurt. I realized there were people off to the side staring at us, and then, when my hearing resumed, I heard Amelia shout, "Karmen! Someone! I need a napkin, oh my god!"

I forced myself into a sitting position as Amelia stepped away. My head felt weird. It didn't hurt too badly, most of my weight was caught on my arms when I fell forward, but there was a certain sting to the upper part of my left eyebrow. I slowly reached up to touch my face.

Amelia was back down on her knees in front of me before I could feel my face. She grabbed my wrist, jerking my hand away from my face. "Stop, don't touch it!" she snapped. Then she reached out with a fist full of napkins and pressed them against my forehead with way too much force. I yelped.

"That hurts!" I growled, jerking away from Amelia. She grabbed me more aggressively then, telling me to stop wiggling. Then she pulled out a small bottle of hand sanitizer and globbed some onto my head. I hissed against the sting.

"Stop complaining," Amelia reprimanded. "You've got a nasty scratch across your forehead. I have to clean it."

I felt bitter, my pride hurt at having taken such a tumble in the first place. I smirked though after a minute. "What, are you worried about me or something, Amelia?" I teased.

Amelia narrowed her eyes towards me. "You wish," she retorted. "I just can't have you dying on my watch. Not sure how I'd explain that to park security."

"Yeah, well, it's your fault anyway that I fell," I replied.

"My fault?" she questioned, sitting back now that she was done cleaning my forehead. "How is it my fault that you're an ungraceful disaster?"

I stuck out my bottom lip in a fake pout, but I didn't miss the way Amelia's lips curled into a soft grin. She turned away from me to hide her smile. She was teasing me, not because she was trying to be hurtful, but because she was having fun with me.

By then, Karmen caught up to us. She offered Amelia her water bottle to help clean off a bit of dried blood around my eyebrow. Once she was done, she sat back again, watching my head intensely before nodding.

"Okay, the bleeding has officially stopped," she stated. "It was just a bad scrape, so I don't think you actually split your eyebrow open. If you did, you'd need stiches, so it's good you didn't."

"Darn," I stated with a snap of my fingers. "I was hoping for a sick scar on my eyebrow."

"Don't," Amelia chastised with a playful finger wag. "I wouldn't have taken you to the hospital."

"Rude," I muttered in mock contempt. "You would have just left me here to bleed out?"

Amelia gave a shrug. "You're more trouble than you're worth," she stated, sticking her tongue out at me.

"What are you, five?" I scoffed, though I stuck my tongue out at her in response. "Karmen would have taken me to the hospital because she's a good person. Wouldn't you have, Karmen?" I asked the pregnant woman standing over me.

"Uh huh," Karmen muttered, seeming bored. "Are you two done flirting? We have five minutes until this competition is over, and I thought you were serious about winning or whatever."

"Flir—flirting!?" Amelia gasped out, choking on spit. She had a full-on coughing fit before stumbling to leap up. "We—we weren't—what are you talking about? Flirting? I wasn't—"

"Come on," Karmen stated, rolling her eyes.

I stood up as Karmen pulled Amelia away, tugging her towards the finish line. I smirked contentedly, noting the blush staining Amelia's cheeks. Quickly, I chased after them.

We reached the finish line and found that Team Piper wasn't anywhere in sight. Triumphant, Amelia and I shared a leaping high-five, and a more subdued high-five with Karmen. Karmen rolled her eyes at us once more, then sat down on a bench, complaining about her feet. Amelia sat beside her, already texting the others about our victory, but was disappointed when they didn't immediately respond. I reclined on a concrete ledge just beside them.

Time was quickly running out for the others. With each minute that ticked by, Amelia grew giddier for the ice-cream reward. She seemed so young and carefree in that moment, completely harmless and adorable. But people were complex creatures. Amelia had just as much of a flame inside her as Eleanor. And Eleanor, she was a puzzle too.

"Penny for your thoughts?" Karmen questioned, breaking me from my trance. I blinked my vision away from Amelia, turning to look at Karmen. "I don't have a penny," she continued, "but I'm just saying."

"I don't know..." I muttered. "I'm just... thinking about winning that ice-cream."

"What's your favorite flavor?" Karmen questioned.

"Oh, um, I don't know. I guess just plain vanilla."

"Boring," Amelia cut in. "Rocky Road is clearly the superior flavor."

Karmen just scoffed at me. "Yeah, I don't believe you for a second. What's really on your mind?"

"Okay, fine, you caught me," I sighed. "I was thinking about what happened earlier... about that guy and his friend that were provoking you... How Amelia and Eleanor nearly got into a fight."

"He deserved more than that," Amelia cut in.

"Yeah, maybe, but I mean, you're a high school teacher," I stated. "You must encounter annoying teens every day. You can't just start fights because a kid's being annoying."

"This guy wasn't just *annoying*," Amelia replied. "He was verbally and physically harassing both Karmen and Eleanor."

"We all do things we aren't proud of," Karmen declared. "Our tempers can certainly get the better of us. But just because a certain side of us comes out on vacation, doesn't mean we don't know how to be professional in our daily lives."

"What a noble thing for *you* to say," Amelia scoffed. "Separating our personal lives from our work lives... I seem to remember an entire semester where you refused to walk down the science wing because you might run into Eleanor."

"That's different!" Karmen huffed. "Besides, I know you took overtime for Nicholas. Some separation of personal and professional, huh?"

"You know darn well it was his birthday and—"

"*Uhh*, hey guys?" I cut in meekly, realizing their argument was starting to escalate. "It's fifteen minutes past the hour, and there's been no sign of the others... What are we going to do?"

"I hope nothing bad happened to them," Amelia muttered.

"I'd say the competition induced someone's labor, but I'm further along than Piper, so I doubt that's the case," Karmen commented.

"Plus, one of them surely would have texted us if Piper went into labor," Amelia added.

"They probably just realized they were losing—since you texted them," I said pointedly to Amelia, "and just went to get ice-cream without us. They might have even gone back to the hotel so we couldn't make them buy us ice-cream."

"*Ugh*, that's exactly something Eleanor would convince them to do!" Amelia shouted in frustration. She frowned and honest to god looked like she was about to start crying. "I just really wanted some Rocky Road in a waffle cone..."

The sad look on Amelia's face hit me straight in the gut. I was filled with an overwhelming need to comfort her, to ease her pain. I hated myself for what I was about to suggest, but I couldn't just stand idly by, watching the glistening in her eyes. I hopped up abruptly and exclaimed, "I'll buy you guys ice-cream, how does that sound?"

"Natalie, you don't have to," Karmen stated.

"No, I want to," I said more confidently. "That's what friends are for, right? And besides, next time, you can buy," I added with a playful wink.

"Well come on then!" Amelia squealed, leaping up and grabbing my arm. "To the ice-cream parlor!"

I laughed as Amelia pulled me forward, only to stop and run back to Karmen, helping the pregnant woman stand before ushering her forward impatiently. I was going to regret my suggestion. Park food was expensive enough just buying for one person. But Amelia's pure excitement was already making it worth it.

As we neared the ice-cream parlor, the evening was setting in. The sun had begun to set, casting a warm glow over the top of the sky. The ice-cream parlor was a good hike from the finish line and once we entered the shop, I could tell Karmen was essentially drained of all her energy. She never voiced a complaint, but she held her back and was walking much slower. I decided it was back to our hotels after ice-cream, no matter how I felt.

Once in the ice-cream parlor, Amelia skipped off towards the counter. I held back a laugh. What fully grown woman would skip to ice-cream? Amelia, evidently. She really intrigued me. Her spontaneity was already near addicting, but also her confidence. She didn't care what anyone else thought of her, and I admired that.

Karmen stood beside me, watching the same display. She chuckled slightly, causing me to turn towards her. When I did, she said, "Amelia turns into a sweet, innocent child around ice-cream and puppies. She's a goddamn cinnamon roll."

That time I couldn't contain my laugh. 'Cinnamon roll' felt like a pretty good descriptor for Amelia's current display. My laugh didn't faze Amelia in the slightest, as she was far too busy drooling over all the flavor options. I just stood and watched her for a bit, but soon enough, Amelia turned back to me, eyes absolutely sparkling.

"Natalie!" she exclaimed. "Come help me pick! I can't decide what I want!"

Karmen dismissively commented that she'd just steal a bite of ours before she turned and went to sit down. I giggled at Amelia, walking over to her side.

"I thought you wanted Rocky Road," I commented, my eyes scanning the colorful bins of ice-cream.

"But, but... they have Triple Chocolate Fudge Brownie! And Birthday Cake! And oh, oh my god, *Apple Pie*!?"

I looked through the flavor list, biting my lip in concentration, trying to decide what to get. Honestly, nothing sounded overly appealing to me. I clearly didn't share the same enthusiasm about ice-cream that Amelia did. I chose to simply please Amelia, because pleasing her would make me happy, and that was all that really mattered.

"Alright, how about this?" I offered. "Why don't we get a scoop of each, and then the three of us can just share?"

"Okay!" Amelia happily agreed.

I turned to the cashier and ordered a scoop of each flavor Amelia had listed. The worker nodded and set about preparing our dish. Amelia watched him intensely, as if he were performing a sacred ritual, and then she turned to me.

"Can... can we get hot fudge?" she asked quietly, tentatively. I nodded, a slight smirk to my expression. She mirrored my smile with a larger grin. "And caramel and sprinkles and a cherry or two on top!?" she then added.

"Okay, okay, geez," I laughed. "You're going to get diabetes eating this thing." Despite my comment, I still turned to the worker and told him to top it off.

The worker finished our dish and returned to the register, ringing us up. Then he asked, "Anything else?"

I glanced to Amelia, expecting her to come up with another topping she desperately needed, like marshmallows or chocolate chips, but instead of paying attention to the conversation at hand, I found her gazing longingly at the waffle cone display. I looked down at the sweet monstrosity we already ordered, then back to the woman who couldn't possibly eat all that ice-cream. With a soft sigh, I turned back to the worker.

"Can we also get one waffle cone with Rocky Road?" I added to the order.

Amelia heard me when I said that, and she spun to look at me in shock. I glanced towards her, a shy smile on my face. I hoped she would appreciate the extra treat, though I was half expecting a snarky remark, maybe like how I was trying to flatter her, or put her into a sugar induced coma. I didn't get either of those, however. Instead, there was a pause where Amelia just stared at me, and then she very suddenly dove on me and squeezed me in the tightest of hugs.

Before I could even process, Amelia was gone. She backed up a step, looking almost embarrassed of her actions, her cheeks tinted pink. I thought to say something, but then the worker was handing Amelia the waffle cone and she was gone, dashing over to Karmen. I paid for the ice-cream, my mind fuzzy, lessening the blow of the cost, which was entirely outrageous.

I brought the sugary mess over to the table with the others. I sat it in the center of all of us, taking a seat.

Karmen took one look at the bowl before curling her lips in disgust. "What in the world is this monstrosity?" she grimaced, poking at the ice-cream with a plastic spoon.

"Don't look at me like that," I stated. "This was all Amelia."

"Fwat? I fwike ice-fream!" Amelia defended, her mouth full of Rocky Road.

We slowly worked our way through the ice-cream. Periodically, Karmen would pick at a small bite or two amidst playing on her phone. Amelia managed to finish off her cone all by herself and then had two bites of each flavor in the dish. After that, Amelia was essentially in a sugary coma, moaning about how she ate way too much. I tried to finish the rest, but it was too sweet for me. I couldn't stomach it. After pushing the bowl back and forth between the three of us, Karmen finally got up with a huff and just threw it away. Then we sat in silence, save for the few groans from Amelia, and I decided it was time to call it a night.

"Alright, you two. Why don't we go back to your hotel and find the others?" I stated, but after the words left my mouth, I faltered. "I mean, well... you two should probably do that. I'll just go back to my hotel, because it's not like I—"

"I already texted Piper," Karmen cut off my awkward ramble. "Evidently, she was hit with a bout of pregnancy sickness, and after that they just decided to call it an evening. They went back to the hotel to rest and watch a movie."

"They could have called us," Amelia muttered a bit dejectedly.

Karmen smirked. "Oh, they didn't want us to worry and rush back... They wanted to let us have some fun. And besides, they figured it would be good for the two of you to get to know each other a little better."

"Natalie and me?" Amelia questioned, almost stuttering as she had when Karmen suggested we were flirting.

"Have they eaten yet?" I questioned, choosing to ignore Amelia. "It *is* almost dinner time... probably some real food with this ice-cream will help us feel better."

"Piper and Ellie 2.0 ordered room service. They got into a little spat with Eleanor though, said she went downstairs nearly an hour ago and won't answer any of their calls," Karmen explained. Then she added bitterly, "She's probably drunk again."

I looked between Amelia and Karmen, not sure what was going to happen. I didn't want to overstep and invite myself to continue spending time with them. Even though I felt we had reached a level of friendship, I didn't want to push it. I thought someone ought to go deal with Eleanor, but I did that yesterday and I felt it was someone else's turn.

As if she had been reading my mind, Amelia suddenly shot out, "We need to do something about Eleanor." She looked Karmen dead in the eyes and stated, "Or should I say, *you* need to do something about Eleanor."

Karmen threw her hands up in the air. "I've done all I can!" she insisted. "She's the one who refuses to talk to me! I tried talking to her yesterday, and we kind of did, but clearly it wasn't enough. I can't help that she got jealous the second she found out I was pregnant. She chose him over me, so I had no choice but to choose my husband over her. I'm just... sick of her! I'm sick of her behavior and her attitude! Maybe I don't even want to mend things. Maybe it's too late."

Amelia immediately jumped at Karmen, shouting something about immaturity and stupidity, but I was hardly listening. I was too busy trying to piece together what had happened, based on little tidbits of information I was picking up, and work that into a way we could convince Eleanor to calm down.

When I came out of my haze of contemplation, I realized Amelia was looking at me expectantly. "Wha—what?" I stuttered.

"Natalie, you should talk some sense into Eleanor," Amelia repeated herself.

"What? Me?" I gasped. "You can't be serious! I don't hardly know Eleanor, let alone the situation."

"You're a new perspective on things," Amelia stated. "We have all tried, and our methods haven't worked, but you can come at it with fresh eyes."

"What could I possibly say to her?" I pushed. "I literally don't know anything about what happened except I guess Karmen and Eleanor have some history together? What am I supposed to do with that information?"

"Well... we could tell you what happened," Amelia offered. She glanced over to Karmen who was being pouty. It reminded me of Eleanor.

"I have absolutely no desire to relive the past several years of my life through vivid storytelling," Karmen huffed. "I'm tired, anyway. I want to go back to the hotel and lie down."

"Yeah, Amelia, you're being unfair," I stated. "It's been a long day. We should just call it a night."

"I could tell Natalie," Amelia then said, refusing to let it go.

"Amelia..." Karmen warned.

"No, really," Amelia pushed. "I've been around through it all. I know the whole story. Plus, I'm an unbiased third source."

"It's not your story to tell me," I told Amelia.

"You know what, fine," Karmen huffed, waving dismissively. "If it'll get you off my back, fine. Tell Natalie whatever you want. It's not going to make an ounce of difference. But I don't care. I just want to go to bed." Karmen pressed her temple when she said that, as if she had a headache. "Please, can we leave now?"

"Sure," Amelia stated, a bittersweet smile gracing her lips. "Let's go back to our hotels. Karmen, you can go to your room and relax. Natalie and I are going to get dinner at her hotel."

"We are?" I questioned, surprised.

Amelia shrugged. "We have to go somewhere to talk, and as you mentioned, it's dinner time. Might as well kill two birds with one stone."

We were all the way to the park exit before I realized that not only was I going to be learning about the feud between Eleanor and Karmen, but I was also going to be having a one-on-one dinner with Amelia.

Yikes.

4.

Flipping Into A Pool Is For Sober People

"I'll pay for dinner," Amelia stated just after we sat down and opened our menus. I glanced down at the prices and decided I wasn't going to argue. "Considering I know what you paid for that ice-cream was beyond reasonable," she added. "And you didn't have to get me the cone, I—"

"Didn't I, though?" I half laughed. "You were making mad puppy-dog eyes at the waffle cones. Pretty sure if I hadn't gotten it for you, you would have been mopey the rest of the trip."

Amelia lowered her menu and pursed her lips at me. I, feeling more confident, winked at her before I hid my face behind my own menu.

We sat in comfortable silence, browsing our menus until our waiter came over. He introduced himself, then asked if he could interest us in any drinks.

"I'll have a raspberry margarita," Amelia ordered. Then she looked at me and asked, "Would you like something, Natalie?"

I was caught off guard. I didn't think drinks were going to be on the table that evening. In fact, the presence of drinks made the entire scenario feel even more like a date to me, and I felt myself heating up, thinking about the implications. I must have waited too long to answer, as Amelia was suddenly ordering for me.

"She'll have a strawberry daiquiri," Amelia said, the waiter nodding and taking his leave before I could say anything. Once he was gone, she added, "Don't worry. Strawberry daiquiris taste like a fruit smoothie. They're perfect first-time drinks."

I frowned. "What do you mean, first-time drink? I've had alcohol before," I defended, which only prompted Amelia to laugh more.

"You could have fooled me," she said teasingly. "Nervously sweating when offered alcohol... sweet and naïve in nature... unexperienced, prudish even—"

"Okay, okay, damn," I huffed. "Just how young and childish do you think I am?"

Amelia continued to laugh at me. "Piper said you're in college, so you've got to be at least eighteen. You couldn't be any younger because there's no way you skipped a grade."

"*Hey!*" I snarled. "What's that supposed to mean? I'll have you know that I *could* have skipped a grade, I just—"

"Calm down, tiger," Amelia practically purred, reaching out a hand which she rested against my arm. Her physical contact immediately shut me up. "I'm teasing you," she cooed.

I fake pouted, pulling back and leaning away from her touch, crossing my arms in defiance. "I'll have you know I'm actually in my last semester of undergrad," I stated. "I'm twenty-two, *above* legal drinking age, and I have indeed had alcohol before."

Amelia grinned, releasing a 'tsk, tsk." She sat back, as I had done, with a smirk on her face. "I don't know, Natalie," she said, looking down at her hands. "I've got five years on you. I don't know if I can associate with *babies.*"

When she said 'babies,' Amelia looked up at me through her lashes, sending my heart pounding into overdrive. She just called me a baby. It was an insult, but the way in which she said it took every bit of malice from the comment. The tone in which she said it gave it an edge which sent a shiver down my spine.

The waiter returned then, giving us our drinks, and taking our orders. And then, it was just me, a choir director, and two alcoholic fruity drinks between us. Amelia absently took a sip of her margarita, and I in turn tried my daiquiri. I wasn't a big drinker by any means, but the drink was good... dangerously good. Amelia sipped her drink again and I sipped mine.

We were halfway through our drinks, not a single word exchanged between the two of us, and I had hardly noticed. I was too busy focusing on calming my racing heart, the heat of my body being cooled by the frozen drink. I broke from my trance when I caught Amelia smirking at me.

"What?" I questioned.

"If you keep trying to pace me, you're going to blackout," Amelia laughed lightly.

I scoffed, realizing we were evenly drinking one sip after each other the entire time.

"This ain't my first rodeo, señorita," I declared.

I should have known the playful edge to my words would get me in trouble. I was challenging her, and knowing how competitive Amelia was, I figured I would live to regret my statement. I watched her pick up her drink, expecting her to take another sip, but instead she downed the rest in one gulp. Then she sat down her glass, wiped off her lips, and looked at me with the smuggest grin.

Game on. I mirrored her actions, chugging the rest of my drink, fighting through the cold headache that surfaced. Most of the rum in my drink settled at the bottom and hit me hard at the end like a whip, but I fought against the reaction to keep from coughing. I didn't want to look like a wuss.

Amelia ordered us refills and I was starting to regret my stubbornness, realizing that wasn't the end. Before I could think to give up, however, Amelia pulled us on topic.

"I guess we should start this conversation," Amelia declared.

"I still don't think it's your story to tell," I stated. "Regardless if Karmen's okay with it, I just... it's not about you, right? So why should you be the one to tell me what happened?"

"Are you telling me you aren't even the least bit curious?" she questioned, waggling her eyebrows at me.

"It's not about if I'm curious or not, it's about principle—"

"Come on, let loose, live a little. Dive into the gossip you so desire to know."

I shot Amelia an incredulous look but dropped my shoulders in surrender. "Fine!" I caved. "But if Karmen or Eleanor gets mad about me knowing, I'm coming after you."

Amelia smirked, content she had won. "Alright, let's see... about five years ago, Karmen and Eleanor both got engaged. Not to each other, but to men. Karmen's husband—then fiancé—is a very conservative, religious dude. His name is even Adam. And they do say opposites attract, but Karmen and Adam are nothing alike. Karmen's mellowed out a bit since she became a mother but growing up, she was like a stereotypical sorority girl: super preppy, vain, and she slept around constantly. There's nothing wrong with that, I just mean... Karmen *loves* sex.

"They somehow fell in love. I guess Adam treated her in a way the other boys didn't. And he wanted a family, which Karmen always craved.

Her biggest dream in life was always to be a mother, and he could provide her with that. There was kind of a deal breaker with Adam, however, and that deal breaker was sex. Because like I said, Karmen *loves* sex, but Adam is very conservative, right, and he believes the only purpose of sex is to create children. He thinks it's sinful to engage in the act and enjoy it if you aren't specifically trying to create life, and pre-marital sex is a big no-no.

"Karmen must have really loved him though, because she was willing to look past all that and wait. Except I guess the lack of sex left her reflecting on her life a lot, and the next thing we know, it's a week before her wedding and she's *freaking out.*

"She was mainly concerned because she'd never slept with Adam and what if he was horrible in bed, yadda, yadda. I mean, I was trying to be logical. He didn't think sex should be pleasurable, because that was a sin, so like, yes, the sex was probably going to be bad. We ended up having a bit of a pitiful laugh about it, and then Kamren made a crack about how it was too bad she was marrying a man, because another woman would clearly know her way around a woman's body, or whatever. And then Eleanor was like, *'I know exactly what would help you feel better about marrying Adam. You need to have sex with another woman, so you won't keep worrying about the what-ifs. You should have sex with me!'*

"Really?" I cut in, not believing everything went down as smoothly as Amelia was making it out to sound.

"I mean, I wasn't *there* when they first decided to have sex," Amelia stated with a shrug. "But it happened somehow, and that's the gist of what they told us. Evidently, they just had sex that one night, nothing major happened—well aside from the cheating but like... schematics. I mean, we're all adults. We might not condone it, but if you want to have casual sex with your best friend, then fine. We'll be mature about it. And then Karmen got married, right, so it should have been the end of it."

"But it... was not the end of it," I guessed.

"Nope, because a week before Eleanor's wedding and she goes, *'You know what I need one more time before I get married? Sex with a woman.'* And for some reason, Karmen went along with it."

I laughed at Amelia's word choice. "Were you there that time, or was that paraphrasing again?" I chuckled.

Amelia rolled her eyes. "Okay, fine, I wasn't there that time either. But I can only assume that's how the conversation happened."

"Fair enough. Please continue."

"So, after that, Eleanor got married. They both were happily married—no, scratch that. I don't think either of them have ever been happy in their marriages, but they were pretending, fooling themselves, I guess. They did all the typical newlywed stuff, and then, before long, Karmen got pregnant and had a baby like she always wanted. But... that's when things started going downhill.

"I guess children can put a lot of strain on a relationship, especially one on such a rocky foundation to start with. Adam refused to have sex with Karmen because he didn't want another child so soon, and Eleanor wasn't having a very good sex life either—probably because she's sexually attracted to women and married a man, but that's just my take. But do you know where they *did* find good sex? I'll give you one guess."

"Each other?" I questioned.

"Bingo. So Karmen and Eleanor started having lots of regular sex to satisfy each other's needs or whatever. And some people are really good at the whole friends-with-benefits things, but I think it's kind of a difficult relationship to have. Feelings are bound to get caught. By then, I knew about their little sexcapades, but Piper didn't find out until she overheard Eleanor telling me she had caught feelings for Karmen.

"Piper wasn't too happy about things. She's very... lawful... and cheating is most definitely *not* lawful, so she told them both to end it immediately. But when Piper wasn't around, I told Eleanor she needed to tell Karmen how she felt. As her friend, Karmen deserved to know what happened, right? Even if the outcome would be bad... and it was, bad that is. But they both ended the sex.

"Eleanor, however, has some unhealthy coping mechanisms, as you've maybe figured out. And they say the fastest way to get over someone is to get under someone else, right? She could have found another woman, but why bother when she had a perfectly good and willing husband at home? Anyway, plot twist of the century, Karmen went crawling back to Eleanor."

"Really? But I thought Karmen wasn't into Eleanor like that... that's why they stopped having sex in the first place."

"Right!?" Amelia exclaimed. "I mean, it obviously didn't go over quite as smoothly as I'm making it out to be. There was a lot going on, lots of feelings bouncing around. But evidently, Karmen missed Eleanor, a lot, and I mean, she clearly missed more than just the sex. They were kind of flirting with the idea of leaving their husbands, finally coming clean, but then... Eleanor found out she was pregnant."

"Wait, Eleanor's a mom?" I gasped.

"Yes, she has a daughter named Vanessa," Amelia confirmed. "And Eleanor was convinced this was a sign that they should definitely leave their husbands and raise their kids together. However, Karmen got to thinking, and she very adamantly settled on a no-divorce policy. I don't really know why or how she reached that conclusion, but point is, she's not going to divorce Adam. Like, she's very adamant about that. Ha, *adamant*, like Adam—"

"Okay, but then why is Eleanor so mad all the time? Because Karmen essentially shot down her proposal?" I asked, too invested to focus on Amelia's accidental pun. "Because Piper told me Eleanor was mad that Karmen got pregnant again..."

"We're getting to that," Amelia said. "But at that point, they ended it for real. They had to because, well, if Karmen wasn't going to get a divorce, what other option did they have? And I mean, I kind of understand where Karmen's coming from. Just because Eleanor and Karmen could legally marry, and just because they could raise the kids, doesn't mean a judge is going to pick them over the husbands, you know? There was just too much at stake. But they were really in love with each other, still are, maybe. And when they broke it off, Karmen swore that her heart belonged only to Eleanor, and even if she couldn't have Eleanor, she would never be anyone else's, not even her husband's."

"Oh, but Karmen got pregnant again," I stated with comprehension. "What were they going to do? Just stay married but never sleep with their husbands again? Wouldn't the men grow suspicious?"

Amelia shrugged. "That's what I thought. But all I know is that Karmen got pregnant again, and now Eleanor's been mad about it since forever. It's getting really old."

"I can imagine."

By then, we had finished eating. Somehow, I was half-way through another daiquiri. Was that my second... or my... fifth? When I looked over to Amelia, she was downing the rest of her margarita. Personally, I was having trouble focusing. I also realized it was difficult to keep a filter on my mouth.

"Is Piper married?" I questioned before I even realized what I was saying.

If Amelia was surprised by my outburst, she made no notion of it. "They're... separated," she answered. "I mean, she'd rather a divorce like *right now*, but her husband's kind of being a jerk about it."

"Oh..." I muttered. "That's horrible. And the baby's just about due too."

"Well, that's the problem of it all," Amelia stated with a shrug. I didn't understand what she meant, but she was changing the topic again before I could ask for clarification. "We should probably figure out your approach for talking to Eleanor about things. Maybe we could... order dessert?"

It was a definite yes to dessert, not because I wanted more food, but because Amelia clearly loved sweets and I couldn't seem to say no to her. Besides, she was paying so...

I found, however, that I didn't really want to talk about Eleanor. At least, not yet. I wanted to get to know Amelia better. If we were on a pseudo-date, I might as well take advantage of that.

"Amelia," I questioned before she could start in again, "why did you decide to become a teacher?"

Amelia looked up at me, a slight curiosity shining in her gaze. "I mean... most people don't perform their entire lives. Some do, sure, but um... well... I guess I always knew deep down that I wanted to teach."

"So, you knew your entire life that teaching was your life's calling?"

"I guess not exactly, not in so few words. People teach for different reasons. Some people teach because they want to inspire young minds and help pass on knowledge to the younger generations. That's why Piper teachers. And I do that too, don't get me wrong, but that's not *why* I teach."

"Then why do you teach?"

"I teach because I want to be there for the kids when they have no one else to turn to," Amelia stated. "I still want to inspire them and help them learn, of course, but it's... deeper than that. I know what it's like to be young and confused, with the whole world turning against you. I want to be the guiding light for my students who don't have anyone else to turn to. I want my students to know they are valid, that what they're passionate about matters, and that they will make an impact on the world, no matter the size. That's why I like teaching high school. The kids are older. They're learning about the real world and branching out from their upbringing. They're all strong little mini-adults just trying to get their foot in the door of the big, bad, scary world."

"Wow, that's... kind of deep," I muttered. I didn't want Amelia to think I was shallow or dumb because I couldn't think of something reasonable to say, but I just felt as if I couldn't relate. I had never made a difference in anyone's life before, yet there she was, inspiring the youths of tomorrow.

I didn't need to worry too much though, because Amelia was getting drunk and doing a good job embarrassing herself, taking the limelight off me.

"But listen, that's not all," Amelia continued. "Come here." Amelia beckoned me closer, and I leaned over the table. She whispered into my ear, "I'm a slut for some good drama, and let me tell you, high school has tons of drama."

I fell back laughing hysterically, my reserve further loosened by the alcohol. "You're a slut for some good drama?" I cackled, wiping a stray tear from my eye. "You're something else! One minute, you sound like the wisest, most mature woman in the world, and the next minute you sound like a high schooler yourself! I'm starting to think you're a real enigma, Amelia."

Amelia gave me a half-hearted shrug with a smirk. "Yes, well, that's the tea," she stated. "What about you? I believe Piper mentioned you're a biology major. Med school?"

"Heck no," I scoffed. "Do I look like doctor material to you?"

"I mean, not particularly, but you never know. What do you plan on doing then?"

"*Umm...*" I froze up. I had been telling people I was planning on going to grad school, but my lack of applications meant that wasn't going to happen. I was then telling people I planned on doing clinical research, but again, my lack of job offerings made that less promising.

Amelia read me like a book. "You don't know," she stated. I eyed her closely, but there was no judgement in her words. I deflated a bit.

"You caught me," I muttered. "I don't know what I'm doing after graduation. I don't even have a job lined up. Maybe this vacation will spark some motivation in me again."

Amelia smiled softly at me. "People act like having a degree sets up your whole life. It doesn't. And I doubt it's what you were dreaming of when you started school, but no one's going to judge you for working at, say, a grocery store for a while until you figure out what you want to do."

"Nice of you to say. Wish my mother shared your opinion," I stated dejectedly.

"And hey, if nothing works out for you, you could always teach," Amelia stated with a wink.

"Yeah, I don't know about that one. I'm not really a, what was it again? Oh yeah, a 'slut for good drama,'" I teased.

Amelia narrowed her eyes at me before wadding up her nearby straw wrapper. She swung to throw it at me, and I jerked to dodge, but instead of hitting me like I thought it would, the paper wad landed right in my drink.

"*Eww*, you play dirty," I huffed, fishing the paper out of my drink. "You sure do act like a rotten kid for supposedly being some mature high school teacher."

"There's a lot about teaching you don't know," Amelia said, obviously proud of herself for her actions.

"I don't think being immature is part of the job description."

"No, but there's a certain playfulness that comes with the territory."

Our desserts came then, which left our conversation a bit stilted. Amelia's attention was clearly on her chocolate fudge brownie, her eyes rolling back in ecstasy every time she took a bite. Before long, we both finished and our waiter returned, bringing the bill as he cleared our plates. Amelia reached for the check and studied it, looking like she was having trouble focusing.

"Honestly, I might be a little drunk," Amelia admitted, glancing towards me. She had a mysterious glint to her eyes that I couldn't place. "You know, maybe walking all the way back to my hotel isn't the best idea..."

"I mean, you could stay in my room?" I found myself suggesting. "I have a single, but I think there's a futon."

Amelia glanced away from our table, and I saw our waiter heading back towards us. "That could work," Amelia commented. "What's your room number?"

It was an odd thing to ask, considering we would both just walk up together. But tipsy me wasn't thinking clearly, believing that was a perfectly normal thing to ask.

"Oh, um... 513," I answered.

The waiter reached our table then and asked if Amelia was done with the bill. She quickly scribbled something down before handing it over to the waiter with a smirk. She glanced at me out of the corner of her eyes as she stated mysteriously, "You can just charge it to my room, number 513."

"Of course, miss," the waiter looked down at the check— "Will that be all?"

"Yes, thank you," Amelia answered with a smile. Then the waiter was gone.

"Wait, hey!" I protested once I realized what had happened. "You said you were going to pay!"

Amelia stood up from the table and winked at me. "Maybe pay closer attention next time?" she teased. "Although, I guess it was hardly fair of me, considering you're totally drunk. Looks like you're no match for pacing me, you light-weight."

I jumped up from the table to defend myself, but when I did, the entire world spun. I grabbed the table with one hand to steady myself, my other flailing arm landing against Amelia. "Oh... my god," I sputtered out.

Amelia laughed, tugging me out of the restaurant. "Let' go take a stroll outside. The cool evening air with sober you up," she stated, pointing towards an exit.

"Sober?" I scoffed. "I'm not drunk. You're drunk."

"*Ahh...* maybe I'm a bit loose, but you're utterly hammered," Amelia answered, pushing me outside onto the hotel veranda.

"Whatever, I am not," I huffed, crossing my arms in defiance.

Amelia laughed again and tried to grab me, but I pulled away, trying to will the world to stop spinning. After several deep breaths of cool evening air, I felt good enough to walk forward in a semi-straight line. We ended up tumbling over to the pool, constantly cracking jokes at each other. I told Amelia that I needed to get to the pool because I needed to prove to her that I could indeed do a front flip. I was too scared to do one over concrete, but I was going to do one into the pool. So, I grabbed the gate to the pool with gusto, jerking on it several times, but it wouldn't budge. I was getting increasingly irritated until Amelia read the sign listing the pool hours.

"It closed nearly two hours ago," she stated with a giggle. "I guess I'm just going to have to keep believing you're a total nerd who could never do a front flip."

"As if a little gate is going to keep me out," I muttered.

I pressed along the fence until I realized the fence ended just off the path and was replaced with dense shrubbery. It might have deterred the average person, but I pushed through the roughage. I emerged poolside victoriously helping pull Amelia through, and then I dashed to the edge of the pool, lining myself up.

"Okay, here we go!" I declared, swinging my arms at my sides to gain momentum.

"Wait, wait, wait," Amelia said quickly, tumbling after me. "Don't be an idiot. Give me your phone and wallet."

"Oh, so first you want a free dinner, and now you're trying to rob me," I scoffed. I bent my knees, poised to jump.

"No!" Amelia stated, grabbing my arm and spinning me back to face her so that I couldn't even accidently fall into the pool. "I just don't want you to ruin your stuff. I'm not drunk, unlike you, so I still have a train of rational thought."

"I'm not drunk," I protested.

"Yeah? Then prove it."

"I'm trying to, by doing a flip into the pool, but you won't let me."

"That's something a drunk person would do!"

"Fine! Then... let me ask you a sober question," I stated.

"A sober question? What does that mean?"

"It's a question that anyone would ask anyone because they're totally sober," I clarified.

Amelia burst out laughing. "Okay, well know I gotta hear what this question is."

"What is..." I died off, squinting at Amelia, trying to think of a totally normal, sober thing to ask. It was really difficult. My brain was running at hyper speed, flipping between Eleanor and Karmen sleeping together, to Piper getting divorced, and then onto Amelia. Before I could stop it, my drunk brain blurted out, "How come you haven't dated anyone in practically a decade?"

"Who told you that?" Amelia questioned. "You're clearly drunk. Give me your phone and wallet."

I lamented, knowing she was right, and handed her my things. "Piper told me," I answered. "Is it true though?"

"Sure," Amelia answered with a shrug. "Let me put all our stuff on a lounge chair, because I foresee this becoming a disaster."

"Okay, if it's true then, why haven't you dated anyone in so long?" I asked again.

"I've been focusing on my career."

"But you've had a stable job for quite some time now, right?"

"I guess you have a point," Amelia answered, heading back over to me after safely tucking away our belongings.

"Do you... want to start dating again?" I questioned softly as she approached.

I noted the internal struggle Amelia was facing. She was naturally confident, naturally cocky. I could tell she wanted to just declare that she was perfectly content being her own independent self, which I was sure she was. But there was a definite hesitancy to her body language.

After a moment, Amelia choked out, "Yes, I'd like to start dating again. Seeing all my friends with someone, I just... I'm lonely."

I could tell that confession was not easy for Amelia. Without thinking—because my brain was too bogged down to think clearly about anything, really—I reached out and pulled Amelia into a tight hug. Unlike our hug in the ice-cream parlor, this hug was long and, dare I say, intimate. I didn't know if my action would be well received, but Amelia didn't pull away and in fact, she wrapped her arms around me and hugged me in return.

When we finally pulled apart, I could tell Amelia was still a bit apprehensive. I felt the overwhelming urge to cheer her up.

"Look, you're like the greatest catch ever," I stated. "Honestly, guys are just intimidated by your confidence, otherwise they'd be all over you." And then, because I had to pry, I added, "And women, they'd be all over you too."

Amelia colored and shook her head violently. "No, I—I mean, that's fine, for them, but I don't, I'm not, I—"

"No women for you?" I asked calmly.

Amelia was fidgety. I could tell there was something more on her mind that she wanted to say, but she was having trouble finding the words. I was about to ask her if she was okay when she suddenly stepped forward and grabbed my hands. I lost all breath from my lungs, my brain losing my train of thought entirely. I almost backed away on instinct, but Amelia held my wrists tight.

"I... um... can you keep a secret?" she questioned quite intensely.

"Of course," I answered instantly.

Amelia leaned into my ear, still holding my wrists tightly. She whispered, "I think... well I think I might like girls in more than a friend way..."

I pulled back slightly, to look into her eyes. I was about to answer, *"Hey, same, it's all good,"* but before I could, Amelia released my wrists and shoved me backwards, sending me tumbling straight into the pool.

I surfaced with a gasping yelp, standing up to find I was in the shallow end. "Hey!" I snapped.

"That was a pretty shitty flip!" Amelia burst out laughing, doubling over she was laughing so hard.

I pursed my lips, but then an idea struck. I waded over to the edge where Amelia was standing, then jumped up, grabbed her hips, and tugged her straight into the pool with me. Her laughter turned into a shriek as she toppled over. Once she surfaced, she started splashing me, complaining about how I wasn't being fair. I leapt away from her, fighting against the water as I tried to run, and she chased after me, still splashing. When I realized my attempt to flee was futile, I turned on her and grabbed her wrists, holding them steady so she'd stop splashing me, and I tugged her towards me to further hold her still.

"Cut it out!" I laughed. "No splashing!"

"You can't make me!" Amelia answered. She tugged against my grip, wiggling, but I held her tight.

"*Uh huh*, sure I can't," I stated, rolling my eyes.

"Whatever, I let you," Amelia muttered.

I poised myself, ready for whatever her next tactic of escape would be, but it never came. Instead, she just stepped closer to me and dipper her head, resting it on my shoulder. I released Amelia's arms, because I was holding them at a weird angle, and she moved her arms up, wrapping them around my back. I mirrored her actions, holding her close, and I started to sway slightly in the water, enjoying the calm atmosphere and Amelia's closeness. She still smelled of vanilla, even with the added scent of chlorine, and it was lovely... intoxicating. Subconsciously, I ran light circles across her back and Amelia nuzzled against my neck, trying to suppress a yawn, but failing.

"Sobering up?" I questioned.

"I wasn't drunk to begin with," she answered.

Amelia made no move to leave our embrace, so I continued to hold her. I could have stayed like that forever. Even though we were fully clothed and in a hotel swimming pool after hours, I couldn't have thought of a better place to be in that moment. I don't know how long we stayed like that, but eventually I noticed Amelia was shivering—despite our closeness—and it was time to get out.

We waded to the stairs of the pool and climbed out, Amelia grabbing two towels from a nearby towel bin. We did our best to wring out our clothes. Between the cool evening air and the pool water, I was feeling pretty sobered up. I looked to Amelia, who met my gaze, and we both smiled.

I continued trying to dry myself off as Amelia looked at her phone, browsing through her notifications. I wasn't sure what time it was, though I didn't feel too tired. I didn't want my night with Amelia to end, but I wasn't sure what else to suggest. Perhaps, however, Amelia was feeling the same, as she came up with a suggestion.

"Would you like to come back to my hotel?" she asked. I looked at her a bit questioningly. "The gang's still up," Amelia continued, trying to clarify. "Eleanor came back, I guess she just wanted some space and got dinner alone. But they'd love to have you if you wanted to hang out. And you could maybe talk to Eleanor, if the topic comes up."

"Sure," I answered. "I mean, I should probably swing by my room and grab some dry clothes first."

"You can borrow a robe from my room."

I felt Amelia's offer was... unnecessary. But I was very interested to see where the night would lead, especially with Amelia steering, so I gave in.

"Alright, sure," I replied with a nod. "Let's go."

5.

Teary-Eyed Confessions

Amelia shuffled around her hotel room. She grabbed herself a change of clothes from her suitcase and threw me a hotel robe. Then, she stepped into the bathroom and left me alone in her room to change.

I striped down to my underwear, contemplating my next move. It would be uncomfortable to wear wet underwear for who knew how long, but was I really willing to be around the others completely naked with only a hotel robe to shield me? I wasn't exactly shy, but I was by no means an exhibitionist. Sighing, I gave in and chose physical comfort over mental comfort, tugging off my underwear and wrapping the fuzzy robe tight around me. I slipped on the pair of complementary hotel slippers as well and hung my wet clothes up in the closet to dry. By then, Amelia emerged from the bathroom. She looked comfortable, in cotton shorts and an oversized hoodie. I also thought she looked rather adorable.

"Don't comment," she warned. "I know I look like a drowned rat."

"I wasn't going to say that at all," I answered.

"Whatever," she muttered, reaching out to grab my arm. "We're supposed to go over to Karmen's room. Her room's connected to Piper's, so that's where we've all been hanging out."

I just nodded and followed after Amelia. We walked into Karmen's room and found her lying down in bed with a damp washcloth over her face, her migraine clearly lingering. Eleanor sat beside her, paging through channels on the TV.

Eleanor was the first to notice our presence: "What in the world happened to you two?"

"Water ride," Amelia muttered out immediately.

Eleanor frowned, contemplating, and then she shoved at Karmen. "I thought you said they walked back with you?"

I went to move past the bed, but Karmen clearly felt my presence as she reached up, gesturing in my general direction. "Is that Natalie?" she questioned.

"*Uhh*, yeah," I answered.

"Thank god," she stated. "Please, Natalie, get Eleanor off my back or so help me I will strangle someone. My head is *pounding*."

I looked at Eleanor who had a bit of a sinister glint to her eyes. "What am I supposed to do?" I muttered. "Amelia, deal with Eleanor. She's your friend."

Amelia sat down on the bed near Karmen's feet. She watched the TV as Eleanor flipped through channels, but after a second, she grabbed for the remote. A small scuffle over the remote ensued, but it ended abruptly when Karmen kicked Amelia in the side. I couldn't help but chuckle.

Two members of the group were not present in Karmen's room, but I noted that the door to the next adjoining room was open, and I heard some commotion coming from inside. A moment later, Piper came storming into Karmen's room, her phone grasped tightly in her fist.

"Why must divorces take so long, and why can't I block Christian right now?" she huffed.

Ellie 2.0 quickly trailed in after Piper. "You can't block him because you need to communicate through your divorce."

"That's what lawyers are for!" Piper declared.

"But just think how much smoother things will go if you're on speaking terms, with the child and all."

"I don't *want* to be on speaking terms with him! I never want to see his idiotic face ever again!"

Piper turned as if she was about to yell something at one of the others, but her eyes landed on me. I knew her anger wasn't directed at me, but I couldn't stop myself from flinching under her intense gaze.

"*Umm*, hi, Piper," I muttered out. "Amelia said it was cool if I hung out over here, but if you're in the middle of something, I can go..."

Piper threw her hands up exasperatedly. "When am I ever *not* in the middle of something," she huffed. She paced back towards her room, grumbling, and Ellie 2.0 scurried after her.

I turned and looked at Amelia and Eleanor before whispering, "What's going on with that?"

"Divorce stuff," Eleanor stated dismissively.

"Did they have a big falling out or something?" I questioned. I hadn't any experience with divorce—luckily, my parents had managed to so far keep their marriage alive—but I didn't think the hostility was normal for a simple break.

"I will not 'calm down,'" Piper declared, quite loudly, from the other room. "He straight up deceived me, Ellie! He's a dumb idiot!"

"I'm not excusing what he did!" Ellie 2.0 snapped in response, Piper's escalating anger clearly getting to her. "All I'm saying is that you can't take your anger out on your child!"

"I don't want the child!" Piper shouted. "I'm not keeping it!"

"Then let him keep the child! It's his too, and if you don't want it, let him keep his own child!"

"That's what he wants though! If he gets the child, he gets away with everything, *plus* he gets what he wants!"

"Is anyone going to tell me what happened?" I questioned, looking between Amelia and Eleanor.

Amelia gave a slight shrug and gestured towards the other room, so I begrudgingly got up and walked to the adjoining door, hovering in the doorway. Piper was sitting on the edge of her bed, her face buried in her hands, and she shook like she might be crying. Ellie 2.0 sat down next to her and rubbed her back. I stepped fully into the room then and leaned against the desk, just watching, letting Piper cry because letting your emotions out was important.

After a while, I cleared my throat. "So, um... do you want to tell me what happened?" I questioned. "You absolutely don't have to, I just—"

Piper looked up at me with puffy red eyes and cut me off. "I don't want to be a mother," she stated firmly. "I have never, not once in my life *ever*, wanted children of my own, and my husband was always well aware of that. It was nearly a deal breaker for him, but in the end, he chose me over his dream white-picket fence family.

"But guys are idiots! A buddy of his convinced him that once a woman gets pregnant, her hormones change everything and override any current feelings with an overwhelming motherly instinct. He said his wife was the same way, never wanted kids, but once she got pregnant, she was ecstatic, and they were already up to child number three. So Christian thought that if he could just get me pregnant, I would thank him later, and he could have that nuclear family he always dreamed of.

"I never wanted kids though, and so I was always very serious and careful with my birth control. And he knew this... It was meditated, everything he did. He woke me up with breakfast, kept me occupied, surprised me with a trip to the park and a picnic. When we got home, I thought I hadn't taken my pill yet, was very positive I hadn't, but when I went in the bathroom, the pill was gone. I must have taken it on instinct and just forgotten.

"Weeks later I was really bloated and sick all the time... finally dragged myself to the doctor's worried I was anemic or something. But no, instead, my worst nightmare had come true. I was pregnant.

"I broke down. I couldn't handle it. I called Christian and begged him to leave work. I didn't know what we were going to do, I didn't think I'd be able to survive the pregnancy and labor. I needed him for support but..."

Piper was on the verge of hyperventilating, panicking as if she were reliving those moments. I jumped up and sat down on the edge of the bed beside her, rubbing her back while Ellie 2.0 held her hand. Once she was calmer, I looked up and found that Amelia had slipped into the room, sitting on the desk. She sent me a soft smile, which I returned. Shortly after, Eleanor came in too, leaning against the desk, and Karmen followed, looking like her migraine was lessening.

"I just... I panicked because being pregnant makes me feel so... so vulnerable," Piper whispered shakily. "It's like I'm not in control... not in control of my body, or the thing growing inside of me. I told Christian I couldn't handle it, that I wanted to... to get rid of it. That was when he lost it.

"In his anger, he told me everything. He said I was supposed to want it then, and when I questioned him, he told me what his buddy told him. From that, I managed to get the rest of the story out of him. He flushed my pill down the toilet while I was eating breakfast, he poked a hole in the condom when I went to the bathroom. And for some unknown reason, he thought that after I found all that out, that I would lovingly fall into his arms, that I would swoon and praise him for helping me complete my womanly duties of carrying a child! He can go to hell!"

After Piper's snap, everyone remained silent. I wanted to comfort her, but I didn't really know how. Her husband destroyed her trust. He tricked her into something she was vehemently opposed to, had violated her and her wishes. I didn't know how to help, but I couldn't just sit there in silence until Piper just sucked it up and waved us off, telling us to not worry about her.

"So, you're getting a divorce, clearly," I stated a bit hoarsely. "And um, well, I know you were very much against having the child, but well, you're kind of far along now so—"

"I've decided to have the kid," Piper stated, cutting me off. "I'm very nervous about childbirth but trust me when I say I'm fully committed to bringing this child into the world."

I nodded. "Alright, well, I guess my next question then, is, regarding the future of the child, what's your plan? Do you want to raise the kid? Full custody? Joint custody? Put the kid up for adoption?"

"I don't want Christian to get the kid," Piper practically snarled, but then she exhaled shakily. "I know that's hardly fair to the kid... a kid ought to be with at least one of their biological parents if possible. But I just... I can't let him."

"Piper, if I may ask..." I began, "why don't *you* want the child?"

Piper wasn't some fourteen-year-old that got knocked up. She wouldn't be a single teen mom struggling through school and work, trying to make ends meet. She was out of school and had a stable job. The next step for thousands of people was to start a family. Of course, family life isn't for everyone; some people don't want kids. But I wanted to know Piper's reasoning.

Piper started tearing up again. "I'm scared," she whispered. "I'm scared of labor, of childbirth. I'm scared of the changes my body will go through. I'm scared the child will have complications. I'm scared I won't know how to take care of it, that I won't love it right. I'm scared that I'll hurt it, mess it up somehow, and we'll be a dysfunctional family. I'm terrified that I'll ruin the kid. I'm scared that I won't be good enough, that it'll hate me. I'm scared it won't grow up to be a good person. There's so much pressure to be a good parent. I don't want to be a mom that no one wants. I don't want to mess everything up."

Everyone was in shock after Piper's confession. Clearly, no one in the friend group had thought to ask Piper such a thing yet. Suddenly, Karmen was standing in front of Piper. She reached down, grabbing Piper's hands, and clasped them tightly in her own.

"We would never let that happen!" Karmen exclaimed. "Look, parenting isn't always going to be easy. There will be bad days. But there are also going to be *really* good days. I'm a parent; I know what it's like. I'll help you and you can help me! You don't have to do this alone. You have all of us."

Eleanor stepped closer and extended a hand to Piper as well. "You know, Piper, I can't honestly say my pregnancy was planned either. But every time I see Vanessa get excited, or she gives me a hug, well... that's just the most amazing thing in the entire world. And yes, things get hard at times and we're going to worry about our kids, but I know that deep down, we won't have anything to worry about, not really, and do you know why?"

Piper sniffed. "No... why?"

"Because you're going to raise your child to love everyone and be so kind, just like you are, and that kid is going to grow up great because they'll have the sweetest mom in the entire world. Karmen and I are going to be wishing our kids were half the person your kid is going to be. Because your kid is going to be a part of you, and you are an amazing person."

Everyone was teary eyed. Ellie 2.0 was crying harder than Piper even, excusing herself off to the bathroom to blow her nose. Amelia, unable to contain herself, jumped up and dove on Piper, pulling her into a tight hug. And then, before I knew it, everyone was piled onto Piper, and I was pulled into the fray as well.

"You're all right," Piper sniffled, slowly pushing us off her. "I just... well I felt so alone after I found out what Christian did. But you're right. I'm not alone." Piper smiled, despite her puffy red eyes. "She's going to be the luckiest girl alive, having all of you as her honorary aunts."

"Wait... her?" Karmen questioned softly.

Piper nodded a bit sheepishly. "Yeah... I found out the sex at my last ultrasound."

Suddenly, everyone was screaming in glee. Karmen grabbed Piper in a tight hug again, squealing, and both Amelia and Eleanor were bouncing up and down excitedly. Ellie 2.0 wandered back out from the bathroom, looking around in confusion.

"What happened? What did I miss?" Ellie 2.0 asked.

"Piper's having a little girl!" Amelia screamed, diving on Ellie 2.0 and dragging her over.

"Congratulations!" Ellie 2.0 grinned, fighting away from Amelia to sit back down on the bed.

"We're each going to have a little girl the same age!" Karmen continued. "They're going to be the best of friends!"

Everyone was laughing and hugging, especially Amelia, who dove on the bed and tackled me, evidently thinking I wasn't participating in the merriment enough. She jerked me up and spun me around the room before Eleanor grabbed me, tugging me back to spin me as well. I felt a bit like a ping pong ball, but I was laughing too hard to care. I had only just met these women, but I already felt so connected to them.

After several minutes of our excited shenanigans, Ellie 2.0 brought up the real issue at hand. "So, um, not that I want to burst everyone's bubble, but what are the plans moving forward with Christian and the divorce... and the child?"

"You can't give her up, please, Piper," Karmen practically begged.

"I'm terrified..." Piper muttered, "but you're right. I can't just give her up. She is my child after all. I think... well I think I want to fight for full custody. I don't want Christian to get her. He doesn't deserve her."

"Are you going to call your lawyer and tell her that?" Eleanor questioned.

Piper glanced to the clock on the nightstand. "I can't right now. It's almost three in the morning. We all need to go to bed."

Amidst all the excitement, I hadn't realized how late it was. Seeing as all the alcohol I had before was entirely crashing out of my system, I realized I was exhausted. Bed sounded pretty darn sweet.

Without much pizzazz, Piper kicked us all out of her room. Eleanor was trying to play nice with Karmen, but Karmen still kicked everyone out of her room too.

Eleanor headed out with Amelia and me, grumbling under her breath. Amelia bumped Eleanor in the bicep, teasing, "Hey, better luck next time, cowboy."

"Whatever," Eleanor mumbled. "Night, guys." Then she slipped into her own room.

"Let me just grab my clothes from your room," I stated as Amelia unlocked her door.

"You can stay with me if you want," she said as she opened the door.

I stepped inside, heading straight to the closet. "I mean, my hotel's just next door, it's not like it's that far of a walk."

"It's three in the morning though, and well... it might be nice to just *not* have to go back outside."

"I don't want to impose."

"You aren't. I'm offering."

"Alright then, I suppose you do have a point," I gave in. I closed the closet door and before I could even turn around, Amelia grabbed me in a hug.

I wasn't sure what the hug meant, but it was long and close and intimate. We stood there long enough that my mind could process the state of my body—which was extreme exhaustion—and I felt myself crashing. My eyelids were so heavy, I could have fallen asleep standing up in Amelia's arms. I yawned and in turn, Amelia yawned, which prompted her to release me.

She went to her suitcase, and I turned to face the only bed in the room. It was so inviting. I fell onto the soft duvet and probably would have been asleep in seconds if not for Amelia.

Amelia sat down beside me on the bed. I was lying on my stomach, so I couldn't see her, but I felt the mattress sink under her weight. I felt Amelia reach out and rest her hand against my back, against the plushness of the hotel robe. Then, her hand began to trace down, easing slowly towards the edge of the robe.

Her sudden lack of contact made me aware that in my barely conscious state, I was enjoying the touch much more than I realized. I rolled over and sat up, looking to Amelia.

"What's your natural hair color?" Amelia questioned, meeting my eyes.

Despite my tired state, it was never too late for sass. "What are you talking about? This *is* my natural hair color," I answered smugly.

"Yeah, sure, just like this is my natural color," Amelia answered sarcastically, pointing to her own head.

"Alright, fair," I answered with a shrug. "My natural color is... a brown color, I guess. I don't know. I've been dying my hair for nearly eight years, I kind of forget."

"Eight years? What colors have you had?"

"Nothing too crazy," I answered. "Well, I mean freshmen year I went bright blue, but that was a mistake. No, it was just natural colors all through high school. College I had more freedom—tried that whole 'grey' phase from a few years back, but that was a nightmare for upkeep. Now I've got this pink situation going on."

"I like your whole 'pink situation,'" Amelia replied, smiling. "It brings out the blues and greens in your eyes. Your eyes really stand out, you know. They were the first thing I noticed when I saw you."

"Really?" I questioned skeptically. "Most people notice the hair first, considering it's *pink*."

"No, I noticed your eyes first," Amelia stated defiantly. She reached forward, straightening out the collar of the robe I was wearing, and once it was fixed, she slowly ran her hand down further, continuing what she was saying. "I first noticed your bright eyes, then your adorable freckles, and then your hair. Then I noticed your style—it's kind of vintage, skater—and I noticed how you carry yourself. You're confident—it's absolutely attractive—but borderline cocky, which is annoying."

I could hardly breathe. Amelia hovered just inches from my face, staring down at me, and her hand came to rest against my abdomen, toying with the belt-tie that held the robe shut against me. I thought she surely had to be flirting with me, and she was so beautiful, so charming... I could just... kiss her. I could just lean up and kiss her, and I nearly did, but then she was gone.

Before my brain could register what happened, Amelia was off the bed and locked in the bathroom. I sat up more fully, blinking in confusion. Had I imagined that? Or better yet, had I dreamt that? I *was* super tired. I easily could have blacked out for a few minutes. But I could still feel the ghosting touch of Amelia's hand on my stomach.

I glanced at the clock and inwardly groaned. It was approaching four which meant a maximum of three hours of sleep if we were hitting the park right as it opened. It probably wasn't even worth going to sleep at that point. But the bed was comfortable, and when I pulled back the covers and cuddled into them, I felt myself giving way to sleep.

6.

The Second To Last Day

"Amelia! Coffee downstairs if you want some. We're leaving in fifteen! Wakey-wakey!"

I blinked several times, trying to alleviate the burning from my heavy eyes. I felt groggy and sick, from lack of sleep, and I regretted going to sleep at all. Pulling an all-nighter would have been far better. Granted, I hadn't done than since sophomore year, but I knew I was capable with some extra shots of expresso...

I realized I should probably get up. I felt rather gross: dirty hair, disgusting teeth and no toothbrush, an oily face covered in smeared makeup, and dirty clothes still damp and smelling of chlorine hanging in the closet. I realized I was still in the hotel robe, which had come undone in the night and had left me rather indecent. I shifted, trying to adjust the robe, but I quickly realized I couldn't because I had one blonde completely passed out and wrapped around me.

Amelia was snuggled against me, her face buried against my bare collar bone, her body flush against mine. Her one arm had slipped inside my robe, resting along the base of my rib cage, and that realization sent my heart speeding up. I flushed, reaching down, and carefully untangled her arm from me, tucking the robe back together. When I released Amelia's arm, she grunted and snuggled up closer to me. I realized I didn't care about getting up anymore. All I cared about was relaxing, closing my eyes, and enjoying this moment for as long as I could.

I must have dozed off because I was startled awake by someone knocking on the door.

"Amelia? You up? We need to get going," Piper called from the hall.

I didn't want Piper—or anyone else for that matter—barging in on Amelia and me in our current state. I figured Piper had a spare key, so I needed to answer to keep her from opening the door.

I cleared my throat and called out, "*Umm*, just a minute," hoping I sounded enough like Amelia to slip by.

"Amelia, who's in there with you? Is that Natalie?" I bit my tongue. Maybe if I didn't say anything, Piper would just assume she had misheard. "Um, well, just come downstairs when you're ready," Piper continued and then luckily, she left.

I still didn't want to get up, and Amelia clearly didn't either, apparent in the way she kept burying her face further into me. However, I was very concerned Eleanor might burst in snapping pictures for future blackmailing, and with Amelia's closeness, I felt like I might combust.

Slowly, I extracted myself from Amelia. "Hey, Amelia?" I questioned, shaking her slightly. "You need to wake up. Come on."

"No, I don't wanna," Amelia whined. She rolled away from me and buried herself into a pillow.

"Look, I don't want to get up either," I declared, retrieving my things from the closet. "But you need to get downstairs to meet everyone and I need to rush back to my hotel to get a change of clothes and well... make myself presentable."

Amelia didn't answer me, perhaps asleep again, but I figured her friends wouldn't let her sleep in forever. I slipped out of the room, opting to take a back-stairway downstairs and a side door out to hopefully avoid the others waiting in the lobby. I went back to my own room, barely aware I was wearing a different hotel's robe.

I didn't know what time it was when I finally headed out to the park. I hardly cared about early access, having been on all the rides multiple times already, so I took my time getting ready. I used the coffee maker in my room, despite it being overpriced, and finally feeling more awake, I headed off.

I was contemplating how I might find the teachers again, but I luckily didn't have to worry too much, because downstairs in the lobby of my hotel I found Piper, Ellie 2.0, and Amelia. Before I could question why they were there, Amelia ran over to me and hugged me abruptly. Just as quickly as she had grabbed me, she shoved me back, snapping, "Hey, it took you long enough."

"I... didn't know you guys were waiting for me...?" I questioned.

"Amelia insisted we wait up for you," Piper stated, ratting out her friend, which Amelia was not happy about.

"I did not!" Amelia huffed. "I just thought, you know, that maybe it would be nice to wait up for you, and Piper agreed! It was basically her idea, even!"

"Of course," Piper answered, humoring Amelia.

"Where're Eleanor and Karmen?" I asked.

"They're on a date!" Ellie 2.0 practically squealed.

"Hardly," Amelia muttered. "They're on speaking terms, but that's about it. And who knows if they'll start fighting again."

"Maybe we'll get lucky, and they'll still be on pleasant terms when we catch up with them," Piper commented. "Either way, shall we get going?"

"You guys really didn't have to wait up for me," I stated sheepishly.

"How else could we guarantee finding you again?" Amelia cooed.

"Look, I don't know. You guys kind of stick out like a sore thumb," I stated with a grin. "I think I would have been able to track you down."

"Friends wait up for friends," Ellie 2.0 declared. "Now come on! We're wasting vacation time!"

I grinned, being pulled out of the hotel by my new friends. I wasn't sure what would happen when spring break came to an end, but for the time being I was content and happy.

With my extra time getting ready, we were no longer early enough for early access. Early access was a perk of staying at one of the park's hotels, letting people in thirty minutes early to start filling the park from the back. Then, when the park opened normally, it opened in the front, evenly filling the park. We ended up arriving as the park opened normally, meaning there was a massive crowd. As we waited in line, I turned to Piper.

"How are you doing?" I asked.

"I'm... hanging in there," she answered. "I've decided to table things until after break and just enjoy my vacation."

"Of course."

I looked to the others. Ellie 2.0 engaged Piper in conversation and Amelia stood on her tiptoes, scanning the crowd over everyone's heads, trying to gage how long the line was. I was curious what the day might hold for us.

"So, what's the plan for today?" I asked the group.

"I'm still really not feeling rides," Ellie 2.0 muttered. "I've filled my excitement quota for the rest of the year... maybe the rest of my life."

"Kill-joy," Amelia grumbled, though it was lighthearted.

"I'm fine to ride things with Amelia if you and Piper don't mind hanging out a bit," I said. "But well, what are we doing about Eleanor and Karmen? Are we going to try and find them or just give them space?"

"I think we should give them some space," Piper stated. "The more time they're together alone, the more likely they'll be to have an open and honest conversation."

"I'm fine leaving them alone," Amelia agreed. "Eleanor has been such a jerk all vacation. Let Karmen deal with her, as far as I'm concerned."

"I think they'll work things out," Ellie 2.0 stated optimistically. "I, personally, believe in the power of love."

"I don't know about all that," Piper commented, "but I'm fine with just going with the flow. I've had more than enough stress in my life lately. Taking the backseat for a day seems like a luxury."

"Alright, it's settled then," I declared. "We'll leave them be and see what happens."

Amelia was still distracted looking over people's heads. She suddenly reached out and roughly grabbed me, not even turning to see where she had grabbed. She grabbed my shirt right in the center of my stomach as well as a handful of skin and jerked me forward.

"Ouch!" I squealed, attempting to fight her off.

She released my stomach only to grab my shoulders. She jerked me in front of her, pointing off into the park.

"Look!" she exclaimed. "They have a breakfast café!"

"I thought you only got this excited about ice-cream..."

"Try any sugary monstrosity," Piper chuckled. "For every pancake she has to have five pounds of whipped cream, a gallon of syrup, and all the dessert toppings."

"Just the thought of that is enough to make me throw up," I stated, pulling a disgusted face.

Amelia was oblivious to our comments. "Can we get food? Pretty please?" she asked, squealing with glee. "I'm so hungry," she continued. "I haven't eaten in hours and *ohmygosh* they have a pancake *and* waffle special today!"

"I mean... I could eat," I confessed.

"I wouldn't mind a bite either," Ellie 2.0 chimed in. "And Piper should always be ready to eat. She's eating for two, after all."

"I'll take that as a yes!" Amelia declared. "Let's go!" She reached out blindly and grabbed my shirt again, but I shoved her off.

"Stop, look at the state of my shirt!" I complained, trying to smooth out all the wrinkles Amelia created. "And we still have to wait in line to get into the park anyway."

Amelia's eyes narrowed, scanning the crowd like a hawk. "Nothing stands between me and a tower of pancakes," she muttered under her breath. Then she grabbed my shirt again, but this time took off, pulling me with her.

"Cut it out!" I shouted, stumbling. "Let go! What are you doing?"

Amelia didn't answer. Instead, she just swiveled me around and shoved me forward into a new entrance terminal just as a new worker walked up and opened it. We scanned our passes and were inside the park seconds later, but we left Piper and Ellie 2.0 behind, still stuck in the line. Amelia and I went inside a got a table while we waited.

Luckily, it didn't take them too long to get in and shortly after we ordered our food. Amelia got the works, as expected, but the rest of us opted for normal, minimal sugar, breakfasts.

Piper seemed pensive. It was understandable, given the night before. Ellie 2.0 would utter out little comments here and there. Amelia seemed enthralled with the atmosphere of the diner. I realized, sitting there, that I knew a fair bit about Piper and Amelia, but virtually nothing about Ellie 2.0, so I vowed to change that.

"What's going on in your life, Ellie 2.0?" I questioned.

Ellie 2.0 looked over at me with wide eyes. "Wha—what do you mean?"

"I mean, what's up? Are you sleeping with your coworker friend, divorcing your husband, or fighting off gay feelings?"

Amelia, who at that exact moment took a big sip of water, started hacking violently. I reached over and patted on her back, but she shoved my arm away. As soon as she could take in air, she snapped, "I am *not* fighting off *gay feelings*, thank you very much!"

"Funny you figured that was directed towards you then," I replied skeptically.

"I like men!" Amelia declared. She looked to her friends for help, but they refused to comment. "I do!" she stated more firmly. "I like guys with, well, five o'clock shadows and... and happy trails leading down to their... well you know... their *apparatus*—"

"Apparatus!?" I howled in laughter.

"I like men!" she stated defiantly.

"Stop yelling!" Piper snapped at us.

"Look, chill out," I huffed at Amelia. "No one said you *didn't* like men."

"But you said gay feelings—"

"Okay, fine, bisexual feelings," I corrected. "Better?"

"No!" Amelia snapped. "I don't like women either! I just like men—"

I sensed the conversation deteriorating, so I turned back to Ellie 2.0, ignoring Amelia. "Anyway, what's going on in your life, Ellie 2.0?" I questioned again, cutting Amelia off. She expressed her displeasure with a taunt snarl, and I cracked a sideways grin in her direction.

"I... um... none of that," Ellie 2.0 muttered. "I just have two dogs and a very nice male fiancé. He's an English teacher too at a nearby charter school. We're planning on getting married this fall."

"*Aww*, that's adorable! It's about time someone in this friend group didn't have any extra drama."

"I don't have extra drama," Amelia stated defiantly.

"Uh huh, sure," I answered, rolling my eyes.

"So sorry to break up the conversation," Piper cut in, "but I have a small child playing kickball with my bladder. Excuse me."

Piper strolled off to the bathroom and the sudden arrival of our food broke up the conversation. I looked over to Amelia's plate, which was a stack of pancakes completely hidden in a layer of whipped cream, next to a stack of waffles piled high with powdered sugar and candied cherries. Amelia smacked her lips, greedily grabbing for the syrup, before further drowning her food.

"*Ugh*," I gagged, looking away from Amelia. "I'm going to have to go eat my bacon outside because it's making me sick watching you eat that mess."

"What are you talking about? This is delicious!" Amelia exclaimed.

I suspiciously eyed Amelia as she took another bite. "Ten bucks says you'll puke on the first ride we go on," I declared.

"Make it fifty and maybe I'll consider."

"Fifty!?" I exclaimed. "Well, someone's cocky. But fine. I'd like to be fifty dollars richer anyway."

"Is everything a competition with you two?" Ellie 2.0 questioned. "You're worse than Eleanor and Karmen. Are lesbians normally this annoying?"

"What!?" Amelia practically shrieked, her cheeks red.

Ellie 2.0 smirked. "I think I'm starting to understand why Eleanor likes pushing your buttons so much."

"Being competitive is fun," I stated with a shrug.

"I'm confident in my strong stomach," Amelia said, "so why would I pass up the opportunity to get some extra cash?"

"Are you making bets over here?" Piper questioned, walking back up to the table.

"Fifty if I don't puke," Amelia answered with a shrug.

"I think it could almost be considered stealing, taking fifty dollars from a poor college student when you have a stable full-time job," Piper said, taking a seat.

"I'm not that poor," I defended. "Did I spend a lot of my savings on this trip... well, yes. And am I currently unemployed? Yes. But I have *some* money."

"You mean you have a financial cushion from your parents," Amelia stated. Her comment wasn't as lighthearted as before and I eyed her oddly, trying to understand her tone.

"I mean, they won't let me starve," I muttered. "Just because I'm going to school full time right now and don't have time for a job doesn't mean I'm not ambitious and able."

Amelia scoffed. "Going to school full time and you don't have time for a job... what a luxury."

"What are you talking about?"

"It doesn't matter. Eat your bacon."

I watched as Amelia turned away from me, focusing on her food. I was confused. I slowly nibbled at my bacon, the table falling silent. I felt like I had said something wrong, but I didn't know what or how to fix it.

After breakfast, things seemed to settle back to normal. Amelia was dying to ride a roller coaster, so she dragged me off like nothing happened, leaving Piper and Ellie 2.0 behind.

Amelia looked... not too great as we waited in line. "Hey, are you okay?" I asked. "I'm sorry if I said something—"

"No, no, you're fine," Amelia answered. "Do you ever have a moment where something will come up and it just... well... it reminds you of a sad time in your past?"

"Oh..."

"But it's fine. Things are in the past," Amelia stated, although she still didn't look well.

"Are you sure you're okay?" I asked again.

"Yeah, I'm good, I—" Amelia cut off abruptly as she turned to the nearest bush beside us in line and promptly emptied her stomach contents. The people around us in line backed up, side-stepping us in line. I reached up, helping hold Amelia's hair back as she gagged again, rubbing what I hoped were comforting circles on her back. I was so taken aback by her sudden vomiting that I nearly forgot about our bet.

Nearly.

"*Ha*! That's fifty dollars for me!" I exclaimed over Amelia's misery.

Amelia gagged again, but then she turned and glared daggers at me. "No, you said I'd puke on the first ride we went on, but we haven't—" she turned away to puke again— "been on any rides," she added, more lackluster.

"Oh, come on!" I whined. "This has to count!"

Amelia stood up fully, though cautiously, and leaned against the rail on the side of the line. She held up a finger, swallowed, then spoke. "*Umm*, no. You can't take advantage of a sick person."

I grumbled a bit but gave in when Amelia pitifully asked if we could go find some water. I couldn't hold a bet over her head when I just wanted her to feel better. We stopped at the nearest concession stand where I chivalrously bought Amelia a bottle of water, then we sat around for a bit to let her stomach settle.

"I'm sorry," Amelia muttered. "Sometimes I forget that I'm getting old, and my body can't handle the sweets I so dearly love."

"First of all, no one could handle the amount of putrid sweets you ingested this morning," I stated. "And then, second of all, you aren't getting old—"

"Oh, well thanks, but—"

"You *are* old."

Amelia looked up for a moment, absorbing what I said, before she narrowed her eyes and reached out and smacked me. "You're so rude!" she huffed.

"I'm just kidding!" I rectified. "You aren't old at all. Old people are kill-joys that talk about 401(k)s and the new spatula they just bought."

"So... Ellie 2.0?"

We both started laughing, lifting Amelia's spirit.

"You're too fun to be old," I continued, once I controlled my giggles. "Old is a mindset, isn't that what they say?"

"There's nothing wrong with being old."

"Well in that case, I guess you're old."

"Stop!" Amelia exclaimed, shoving my arm.

With Amelia feeling better, we decided to head back and find Ellie 2.0 and Piper. The concession stand we went to was a bit out of the way and we took our time wandering back, just enjoying each other's company.

Suddenly, something caught my eye. Using my Lesbian Doppler Radar skills, I easily homed in on a lesbian couple just off to the side of the path. I often spotted adorable couples and seeing queer couples out in public always warmed my heart. This time though it was different, as I knew this couple.

Not too far ahead of us were Eleanor and Karmen, hand in hand, strolling along. When I saw them, Eleanor turned, and we nearly made eye contact.

"Oh shit," I squeaked out unintentionally. I grabbed Amelia's arm and jerked her back to the side, Amelia yelping as we ducked down.

"What just happened?" Amelia gasped as I pulled her into a gift shop.

"Over there," I stated, pointing out the window. "It's Eleanor and Karmen."

Amelia squinted out the window, trying to spot the others. Karmen and Eleanor stopped just across from the giftshop and sat down on a bench. They seemed to be on friendly terms, at least. Karmen was smiling. Eleanor had her hand resting on Karmen's knee.

"Rude of you to just tug me in here," Amelia stated.

"I didn't want them to see us because then they'd come over and we'd never get them alone again," I defended.

"Well... they aren't fighting," Amelia observed. "But Karmen seems a bit dismissive. Did you notice that?"

I looked back out at the pair, noting that what Amelia said seemed to be true. When Eleanor tried to get extra close to Karmen, Karmen would turn away. It seemed innocent enough, but I figured Eleanor would eventually catch on that she was being snubbed, and then she'd be bitter all over again.

"Oh shoot! It's Ellie 2.0!" Amelia gasped, pointing out the window frantically.

Amelia shoved me towards the door, and I stumbled out, roughly grabbing Ellie 2.0 by the shirt sleeve, tugging her back inside with us. Ellie

2.0 shrieked, which I should have expected, but she noticed Amelia quickly enough to quiet down.

"Goodness gracious!" Ellie 2.0 spat. "You two gave me a heart attack!"

"We didn't want you to run into Eleanor and Karmen," Amelia declared, pointing towards the others.

Ellie 2.0 looked out the window and shrugged. "So?"

"We want them to work things out on their own," Amelia explained.

"What happened to Piper?" I asked.

"Bathroom break again. She was getting a bit cranky, wanted some time alone. She told me to not wait up for her and to come find you two. Frankly though, I'm not about to hide out in here. It's a nice sunny day out. I want to be outside."

She turned to leave but Amelia grabbed her while I gasped, "No, no, no, wait!"

Ellie 2.0 stopped and pointed outside. "Well, would you look at that," She declared.

I turned, following her line of sight, and saw none other than Piper now standing with Eleanor and Karmen.

"Well... I guess we found Piper," Amelia muttered.

"So much for keeping Eleanor and Karmen alone," I huffed.

After a moment of the three of them being engaged in conversation, Piper turned and pointed directly at us as we stood in the window, effectively blowing our cover. Barely a second later, Eleanor was over and tugging us back out into the sunshine.

"What are you guys doing spying on us?" Eleanor questioned.

"We weren't spying," Amelia declared.

"Now, now," Eleanor tsked, "I can't have the two of you getting off too easy, now can I?"

"What is she talking about?" Ellie 2.0 asked Karmen and Piper.

"I want to hear all about how this morning went... and last night too if you catch my drift," Eleanor stated, winking at Amelia.

"What are you talking about?" Amelia grumbled. "We all stayed up late and got up at the butt crack of dawn. How do you think our mornings went?"

"You're not fooling me," Eleanor chuckled. "I bet you two weren't doing much sleeping at all last night."

"What are you saying?" Amelia demanded. She was bright red in the face and the tops of her ears were scorching.

"I'm not saying anything. Your actions speak louder than your words anyway."

"What actions!?"

"You mean besides the fact that you're blushing like a fiend right now? Fine, we all know there was more than one occupant in your room last night, Amelia. No sense trying to deny it." Eleanor smirked impishly. She turned to me and reached out, grabbing me in a teasing headlock before she ruffled my hair. "Good for you, Short Stack," she declared. "How was your night, kiddo? Bet you had an awful lot of fun last night after the rest of us went to bed."

I pulled away from Eleanor, confused by the nickname, but that was hardly the point.

"I don't know what you're talking about," I stated as confidently as I could, though I was blushing just as badly as Amelia was.

"What are you *talking* about?" Ellie 2.0 whined exasperatedly. "It was so late last night we all just went to bed! I mean... we did, didn't we? Piper? Karmen?"

Piper remained silent, refusing to get involved. Karmen, however, cracked a small smile.

"*Ahh*, Eleanor, come on, leave them alone," Karmen stated.

"I'm just trying to get some answers here!" Eleanor pushed. "Like... how did Amelia know to wait for Natalie back at her hotel? Wouldn't it make sense to assume Natalie left for the park the same time we did? Unless, of course, they saw each other this morning and said otherwise."

"It—we just thought—Piper said it was—" Amelia tried to choke out an excuse, but she couldn't manage proper speech.

"Stop denying it, Amelia, I *know* you two spent the night together," Eleanor stated.

Amelia snapped, getting ahold of herself. "So what if we did!?" she shouted. "There's nothing wrong with two fully grown adults sharing a room platonically!"

Eleanor burst out laughing. "Platonically!? Platonically my ass! You're always making such heart eyes at other women, it's about goddamn time you finally shagged one!"

"Why are you being like this?" Amelia practically pleaded, her voice cracking, and I realized she was about to burst into tears.

I didn't understand what any of this was. Personally, Eleanor ragging on us didn't bother me. I probably would have done the same to my own friends, regardless of what the truth was. But it was very clear that what

Eleanor said was greatly bothering Amelia and her jabs seemed to get harsher and harsher. Suddenly, the only thing I cared about was breaking up Eleanor and Amelia.

I harshly grabbed Amelia's arm and exclaimed over Eleanor, "I just realized there's a water ride I haven't been on yet! Come on. We have to complete the circuit!" Then, before Amelia could question me and before Eleanor could stop us, I ran off, tugging Amelia away.

While we waited in line for one of the water rides, Amelia seemed rather down. She didn't cry, luckily, but she was clearly lost in thought.

"Hey, look, don't listen to Eleanor, alright?" I stated. "I think she just likes pushing people's buttons. She shouldn't be such a jerk, but just, don't dwell on it so much, alright?"

Amelia glanced towards me, biting her lip in contemplation. "I'm kind of used to it," she answered after a pause.

"Does it... well does it bother you when your friends insinuate things about your sexuality?" I asked.

Amelie scoffed. "That's just what friends do. We're always making cracks about who's getting laid and who has the best sex life. That's what friends are for, right? To always have your back and to know all the dirty little secrets of your bedroom life."

"Sure, but does it *bother* you?" I asked again, emphasizing my point. "Because, look, I've been out since the beginning of college. I'm used to the jokes. They don't phase me anymore. But I know they used to make me uncomfortable, and I know that they make other people uncomfortable. So, if it bothers you, I can promise you that at least *I* won't joke about it."

"I... thank you."

"No problem."

We tackled the water ride. I disappointingly hardly got wet at all, but when we spun around one corner, a wall of water flew up and crashed down directly onto Amelia, completely soaking her. I roared with laughter, and she smacked at me, threatening to hug me when we got off the ride.

"You look like a drowned rat!" I laughed, skipping away just out of reach of Amelia once we were off the ride.

"Stop, it's not funny!" she stated, though she was laughing. "I'm absolutely freezing! Be a gentlewoman and give me your jacket!"

"What? No way! I don't want you getting my hoodie all wet!"

"This is all your fault!" she continued. "You were the one who wanted to ride that thing! The least you could do is help me not freeze to death!"

"You're not going to freeze; it's nearly eighty degrees out here!"

"Please?"

I rolled my eyes, coming to a stop. "*Ugh*, fine," I gave in, pulling off my hoodie. "Frankly though, you're annoying."

"Uh huh, such an articulate come back," Amelia answered with a smirk, tugging my hoodie over her head.

Amelia and I ended up spending most of the day together alone. Considering how easily we had been running into each other, I figured the others were giving us space. Maybe this was because Amelia was really upset earlier, but I thought it was because they were pushing Amelia and me together in much the same way we were trying to push Eleanor and Karmen together. I didn't mind though. We rode rides, laughed together, browsed gift shops, and just genuinely had a good time.

We got along well. Some people you just seem to click with, and I guess Amelia and I just clicked. Our sense of humor was nearly identical. We were getting to know each other better. And I liked the other teachers a lot too, even if Eleanor sometimes pushed too far. I would have been happy hanging out as a group, but I cherished the alone time I got with Amelia as well.

In a way, it felt like we were on a date. We didn't hold hands or kiss or anything—nothing like that—but we took turns buying each other snacks and we did seem to bump shoulders rather often. Sometimes I felt like she wanted me to hold her hand, or maybe kiss her... just make some sort of move, but I kept second guessing myself. I didn't know what she was comfortable with, especially after how she reacted to Eleanor, and I didn't want to upset her if we weren't on the same page.

I found myself then thinking about tomorrow. Tomorrow, my newly acquired teacher friends were leaving. They wanted to get home before the weekend to prep for class whereas I was staying through Sunday to maximize my vacation time before begrudgingly returning to school. That meant tomorrow was my last day with them. If I was going to make a move, it was now or never.

Part of me wanted to see where this—whatever you wanted to call it— would go. I wanted to tell Amelia that I liked her, that I didn't want this to be goodbye forever. But another part of me, the majority, really, didn't think we'd mix outside of a spring break vacation. They were successful teachers, and I was a nobody college kid with no planned future. Maybe that night I could make a move... sleep with Amelia once just because. She might be down to experiment. But when I looked at her and I saw her smile, her eyes just absolutely sparkling, I knew I never could. I wasn't a one-night stand kind of person. I put too much emotion into everything, unfortunately. It wasn't meant to be, and that was fine.

Late into the afternoon, Amelia and I settled down on a bench. We were munching on candy watching people walk by. The park would close soon enough, after some late-night show, but with the way our energy levels were crashing, I wasn't sure we'd make it that long. The more tired Amelia got, the more affectionate she became. She leaned into me, chewing on a piece of candy while she absentmindedly played with my hand that was lying in my lap. To me, the rest of the world no longer existed.

Amelia saw something then, however, and grumbled, "Great," under her breath.

I looked up, noticing Eleanor approaching us from across the way. She waved at us. Amelia ignored her, being sour, but I waved back to be polite.

"Hey, be pleasant at least," I told Amelia. "But if she starts pushing buttons again, we'll just leave."

"I'm sorry," Eleanor called out to us. Amelia quickly sat up, pulling away from me, and I sat up straighter myself. Once Eleanor reached us, she stopped just in front of us and reiterated what she said. "I'm sorry. I was being awful earlier, and I said things that made you guys uncomfortable. I'm sorry. I just... well I guess there's still a part of me that's insecure about my sexuality. I never planned on things to happen with Karmen the way they did, and then Amelia found out, and then suddenly everyone knew. And Piper was always in my face about it, telling me what I should be thinking and feeling and what I should do... I never had time to really figure it out for myself. But when it surfaced that, I don't know, Amelia might kind of maybe like women or something, I felt like I could take the spotlight off myself and throw it on you guys. Then you'd be the new gossip and I could just... fucking figure out things without Ellie 2.0 constantly being like, *'Oh my gosh, just talk to Karmen, you two should just make up already. You're such a cute couple and shit.'*"

"I don't think Ellie 2.0 would say shit," I interrupted with a small smile.

"Okay, whatever, but you get my point. I wasn't thinking about how I was making you feel because I just liked having the focus off me. And well... Karmen's always sort of been my moral compass, so when we weren't talking, I got a bit nastier—"

"You think?" Amelia scoffed.

"I'm sorry," Eleanor stated again, and it sounded like she really meant it. "Karmen and I have been talking again though, and she made me realize that I was making Amelia feel exactly how I always felt: like I was in the spotlight and couldn't see. So, for that, I am truly sorry."

Slowly, after a moment, Amelia answered, "...Thank you."

"And look," Eleanor continued, in all her grace, "I don't know if you two like each other or if you're fucking or whatever, but I'm going to shut up about it. If either of you want to talk about things with me, that's cool. Otherwise, it's whatever. Consider this topic tabled."

"Thanks," I agreed with a nod.

I looked to Amelia. She was blushing softly, but also smiling, which was a good sign. I glanced over to Eleanor then and realized she looked downright exhausted. There was clearly a lot going on in Eleanor's life and her fight with Karmen was wearing her out. I felt like we all benefitted from our open and honest conversation with Piper, and now this conversation... communication was important in all aspects of life. I couldn't force Eleanor and Karmen to talk to each other, but I was capable of talking to Eleanor myself.

"Hey, Eleanor?" I asked tentatively. "Would... *you* like to talk?"

Eleanor snorted. "What do you mean?" she questioned.

"I mean... talk about gay stuff," I clarified as well as I could. "I've been out for several years. I've got some experience in this category. I just thought it might be helpful for you to have someone to talk to, just so you can unload and ask questions or just, well, talk with someone other than your friends."

Eleanor seemed very taken aback by my offer. She shuffled her feet for a moment before muttering out, "I mean... I don't know... I guess if you'd be willing...?"

I turned to Amelia. "Would it be okay if we...?"

"Of course," Amelia answered, waving us off. "I think I'll just head back to my room anyway. I'm super tired."

"We could go back to my room to talk," Eleanor stated. "That way we can all walk back together."

"Sure."

"Sounds good to me."

We headed off towards their hotel. Amelia sent me an odd sort of look that I couldn't quite place. It was probably just because I was finally going to talk to Eleanor like Amelia had been wanting... probably...

When we reached the hotel, we stalled at Amelia's room.

"What's the plan for tomorrow?" she asked me.

"I don't know. When are you guys heading out to the park?"

Amelia shrugged and looked to Eleanor.

"I haven't a clue," Eleanor answered. "Ellie 2.0's the one who planned everything and Piper's the one who keeps us on track. I just go with the flow."

"Well then I guess just come get me when you're heading out," I decided, turning back to Amelia.

"What room are you in?" Amelia asked.

"What? You don't remember my room number from dinner?" I quipped. "Were you perhaps more drunk than you let on?"

"Hilarious," Amelia answered, rolling her eyes. "Just remind me."

I reached into my pocket and pulled out my spare room key, passing it to Amelia. "513," I stated. "No promises I'll be awake, so just come in and shake me a few times."

Amelia grinned. "Alright, see you tomorrow."

Amelia slipped into her room, and I headed down the hall after Eleanor. We settled into her room, Eleanor leaning against the bed, and I sat at the desk.

"So, what was that all about?" Eleanor questioned with a smirk.

"What was what all about?"

"You know... with Amelia," Eleanor said pointedly. "I guess Amelia's sexuality is still up in the air, but I know you're a full-blown homosexual, so what gives?"

"Nothing. I don't know what you're talking about."

"I said I wouldn't keep bringing it up around Amelia, and I won't, because she's clearly uncomfortable with it. But you're a different story. And she's wearing your hoodie, is she not?"

I had completely forgotten about my hoodie, but still, Eleanor was grasping at straws the way her eyebrows were wiggling.

"I know what it looks like, but seriously, she was cold. I was just being nice," I answered cautiously.

"Okay, sure," Eleanor replied, though she didn't sound convinced. "And do you like her?"

"Sure. Amelia is funny and fun to hang out with. All of you are."

"Do you think she's attractive?"

I felt my face heating up. "I... I mean... I feel like that's a well-known fact, that Amelia is... good looking..."

Eleanor smirked. "We're leaving tomorrow, you know. So, are you going to '*tap dat ass*' while you have the chance?"

I let out an irritated huff. "Listen!" I snapped. "First of all, I do not 'tap dat.' Women deserve more respect than a quick horny fuck. I happen to really respect women and all they can offer physically. I don't view sex as just a fun quick hook up, but rather as an emotionally loaded commitment. You can make fun of me all you want, but that's how I feel. And second of all, most importantly, I don't want anything Amelia doesn't want, this included."

My nostrils flared as I breathed heavily, Eleanor just watching me. Finally, she chuckled lightly and stated, "I get why Amelia likes you."

My heart pounded slightly and feeling a bit panicked and perhaps trapped, I crossed my arms defiantly, huffing, "We're supposed to be talking about you anyway, so I'm changing the subject."

To my surprise, Eleanor didn't fight this. She just leaned back slightly and shrugged. "What do you want to talk about?"

"Anything," I answered, "but if you're looking for some direction, I wouldn't mind hearing your take on what's happening between you and Karmen."

"Look, I loved my husband, alright?" Eleanor suddenly snapped, but I could tell she wasn't angry at me. "But well... it's hard to know if you just love someone or if you're *in love* with them. There are so many different kinds of love—love for friends, and family, your parents, your children, and *then* there's love for your partner. They're different, but all still love, so sometimes it's hard to figure out which version of love you feel for someone. It's particularly hard because we live in such a heteronormative society. Girls and boys can't *just* be friends. There's always got to be feelings. And that's essentially what happened to Matthew and me.

"We were good, no, great as friends. But everywhere we went, everyone just assumed we were dating. After a while, we kind of just figured we *should* date, since that seemed to be what everyone else thought we should do. And so, we did.

"Maybe Matthew really did fall for me, I don't know. I think if I asked him, he'd instantly say he did, but I wouldn't ever know if it was true, or if he just convinced himself it was because that's what we were supposed to do. And I loved him, sure, as a friend, but I was never really attracted to him. I mean, anyone can sit on a dick, guys and gals alike, but that doesn't mean I lusted after him. But Karmen... I mean, you probably get where

I'm coming from. Girls are hot as fuck. And after I met Karmen at work, I just kept daydreaming about her."

"Daydreaming like... cuddling her or eating her out?" I cut in, trying to figure out if Eleanor had feelings, or if she just wanted sex, since the two were vastly different.

Eleanor hesitated for a moment before responding. "At first it was just sexual, and it remained that way for a while. But then, well, it started getting more emotional, at least for me it did. I love Karmen. I know I do. I love her like a friend, but also as a lover."

"Does she know?" I asked.

"Yes."

I waited, but Eleanor didn't elaborate. "Okay, and?" I questioned. "I hardly doubt Karmen didn't have a single thing to say in response to you pouring your heart out to her."

Eleanor sighed. "I think our timing has just always been bad. I mean, we first slept together just because the sex was good. But then we got married and pretended our husbands were satisfying our needs, but of course we broke. Then we were just having sex because the sex was better. And I mean logically, the next thing would be to leave our husbands because what were they offering us, really? But Karmen... she's always really wanted kids.

"I'm not holding it against her. Having children is a big part of most women's lives, and she was married, of course she'd have a kid with her husband. But having a kid just complicated things. Karmen didn't want to leave her husband for the sake of their son. And she hurt me, so I turned to other means of coping and well... got pregnant.

"I wanted her to leave Adam. We could raise our kids together! But she talked me down, explained how divorce could really hurt kids and whatnot. At the end of the day though, we still loved each other and *not* our husbands, so we promised each other that it was over with them. We'd make our marriages work but we wouldn't be physical with our husbands because we loved each other, not them. But she lied to me, because she got pregnant again!" Eleanor ended her declaration with a shout and angry huff. Tears welled in her eyes, but she fought them back furiously.

I stood up from the desk and walked over to Eleanor, sitting down on the bed beside her. Slowly, I reached out and rubbed her arm comfortingly.

"How did Karmen lie to you?" I asked softly.

"We promised we weren't going to sleep with our husbands anymore because we loved each other! But she did it anyway!"

"Right..." I muttered. "She lied to you because she never actually loved you and she just wanted to hurt you." I didn't believe what I said, I was being sarcastic. I hoped Eleanor would pick up on how irrational her conclusion was.

"Yes!" Eleanor shouted immediately, but then she stilled, shaking her head. "No... I know why she did it. She told me. But I'm stupid and self-destructive and I always ruin anything good that happens to me."

"Why did she do it?"

"Adam knew."

"Karmen's husband?" I tried to clarify.

"Yes."

I squinted my eyes in confusion. "Wait, really? I just figured the guys knew all along. I mean, the whole friend group knows, how did you keep it from your husbands?"

"We weren't stupid," Eleanor scoffed. "Matthew *still* doesn't know. Though I'm going to tell him soon. But Adam found out, and he's super religious and he doesn't believe in divorce, right, so he was willing to just look past it... assuming Karmen got help. He thinks she's tormented by sin, sent her to some church counselling. I was so worried for her. She's okay, luckily. But Adam was really pushy about needing proof that it worked... she had to sleep with him to appease him so he wouldn't get suspicious."

"You know Karmen didn't do it to hurt you, right? She had to do it for the sake of her family."

"She told me before she did it. She was really torn up about it. I told her to just leave him. I'd walk out on Matthew too, right then and there. But she was so afraid for Michael, her son. I was selfish though, refused to look at the bigger picture, just wanted her to myself. We got into a huge fight and stopped speaking after that. And god, what luck that she got pregnant too."

I roughly squeezed Eleanor's arm. "You really hurt her," I stated seriously.

"I know. I never meant to hurt her. I love her so much, Natalie! I love her so much it hurts! I just—I want her all to myself. I would treat her so much better than her fucking homophobic husband. She deserves better!"

"I might not have known you guys for very long," I stated, thinking about all the interactions I'd had with them over the past several days, "but

I am very confident in saying this: Karmen loves you too. But you have to realize she's a mother and I'm guessing her relationship with her husband is a lot different than your relationship with your husband. She has to think about what's best for her kids, even if that means sacrificing her own happiness."

"But it's insulting to me! I want her to divorce Adam so we can raise our kids together! I would be the best mother to her children, and she's always been so good with Vanessa. We would raise an amazing family together! But she doesn't trust me!"

"I don't think that's it," I offered meekly. "I'm sure she thinks of you as a wonderful mother. But just because you get divorced doesn't mean you automatically get the kids. I'd imagine Adam would fight for custody, and as shitty as it may be, I'm pretty sure Adam would win full custody in court."

"Why? He could win joint custody, or maybe—"

"Karmen would be fighting an uphill battle against the sexist, racist, homophobic legal system. Karmen was the one having the affair, and not only that, but she was sleeping with another woman. Even if you managed a completely non-homophobic team, Karmen still cheated on Adam and that's a bad role model for children. Adam is a religious man... never did a 'bad' thing in his life. Comparing the two, Adam is the model of purity and Karmen is, well... the epitome of sin. Adam would win full custody if he really fought for it, and I'm guessing Karmen knows he would fight. I don't know how Karmen would cope with losing her children..."

Eleanor sat back, processing. "I'm such a fucking idiot," she muttered under her breath. Then she jumped up suddenly and grabbed her cell phone, making a call.

"Where are you?" Eleanor gasped into the phone. "Can you meet me outside the hotel in like... five minutes? I really need to talk to you." There was a pause, and then, before Eleanor ended the call, she added, "Thank you. I'm really sorry."

"Let me guess," I stated, "you're going to talk to Karmen."

Eleanor nodded, hardly able to stand still. "Thanks, Natalie. I, well... you're pretty okay, I guess."

I grinned, watching Eleanor fidget. "Go get your woman," I stated, standing, and pushing Eleanor towards the door. Eleanor grinned back at me before she turned and dashed off down the hall.

7.

A Bittersweet Goodbye

I was having a fabulous dream. I hardly remembered the details upon waking up, but it involved a picnic of all my favorite foods and well... Amelia. We were laughing, talking, and gazing up at the sky. And then, she kissed my cheek. I blushed like a bashful fool and upon seeing my blush, she laughed.

"You're beautiful," dream Amelia declared. Then she kissed my forehead.

Her kiss was soft and warm against my temple. I smiled contentedly. Then, my dream world grew hazy. Slowly I yawned, blinking the real world into existence. Then I realized with a start that Amelia was sitting right beside me on my bed.

I shot straight up, gasping, "What are you doing in here!?"

Amelia smirked, fighting back a laugh, and held up my spare room key. "You told me to come wake you up, remember? Now come on. We've got a big day ahead of ourselves."

I narrowed my eyes suspiciously, faintly remembering the very real feeling of a kiss on my temple. "Pretty sure I told you to shake me awake," I stated.

She shrugged. "This was more fun."

"Did you... kiss my head?"

"Oh, you wish," Amelia laughed. She stood up from the bed and reached out towards me. "Come on. Let's go grab breakfast."

Amelia seemed to have learned from her pitiful breakfast display the morning before. She only ordered a stack of candied waffles and I noted she was taking it easy on the syrup.

Piper looked terrible. There were bags under her eyes, and she was practically glued to her phone. She kept running her fingers through her hair and biting at her lip. I reached over and poked her gently with my fork. "Hey, are you okay?" I questioned softly.

"Lawyer stuff," she muttered out. Then she immediately began typing on her phone again.

"I thought you were waiting until after vacation to get into that?"

"I couldn't wait. I... I just want everything to be taken care of and done, no more of this waiting. I already set up three meetings next week, two with my lawyer, and we have a sit down with Christian... and oh gosh, the interviews are coming up, I totally forgot—"

"Hey, you need to breathe," I chastised. "None of that is getting done with you in Florida for the next couple hours, so you might as well just turn off that phone and enjoy the last of your vacation."

Reluctantly, Piper lowered her phone, nodding. I pushed a piece of bacon towards her, which she also took.

I relaxed and turned back towards the rest of the table. Ellie 2.0 was telling Amelia a story about her dogs. Karmen was listening in, munching on food herself, and Eleanor was... lost in thought. I peered around Karmen to get a better look at Eleanor. She pushed her food around on her plate, not actually eating it, and she definitely wasn't listening to Ellie 2.0's story. It worried me. I was afraid the talk Eleanor and Karmen had last night didn't go well.

The teachers were leaving around four in the afternoon, hoping to beat the traffic on their drive home. I was sad I wouldn't get another full day with them, but I took what I could get. We decided to all hang out as one big group. That meant we didn't really ride any rides, but we browsed giftshops and just relaxed.

In one of the stores, I noted that Karmen had stepped away from the others to look through some clothing. I quickly darted over towards her, flicking at some clothes on the rack as well.

"So, how are you doing?" I questioned as nonchalantly as I could.

"Good... fine," Karmen answered.

"Really?"

"No, I'm miserable," she uttered, and then she froze, biting at her knuckles.

"I'm so sorry!" I barked out. "I shouldn't have pushed Eleanor to talk to you, and—"

"No, no, no, we needed to talk. I am so grateful for everything you managed to do for us in just a few days, Natalie," Karmen replied. "I never want to lose Eleanor from my life. And with the way we were acting, it was very possible that I *was* going to lose her. But we talked and... and I don't think I'll lose her, not in that sense. The conversation last night was good."

"But... you're miserable."

Karmen glanced over her shoulder, then turned closer to me. "I wish—god, I *wish*—I could just drop everything, leave everything behind and be with Eleanor. I'm not in a happy relationship, frankly, it's a very toxic marriage. But what can I do? I can't lose my children, Natalie, they're my life. And I love Eleanor, but I can't choose her over my children."

"You... can't be together..." I muttered dejectedly.

"Adam has so much against me, I don't... I'd have to have a spectacular lawyer and I just, how could I afford that? I make good money but I'm still just a teacher!"

"I'm sorry," I offered. It was pitiful and unhelpful. I left Karmen a bit awkwardly, heading straight across the shop towards Eleanor.

Eleanor was alone as well, leaning against the wall in the corner, absorbed in her phone. I walked right up to her and pulled her phone down, forcing her to look at me.

"What's your game plan?" I stated harshly.

"What?"

"Your plan, with Karmen. You want to be with her and she wants to be with you, but the court... you'll need a really good lawyer and—"

"Yeah, we talked about all that last night," Eleanor cut me off. She turned her phone around to face me and shoved it at me. I looked over the webpage that was open on her phone, but I couldn't comprehend what I was reading, at least not that fast. Eleanor filled me in, however. "He's the best custody lawyer in the whole state... has success with Latina mothers and is even a strong advocate for the queer community. He also costs like a whole year's worth of income."

"How... are you—*can* you—afford it?"

"If we sell the house and Matthew lets me keep half, and the divorce hearing... sure. It'll be a tight few years, but it's entirely worth it to me. I'm just... I'm moving some funds around."

"Okay, and Karmen...?"

"I'll tell her in a bit."

Before more could be said, I felt a pair of hands on my hips, and I was spun around to face Amelia.

"Look at this!" Amelia gasped, clutching a stuffed animal in her arms. "Is this not just the absolute cutest thing you've ever seen?"

"It's... yeah, very cute," I replied. I couldn't tell what animal it was. It was cartoonish with massive eyes and too much sparkle... didn't look realistic at all, but I could see how Amelia would find it cute.

"It made me think of you," Amelia continued. "I... I don't know why. Maybe it was the eyes, since they're blue, or maybe just because you seem like a leopard kind of person to me—"

"That's a *leopard?*" Eleanor gasped behind me. "I thought it was a rhino."

"Oh, it's not a *rhino!*" Amelia snapped, smacking at Eleanor. I kind of agreed with Eleanor on that one though. "It's a leopard and it reminded me of you, Natalie. So, um, here." At that, Amelia shoved the stuffed animal at me, and I scrambled to grab it.

"Oh, um, thanks," I stated. "I just, well I already bought a souvenir and I kind of promised myself I'd only buy one thing, so I don't think I'll be able to buy it—"

"I already bought it," Amelia quickly explained. "It's... it's for you. A gift."

"*Ohh...*" I muttered, my cheeks heating up.

"You don't like it!" Amelia gasped. "I'm sorry. I guess it is kind of ugly. I'll just... I'll just return it."

"No!" I practically snarled, jerking the toy away from Amelia. "Don't you dare! This leopard is absolutely, utterly amazing, and I will treasure him for the rest of my life."

Amelia and I just stared at each other for a moment. I looked into her eyes, my heart pounding. The last day I'd ever see her... a goodbye in only an hour... a goodbye forever. Would it make a difference if I told her how I felt? How *did* I feel? What was I feeling? Was it worth pursuing?

"Ahem, *gay,*" Eleanor coughed out behind me.

"Eleanor!" Amelia snarled.

Eleanor held up her arms in surrender. "Just stating an observable fact."

"Come on, ladies," Piper stated, walking up to us. "Ellie and I have decided we'll grab a quick bite to eat before we hit the road, and then we need to get going."

We ended up getting pretzels. I couldn't stop staring at Amelia the entire time. I needed to say something to her, but I didn't know what. I didn't know what I wanted to say. Then, before I knew it, we had finished our snack and I was walking towards the exit of the park with them.

We stepped onto a bridge by the park exit, one I had walked across many times before during my many loops around the park. Amelia pulled towards the side of the group so she could look down at the koi fish in the water below. I followed her, watching as she pointed at her favorite of the fish.

Suddenly, Eleanor exclaimed, "Everybody stop. There's something I need to say."

Amelia and I turned, curiously looking towards Eleanor. Piper and Ellie 2.0 were nearly all the way across the bridge, so they turned and came back several steps. Eleanor stood in the middle, just a stride away from Karmen.

"I need to apologize," Eleanor began. "I need to apologize to each and every one of you. These past years I've learned that I'm not any good at processing emotions. When I'm hurting, I lash out and take it out on everyone around me. And that's a really shitty thing to do—"

"Language—" Piper warned, but Ellie 2.0 grabbed her arm and urged her to be quiet.

"Look, I thought this vacation was going to be miserable. I didn't want to go. I was upset, hurting... I didn't think I could stand to be so close to Karmen for so long. But then... well then this pink-haired *kid* just pops up and she's like an old sage, dropping wisdom here and there—"

"Do *not* give me so much credit," I muttered.

"Yeah, she's not *that* great," Amelia added.

"Natalie—" Eleanor turned towards me— "thank you. You... well somehow, you're just... good at getting people to talk and sort out their feelings. I don't know how you do it, but I'm eternally grateful. Because without you, Karm and I wouldn't have talked—"

"*Aww,* you have a nickname!" I cooed, to which Amelia elbowed me in the ribs.

"Don't interrupt," Amelia huffed. "Let them have their moment."

"Yeah, I, um..." Eleanor turned back to face Karmen. "Karmen, I told you this last night, but I need to say it again because it's the most honest and truthful thing I've ever admitted. I'm in love with you, terribly so. I can't imagine my life without you. When we fight, I'm devastated. When I fall asleep without you, I'm empty. Vanessa loves you and Michael. I love when we're together with our kids. You know I love Matthew, but not like this. When I picture my future, it's not with him. It's with you, Karmen. I *need* you."

Karmen shook her head slightly, biting at her knuckles again. She removed her hand just long enough to choke out, "Eleanor, honey, you know... we can't—"

Eleanor reached into her pocket and pulled out a slip of paper. It was folded in half, so she unfolded it and smoothed out the wrinkles. Then she took a step forward towards Karmen and held out the paper.

"Divorce Christian," Eleanor stated. "I found the perfect lawyer, the best in the state, and he'll help. He'll make sure you don't lose your kids. I don't want to lose them either, okay?"

Karmen took the paper from Eleanor's hands and looked it over. "Eleanor, I can't—fifty thousand dollars!?"

My eyes widened. It was a check.

Eleanor reached out and folded Karmen's fingers over the check. "Take it. Think of it as an investment into our future... our children's futures."

"But... but Eleanor—"

"No, no buts. No more buts. We've always had excuses, but not anymore. I'm giving you an out. And I will always fight for you and this family, because I love you more than anyone in the entire world."

Karmen flung her arms around Eleanor, and they crashed together. They kissed each other passionately before Karmen pulled her head away and buried it against Eleanor's shoulder. Karmen was sobbing, clutched tightly in Eleanor's arms.

"O—Okay," Karmen uttered weakly. "Yes... yes, I... I love you too. I want this. I want a family with you. Please just... don't leave, don't let go."

Eleanor squeezed Karmen tighter. She too was sniffling, trying to fight back her tears, but she was failing. A tear escaped, running down her cheek, and she jerked away from Karmen, cursing, "*Ahh,* damn this spring weather and my stupid allergies."

"You're not fooling anyone!" Amelia shouted, and in turn I elbowed her in the side.

"*Let them have their moment,*" I mocked Amelia's earlier words, receiving a glare.

"Why you little—" Amelia reached out to maybe pinch me, but I dove away from her. She gave chase and I ran circles around the others, squealing.

Eleanor reached up and ran her fingers through Karmen's hair. "I'll be right by your side the whole way through. We're not going to let Adam keep the kids from you."

Piper reached out and grabbed my wrist as I attempted to dash past her. "Stop being idiots, you two," she stated, pulling me to a stop. Then she smacked at Amelia's wrist to get her to stop chasing me.

"Amelia started it," I mumbled, but Piper glared at me, and I shied away.

Piper took a deep breath and then cleared her throat. "Well, ladies, it's certainly been a day, that's for sure. But well... it seems our departure time has arrived."

Very suddenly, I was engulfed in a group hug with five high school teachers all squeezing the life out of me.

"Bye, Natalie," Ellie 2.0 gushed. "Good luck in your last semester and the rest of your life. I know you'll do great things!"

"Yes, goodbye, Natalie," Karmen stated with a smile, her eyes still watery. "Thank you for everything you did for us. It was a real pleasure meeting you."

"Bye, Short Stack, and thanks again for the talk," Eleanor said, patting me on the back. "I'm never going to forget how you helped us... helped me. Thank you."

"Bye, guys." I grinned sadly. We hugged one last time before Ellie 2.0, Karmen, and Eleanor turned and headed off towards the parking lot.

Piper reached out, taking hold of my shoulders before she turned me around to face her. "Natalie... you have very great potential inside you. I say that as a teacher, but also as your friend. Don't forget that, okay? And thank you for helping not just Karmen and Eleanor, but me as well. Even though we've only known each other for a few days, you have made a really big difference in our lives."

"Bye, Piper," I said, pulling the woman in for a hug. "Good luck with the baby and everything else."

"Goodbye, Natalie," Piper added one last time before she turned and followed after the others.

I watched them walk off for a moment before I turned back to Amelia. "Well... are you going to say goodbye, or what?" I questioned.

Amelia smiled at me. It was a sad smile, but still full of warmth. Then, she tackled me in another hug. While she hugged me close, she whispered into my ear, "I'm really going to miss you."

I squeezed her tighter. "I'm going to miss you too," I agreed. "You guys are the most fun, albeit weird people I've ever had the pleasure of meeting. Although... y'all got too much drama."

Amelia pulled back from me, laughing. "You know you like it," she stated with a wink.

"Maybe, but you can't prove it."

Amelia smiled bigger at me, nodding slowly. She took a step back, still just grinning at me, gazing like she was trying to memorize every part of me.

"Amelia, come on, let's go!" Eleanor shouted.

"I'm coming!" she yelled in response.

"You better go," I said, although I didn't want her to leave.

"Yeah..." Amelia turned to leave but she stopped, spinning back to face me. "Oh, and, um... well... I *did* kiss your forehead to wake you up this morning. I just... I couldn't help myself."

"Amelia, come on! Ándale, ándale!" Karmen shouted.

Amelia spun on her heels, taking off at a sprint after her friends before I could say anything else. And then they were gone, lost to a mob of people coming and going from the park, and I was left standing there alone.

Part 2.

Pitfalls & Redemption

8.

Job Hunting Through DM's

Somehow, the park didn't sound enticing anymore. I'd been on all the rides; I'd eaten most the food; I'd seen all the shops. Sure, I could find things to occupy my time, but it wasn't fun anymore. It wasn't fun because I didn't get Amelia's and Eleanor's enthusiasm, and Ellie 2.0's worry, and Piper's groaning. It wasn't fun anymore because I was alone.

Yes, I went to the park to be alone. Yes, I went to escape people and find myself, like a mission for enlightenment in all the wrong places, yet somehow, I had met five beautiful, amazing women, grown attached to them, and then they just left.

I missed Piper's all-knowing smirks and disapproving gazes. I missed Ellie 2.0 trying to make peace and be innocent, but also sneaking in little jabs every now and again. I missed Eleanor antagonizing us, as annoying as it was. I missed Karmen with her excessiveness and comforting glances. And I missed—oh god did I miss—Amelia.

I missed Amelia's stupid sense of humor and her relentless teasing. I missed her ability to make everything into a game and a competition. I missed her overeating sweets and getting sick, missed her drunken laughter, missed her eyes, the features of her face, her closeness to me. Why didn't I say something before she left? Why didn't I tell her how I felt, that I at least felt *something* for her? Rejection would have been better than just the haze of 'if only.'

I cuddled the little toy leopard Amelia gave me almost religiously. Even though it did sort of look like a rhino, and even though it was kind of ugly, I didn't care, because Amelia had gotten it for me.

When Sunday afternoon rolled around, I was more than ready to break free of my captivity in Florida. The vacation I so longed to use as an escape had now become my shackles. I was ready to return to school with a newfound boost. I was ready for classes, homework, exams... anything life could throw my direction that I could use as a distraction from the memory of *those women.*

Back at school, I reunited with my roommate and truly best friend at college, Lizzie. She had an eventful break, something about some hot guy she hooked up with. By the time she finished her tale, it was too late for me to tell her about my break, so I just let it go.

I quickly fell back into the routine of school. The excitement of a change of pace and distraction from Florida died about the first day I was back in class. I wasn't enjoying school. I was just going through the motions to graduate. It was monotonous. I didn't feel motivated or driven. During the day, I was pulled between classes, homework, and social interactions, but at night, I fell victim to my thoughts again.

Why hadn't I asked Amelia, or any of them, for their phone numbers? I just wanted to stay in contact, wanted to know how the divorces went, and learn more about the love life of Eleanor and Karmen. I wondered how Amelia was doing, if she was kept awake at night thinking about me the same way I thought about her.

I didn't even tell anyone about my vacation, save for the polite response that it was 'nice.' Brining up anything about Florida was too personal, too close to the women I missed so terribly. I could hardly bear to talk about such things.

By a week in, I was doing better. My sleep was improving. I spent more time studying and less time victim to my thoughts. I hung out with my friends more, made dinner and laughed with Lizzie. And sometimes I thought, yeah, I'll be okay.

Inevitably, my mother called me. She harped on me about my future plans, and we came to a compromise. I'd look online and apply to five jobs every day. The first jobs I found were biology related. They were left with unreturned phone calls and no interviews. Then, I widened my search. Upper-level jobs in different disciplines, but still stuff I could do. And when that didn't yield a job, I started applying for anything and everything, even minimal wage jobs at retail stores and fast-food restaurants.

One day, my phone started pinging—a lot. I was in the middle of working on a project when I finally picked up my phone, only to see that I had a bunch of new followers on my social media accounts. It wasn't anything crazy, like I had suddenly gone viral overnight, just a handful, about a dozen, but that was weird for me. Only my family and friends followed me online, and since I hadn't made a bunch of new friends in person lately, it was odd. And the people following me... I didn't recognize any of their names.

And then I saw it: one fateful DM, one direct message from one of my new followers. I didn't recognize the person, didn't even bother to look at their profile. All I saw was the message which read: *"Job position available. High school biology lab coordinator. $20/hr. No Master's required."* And then I clicked on the link and submitted my application, because why not? Even if it was just spam, it wasn't like it could hurt.

Monday, I woke to the sound of my phone ringing. Groggy, I pulled myself up, blinking several times, trying to orient myself. The ringing was not in fact my alarm clock, and it was actually nearly an hour before I normally got up for classes. I looked to my phone. It was an unknown number, but because I had been applying to so many jobs, I knew I should answer it. I sat up fully, trying to sound more awake than I was.

"Hello, Natalie Benton," I stated, trying to suppress a yawn as I answered my phone.

"Hello, yes, I'm the secretary at Elk Creek. I saw that you submitted an online application for our lab coordinator position, and I was just calling to inquire if you were available for an interview?"

An interview! My eyes widened. "Yes, um, yes, an interview, yeah," I stated, trying to reel myself back in.

"Great. Are you available tomorrow at eight?"

"Yes, I'm available. In the morning?" I clarified.

"Yes. We like to conduct our interviews during the school day, so you can get a feel for how daily life is like around here. And also, our very devoted biology teacher would like to meet you during her free period at nine."

"Okay, perfect, eight in the morning."

"Fantastic. You can park in the student lot, and then just ring the bell on the front doors by the office, and I'll let you in. See you tomorrow!"

The line clicked dead. I lowered my phone. I had... an interview! Now that wasn't a full job as of yet, but it was further than I had managed to get with any of my other applications! And, yeah, I'd have to miss some classes tomorrow, but whatever! I had an interview for a job! For a job at...

Fuck, I realized I didn't remember where the lady said she was calling from. Panicking, I tried to remember the conversation. There was um... student parking... and a... a biology teacher... and... the lab coordinator! That was the application that someone DM'ed me about on social media!

I sat on my bed frowning. Maybe they were a friend of my mother's and she asked them to send me that application link. Either way, it was time to do a little research, because I planned on nailing that interview tomorrow!

From my DM's, I discovered the name of the company, or rather, school, where I applied: Elk Creek. Elk Creek was a college preparatory high school only about two miles off my college campus. It was situated in the snootier part of the city, a predominantly white, rich neighborhood. The houses there were mansions and all cost more money that I could conceptualize. From that alone, I didn't think I'd fit in too well... and probably wouldn't get the job.

I ended up going down a rabbit hole on my phone as I looped between my classes. There were dozens of news articles about Elk Creek pouring countless resources, both time and money, into helping a poor nearby middle and high school known as Byram. Byram was in the quote-unquote 'bad neighborhood' of the city. The neighborhood was predominant black, very poor. The school was struggling with money, dropout rates sky high and not enough resources to provide a good education.

Elk Creek was doing a lot for them, though. Elk Creek donated money to improve Byram's facilities, and they also hosted afterschool classes in their own building for the students of Byram—for *free*—so even those less privileged kids could get an equal education.

I was entirely perplexed. What connection could Elk Creek have with that school in that they would pour so much time and money into helping them? Elk Creek wasn't a religious affiliated school, wouldn't have a religious reason for volunteer work and giving back to the community. I couldn't imagine the snobby millionaires who sent their kids to Elk Creek donating money to help poor black kids. If anything, I just wanted to know more.

The following day I put on my best interview outfit, which at its best was some slacks and a blouse I got from a thrift store two years ago. I thought I looked presentable, however. Then I hopped into my car, plugged the address into my phone's GPS, and I was off.

Elk Creek College Preparatory High School was housed in an old boarding school that had been restored. The outside was tall, dark, and majestic. I suddenly felt very intimidated. I knew from my research that Elk Creek's tuition cost for a year was nearly double my college tuition at a state school. The education had to be pretty fantastic to warrant that cost. I was always a decently average student, but that was in public school. The students inside that I would be teaching—should I get the job—were already, without a doubt, far smarter than I could ever hope to be.

I nearly chickened out. It was just an interview; I didn't owe these people anything. I would just look like a jerk for not showing, but who was I kidding, I wasn't going to get the job! But there was a small part of me that was like, 'What if?' What if I did get the job? It would be job security for summer and next school year, and it paid really well!

I got out of my car and buzzed in at the office. While I was waiting for the secretary to come open the doors, I suddenly remembered my hair! It was *pink*! If I didn't get this job and told my mom, she would definitely blame my pink hair! And I was apt to agree with her. No way this rich school was going to want a kid with pink hair teaching their rich children!

"Ms. Benton, it's so great to meet you in person," the secretary grinned, opening the door. "We always love it when we get fresh college graduates applying. They always have so much spunk, so much drive, and the students always love them. I think they can relate better because you're closer in age."

"Thanks for having me."

"Of course, of course! Please, follow me. Our principal always conducts the interviews and I sit in taking notes, but don't mind me at all! We're just going to ask some questions, have a nice little chat, is all. And then our dear biology teacher—she'll really be like your supervisor—she wants to meet you too, of course. And she usually gives a little tour of the school." She sat me down on a chair in the school office. "Can I get you anything to drink?"

"A water would be nice," I answered.

While I waited, I tapped my foot nervously and looked around the office. Everything inside the school reminded me of an old-fashioned rich mansion. The floors were a polished dark stone and the walls a deep mahogany. The lights out in the hall, which I could see from where I sat, were miniature chandeliers. The drapes that adorned the large, floor to ceiling windows, were a dark red velvet. Just out in front of the office was a fancy sculpture, like something from ancient times you would see behind ropes in an art museum in France.

Three students ran past the statue and darted into the office. There were two boys and one girl, all in full uniform. The boys wore grey slacks, the girl a grey pleated skirt. They all had on a button-up long-sleeve white shirt under grey sweater vests, with red accents, and a red tie. The girl also wore tall socks that matched her sweater vest, and they all wore black dress shoes.

It felt like a European boarding school.

"Okay, we're ready for you!" the secretary stated, startling me. I stood, nodding, and followed her into a back office.

I was greeted there by the principal. I talked about myself first, about my education and aspirations. I played it off and said I wanted to go to grad school, but also would possibly like to teach, so when I saw this job opening, I just had to apply, see if teaching was really for me. In reality, I didn't want to do either of those things. I liked biology, and I liked talking about biology. I figured I could do the job just fine. But for the rest of my life? No thank you.

She asked me how I would handle certain things in the classroom. Asked me how I felt about certain things, where I went to high school myself and if it was anything like Elk Creek. I didn't figure I could lie my way through that, so I was just honest. Then the principal asked if I had any questions.

"I do, actually," I replied. "I was doing some research on Elk Creek when I applied for the job, and I couldn't help but find that you do a lot of work helping out Byram?"

"Oh yes," the principal stated with a nod. "I never thought that initiative would go over as well as it has. There's a reason, you know, that schools in white neighborhoods do better than those in black neighborhoods. It's all prejudice and economics and whatnot, years of systematic oppression put in place. But by god do we have some passionate teachers here... passionate teachers that inspire passion in their students, who then work magic on their parents to get the donations."

"You have an afterschool program with Byram, right?"

"We do. Many of our teachers stay late for an extra hour or so to teach the students of Byram for free. We've got all sorts of science labs, history classes, math tutors, a theater group, and now a literature class, even."

"If I got the position, could I help with the afterschool program?"

The principal sort of smirked at me. "I think that would be just fantastic, Ms. Benton," she stated. "The biology teacher you'd be working with, she's very active in the afterschool program. I think she'd love to hear that you're interested."

"Oh yes, she's a wonderful woman," the secretary added.

"Just a little more information about the position," the principal continued. "So, the biology teacher we keep mentioning, she's really over worked, frankly. Not even accounting for the afterschool volunteer work, she teaches three biology classes and two labs: our intro biology that all freshmen take, an advanced biology open to the older students, and then a disease related course. The labs go with the two main biology classes. She just has too much going on and needs help with the labs. So, you'd technically be working under her, as the labs relate to the course work she's teaching. But what we're thinking is if you could maybe start supervising the afterschool labs until you graduate, just to get a hang of things, then over summer you could shadow her summer classes, and then hopefully by next fall you'd be able to step in full time."

"Sounds perfect," I replied.

"Okay, great. Then I'll just go page the biology teacher so you can meet her, and then she wants to give you a tour, show you the classroom and labs and stuff."

"Of course."

The principal slipped out of the room to page my would-be supervisor and I was left in her office with the secretary.

"I think you'd really fit in well here," the secretary rambled. "We have another young teacher who just started here not too long ago, fresh out of college, just like you, and the students adore her. Your energy too it's very... it fits well with the energy we have here at Elk Creek. And your passion for volunteer work already? Why, it sounds like you're already one of the teachers!"

I ran my hand through my hair. Best not jinx it, but I felt the interview was going rather well.

The principal stuck her head back in. "Classes just switched, not sure if you heard the bell, but she's on her free period now. She said to just show you down to her room—"

"Oh, I'll take her!" the secretary jumped at the opportunity, already pulling me out into the hall. "I do hope you hit it off with our Ms. Kegan. She's such a nice and loving young woman. She's going through a bit of a rough patch, that's why we figured she could use a little extra help, you know. Oh, but she's wonderful! Sorry, don't mind my chattering! Anyway, here's her classroom." She knocked on the open door, leaning into the room. "Ms. Kegan," she called, "your little interviewee is here to meet you."

"Come in," the biology teacher answered from inside.

The secretary gestured for me to enter, giving me a thumbs up as she turned and headed back towards the office.

I stood taller, taking a deep breath. All I had to do was impress this one last person, and then surely, I could land this job. I just needed to be grateful, thankful, show interest and curiosity, mention the volunteer work... I stepped into the room, fully prepared to give it my all, but the second my eyes fell on the biology teacher, all thoughts instantly vanished from my mind.

"Welcome to Elk Creek, Natalie," Piper stated, grinning impishly. "Cat got your tongue?"

"What—how?" was all I managed to choke out.

"I have a need for an assistant, you need a job... looks like things just happened to work out for the better."

"I... oh my gosh!" I finally gasped, running straight up to her before I grabbed her in a hug. "How are you doing?"

"Fine, fine. Life's been a hectic mess and I'm ready to get this kid out of me, but you know."

"Wow, it's... so great to see you again! I just... why aren't you surprised to see me?"

"I looked at your application," Piper explained. "I approve all applications before we call for interviews. I remembered your name, obviously, and found your application was quite substantive. I think you'd really be a good fit for this position. Though... from what I heard from Amelia, I didn't think you were interested in teaching."

"I thought I'd give it a go," I answered. "Amelia had a lot of good things to say about teaching, so..."

"Well in that case, shall we take a tour of the school?"

"Oh, I thought it was just the labs—"

"Yes, but I'm offering you more, as a friend," Piper replied.

"Then say no more. Lead the way."

We wandered back out into the hallway, and I quickly forgot that I was supposed to be in an interview. I noticed then, more clearly, that Piper, though I recognized her easily, didn't look anything like how she had in Florida. In Florida, she dressed casually, like a white suburban mom out for a morning jog (aside from the pregnant belly). Now though she was formal, like a businesswoman, dressed modestly in a dress and kitten heels.

I muttered out, "This is like culture shock," before I could stop myself.

"*Mmm,* not quite what you expected when you met us in Florida, huh?"

"No," I admitted.

"People aren't two-dimensional creatures," Piper stated. "We try to remain true to ourselves, but we have to carry ourselves a bit differently at work. That's the most exhausting thing about working with the children of rich parents... you should hear some of the flim-flam I say at parent events. We have to act a certain way to please them though, keep the donations pouring in, and we try to do right by their money."

"Like the afterschool program," I cut in. "I read up on Elk Creek before I came for the interview. I really like what you do to help Byram, and I want to be a part of that, I just... I don't understand why."

"It's a fairly recent development around here, actually. Eleanor was the one who made such a push for it. It's her drive that got the program going and keeps it up and running."

"Wait, Eleanor started that partnership?"

"It's very close to her past. And actually, this is her classroom, if you want to stop in and talk. She's got a prep period right now too—we try to coordinate our free time."

"Of course!" I answered, not even waiting for Piper. I just burst straight into the classroom, gasping out, "Hey!"

Eleanor was seated at her desk, her back to her door. "Hey, what's—" she began, swiveling, and then her eyes landed on me, and she gasped. "Natalie?" she questioned.

"Hey! How's it going?" I asked, walking over to her.

Eleanor pulled me into a hug when I was close enough. "Short Stack!" she exclaimed, ruffling my hair. She looked back to Piper. "What is Natalie doing here?" she questioned.

"Technically, this is an interview," I answered, remembering my place.

"And she's acing it, quite frankly," Piper replied.

"For that lab coordinator position, yeah?" Eleanor said. "That's just fantastic that you're interested."

"She wants to hear more about the afterschool program, wants to help out," Piper explained.

"Oh yeah, for sure," Eleanor answered. She gestured for Piper and me to sit down in two desk chairs, then she pulled over her own chair and sat down across from us. "I'll tell anyone who's willing to listen about the program. I think it's something all well off schools should be doing. We need to sort out the education system in America, and if the government can't sort it out, we'll do it ourselves."

"That's pretty ambitious," I stated.

"The issue's really near and dear to me. I spent a good chunk of my childhood living in the slums where Byram is. The school's an utter shit show. They don't get any funding and all the bad teachers get stuck there because the parents aren't complaining. By god, if a lemon got stuck here, could you imagine the outrage, Piper?"

"What's... a lemon?" I questioned.

"It's an education term, the 'dance of the lemons,' or 'passing the trash,'" Eleanor explained. "Teachers get tenured and can't be fired—lemons—but they're terrible at their jobs, don't care about teaching anymore. They can't be fired so they just get shuffled through the system. If a lemon ends up at a well-cared for school, the lemon quickly gets shoved along. But at a school that doesn't have the resources or time to care? Elk Creek is private, so we as teachers don't get the job security of tenure, but we don't have the nightmare of lemons either... Luckily we have a very ambitious team. But Byram's just a public school.

"I went to Byram for a while. If I had stayed there... I wouldn't have graduated. And even if I had managed to survive all four years, I never would have gotten high enough ACT scores to get into college. Some stuff went down with my parents, and I was put in foster care. It got me out of Byram, but... it really took a mental toil on me. But then my grandmother found me and took me in. Funny thing about my grandmother... she's a very well to do white lady and she got me a proper education.

"Once I turned my life around, I always knew I had to get back to Byram and help those kids. Those kids deserve all the same opportunities that the white kids get going to school here. In America, good education is treated like a privilege, but it shouldn't be. It's a right. Every child, no matter their background, where they're from, how much money they have, the color of their skin... they all deserve access to not just *an* education, but a *good* education."

"Your passion is so... admirable," I stated in awe. "The fact that you even managed to convince a rich private school to donate time and resources to a poor school is... amazing."

"Well, it certainly wasn't easy," Eleanor scoffed. "But look, the staff here, we care. We've all struggled in life, and we understand to some degree. We want to help. Convincing the racist rich asshole parents that a tenth of their donations should go to a black kid in need? Well, that's the real uphill battle. But I love what we do, and I love all the children so much—our students and the students at Byram. All of them are going to grow up and make their own difference in the world, and I'm so proud of all of them."

"You're doing really great work."

"Well, we better continue on with our tour," Piper stated.

"Looks like we're moving on," I said, standing with Piper. "It was really great seeing you again. Hopefully I'll see you around," I told Eleanor.

"Later, Short Stack," Eleanor declared, waving as Piper and I left her classroom.

As we continued down the hall, Piper acted more like a proper tour guide. She explained what every room was, giving little tidbits here and there. Before long, we looped around to a large, grand, central staircase lined with red velvet carpet. We left the downstairs science and math wings, heading upstairs to the other classrooms. We passed both Karmen's and Ellie 2.0's classrooms, though they were teaching. Piper said I had to wait around until the start of next period so I could say hi to them, though.

I felt very out of place. Even my very best outfit was cheap in comparison to everything about the school. I also felt very under accomplished next to the teachers. They all had passion and drive... used their skills to accomplish so much good. What had I done? Nothing. Wasting my time in college picking a major for a field I didn't even want a job in.

We rounded the tour off back on the first floor with the impressive cafeteria and gymnasium. With every step we took, I got more nervous. I was uncomfortable with the atmosphere—the formalness of everything— but I also realized I was anxious about seeing Amelia again. Every classroom we passed meant there was one less thing standing between me and Amelia, every step meant one less foot of distance.

"And finally, the new hall," Piper stated, steering me away from the cafeteria. "Amelia has class right now so—"

"Oh, well, I don't want to interrupt," I stated quickly.

Piper paused, looking back at me a bit oddly, before saying, "You won't be a bother, rest assured. I'm sure you'll be a very welcomed interruption. Now come along."

I nodded meekly, hurrying after Piper. At the end of the hallway, we came to an archway we hadn't previously passed. When we stepped through, things instantly felt different. Unlike the rest of the school with its dark demeanor, this wing was bright and inviting, all white marble and royal blues. The ceiling was higher, the chandeliers bigger. Marble lion busts lined the pillars going down the sides of the hall.

"Well... this is fancy," I commented as we walked. To my right was a pair of massive doors. Above it hung a golden plague with a donor's name and the word 'Auditorium.' It was a theater, though I couldn't see inside.

"It's a brand-new wing. Construction was just finished over winter break," Piper explained. "Amelia is an award-winning choir director. She brings in a lot of money for the school. Granted, we didn't *need* a new wing and Amelia begged them to use the money on other things, but the board won out. What better way to show off that your choir won a five-million-dollar grant than by adding an entirely new addition?"

Screech.

My body froze. Piper trailed on without me, lost in her explanation, but I was floored. Award winning? Five-million-dollars? I couldn't comprehend even a tenth of that much money.

Piper stopped, realizing I wasn't following her. "Are you okay?" she asked, walking back over to me.

"I—I can't talk to Amelia!" I gasped out. "It would be like meeting the queen! I'm not qualified to even stand in her presence!" I was freaking out because of Amelia's accomplishments. I was happy for her, proud of her, but I wanted to impress her. Nothing I'd ever done or could ever do would stand up against her though. I was just... a nobody.

"Natalie," Piper stated slowly, resting her hand on my shoulder reassuringly. "We all have major ambitions in the workplace and strive daily to achieve them. Just like Eleanor works so hard on the afterschool program, Amelia works hard to direct her choir to success."

"I know, but five-million-dollars!? Do you know how ridiculously large five-million-dollars is? One time, when I was seven, I won a pie eating contest at the state fair and got five bucks! That's my claim to fame!"

I turned, ready to bolt straight out of the school, straight out of my chances at a *job*, but Piper grabbed my wrist and pulled me back.

"Oh no, you don't," Piper huffed. "Could you imagine if Amelia found out you were here today and didn't stop in to see her? No, no, I'm not dealing with her moping for another day. Listen, Natalie. The woman you met on vacation? That's still Amelia. That's the same woman at the end of the hall, in her classroom, teaching. She's still the same person."

"I know, but—"

"No buts. You're coming with me and we're interrupting Amelia's class whether you like it or not."

Piper tugged me the rest of the way down the hall. She gripped me tighter as she slowly pushed open the classroom doors.

I felt my breath leave my body. Nothing could have prepared me for the scene we walked in on. Immediately my eyes were locked on Amelia—her back turned on us—in all her adorable glory, gorgeous as always, just as I had remembered her. She was dressed more professionally, like the others, but she was still that bubbly goof I met in Florida, jumping and dancing in front of her students, who stood tall and proud on several rows of risers.

The class sang gallantly, every student focused on their director. Amelia gave them hand signals as she danced around. There was no boredom in that classroom, only pure enjoyment, and a deep love that you could actually feel, floating in the air. The choir sounded angelic. Suddenly, I could understand the five-million-dollar grant.

Amelia was damn good at her job. It was clear, evident in the way the students sang, that they loved what they did, and they wanted to do their best for their teacher. She had inspired them.

Currently, Amelia was front and center of the risers, her back to Piper and me. She was focused on a single boy who was singing a solo while the rest of the choir did backup and harmony. His hair and eyes were dark against lighter skin, around two feet shorter than everyone else in choir. He also looked like he couldn't possibly be older than ten, but surely, he had to be at least a freshman. He sounded really good. I didn't know much about the technicalities of voice, but I thought he had a professional career lined up ahead of him for sure.

As the song went on and the boy's solo finished, the rest of the choir got louder. Amelia then snapped her attention to a group of boys immediately to her left. "Tenors!" she snapped loudly above the music. "If you don't sing up, I'll be forced to dab!"

A girl in the far back row, with strawberry blonde hair and glasses, completely stopped singing to shout, "Don't you dare!" Several heads nodded in agreement.

Amelia's silly threat about 'dabbing' was about as internet meme humor as one could get—an old meme, old and cringey—but it clearly worked on her Gen Z students as the volume of the tenors about tripled.

I glanced back to Amelia and the tenors, and my eyes were caught by two redheads that had to be twins. They kind of all... looked familiar? Which was super weird because I was positive I didn't know any of them, not the ten-year-old looking boy, not the strawberry blonde girl, and definitely not the red-headed twins.

Amelia laughed maniacally, waving her hand out at the tenors. "Okay, okay, thank you! But bring it back down about two notches." As she said this, she made a motion like she was turning down an invisible volume dial.

Just when I thought the choir couldn't get any better sounding if they tried, Amelia suddenly and very dramatically pointed to a group of girls. She exclaimed, "Sopranos! Your volume! What did we talk about? Don't make me—oh! Oh no!" And then, in the most dramatically embarrassing display, Amelia threw her entire body into a dab, burying her face into her elbow and throwing her other arm out behind her. When she did this, the entire choir immediately stopped singing to groan in frustration and annoyance.

"Dabbing is so two-thousand and late!" the tiny boy with the solo shouted out, cupping his hands around his mouth.

Amelia stood up straight, laughing, and skipped over to the stereo system, turning off the music. Then she turned back to the sopranos, her hands on her hips disapprovingly. "Shannon, what was all that about?" she tsked. "You were the one complaining about the dab, but look where we are."

The strawberry blonde girl with glasses, Shannon, rolled her eyes in response.

With the pause in singing, Piper chose that time to alert Amelia to our presence. And to be fair, I nearly forgot we were crashing her class and not just observing her in her natural element.

"Oh, Ms. Lewis, I have someone here who wants to see you," Piper called from the doorway.

Amelia turned around in question, as did the students. Before anyone could say anything, Amelia realized it was me and she let out a loud squeal, immediately racing straight over to me. I was engulfed in a tight hug. She started swinging me side to side as she squeezed me tight. I clamped onto her shirt to keep from falling over, finally managing to pull away before we both lost our balance.

"And hello to you too," I muttered, wearing a shy smile on my face.

"How—I—why are you here?" Amelia continued to squeal.

"She's interviewing for my lab coordinator position," Piper stated.

Amelia grabbed my shoulders tightly and stared at Piper. "She's getting the job, right?" she questioned incredulously.

Piper cryptically shrugged in response. "I'll let you two catch up. Send her back to my room when the period ends, alright?"

"Okay," Amelia stated, nodding enthusiastically.

As Piper left, Amelia grabbed me and jerked me to the front of her classroom. I noticed the students were whispering loudly to each other about the interruption, and rightfully so.

"Class!" Amelia exclaimed. "This is Natalie! Natalie, this is my honors choir!"

There was a collective chorus of 'Hello, Natalie,' followed by more muted whispering, before the boy with the solo marched straight down from the risers and right up to me. I towered over him, as he literally looked ten, but he thrust out his hand like a mature man. I reached out and took the offered hand a bit hesitantly, but he shook it strongly.

"My name is Nicholas. It's very nice to meet you, Natalie," he said surely, his voice not yet deepened by puberty. "You met Ms. Lewis over spring break in Florida, correct?"

"*Umm*, yeah," I answered, glancing sideways towards Amelia.

"It *is* her!" I heard someone from the risers gasp. The room erupted into whispers again, and I wondered just what all Amelia had shared with her choir about her Florida vacation.

"You're still in school, right?" Nicholas stated.

"Yeah, I'm in my last semester of undergrad."

After I said this, Shannon leapt up from the risers, exclaiming, "You're not too much older than us, then. I'm a senior." She pranced down off the risers and straight up to me as well. "Hello, I'm Shannon," she introduced herself. "Can you tell us what college is like? Is it any different than high school? What sort of things can we expect?"

I softened a little, realizing that these smart students, whom I was so intimidated by, were really just kids, no different than I had been four years ago. I started talking about college life, feeling like an older sibling imparting knowledge to my young pupils. Amelia sat down on the bench of a black grand piano and just listened to our conversation, watching. After a bit, I nearly forgot she was there.

Before I knew it, the bell rang, and class was over. The students bid Amelia a fond farewell, exiting the room as Amelia lovingly sent them off.

Nicholas went up to Amelia before leaving and asked, in the most professional way, "Are you eating lunch with us in the cafeteria, Ms. Lewis?"

"Of course!" Amelia instantly exclaimed, but then she looked over at me. "Actually, are you hanging around for lunch?" she asked me.

"Oh, no, I just—um, I don't want to upset your routine," I answered.

"You should bring Natalie to lunch in the cafeteria," Nicholas stated.

"You should hang around for lunch. I'll pay," Amelia said. "It'll be fun. Now run along, Nicholas, before you're late for your next class."

"Alright, goodbye, Ms. Lewis," he stated. Then, he turned and looked at me. "It was nice meeting you in person, Natalie. I'll see you both at lunch." Then he trailed out of the classroom after his peers.

Once the room was empty, save for Amelia and me, Amelia bounded right over to me, giddy and bouncy, and pulled me into another hug. "I'm so excited you're here," she stated genuinely.

I relaxed into her touch. "I'm excited to see you too. Though I'm a bit concerned how much you told your class about the spring break trip..."

Amelia laughed off my comment, pulling me out into the hall by my hand. "I promised to get you back to Piper's room, and I don't want you getting lost," she stated. The second we passed through the doors and into the hall, Amelia released my hand. I wasn't sure if I was glad or disappointed.

"That was my honors choir," Amelia explained as we walked. "I don't want to brag, but they're really the best of the best, and they deserve recognition for all their hard work. I spend so much time with them, recruiting them from middle schools, practicing hours upon hours every week... they're like my second family. I firmly believe it's not just drive, but also our closeness that helps bring home wins."

Before I could really stop myself, my big mouth slipped out, "Wins like your five-million-dollar grant?"

Amelia blushed slightly at the mention, but quickly brushed it off. "Winning isn't about the prize, it's about the journey... the friends you make, the skills you perfect, and the relations you build along the way. I've grown so close to my honors students... they *are* my family. That's the important part."

After she said this, we found ourselves back at Piper's classroom.

"You're going to get the job," Amelia stated confidently.

"I don't know," I answered. "I'm not really qualified to teach, and frankly, I'm not so sure I fit the atmosphere here."

"Don't be ridiculous," Amelia chastised. "You fit in with us perfectly, and *we* fit in here. The appearance of the school isn't the same as how we run it. And of course you're qualified for the position."

"How do you know?" I muttered dejectedly.

"Besides," Amelia continued, "if Piper doesn't give you the job, I'll never let her live it down."

I trailed into Piper's classroom, my stomach in knots. I *really* liked Amelia. She was funny, goofy, ambitious, driven, adorable, everything... she had it all, everything I ever wanted in a partner. But she was also so *out of my league.*

"Unless you've got somewhere you need to be," Piper stated as I walked up, "I think you should hang around and observe my biology class this period. And then, well you might as well hang around for lunch. Our cafeteria has rather fantastic food."

"Sure, I'll hang around," I replied. Besides, I figured if I dipped out of lunch with Amelia, it would crush her, and I wasn't about to do that.

At the end of the period, just as the bell rang, Ellie 2.0 and Karmen came into Piper's room, greeting me.

"Eleanor told me you were in the building," Karmen stated with a grin as Ellie 2.0 hugged me. "Piper was trying to keep you all to herself, I see."

"She's interviewing for a position working *with me,*" Piper replied.

"That's so exciting you're going to be working here!" Ellie 2.0 stated.

"Now, I don't have the job yet," I uttered.

"Oh please," Karmen said, rolling her eyes. "Piper's nowhere near stupid enough to not give you this position. If Amelia were to find out, she'd flip her lid, and she's been annoying enough as is."

"Annoying?" I questioned.

"Yes," Piper, of all people, agreed. "She's been downtrodden and mopey ever since we left Florida—left *you* behind."

"Never thought to grab your phone number, just let you go, her only remembrance of you the hoodie she stole from you," Karmen continued wistfully.

"Wait, *that's* where my hoodie went!?" I exclaimed. "Man, I've been looking everywhere for that!"

Suddenly, Amelia stuck her head into the classroom. "Don't any of you even *think* about stealing Natalie away for lunch!" she declared. She skipped into the room, grabbing my arm. "Natalie is coming to the cafeteria with me and we're going to eat lunch with the choir kids."

I spun a bit as Amelia jerked me into the hallway, just barely locking eyes with Karmen. She smirked, mouthing the word, '*Sorry.*' What had I just gotten myself into?

"Just so you're prepared, the cafeteria is a madhouse," Amelia told me.

As we rounded the corner, I confirmed that Amelia was indeed correct. There were teenagers everywhere, shouting, dashing between tables. "It's hectic," Amelia gasped, "but I love spending the extra time with my students, getting to know them better when we're not working." In under two seconds, nearly a dozen kids ran past, greeting Amelia with a chorus of 'Hey, Ms. Lewis!' Amelia fluidly pulled me into the food line, still carrying on conversations with students and the lunch staff.

Once we had our trays, I followed Amelia out into the sea of tables and towards one at the far back of the cafeteria. Unlike the tables at my high school, which were old, rectangular, and falling apart, these tables were nicely polished dark wood in a circle, surrounded with cushioned dining chairs. About a dozen choir kids were already sitting around the table—I recognized them from class. Amelia sat down next to Shannon, and I sat down beside her in the only remaining chair next to Nicholas.

"I saved you both seats!" Nicholas proudly stated. "Arthur got a bit huffy about it though because they said it was their week for table number one, but I told them it was a special occasion, and they could have the seat back tomorrow."

"Wait, what's this about table number one?" I questioned. "I don't want to mess up any sort of seating arrangement..."

"We have too many members to all sit at one table," Nicholas explained. "We have four tables. Table number one—this table—is where Ms. Lewis always sits, because she's our director, along with the choir's president and vice president, Shannon and me respectively. The other members rotate on a tri-weekly schedule, so everyone gets a chance to sit at table number one."

"Wow that's... intense..." I muttered. "And well, I guess thank you for letting me sit here. I don't really feel like I've earned the position but thank you."

"But of course you have!" Nicholas scoffed. "You're Ms. Lewis' best friend! And we're all very excited to finally meet you in person!"

"That's concerning," I stated emphatically, "because that means Amelia, um, Ms. Lewis, has been talking about me. And that's scary."

Nicholas stared at me oddly for a moment before declaring, "You're funny."

"*Umm...* thanks?"

"But yes, Ms. Lewis talks about you a lot," he added.

"*Ohh*-kay!" Amelia cut in abruptly, clapping her hands together. "That's a bit of an exaggeration. I don't talk about Natalie that much!"

"No, of course not." Nicholas rolled his eyes.

I glanced towards Amelia skeptically. "What all has she said about me?" I questioned.

"Well, she told us how you met," Shannon answered. "When she was in line for a ride. She said she was, um... entranced I believe was the word she used—entranced by your eyes. She said they were the prettiest mix of blue and green."

"I don't think I said 'entranced,'" Amelia muttered out, her cheeks slightly pink.

Nicholas then grabbed my jaw, roughly jerking my head around to face him. He climbed up on his chair so that he was on his knees, holding my head as he stared right into my eyes.

"You do have really pretty eyes," he stated in agreement, releasing my head. I quickly pulled back from him.

"She also said you had pink hair," Shannon added. "I don't know though; I think it's more of a salmon shade..."

"Ugh, Shannon, we talked about this!" Nicholas groaned. "Her hair is *rose gold*! It's the newest trend in fashion, haven't you heard?"

"It's actually just faded pink," I uttered.

"Oh please," Nicholas huffed. "You listen up, Natalie. Your hair is the most perfect shade of rose gold. Just tell it like it is! Be proud of your shade!"

"Wow, okay."

A boy from across the table cut in, "Hey, don't forget about the freckles."

"Yeah!" one of the redheaded twins cut in. "Remember the freckle tangent of last Wednesday?"

"Oh my gosh, I can't believe we nearly forgot about the *freckle tangent*!" Nicholas wailed. In his excitement, he leapt up from his chair and slammed his hands down on the table. "Ashley was showing Anna how to use makeup to create faux freckles before practice, and Ms. Lewis went on a twenty-minute tangent about how Natalie has just the best freckles in the entire world."

"She said they were like stars in the sky... just as beautiful as every constellation known to man," Shannon added wistfully.

"Stop! It was not twenty-minutes!" Amelia huffed. "It was like... two seconds of a passing comment, is all. And I hardly said anything so... so... poetic!"

"I find that hard to believe," I stated. "I mean, they called it the freckle tangent of last Wednesday. That sounds a lot more detailed than two seconds."

"The freckle tangent was ridiculous, but let's not forget just how often Ms. Lewis brings up Natalie in the first place," the other redheaded twin commented.

"Oh, every day," Nicholas stated. "James had biology homework, oh, do you know who's a biology student? Natalie."

"Katie wanted to get ice-cream after practice," Shannon stated with a grin.

"Oh, you know who likes vanilla ice-cream? Natalie does!" another girl at the table exclaimed.

"Look guys, I learned how to do a backflip," one of the boys commented.

"Did you know, Natalie claimed she could do a front flip?" Nicholas cut in again.

"Okay, *okay*!" Amelia shouted over her students, trying to get them to stop. They all sunk back in their chairs, laughing heavily. "I might maybe kind of bring up Natalie *sometimes*!" Amelia admitted. "But I bring up a lot of things and a lot of people every day."

I smirked at Amelia who was clearly embarrassed for being called out. I didn't mind it. All those nights I had lied awake, thinking about Amelia, wondering if I was on her mind as much as she was on mine... well now, I had confirmation. Amelia was definitely thinking about me at least sometimes.

"It was downright depressing when we learned she had no way to contact you!" one of the girls declared. "She didn't even know your last name. Isn't that just the worst? You're clearly her best friend, Natalie, and she lost you!"

"So that's when we decided to form the Find Natalie Committee," Nicholas stated.

"The what now?" I questioned.

"We had to track you down so you could reunite with Ms. Lewis," Nicholas explained. "We asked all the teachers who went on the trip with Ms. Lewis, trying to figure out a way to contact you."

"We learned your last name from Ms. Kegan, thanks to James," Shannon explained. "And some easy internet searches helped us learn that you went to school at GSU, right next door practically!"

"I wanted to come find you in person," Nicholas declared. "I was so close to convincing my parents to let me take a tour of GSU, destined to find you, Natalie. But my parents kept pushing back because it was a '*state school,*' and why should I settle for GSU when I could have '*Harvard.*'"

"We settled on just sending you a DM, because we found your social media accounts," one of the twins clarified.

"We knew there was a position opening up to help Ms. Kegan with the biology labs, and we knew, from Ms. Lewis's rambling, that you were a soon to be college graduate with a biology degree. We figured why just bring you back when we could get you *hired* at Elk Creek!" Shannon said.

"And obviously it worked," Nicholas added, "because you opened my DM, applied, *and* came here for an interview."

My eyes widened in sudden realization. These kids looked familiar to me because they were the ones who had flooded my social media accounts, following me! It was Nicholas who sent me the somewhat cryptic DM about the job opening at Elk Creek.

"You guys stalked my social media accounts and DM'ed me a job opening here, just so I could reunite with your teacher?" I questioned incredulously.

"I didn't put them up to this," Amelia stated, her hands in the air. "I had no idea."

"We had to!" Nicholas forced.

"Of course we did!" Shannon agreed. "Ms. Lewis means the world to us, and she obviously missed you so much! We had to find you for her!"

"Ms. Lewis is our family," Nicholas added, walking over to Amelia before he pulled her into a hug. "We just want her to be happy!"

"Guys, stop," Amelia muttered, though she was smiling. "You didn't have to find Natalie for me."

"Sure we did! You're already so much happier now that you two have been reunited!" Nicholas exclaimed with glee as he returned to his seat. "And now Natalie is going to be around here all the time!"

"I, um, still have to get the job," I stated. "This is technically just an interview."

"Oh, but you *have* to get it!" Nicholas protested, pouting.

"And she will," Amelia stated, winking. "I can pull some strings."

"So, you're going to be around everyday then?" Shannon questioned.

"Well, I think technically I'm just going to be helping with the afterschool labs until I officially graduate. I still have classes," I stated. "But I'd be here after school every Thursday."

"But that's not fair!" Nicholas protested. "Shannon and Xavier have voice lessons here on Thursday, but that's when I have piano lessons, so I can't hang around!"

"I mean... I do finish classes by eleven on Thursday... I guess I could always swing by at lunch time and spend the rest of the day here," I offered. "As long as that's okay with your principal."

"You can sit in for our choir classes," Nicholas exclaimed, turning to Amelia with puppy-dog eyes.

Amelia laughed. "Alright, alright," she gave in. "I'll let Natalie sit in for our classes once a week, so long as you all promise to not bother her and not get distracted."

"We promise!" Nicholas answered for everyone. Then he turned to me and stated, "You're just going to love it here, Natalie!"

After lunch, my interview was technically finally over. Piper offered to let me sit in for her remaining classes if I wanted, however, and I decided I probably better. After her last class, she walked me through the lab, showing me stuff and explaining basic procedures.

Then, she finally turned to me, smiled, and extended her hand for me to shake. "Welcome to Elk Creek, Ms. Benton," she stated.

"You mean, I got the job?"

"Of course. You had the job the second I finished reading your application."

I let out a sigh of relief. "You have no idea how glad I am to have this position," I muttered.

"I do believe you'll be a fantastic fit around here. And I know teaching was never really on your plate, but I think you'll find that you'll excel on that front as well. I'm a pretty good judge of character and it seems many students have already taken quite the liking to you."

"I sure hope so."

Piper walked me out of her classroom and out into the hall, mentioning details about when I needed to come in, and how I needed to fill out paperwork in the office before I officially started working. I mentioned the choir and she said it wouldn't be a problem if I wanted to sit in during some classes.

"Call it researching how to be the best teacher you possibly can be," Piper stated. "It might not be biology, but if there's anyone who can teach you the art of teaching, it's Amelia. I trust you'll be in good hands."

And speaking of Amelia, she rounded the corner into the hall just about then. She stopped near Eleanor's classroom, talking to Nicholas. Piper followed my line of sight and just grinned.

"May I just bring up the fact that Amelia hasn't stopped talking about you since we left Florida?" Piper stated. "You should go talk to her."

Before I could say anything, Piper ushered me off. As I approached them, Nicholas spotted me first and greeted me.

"Hello, Natalie. I do believe your hair is just absolutely fabulous."

"Well?" Amelia questioned, looking towards me. "Did you get the job?"

I nodded. "Of course, I did."

Amelia's smile grew even larger, and Nicholas clasped his hands together excitedly. "Fantastic!" he exclaimed. He looked to Ms. Lewis questioningly for a moment before he turned back to me. "May I hug you?" he asked.

"*Umm*, sure," I answered, leaning down a bit to awkwardly wrap my arms around the shorter boy. Nicholas was by no means shy. He squeezed me tightly before letting me go.

"I'm very glad we found you and that you applied for the position. I like you, Natalie, and you make Ms. Lewis happy, so in my book, you're good."

"Well, I'm glad you approve," I said with a slight chuckle.

He turned back to Amelia, giving her a quick hug too, before bidding us both farewell. Then, he bounded off down the hall.

Once he was gone, I decided I just had to ask. "Is he really a freshman?"

Amelia laughed, shaking her head. "He's actually twelve, but he skipped four grades because he's a genius. So technically, he's a sophomore."

"Oh... my gosh."

"But hey, congratulations on landing the job," Amelia stated. "I know you were worried about what you were going to do after graduation and well, I know you don't really want to teach, but... is it selfish of me that I'm really glad you got a job here? I um... I *really* missed you."

"I really missed you too," I admitted honestly. "I won't really start full time until next school year, but at least I'll be around Thursdays. Maybe we could... do something after lab gets out?"

"I have voice lessons until five on Thursdays."

"That's when lab ends, so..."

A large grin grew across Amelia's face. "Then I'd like that."

"Would you, um, like to exchange phone numbers? Just so it's easier to stay in touch and stuff?"

"Yes!" Amelia shot out perhaps a bit too eagerly. She struggled to pull her phone out of her skirt pocket, too giddy, but she managed and passed her phone to me. I put my contact information in and handed her phone back to her, our fingers brushing, and we nearly dropped the phone straight on the floor. Amelia blushed, again struggling to tuck her phone away, and she sputtered out, "I'll see you Thursday, Natalie," before she turned and quickly walked away.

I watched her go, my heart beating rapidly as well. Before I could return to Piper, I heard Eleanor talking behind me.

"God, when will those two realize they're head-over-heels in love with each other?" Eleanor commented. Her words made me blush and I held my cheeks, trying to will the heat to go away as I composed myself.

Finally, I turned and went back over to Piper, who was now standing with Eleanor.

"I don't want to hate on the embarrassing exchange that I just witnessed," Eleanor hummed, "but maybe you should have tried something like this." From her back pocket, Eleanor procured a black permanent marker. She popped the cap off with her teeth, smirking as she grabbed my arm. Then, she wrote two phone numbers on my inner forearm.

"What... the heck?" I stated.

"My number and Karmen's," Eleanor replied. "I would write Piper's and Ellie 2.0's, but I don't have their numbers memorized."

"Oh, well I can fix that," Piper replied, stealing the marker from Eleanor before writing down two more phone numbers on my other arm.

"I look like a mess!" I huffed. "Couldn't you guys just enter your numbers into my phone like normal people?"

"*Aww*, but where's the fun in that?" Eleanor said with a wink. "Text us later so we can save your number."

"If you're lucky," I muttered half-heartedly. Then, Eleanor pulled me into a headlock and ruffled my hair.

9.

The Lonely Leader

Since getting their numbers, by Wednesday afternoon, I had already threatened to block Eleanor three times. She was annoying in a ridiculous way, always teasing, and sending me dumb stuff. Karmen wasn't much better, frankly, though I could, between the teasing, get some actual information from her.

Eleanor finally told her husband about the affair and asked for a divorce. He was caught off guard, but not too surprised. Evidently, he said he always thought Karmen and Eleanor were extra close. He was very understanding and cool with everything, agreed Karmen's husband was shitty. He wanted joint custody of their daughter and wanted to remain friends despite everything. He even decided to help Eleanor and Karmen get a good custody lawyer.

In the meantime, Eleanor and Karmen were looking for a nice house out in the suburbs. Karmen wanted to get out of her house with Adam as soon as possible. Until better housing arrangements could be found, Matthew decided it would be best to let Karmen stay with them, but she still periodically had to return home for her son.

As much as I was inquiring for updates, Eleanor and Karmen were prying into my own personal life. They learned just about every part of my school life—academic and social—and I even told them about my family—being an only child to an ER doctor and a firefighter.

I checked in on Piper to see how she was doing. She told me she was just dealing with lawyer stuff. She moved out the day after she learned the truth from her husband, the same day she took off her wedding ring and went back to being called Ms. Kegan. She wasn't in a good enough place to get her own home, but Ellie 2.0 and her fiancé, Cliff, were nice enough to let Piper stay with them.

I actually found out most of that from Ellie 2.0, who was far more talkative than Piper—I think she was just less stressed. She said Piper kept insisting she'd move out soon, but Ellie 2.0 was planning on having her hang around through the birth of the baby. They wanted to help Piper out with the kid, and I was starting to think Ellie 2.0 would win out on that argument.

Amelia didn't text me until Wednesday night, not that I was waiting or anything. I missed all my classes Tuesday for the interview, so I had a lot of work to catch up on. I was reading through a paper when my phone buzzed. I was gracious for a distraction, but if it was another ancient meme from Eleanor, I was going to block her. Instead, it was a text from Amelia.

Her text read: *'Hey, Rose Gold.'*

Noting her reference to Nicholas's description of my hair color, I greeted her in much the same way: *'Hey, Platinum Blonde.'*

I put my phone down to go back to my homework, but my phone chimed again immediately. I unlocked it to read Amelia's new message.

'What are you up to?'

'Homework,' I responded.

'You should go to bed. It's late.'

I glanced at the time. It was approaching midnight. I still had a lot of work to do, but I was past the point of caring. I closed my book and leaned back in my chair, picking up my phone again.

'Thanks, mom,' I mocked. *'I can say the same to you. It's late. You should go to bed.'*

'I can't sleep.'

'Something wrong?'

Immediately, Amelia's 'typing bubble' appeared. I watched it bounce up and down for several minutes, expecting a very long response. Instead, when the message came through, it only read, *'I probably just drank too much coffee.'* I frowned. There was definitely something on her mind and this was only a lame cover story, but I didn't want to pry.

'Coffee is nasty,' I chose to answer.

'I have mine with chocolate. Coffee, hot chocolate, chocolate milk, and cream.'

'That's worse than normal coffee but doesn't surprise me at all.'

'It's really good. You're just bitter. Maybe if you ate more sugar, you'd be sweeter ;)'

I rolled my eyes at Amelia's winky-faced emoji. *'Doubtable.'*

'I'm excited to see you tomorrow. You're going to do great.'

'I'm excited too, a little nervous. What do you want to do afterwards?'

'Get dinner.'

'Why does that not surprise me? You always want food.'

'Food is really good,' Amelia defended, which was hard to argue. *'We should probably get to bed. I just wanted to check in.'*

'Yeah, sleep is important. See you tomorrow.'

'Goodnight, Natalie.'

'Night, Amelia. Sweet dreams.'

I held my phone in my hands, contemplating. Before I could dwell too long, I opened up my favorite social media app and searched for Amelia. Because her number was saved in my phone, the correct Amelia Lewis popped up easily. I browsed through her page. There were pictures of her and her teacher friends and of her and her students. Several of her students, including but not limited to Nicholas and Shannon, had posted comments on her profile, and liked most of her posts.

Her 'about me' section was a bit lacking. It listed her name and birthday and that she wasn't currently in a relationship. I thought about what Piper said, how she hadn't seriously dated anyone in a decade. It was crazy that she was still single. She was perfect. She literally didn't have any flaws.

Well... that was an exaggeration. I could think of a lot of flaws Amelia had. For instance, she was whiny and sarcastic. She was pouty, probably spoiled, and really competitive.

I shoved my phone under my pillow before I dove on my bed and smashed my own face against the pillow. I was trying *really* hard to not like Amelia. It was so difficult though. She was everything I wanted in a girl but liking her felt wrong. I could barely comprehend the life she was living, and I couldn't imagine a world where I fit into her life.

Maybe after I got to know Amelia better, as a friend, I wouldn't be so interested. Surely this was just a stupid little crush that would come to pass as all crushes do. Yes, that seemed like a solid plan.

The following morning after my last class of the day, I swung my backpack up on my shoulder and headed out of class. I made it exactly ten steps out of the building before I heard someone shout, "Natalie!" I stopped and turned just in time for Lizzie to collide with me, grabbing my shoulders.

"Dude, we have to go to the quad!" Lizzie practically yelled in my face. "Ted ran into Josh like five minutes ago, and Josh said they're giving out free donuts! He got an entire box!"

"*Ahh*, I'd love to, but I can't," I answered, heading for the parking lot.

Lizzie followed close behind me. "You? Turning down free stuff? What's wrong with you? Are you sick? Feverish?"

"No, I just have work."

"You got a job!?"

"Sure did," I answered. "I can't wait to tell my mom. Maybe she'll finally get off my back."

"Where'd you get a job at? Is it fun?"

"It's a lab coordinator position at a local high school—Elk Creek. Anyway—"

"Elk Creek? Isn't that the really rich uppity school?"

"Sure is."

"How on earth did you, looking like this—" she gestured up and down my body— "get a job at Elk Creek?"

"Well actually, a student there DM'ed me the application link, but I guess I'm sort of friends with some teachers there? So, I think that's how I got the job."

"How'd you make friends with teachers at Elk Creek?" Lizzie asked incredulously.

"Well, I met them over spring break—"

"Oh my god, you never told me about your trip! How was that lone vacation? I know you said it was to find yourself or whatever, but I still think you just wanted to get laid—wait! Did you *sleep* with a teacher at Elk Creek?"

"Wow, you need to stop jumping to conclusions," I declared, reaching my car.

"Listen, you can say I'm reaching at nothing here, but you're blushing."

"I am not!"

"You most definitely are."

"Look, I need to get going. We can talk about this later."

"Fine, but I expect mad deets on these teacher friends of yours," Lizzie demanded.

"Alright, look, if you're going to shorten details to 'deets,' you won't be getting any more information out of me," I stated, slipping into my car.

"See you when you get back!" Lizzie hollered, skipping back away from my car.

I groaned, banging my head against my steering wheel before I turned on my car and headed to Elk Creek.

At the school office, I filled out a bunch of new hire paperwork. It was lunch time, and the choir kids were likely expecting me back at table number one. The secretary offered to walk me to the cafeteria, but I declined, insisting I knew my way around after Piper's tour.

Except... I didn't. I clearly wasn't paying that much attention during the tour, because I very quickly found myself lost in the empty halls. As I walked around, I took in the embellished atmosphere of the place. I looked down at myself compared to the décor, and even thought about the student uniforms. I felt like I was in rags compared to them. The more I walked around, the worse I felt. And then, I tumbled directly into a marble lion bust.

It was the new choir wing! Even more beautiful and majestic and *rich*, unlike me. I stopped before the closed theater doors in the new wing. Feeling curious, I slowly pulled open the door.

The theater was beautiful and large. The lights were off, so all was dark except the sliver of light sneaking in from the hall through the door I cracked open. The stage was too far away to make out any details, though I did notice a balcony rim. The second story would explain the extra high ceiling in the new wing. Everything was detailed with gold, light catching the reflective sparkle all over the room. The seats were a dark red velvet, just like the curtains hanging in the rest of the school. I couldn't keep my mind from wandering, thinking about pressing Amelia against one of those velvet chairs, kissing her, tasting her lips on mine....

I turned abruptly, tearing out of the auditorium and straight down the hall. My heart was pounding. I already had a bad habit of freaking out at the mention of intimate activities—which was perhaps a bit pathetic, considering I had slept with a few women already and never freaked out in bed—but feelings and intimacy freaked me out. That was likely why I hadn't managed to pin down a solid relationship, one that didn't end with walls up and cold shoulders.

Without thinking, I slammed open one of the choir room doors. I needed some time alone to just calm down, but instead of being met with an empty classroom, I was met with a blood curdling scream.

The scream scared me. I fell back against the now closed door, looking around in panic. My eyes fell on Amelia where she sat at her desk in the front corner of the room, her hand pressed firmly against her chest, breathing heavily.

"Oh my god, you're in here," I exclaimed unceremoniously.

"You gave me a heart attack!" she shouted in response.

"Sorry," I uttered.

I felt myself relax. Even though thinking about Amelia and thinking about *feelings* with Amelia freaked me out, being in her actual presence was always calming. Slowly, I sauntered over to her desk. She had papers strewn about her desk and on the corner sat a boxed sandwich from the deli, entirely untouched.

"Why did you just... barge in here like that?" Amelia questioned. "You practically broke the door off its hinges."

"In my defense, I didn't know anyone was in here," I answered. "I figured you'd be at lunch with everyone else. Why aren't you, by the way?"

Amelia let out a low sigh. "I needed to get some extra work done today. I decided to just eat in here while I worked."

I looked down at the untouched food once more. "I think that would require you to actually pick up the food and take a bite."

My comment got Amelia to crack a grin. "Fair point," she replied, "but I'm too stressed. God, there's so much math. Math stresses me out. And I can't eat while I'm stressed." She reached for some papers, fiddling with them. "Have you eaten lunch yet?"

"No, I came over straight from class."

"You should grab some lunch then. Did the office get you an ID card? You can take mine and get lunch if you want."

"No, I'm covered, they set up my account," I answered.

Amelia watched me for a moment as I made no attempt to leave. "But... you're *not* getting lunch?"

"I um... don't know where the cafeteria is," I answered meekly.

"I can show you—"

"No, really, it's fine. I had a granola bar about an hour ago between classes. I'm good. And besides, I don't want to be a bother while you're trying to work."

Amelia shook her head, smiling fondly. She reached down and slid the boxed sandwich towards me. "It's chicken salad, if you're into that kind of thing," she stated.

"Oh, I can't eat your lunch," I quickly said.

"I'm not hungry, like I said, so you might as well eat it, otherwise it'll go to waste."

A bit hesitantly I reached out and took the sandwich. I was actually very hungry, and I didn't feel like refusing and just staring at the untouched sandwich for the next hour.

Amelia told me to pull up a chair, so I retrieved one from several stacks in the back of the room. As I did, Amelia got up and turned on some music before she returned to her work. I sat, eating the sandwich, listening to the song. I didn't know it. It was classical, sort of like an opera but without singing.

"What is this song?" I questioned after another bite.

"Rameau."

I looked over at Amelia as a particularly aggressive part of the song hit. It was a... bop. And Amelia said the guy's name with such flare—well, I assumed it was a guy.

"It's... classical, I guess?" I questioned.

"Yes, some of Jean Philippe Rameau's opera and ballet intermezzos."

"I know... some of those words."

Amelia laughed. "He's a pretty important eighteenth-century French composer, but more importantly, he's my favorite classical composer."

"Oh, I didn't know people had favorite classical composers," I replied. "But it's good. I always thought classical music was boring and dull but this... this is *bopping*."

"If you like this, then I'll have to play *Hippolyte et Aricie* for you sometime."

Again, the flare of the name, the perfect pronunciation. "Can you speak French?" I questioned, just dying to know.

Amelia flushed slightly. "I have... a complicated relationship with French," she replied. "The pronunciation mainly comes from singing in other languages."

I gave Amelia an odd look. How could someone have a complicated relationship with a language? I didn't want to be a huge distraction though by bringing up a bunch of feelings or anything, so I returned to eating the sandwich. I glanced down at the papers tossed on her desk. I leaned forward, struggling to read it upside down.

"Is this a New York Hotel?" I questioned. "A... five-star hotel?"

"*Hmm?*" Amelia questioned, turning to look at what I was reading. "Oh, yes."

"Are you going on another vacation?"

"No, it's for Nationals."

I waited for Amelia to elaborate, but when she didn't, I prompted, "What's Nationals?"

"A singing competition," Amelia explained. "The honors choir won Regionals and Sectionals, so now we're off to Nationals. If we place there, then it's off to Worlds."

"So, the whole choir is staying at this five-star hotel then?"

"Yes. Rich parents don't like their spoiled rich kids staying anywhere but the best."

"Well, that's snobbish."

"But truthful. Pick your battles. If the parents are willing to pay, I'm not going to risk angering them by refusing."

"So, who all's going? Just you and the honors choir?" I questioned, grabbing the hotel reservation so I could get a better look.

"Yes, us and a few chaperons. The competition is in a couple months."

"And you have to do all this prep work by yourself?"

"Yes, that's why I'm in here making sure everything is finalized instead of eating lunch."

"I could help you," I offered. "I'm pretty good at paperwork, believe it or not."

"Sure, I suppose, if you're offering."

"I am, under one condition."

Amelia groaned lightly. "I knew there'd be a catch."

"Let me come to New York with you," I stated, grinning largely.

"*Hmm...* that's a bold demand, pretty greedy," Amelia stated in reply, leaning back in her chair. She stared at me as she held her pen between her front teeth. I found myself distractedly staring at her mouth, her tongue... "We already booked the rooms though. You'd have to get a room elsewhere and it would probably be outside of the city since bookings have to be made months in advance, sometimes years even."

I flipped through the reservation papers, looking at the list of students and chaperons, running some math in my head. "Let's see, forty... a double room with two full beds holds four kids per room... works out to ten doubles, perfect. Two extra doubles for chaperons, I'm assuming. And you... in this single?" I pulled out the reservation for the single room at the back of the stack. "*Hmm,* a single has a king-sized bed... interesting. Pretty sure two people could fit very comfortably in that bed."

"What are you getting at?" Amelia questioned.

"You didn't seem to have any qualms about sharing a bed with me in Florida," I stated.

When I said this, the door to the choir room was shoved open. Amelia jumped straight up and out of her desk chair, turning away from me and the door, covering her face with her hands. I turned around to see who had just barged in, only to find Nicholas bounding over.

"Natalie!" he gasped when he saw me, running straight up to me. "I forgot you were coming back today!"

"Yep, just spending some time with Amelia, um, Ms. Lewis before class starts back up."

"Did Ms. Lewis tell you about our Nationals trip?" he questioned, looking at the papers still in my hands.

"Yeah, I heard you're going to New York."

"Yes, it's going to be so much fun! And—*ohmygosh* wait! Do you know what I just thought of?"

"What?"

"You should totally come to New York with us!" Nicholas exclaimed. "Ms. Lewis! Ms. Lewis, please can Natalie come to New York with us? Please, please, please, oh *please*? Shannon really likes Natalie, and the twins are just dying to get to know her more. And you know our trips are our greatest bonding time, so it would be just perfect for Natalie to come with us. Plus, you know—"

Amelia, turning and removing her hands from her face, cut Nicholas off. "It would be nice to have Natalie join us, but unfortunately, we don't have enough room."

Nicholas frowned. "But you said we were taking two buses, so we'd have plenty of space!"

"Yes, but we don't have enough space in the hotel."

"Can't she stay in your room?" Nicholas asked with shinning puppy-dog eyes. "Pretty please, Ms. Lewis, can't she come?"

After a minute, in which Nicholas did not take the pleading look off his face, Amelia caved. "Okay," she answered meekly. "Natalie can come."

"Yes!" Nicholas screamed, grabbing me in a rough and tight hug before quickly releasing me, dashing over to Amelia who he hugged just as hard. He chanted 'thank you' as he jumped up and down.

"Of course, Nicholas," Amelia answered, smiling softly, hugging the boy back.

"Can I stay for concert choir?" Nicholas questioned, pulling away from their hug.

"You know you need to rest your voice."

"Please? Just for warm up exercises?"

"And what class would you be skipping?"

"College algebra."

"That sounds like an important class, Nicholas. Don't you think you maybe shouldn't skip it?" Amelia suggested.

"It's just algebra," Nicholas protested.

"Yeah, it's *just* algebra," I added, a snicker in my voice.

Amelia shot me a glare, as I wasn't helping the situation. "*College* algebra," she corrected.

"But it's not... college calculus," I pointed out with a shrug.

"Exactly!" Nicholas exclaimed in agreement.

"Oh, well, I can't argue with *that* logic," Amelia replied, rolling her eyes. "I can't win against you two. This is a bad combination."

Nicholas let out a squeal again before running over and giving me an enthusiastic high five. He grabbed the handles of the chair I was sitting on and leaned forward, staring into my eyes aggressively.

"I like you," he stated.

"I... like you too," I answered, uncomfortable with his proximity.

"I also like that Ms. Lewis likes you," he then added, falling back away from my chair. When he said this, Amelia started coughing violently and excused herself so she could get some water. Once Amelia was out of the room, Nicholas grabbed my arms.

"Are you coming to lunch next week?" he asked.

"Sure."

"Don't let Ms. Lewis come."

"Wait, what?"

"Don't let Ms. Lewis come to lunch. We only want you," he clarified.

"That sounds really sketchy, you realize that, right?" I said. "You guys don't need to interrogate me, okay? And if you want to get to know me better, Ms. Lewis can be around, I—"

"It's not that. We want to talk *about* Ms. Lewis," Nicholas quickly amended. "*Shh,* she's coming back."

Amelia came back in, and Nicholas backed off me. Amelia was acting bashful, which only confused me. What did she have to be bashful about? Maybe that's what the choir kids wanted to talk to me about.

Soon, the bell rang, and the next class began. Tuesday, I wasn't at all prepared to witness Amelia teaching. Now, I knew what to expect, yet somehow, she managed to keep impressing me.

I turned my chair to face the risers. Nicholas stepped up onto the risers as the other students filed in, collecting sheet music from a stand near the door as they entered. Amelia sat at the black grand piano, greeting everyone as they entered. The students of the concert choir were less... intense than the honors choir.

Once class actually started, they did vocal warmups. I was never in choir, nor did I know anything about singing, but they sounded like scales, tongue twisters, and breathing exercises. The students knew the warmups well—they likely had been doing them since the start of the year—and therefore Amelia's directing was a bit unnecessary. However, Amelia was still full energy from her place at the piano. She either played scales along with them to keep them on pitch, or just hit a cord at the start, but it was always done with excessive excitement. And she sang along with them.

After warmups they shifted to the music they were working on, and Nicholas was sent over to sit by me and rest his voice. He started working on homework and I turned my attention back to the choir and Amelia. Even though the entire choir sang, I still heard Amelia's voice over theirs— selective hearing. At the piano she swayed to the beat, content in her space with the music... so happy, so beautiful.

I couldn't be her friend.

I wanted to be, of course. I wanted to be her friend rather desperately. But I couldn't *just* be her friend. This crush I felt... it was different from all the childish crushes I had before. There was a bashful glee in a crush, a desire to see but not so much touch anything beyond a daydream. But this... these feelings... I wanted Amelia *desperately.* If I had been anywhere near her in the moment, I wasn't sure I'd have the will power to keep myself from reaching out to her. I wanted to run my hand down her arm, snake my hands around her waist, lean my head against her shoulder. It was only a matter of time before this intense desire to be near spread to less platonic desires. I was already, after only a few weeks since meeting her, teetering on the line between platonics and romantics.

I was terrified. I didn't want to mess things up. What if Amelia didn't feel the same way? Or what if she just felt... less? I didn't want to ruin things between us, ruin what I had with the other teachers by extension. I wanted this job, *needed* this job. I couldn't mess all that up before it had even really started. I had to keep my feelings under control.

"What's with the drool?" Nicholas asked in a hushed whisper, snapping me out of my thoughts. "Haven't you ever heard Ms. Lewis sing before?"

I wiped at my chin, gawking at the boy. "I'm not drooling," I stuttered. "It just... the choir sounds good, that's all."

Nicholas looked at me skeptically. "You were staring right at Ms. Lewis," he stated. "You don't need to feel bad about it. She's an amazing singer and spectacular pianist."

My eyes wandered back to Amelia. "Yeah... she is," I muttered out wistfully.

"I know you two technically just met, but I can tell you both really connect," Nicholas went on. "Some people just do, connect and fall into place right after meeting each other. I can tell just by the way you talk about each other. Ms. Lewis, well she's a happy, giggly, playful person all the time. Sometimes it can be difficult to know when she likes someone, verses when she's just being herself. But sometimes when she talks about you, or when other people bring you up, she just gets... *quiet.* I've never seen anything that made that woman go quiet. So, I just have to figure you must mean a lot to her, no matter how short of a time you've know each other."

I frowned slightly. "Do you really think so?"

Nicholas nodded. "I can't get as good a read on you, only because I hardly know you. But I can tell you're greatly intrigued by her. You look at Ms. Lewis the same way half the choir does: in awe and admiration."

"Well... that's one way to put it."

"I think it's really special you got a job here with her. You should make the most of this opportunity."

"What do you mean?"

"Just... well spend time with her. Be a good friend. Text her, call her. I know you got her number, trust me, she hasn't shut up about it. Yesterday she was beside herself all day: 'When should I text her? I don't want to look pushy. Should I wait a full day? Should I just text her now? Would it be weird to just text her out of the blue? Should I have a reason?' She literally wouldn't shut up about it." Nicholas rolled his eyes.

I blushed slightly. It felt nice knowing Amelia was overthinking things like I was. "Why do you want me to talk to her so much?" I asked Nicholas.

He gazed longingly over at Amelia. "Because, Natalie... she seems happy and content, sure, but once you really get to know her, you'll see that she's lonely." He turned back to me, sighing. "I just want you to be a good friend to her. She means a lot to me. I've known her since I was eight and no matter what I've gone through, Ms. Lewis has always been there for me, right by my side through thick and thin. She's always there for all of us. That's the thing about her, Natalie. She always puts others first. She deserves someone in her life who's willing to put her first, treat her how she deserves to be treated. And well... I think you're just that friend she really needs."

"I'll try my best," I answered.

Nicholas nodded, a soft smile on his face. He went back to his homework, and I went back to watching the choir. Amelia still mindfully played the piano, though she stopped singing to listen to how her choir was doing. I looked to her and noticed she was looking straight at me, smiling when our eyes met. I was in awe once more. Not only was she playing the music from memory, but also without looking at the keys. I wanted to capture that moment forever.

Slowly I pulled out my phone, never breaking eye contact with Amelia. I held up my phone, and before the moment was lost, I snapped several pictures of her.

When Amelia saw what I did, there was a loud *clang* against the piano as she hit about three wrong notes. She promptly stopped playing, sliding back from the piano, and dipped her head. Without music, the choir died off.

Nicholas looked up in question. "What happened?" he asked in a hushed whisper.

"What um... what's the time?" Amelia muttered, still holding her head.

"There's like ten minutes left," someone from the risers answered.

"Let's take a break then, *hmm*?" Amelia offered, finally looking up at her class. "You can have phone time until the period's over."

Amelia stood up from the piano as the entire class sat down on the risers, reclining, already pulling out their phones. Amelia marched to her desk and grabbed her own phone. Nicholas opened his mouth to ask her what was happening, but that was when she grabbed *me* by the collar of my shirt, pulling me up from the chair. Harshly, right into my face, she demanded, "Hall. Now."

Before I knew it, we were alone in the hallway full of lion busts.

"You took a picture of me," Amelia stated, finally releasing my shirt, only to push me back against the wall near the choir room doors. "Why?"

Feeling oddly bold, I replied with, "Because you're cute."

Amelia smiled, but she pushed me back again, harder, pinning me against the wall with her arm. "Yeah? Well two can play at that game," she stated. Before I could prepare myself, she took a picture of me. Out of my reach she turned her phone around and showed me the picture.

"At least take a decent picture," I huffed. "Here." I pushed against Amelia until she backed off and let me move. I pulled up the picture I had taken of her on my phone and showed her. "Now this... this is a *good* picture."

I tilted the phone back my direction, lost in the image. Amelia was adorable, happy and innocent sitting at the grand piano, head cocked slightly to the side like a puppy.

While my guard was down, Amelia snapped another picture of me, laughing.

"Stop," I whined. "Those are all going to be so ugly."

"You could never look ugly."

"Flattering, but inaccurate," I replied. I stood up straight, taking a step towards Amelia, and I pushed her like she had pushed me. "You're the one who could never look ugly, no matter how hard you tried."

Amelia scoffed, backing a step away from me, but this only prompted me to take another step towards her. "You've never seen me cry before," she answered. "I'm a very ugly crier."

"Well, no one looks like a model while crying," I answered. "But I'm sure you're a cute, ugly crier."

"That's impossible."

"Is not." Another step backwards...

"Is too." Another step forward.

"We'll have to test it," I stated. "What's something that makes you cry?"

"Rude. You shouldn't be trying to make me cry." A step backwards.

"It's for science." A step forward.

"I don't cry at work."

"Bet. Dogs dying?" A step forward now.

"You're going to need more backstory than that to get tears out of me." A step backwards to compensate.

With one more step, I pinned Amelia against the opposite wall, just like she had pinned me earlier. I pushed against her, my forearm pressed against her sternum to hold her there, and her snarky remarks instantly stopped, her eyes fluttering shut. My remarks stopped too. I was too busy watching her, looking at how her face relaxed, but feeling how her body tensed underneath mine.

"Lauren said she'd fire Karmen and me if she caught us macking on school property one more time, but I feel like the warning should apply to the two of you as well."

As if burned, Amelia's eyes snapped open, and she shoved me of her. I stumbled back, noting that Amelia's face was beat red. I turned and looked down the hall only to find Eleanor walking up to us, smirking.

"Don't you have a class right now?" she asked Amelia.

"She ended class early," I answered.

"Yeah, so you two could get extra friendly in the hall."

"We weren't doing anything," Amelia choked out.

"Yeah, sure, and I've never had my tongue between Karmen's legs." Eleanor rolled her eyes. I coughed at Eleanor's sudden vulgarity. "All I'm saying is, whatever you two were just doing could be taken *way* out of context. You should have seen what it looked like. Too bad you don't know the passcode to my phone, otherwise you could look at the picture."

"What!?" Amelia gasped.

Eleanor's grin widened. "You think I wouldn't take a picture of such gold? Please."

Amelia looked downright mortified.

"Delete that picture," I warned, pointing an accusatory finger at Eleanor.

"Yeah, and *you*," Eleanor added, pointing right back at me, "have a job to be doing. Piper sent me down here to get you. You need to start setting up the lab."

"See you at six," Amelia muttered out, waving at me as Eleanor pulled me off down the hall.

Once we were off and Amelia was back in the choir room, Eleanor said, "It's none of my business, but you could have cut the sexual tension between you two with a knife."

"There was no sexual tension," I huffed.

"Yeah, keep telling yourself that," Eleanor stated with pursed lips.

10.

Gut Throwing Contest

The first lab at my new job was, unfortunately, a cat dissection lab. Because Piper was helping me get adjusted, she had already drafted up the packet of questions for the students to answer as they did the lab. I picked one up and paged through it after everything was set up. Piper startled me when she stepped into lab.

"School's over," she stated. "The kids should get here in about fifteen minutes. How does the lab look?"

"Fine. I took a dissection lab freshmen year, back when I thought I wanted to become a doctor," I replied. "It shouldn't be a problem. I just... don't like the smell."

"No one does, but I find that after a while, your nose adjusts. How was your day?"

"Fine."

"Just fine?"

"I've just um, got some stuff on my mind, is all."

Piper sat down at one of the stations and patted the stool next to her. "Take a seat," she said. "We've got some time to kill. Tell me, what's on your mind?"

"I just... Nicholas was acting weird today, and he said some stuff, and... do you know Nicholas?"

"Little child prodigy?" Piper questioned and I nodded. "Amelia and Nicholas have a very strong bond, sort of like an older sister and a younger brother."

"He's terrifying."

"Likely just because you're encroaching on his friend. He surely just wants to make sure you're worthy of her time and aren't going to hurt her."

"I don't want to hurt her," I answered honestly. "Unless, well, it's just teasing, you know. She can be really mean and sarcastic sometimes. She has it coming."

"Of course. Explains today."

"What?"

Piper smirked, pulling out her phone, tapping around before she extended it for me to see. There, in all its blackmail worthy glory, was the picture Eleanor snapped of Amelia and me earlier. The picture was blurry, but I liked it nonetheless. I had Amelia pinned to the wall—I rather liked the look of it—and we certainly looked like we were about to kiss.

"Clearly, I pinned her because she was being argumentative," I defended, crossing my arms defiantly.

Piper pulled back and looked at the picture again herself. "By the looks of it, I'd say that's exactly what Amelia wanted you to do."

I let out a heavy sigh. I wasn't fooling Piper. I wasn't even fooling myself. All I was doing was living in denial of my feelings, but it was stupid. Playing mind games and making others guess what you're feeling is petty and childish. I certainly hated when girls acted that way; it was a waste of time and annoying. It was hypocritical of me to act the same way. And yes, it was scary to be open and honest, but maybe if I started by opening up to Piper, it wouldn't be so bad.

"Okay, fine," I murmured a bit hostily. "I like Amelia."

"I know you do," Piper answered. "You're not good at hiding it."

"It terrifies me."

"Because you're intimidated by her accomplishments?"

"Of course! She's so successful and I'm proud of her for that, but I just... I want to be able to square up to her, be able to pull my own weight. I'm just a broke kid though."

"Not a broke kid, a broke college educated woman about to get her degree," Piper replied. "Do you think Amelia accomplished all this while she was in college? Of course not. She went to school and struggled just like you. But she has drive, and you also have drive. Some things just take time, Natalie."

"I guess so. I don't know. And well, I guess it's more than that too. It's feelings in general. I've never really been the best at romantic relationships. I'm scared I'll mess things up and make things worse."

"Everyone's scared to get hurt and unfortunately, there are no guarantees in life," Piper uttered. She grew reflective for a moment before she stood. "The students should be arriving. All ready?"

I stood as well. "Of course."

"Good luck then, though I doubt you'll need it."

My first ever teaching experience, running a lab, went decently well. I introduced myself as Ms. Benton, but it sounded way too weird to me, so I told the students to just call me Natalie. I trailed around between the bench stations watching as the student groups from Byram cut open cats, labeling organs and organ systems. I helped them answer some particularly hard questions in their packets. And then, I overheard some arguing.

"I told you, I put it right there."

"Well, it's not *right there*."

"How can you just lose a liver?"

"I didn't lose it! It put it *right there*!"

"What's going on?" I interrupted.

"Demarcus lost our liver, and we need it for this diagram," one of the girls stated.

"I didn't lose it!" Demarcus protested. "I put it right there on the tray with all the other organs!"

"Yeah, right. He doesn't even know what a liver looks like. He probably thought it was the lung."

"Well, if that's the case, then you never even took out the liver!"

I looked inside their cat carcass and noted it was void of all organs. "Okay, well..." I spun circles looking around the room. "Has um... has anyone seen a cat liver lying around?"

"Yeah, we each got one," some boy called from across the room. "They come out of the cats."

"Right, but does anyone have an *extra* liver? This group is missing their liver."

"Maybe their cat ain't got a liver."

"Yeah, right, dumbass," the girl beside me shouted. "Our cat wouldn't'a been able to live without a liver!"

"Well, your cat looks pretty dead to me, Nia!"

"Hey, stop!" I demanded, trying to mediate.

"Montrell has two livers," a girl across the room accused. "He botched up cutting out their heart and I caught him trying to steal our heart. I bet he did the same with the liver."

"I didn't steal no liver!" Montrell shouted. "And you were the ones who messed up the heart, not me!"

"Alright, everyone, stop!" I shouted. "Who's finished the page in the worksheet about the liver?" A group near the front raised their hand. "Okay, since you're done with the liver, let this group borrow it so they can answer the questions. Problem solved."

Or so I thought. About ten minutes later, more commotion was coming from Montrell and Nia.

"You asshole!" Nia shouted.

I turned, about to tell them to mind their language, when I saw Montrell throw a kidney at her.

"This shirt cost me thirty dollars, you shit-face!" Nia screamed again, some body fluids now staining her shirt. She turned, grabbed the nearest organ from her bench, and chucked it straight at Montrell before I could stop her.

"No, stop, no throwing organs!" I hissed, diving at Nia and batting her hands away from the lab table. I followed up by chastising Montrell, asking what had possessed him to throw an organ at Nia.

"She keeps accusing me of shit!" Montrell huffed. "She's just dumb and doesn't know how to do the lab, so she keeps trying to blame me."

"Don't call her dumb," I declared. I turned back to Nia. "Is it true? Do you keep blaming him?"

"No! He's the one who doesn't know what he's doing and keeps messing up, trying to blame me!"

I turned then to the other students at the lab station. "Alright, what actually happened? Come on, one of you has to know."

I was met with complete and utter silence. No one would look at me.

"Alright, listen up, everyone," I stated, gaining the attention of the entire classroom. "Everyone gets a warning for now, but for the record, it is *never* okay to throw organs *ever*. You shouldn't throw *anything* in lab, alright? If anyone acts up again, it's a mandatory and very boring lab safety lecture before you're allowed back in class, alright? Now finish your work." I turned to Montrell and Nia. "You two are not allowed to be within ten feet of each other in any lab after this. Do not try me."

The students dove back into their work. Montrell sat and pouted for the rest of the lab, not doing any work, so his marks would definitely be lower than his classmates, but I didn't have the energy in me to mediate that. I'd have to talk to Piper and the others about disobedience in the classroom before I'd know how to handle that.

After Montrell's and Nia's spat, there was a huge mess of formaldehyde on the floor, along with little bits of organs. I was midway through bagging up some pieces of intestines when a girl knelt beside me and started to help me.

"Oh, you don't have to do that. You need to finish your work," I stated, looking over at the girl.

"It's okay," she answered, "my group finished already."

"Oh." I stood up and looked at her bench station. Sure enough, the other girls in her group were chatting quietly, sitting patiently until they could turn in their packet and leave. I turned back to the girl. "Well... thanks. And good work finishing up early."

"It was an interesting lab, not even counting the gut throwing. My friends and I really like science... and animals. It's sad to see dead cats, but I know they'll help us learn about their bodies so maybe someday we can help alive cats."

"Yeah, exactly," I answered. "What do you want to do? Do you want to work with animals?"

She nodded bashfully. "I want to be a veterinarian."

"That's awesome!"

"But—" she cut me off— "I don't know if I'm smart enough, or if I could afford the schooling."

"At least you have the passion. But you're right. The world is hard. I used to think I wanted to be a doctor—though I think that was mostly just my mom projecting on me—but then I went to school, and my grades were just... not good enough."

"You're honest. Most adults I talk to just say if I try hard enough, I can do anything."

"I'm just trying to be realistic," I replied. "Just because you have all the drive and determination in the world, doesn't mean you're good at taking standardized tests... or have the money to afford schooling."

The girl extended her hand to me. "I'm Aniyah, it's nice to meet you."

"Hi, Aniyah," I answered, shaking her hand.

At the end of lab, all the students had to report to me before they left. I made sure their packet was completed and their station was cleaned, and then I asked each student a random question or two about the lab, just to make sure they were all equally contributing and learning. Until they got the question right, they couldn't leave, even if that meant going back through the packet and reading up on things.

Everyone did well, even Montrell who actively stopped participating. I was glad. I didn't have any teaching experience, got this position on a whim, and didn't know how to deal with problem students at all, so I was glad it worked out as well as it did.

Piper swung by just to make sure all went well, and I purposefully didn't mention the gut throwing. She had to hurry off as she had a meeting with her lawyer, and I bid her farewell. I checked the time then and turned to head off to the choir room, but Amelia surprised me when she poked her head into lab.

"Hey, lab coordinator," she stated, smiling at me.

"Done with voice lessons?" I asked.

Amelia nodded, stepping into the room. "Yep. How did lab go?"

"If Piper asks, it went smooth as butter, and everyone was perfect."

"But if I'm asking?"

"Two kids got into a cat-gut throwing contest," I sighed. Amelia tried to repress her laugh but failed miserably.

"That's bad," she stated, still laughing. "Real bad."

"I know, but I handled it," I answered. "I might not be the best at handling a classroom yet, but I really enjoyed it. I liked watching the students learn. It was very rewarding."

"That's basically teaching in a nutshell."

"I think I want to learn more about teaching... get better at it."

"Good, that means I'll get to see you once a week."

"Yeah, I mean..." I shuffled my feet. "We could see each other more often too. We do live in the same city after all. I mean, if you want to."

"Of course. It would almost be a crime to not meet up from time to time."

"Right."

"Well, should we get going? I'm starving. There's this great Italian place on Main Street I thought we could go to, if that's alright with you."

"Sure. I'll drive."

"Oh, I kind of thought we'd drive separately and just meet there."

"Right, of course!" I exclaimed, an edge of nervousness to my voice. "That would be best... definitely most convenient."

"So... I'll see you over there?"

"Yeah."

"Okay."

"Sounds good."

"Okay, cool."

"Cool."

"Right, so um... see you soon," Amelia said a bit stilted, excusing herself out of the lab.

We were likely parked near each other in the parking lot, so it would have made more sense to walk out together. But I already made things awkward, and I didn't want to make them more awkward by running into her again in the parking lot, so I just stalled.

A minute later, while I was still awkwardly wasting time in the lab before leaving, I got a text message from Amelia. It just read: *'Sorry.'*

'For what?' I sent back.

'For being weird.'

'You weren't being weird.'

She didn't respond after that. Logically, she was likely driving, but my mind jumped to the worse possible conclusion. She must think I'm a blundering idiot. I just didn't understand it. We never struggled to get along in Florida, even when we were basically flirting. I felt an overwhelming pressure now.

I felt I needed to prove myself to Amelia, that I had to be someone more accomplished than I was. I needed to be spectacular so Nicholas would know I was good enough for Amelia. I needed to figure out how to maintain a relationship, so I didn't crush Amelia—if she even liked me after that horribly awkward exchange—and ruin everything between all the teachers.

I should just ask her if she likes me. That was the straightforward, mature, adult thing to do. I was honest with Piper, so I needed to keep being honest. But there was something so scary about putting yourself out there. It was the fear of rejection that I would have my own heart utterly crushed.

When I arrived at the restaurant, it took quite some time to will myself out of the car. Eventually, I got up the confidence and headed straight to the front doors, jerking them open, expecting to find Amelia, but a couple was exiting as I got there. I stepped to the side to let them exit and then I just... froze. I couldn't force myself to go inside.

I couldn't do it. *What* couldn't I do? What was this? It wasn't even a date, technically, we hadn't specifically said. Did Amelia think it was a date? Was she expecting it to be a date? Was it just us getting dinner after work as a couple of friends?

Someone tapped me on the shoulder, and I nearly jumped out of my skin. I spun around, my fist up as if I was going to punch the person—though I'd never punched anyone in my entire life. But then I was looking into the gorgeous amber brown eyes of the woman who stopped me dead in my tracks on vacation. All worries vanished from my mind as Amelia smiled at me.

"Sorry, I guess I startled you," she said, almost a whisper. Then she held up a pager. "Our table is ready. Perfect timing, I guess."

They seated us in the back corner of a room surrounded by other two-person tables. The restaurant had a dark and moody atmosphere. Everyone around us looked like they were on a date. It *felt* like a date. But we were just friends... just friends getting a bite to eat after work.

We ordered our food, very little muttered conversation between us. Amelia kept fidgeting, looking down at her lap, messing with her hands. She would glance up, every now and then, a shy expression on her face. I wanted to say something, anything, but my mind was blank and my anxiety high.

Suddenly, I remembered what Nicholas said to me: "*I've never seen anything that made that woman go quiet.*" Maybe he was right. Maybe I really did mean something to Amelia. I needed to stop being such an idiot. I needed to relax and remember how I felt back in Florida.

"You know... the last time we had dinner together, we got completely hammered," I stated.

Amelia stared at me for a moment before cracking a grin. "*You* got completely hammered," she corrected.

"You were drunk too."

"It was all a front to make you feel better, since you couldn't even walk straight."

I laughed deeply. "That's not a comment on me being drunk, that's my natural state. I can't do *anything* straight."

It took Amelia a second to catch what I was saying, but when she did, her cheeks flushed. She composed herself, then answered, "Maybe your natural state wasn't helping, but you were still drunk."

I watched Amelia peculiarly. She admitted to me in Florida that she liked girls, but there was clearly still hesitancy. I knew what that felt like, to be questioning, and struggling, fighting with internalized homophobia and all the societal pressures.

"Do you remember what you told me that night?" I asked.

"Of course, I wasn't drunk," Amelia declared. "I told you about Eleanor and Karmen."

"No, after that. After we left the restaurant."

"When you claimed you could do a front flip into the pool?"

"Yes, and I *can*," I added. "But do you remember what you told me right before you shoved me into the pool?"

Amelia blushed again and wiggled in her seat, but she held her eye contact with me. "Of course."

"I promised I'd never tell anyone," I continued. "I haven't and I won't. Although... I think your friends might have already guessed it..."

"That's fine! They can speculate all they want," Amelia said hurriedly. "I haven't told them because I don't—well I'm not sure if—I just think I might—"

"Hey," I said calmly, reaching across the table and taking Amelia's fidgeting hands in mine. "You don't have to say anything right now. You don't have to figure things out now, or label yourself, or anything. But I just want you to know that no matter what you discover, no matter what you decide, that it's... it's chill."

"It's... chill?"

"Yeah, like it's not a big deal," I replied. "I mean, I'm sure it feels like a big deal to you, and in that sense it is. It's very important to you and something you've got to figure out on your own. But it's not the end of the world. You have tons of people in your life who love and support you unconditionally. In the long run, it's just a small piece of who you are. So, like... don't stress."

Amelia stared at me, her eyes wide. I slowly released her hands, about to ask if she was okay, when she suddenly leapt up from our table. She dashed to my side before leaning down and engulfing me in a tight hug.

"Thank you," she mumbled into my neck.

"I... it's... of course," I answered, surprised by her actions. Quickly, she shuffled back to her own seat.

Our food came and conversation flowed easy. In many ways, it felt like we were back in Florida, though we talked about other things. Amelia shared information about the friend group, and I talked a bit about school and my friends.

Eventually, our conversation shifted to Amelia's choir. She spoke of her students like a proud parent would their own child. I could have listened to her talk about her job forever. The sparkle in her eyes made everything worth it.

Amelia told me about Nicholas, amazing and boisterous Nicholas, who wanted to be a Broadway star with a philosophy degree. His family disapproved, however, and was pushing him to become an engineer, or a doctor, or a lawyer. His father was the hardest on him. He thought singing frivolous and queer, a waste of time and potential. He thought it was hardly appropriate to dedicate so much time to singing when a person couldn't amount to anything doing it.

"He said that to my face during parent-teacher conferences," Amelia stated. "Can you believe he had the gall to say to my face that I'm unsuccessful?"

And Amelia confirmed my suspicions that Nicholas wasn't one hundred percent straight.

"He's twelve, he's young, he's still discovering himself," Amelia explained. "But he knows. At school, he doesn't hide it. He's flamboyant naturally and his father hates it. He's very homophobic. Unfortunately, I deal with that a lot... students questioning their sexuality, living with very homophobic and transphobic families."

The red-headed twins fit into that narrative. They weren't as overly passionate for the stage as Nicholas was, but they loved choir because that's where they found a family of like-minded people. They preferred fashion and interior design—those were their passions—and they put together costumes for the choir performances. Their father was very homophobic as well, hateful of their 'girly' passions. One night he discovered they had smuggled a sewing machine into the attic, and he destroyed it in a fit of rage, and signed them up for the football team the next day. And he forced them to come with him to the gym every week.

"It's awful," Amelia stated, shaking her head solemnly. "Everyone should workout, that's not what I'm saying. It's just... the boys get bullied. They aren't too roughed up on the football team, just because Elk Creek has such a strict no bullying policy, but when their dad takes them to the gym... their dad's friends rail on them. They shove the boys around, mock them, insult them. Every day I swear I see more bruises on them. They always give me the same story: 'I hurt myself at the gym' – 'shouldn't have gone so hard at the gym.' But I know it's those filthy friends of their father."

Shannon was suffering too, though she wasn't dealing with a homophobic father. She loved singing, as much as Nicholas did, and her parents supported it... until they realized how attached she had become. They didn't believe it was a sustainable career. Her mother was pressuring her into medical school and often forced Shannon to miss singing practices to visit colleges and interview.

"It's not ideal that she's missing so much practice, but what can I do?" Amelia sighed. "I can't kick her out of choir; we're her family. She needs us now more than ever. And I can't mention it to her mother, because she'd just get angry and force Shannon to quit choir all together. I couldn't do that to her."

Amelia continued talking about her students. She knew everything about all the honors choir students, and a lot of tidbits about the concert choir kids. As she spoke, the names just bounced off my ears, but Amelia remembered. She remembered each and every one of them.

As I listened, I realized their stories had a common thread. Despite how prestigious the honors choir was, no matter how many awards they won, the choir kids were outcasts. They had a good school community—I figured my teacher friends were to thank for that—but they had rough home lives. It sounded like nearly all of them experienced some type of abuse from their immediate family, be it physical, verbal, or emotional. And Amelia was stuck right in the middle of it. She knew her students were being abused, but she was helpless to stop it. Causing a scene would either get the students pulled out of Elk Creek, or it would get Amelia fired.

What Amelia could do for those kids, however, was create a safe space for them and be a loving parental figure when they needed one the most. She let them know not only that their passions were amazing, but that they as people were valid. She listened when no one else would. She gave her students hope and a reason to keep fighting.

"Piper... I think she tries to understand," Amelia muttered. "She would stay late after school if a student needed her—we all would—but she doesn't understand how I can and would dedicate all my free time to my students. She thinks there's a line set in stone. There's the student's life at school, and the student's life at home. And I get that, I understand that, but I think the line's blurry. I think... I think sometimes you have to cross it. But... well if it wasn't for Karmen, I would have been fired last year."

"Really?" I questioned softly. "What did you do?"

"It was Nicholas' birthday, a Saturday, barely three days after the twins had their sewing machine smashed. I was afraid, no, *terrified*, that something might happen to the twins with the rages their father threw. And Nicholas' parents found his diary the day before. They were livid. They told him he couldn't have a birthday party because he got an A- on his history report, which maybe was part of it, but I know it's because of what they read in his diary. They locked him in his room. You have to understand, Natalie. I was afraid for their lives, their emotional wellbeing. I couldn't just sit at home that weekend and do nothing.

"Shannon and I picked up the twins. I couldn't be seen, so Shannon made up a lie about a group project to get the twins out. Then we went for Nicholas. We knew we could never persuade his parents, so we broke him out. That night we climbed up on the roof and snuck him out his bedroom window.

"We drove out of the city to the countryside, found a patch of woods where we could pitch a tent. We stayed up all night. I told them I loved them. I do. I do love them. I wished I could have done more. They told me I had already done so much for them, that I was the best thing that ever happened to them..."

Amelia had to stop at that point, as she was nearly sobbing. She shook, taking a deep breath to calm herself. Then she continued.

"The parents found out, of course. Everything I did was, if not illegal, very against my teaching contract. Karmen... is a surprisingly convincing liar when she wants to be. She covered for me, made up a story about how I was with her all weekend. Luckily, the parents bought it—thought their kids were lying, maybe, but luckily the consequences on them weren't horrid. Karmen knew where I was coming from, understood, but she had some very strong words for me. There are just... there are things a teacher can't do, no matter how hard she wants to."

I pushed my food around on my plate. I was new to teaching. I didn't have a strong connection to any of my students, which I only met earlier that day. And maybe I didn't understand the love Amelia felt for her students, but by god did I wish I had a teacher like Amelia growing up. I remembered all the nights I cried myself to sleep, wishing I could be somewhere else, wishing I had someone else to tell me it was going to be okay. I wanted to help those kids. I didn't know how, but I wanted to. If Amelia asked me tomorrow to take Nicholas to another country far away from his shitty father, by god, I'd do it and I'd never look back.

We transitioned back into less emotionally charged topics. Amelia talked about a dinner dish she made the other day. I told her that my favorite food was cranberries, and she told me I was weird.

"Not like plain, I mean, baked in things," I corrected.

"You're still weird."

We talked more about baked goods and cranberry nut bread, which is what sparked my love for cranberries in the first place. We talked about Florida a bit. Eventually we finished and Amelia paid, admitting that the little gag she played on me in Florida was pretty rude, and she owed me. Then we talked about the teacher friends again.

"What do you think Eleanor will blackmail us for?" I questioned.

"Oh, you mean the picture," Amelia muttered.

"Yeah. Did you see it?" I questioned. Amelia shook her head. "Piper showed it to me. It's actually a really nice picture. I wouldn't mind having a copy."

"When I... well when I pulled you out into the hall, I didn't mean—that is to say—"

"Were you uncomfortable?"

"What?"

"In the hall? When we were teasing each other, and I pushed you against the wall. Were you uncomfortable?"

"No," Amelia answered.

"Neither was I, so I think everything's okay," I stated.

Amelia stared at me for a moment before nodding resolutely.

Eventually we realized the time and decided we needed to get going. Outside, a light, cool, spring breeze met us, the smells of spring in the air all around us. A tension hit me almost instantly, memories of first kisses after first dates in restaurant parking lots, sun having set long ago, a carryout container in your hand.

"Let me walk you to your car," I offered.

There was no reason for me to, but Amelia didn't complain. As we neared her car, I first noticed it was a pristine white SUV, very practical. But then, as we got closer, I recognized the logo.

"A Porsche?" I questioned. There was a hint of disgust to my tone. Not because it was a bad car, just overly flashy. Amelia didn't strike me as the type to own such a car. And besides, she was a teacher. How did she afford such a thing?

"I don't own it," Amelia stated, glancing towards me when she heard my tone. "It's the school's. They give us loaner cars for appearance's sake... trade them in for the newest model every year."

"It's... fancy," I muttered.

"It drives well," she answered with a shrug. "It's too flashy... I'd much rather buy a little car, used even. But I get this one for free so... I'm not going to pass that up."

"You're really saying you'd take a beater over a Porsche?" I questioned skeptically.

Amelia was quiet for a while before she finally spoke. "I grew up in New York City," she said, growing longingly reminiscent. "My parents were both lawyers, though my father retired into business. He had three sons with his first wife—my stepbrothers—but they were all in high school when I was born. They all went to law school and joined my father's firm. It was... hard to connect with my family. During the school year, everyone was always busy working. I spent all my time with a nanny. I was comfortable. They made sure I had a home, food, and plenty of money to spend on whatever I wanted. But I don't think they ever stopped to wonder if I knew they loved me. I... well I still question if they ever actually loved me.

"Summers weren't any different for them. They were still constantly working. Over summer though they sent me out into the country to stay with my dad's mother on a quaint farm. I liked it there more. I felt loved, *knew* I was loved by my grandmother. But in the city, even though I had everything, I felt like an orphan. I was alone. I don't like flashy things or money even, really. They remind me of my parents... cold and distant. Love, happiness, friends, and family will always be more important to me than money."

"My um... my mom's an ER doctor and my dad's a firefighter," I commented. "Mom works weird hours and dad spends five days at the station with only two days off. I never really saw either of them growing up. I was stuck with babysitters a lot. Coming to college, I just... well I feel like I hardly even know my parents."

"It's hard growing up with parents that are never around," Amelia agreed. "It's like you lost them, but they're still there, so you can't grieve them and just move on. But they don't act like parents. They aren't ever there when you need them the most."

"You had your grandmother though."

"Yes." Amelia smiled. "She taught me so much... how to have fun, how to have compassion for others, how to bake... and she taught me how to sing. I was expected to follow in my stepbrothers' footsteps, join the law firm, or in the very least, take over the business side of things. But, I hate math. I'm terrible at it, and I couldn't keep my GPA high enough for law-school."

"I can relate. My mom pushed me towards medical school, and with a biology degree, everyone just sort of expects you to become a doctor. But my grades are too low. And I just... what can I do with a biology degree anyway? Go to grad school? I doubt my grades are high enough for that either."

"I firmly believe that when there's a will, there's a way," Amelia replied. "But if you aren't passionate about what you're doing, it's really hard to find that 'will.' I was never passionate about law or business, but I was and am passionate about singing and acting. My parents weren't happy about that. They weren't going to pay for my education if I was pursuing the fine arts. And, as I mentioned, my grades were too low for academic scholarships... need based was never an option, my parents are filthy rich. But I was determined, so I made my own way. That was the worst year of my life, going to school full time and working two jobs on the side."

"How did you manage that?"

"Like I said, when there's a will, there's a way. Since I was passionate about music, I was willing, and found a way," Amelia explained. "I really lucked out though... managed to win a music scholarship after my sophomore year of undergrad. That helped me from burning out, because I was barely hanging on. And then, the greatest blessing of my life... I won a singing competition for a full ride to Julliard."

I was by no means educated in the world of singing, but the name Julliard sort of stuck out the same way the name Harvard does.

"Isn't that like... a super major important prestigious school?" I questioned.

Amelia nodded. "It's a great name to have tacked onto you diploma. Of course, it's competitive and hard. They push you to really become your best self. It's a good, no, great education. And I just... well I never thought I'd end up here. I didn't dream of becoming a teacher as a kid. I never wanted to be the failure of the family. I never thought I'd find a place where I belonged, surrounded by friends, doing a job I love. I didn't know I could find a way to use the success I found to better the lives of others.

"I guess what I'm saying is, it's okay to feel lost in college. It's okay to question everything you grew up on, every word your parents ever said to you, because they aren't always right. It's natural to start seeing the corruption in society once you leave home, to realize that America isn't perfect like they always told you it was. It's good to recognize all the shitty things society pressures us into thinking and saying and doing. It's okay to not know who you are or where you belong in all that. It's not forever though. Things will work out, they always seem to."

"I just... I wish I knew what I was passionate about," I whispered.

"You'll stumble into it one day," Amelia stated confidently, "headfirst and unsuspecting."

"Thank you." I opened my arms, offering a hug, which Amelia happily obliged in, wrapping her arms around me.

"You're... really wonderful, Natalie," Amelia said, her chin resting on my shoulder.

"Thanks. I think you're really wonderful too, Amelia," I echoed.

Amelia pulled back a bit, but left her arms wrapped around me. She peered into my eyes, our faces so close. She felt like warmth and comfort. I couldn't think of anything else except her. I couldn't even think about telling her how I felt, because all the coherent thoughts in my mind were replaced with a rhythmic chant of *"Amelia, Amelia, Amelia."*

She removed one of her hands from my back and pushed a strand of pink hair out my face, tucking it behind my ear. Her hand lingered there, hovering against my ear for a second. Then she cupped my cheek, and shut her eyes, leaning just an inch closer to me.

There we were, frozen in time. I wanted to lean towards her, to feel her breath against my lips. I wanted to see if she would part her lips, move towards my mouth. But I couldn't... I just couldn't move.

Amelia took a step back from me. My breathing caught up to me as if time resumed itself around us. Amelia went to her car and opened the door, turning back to look at me.

"I'll see you next Thursday, then?" she questioned.

"For sure," I replied, nodding.

11.

Rainy, Late Night Phone Calls

Lizzie bombarded me when I returned home to campus. I should have expected it. She certainly wasn't going to let me have any peace and quiet until I obliged her.

"Come on! You hardly told me any good gossip. I'm basically dying here!" Lizzie whined.

"Did you stop to consider," I said, taking a seat on my bed, "that I haven't got any good gossip to tell?"

"You totally do though," Lizzie continued, not letting me get away. "No one goes on vacation alone only to befriend a bunch of teachers that all just happen to work at a leading high school, then gets a job with them, and doesn't have even an *ounce* of gossip to tell! Come on! Tell me about them!"

"Okay, fine, since you clearly aren't going to let me get away until I tell you," I caved. "I guess, well, I'll start with Piper to begin with. She's the biology teacher and my supervisor. She teaches a bunch of classes and labs, and is pregnant and getting a divorce, so the principal wants to help her out. That's where I come in, with the position I just got."

"Nice, good for you. And yeah, she definitely needs some help."

"There's Ellie 2.0—"

"You call her 2.0?"

"Yeah, it caught me by surprise too. There's two Eleanor's and she came second so I don't know, the weird nickname stuck. She's honestly the calmest, just because it sounds like she actually has her life together and met a good guy. She's engaged. I think they both teach English, which is cute."

"Totes adorbs."

"Please don't say totes... or adorbs for that matter."

"You're just an old fart."

"Anyway," I stated, rolling my eyes, "Karmen and Eleanor—that's the other Eleanor I was talking about—"

"I know, you literally just mentioned it."

"Okay, if you're going to be sassy, I'll just stop talking."

"No, please!" Lizzie whined. "I promise I'll behave. Please, go on."

"As I was saying, Karmen and Eleanor hella have the hots for each other, but they're both married to guys."

"Hey, if I can't say totes, you can't say hella."

"I'm telling the gossip, I can say what I want," I responded defiantly. "They've been having this huge affair for years, both had kids with their husbands, Karmen's pregnant again. But now they're both filing for divorce and working out custody. Then maybe after that, they'll get married to each other. Not sure."

"Amazing!" Lizzie clapped. "Hooray for marriage equality!"

"Yeah, and then um, Amelia's the choir director there." I looked away from Lizzie, rubbing at the back of my neck. I could still feel the ghost touch of Amelia's fingers against my face.

Lizzie read right through me. "Ohh... *that's* the one you slept with," she stated.

"I didn't sleep with any of them," I defended.

"Yeah, I actually believe you. You're a huge coward and there's no way you could bang successful Elk Creek teachers."

"Well, I don't—I mean—"

"But you still think she's super-hot." I felt my cheeks flush. "And you have a crush on her!" Lizzie added, teasing.

"And I have a crush on her," I repeated under my breath, but Lizzie heard me.

"I was right!" she exclaimed. "I just *knew* you had the hots for at least one of them! Tell me about her!"

"She's just, um... adorable. And she's sassy and confident, I don't know," I muttered, shrugging.

"Well... I hope it works out for you then," Lizzie declared, nodding. "And I know I'm straight, but if you need any flirting pointers—"

"And... I'm going to bed."

Another graduation party for one of my peers penciled onto my calendar... They were going off to Harvard law school. One of my friends from back home called and said they got accepted into their dream job right out of school. Even Lizzie had job opportunities lined up.

My mother was pleasantly surprised that I managed to find a job. She didn't know the area, but definitely researched Elk Creek after I told her, because I got another phone call about how great an opportunity it was, and how I shouldn't mess it up. And I was... happy I got the job.

I was mostly excited that I got to work with my teacher friends. And I did think there was something wonderful to be said about teaching, but I just... was I passionate about it? Did I want my career to be teaching?

Before spring break, I scheduled a career counselling appointment for when I got back. My mother told me I still needed to go, for long term planning, so I went just to humor her. They helped with your resume and interview skills, but also helped find career choices that matched you. I went in with an open mind, but left feeling awful. They kept asking about what things I liked to do, what hobbies I had, what interests I had, what activities I enjoyed, but the problem was, I didn't have any! I went home, did homework, and streamed a movie or two, then it was bed, rinse, and repeat. Every biology and science related field they suggested sounded horrible. I didn't want to work in biology! But that's what my degree was going to be in!

The meeting was late, and it was a real struggle, so I didn't get out until nine that night. I was dragging my feet walking home. I felt like a loser. Who goes to college, picks a major and hates it, and then just finishes the degree without changing majors? I wish I could have gone back in time and forced sophomore me to change my major. But to what? What would I have changed it to?

It was misting outside, a foggy night, very few other students out and about. I didn't have an umbrella, not that I really needed it, but I would be pretty damp by the time I got home. I needed to get home and sleep; it was only a Tuesday and I had class tomorrow. But for some reason, I just wanted to wander. I wanted to stay out in the mist, in the fog.

I wandered, alone, in the dim light from campus streetlamps, clouded over with fog. I pulled off the beaten path, walking back closer towards the buildings where the gardens were nicer. Down a pathway between two buildings, I found my escape from the rain under an overhang. It was over a back-exit door—locked—and a single light by the door flickered, orange and aged.

I didn't know what to do. I felt like I was running my future into the ground before it had even started. I decided I needed to talk to someone, just talk about my thoughts and my options, maybe hear some opinions. I sat down on the wet concrete under the overhang, ignoring the damp, and pulled out my phone. I wasn't sure who to text. My parents were not an option... Lizzie would just want to know where the hell I was. My friends back home were all moving on... my other friends at college were too. In the end, my finger hovered over the contact name of a more recent friend, the name of someone that made me feel comfortable and safe. Even, dare I say, loved?

Eww, too many feelings, gonna vomit, gross. Had to fix that real quick.

I tapped on Amelia's name and pulled up the keyboard to text her.

'Hey, what's up, fucker?' I typed. I stared that the words without sending it. That was a weird and really shitty greeting, even for me. I changed my message to read, *'Hey, what's up, basic-choir-babe?'* That was... still weird. A simple hey would suffice plenty. I went to erase the weirdness from my message, but my finger slipped, and I accidently sent it instead.

I received a response near instantly: *'Basic-choir-babe?'*

'Umm, Freudian Slip?' I offered meekly.

'That means you still think of me as a basic-choir-babe.'

'Well, it was originally going to be 'what's up, fucker,' so be glad you got basic-choir-babe instead.'

'I'm not sure which is worse.'

'Both are bad. I'm just being stupid. Sorry.'

'Don't be. I'll do something just as stupid someday, and then we'll be even.'

'You didn't answer my question though,' I prompted.

'What question?'

'What's up, doc?'

'That wasn't the question. You said, 'what's up, basic-choir-babe?''

'Okay, yes, we covered that. But you still need to answer the question.'

'I'm just relaxing. I'd be asleep by now if I wasn't an insomniac.' And then, immediately after, Amelia added: *'Or it's the caffeinated coffee I drank twenty minutes ago.'*

'It's definitely the coffee. Why did you drink coffee right before bed?'

'Because I'm addicted?'

'Isn't that why they have decaf?'

'Decaf tastes nasty.'

'ALL coffee tastes nasty.'

'I'll convert you someday. What are you up to?' Amelia inquired.

'Sitting out in the rain.'

'Why?'

'Been thinking a lot about my life and what I want to do with it... kind of wanna die.'

Amelia didn't reply for several minutes. In my head, I tried to justify her sudden silence. For instance, she was getting a snack, or brushing her teeth, or maybe she was peeing. But the thought that she just didn't care enough to listen to my problems was forefront in my mind. I was bothering her. I never should have texted her. I was ready to give up, lie down on the wet ground and stay there until I caught pneumonia.

But then, my phone lit up and buzzed.

"Hello?" I questioned, realizing Amelia was calling.

"Are you crying?" was the first thing out of her mouth.

"No," I answered, stronger. I slid back so I could lean against the wall of the building.

"Oh, you just sounded like maybe you were, and from what you said I just... well I just wanted to make sure."

"No, I'm... okay. I mean, I'm frustrated and really stressed. I just... I feel like I'm at a loss."

"That's normal, you know," Amelia assured me. "People are all sorts of stressed these days. It's perfectly normal to feel hopeless."

"I felt like this back in high school too," I uttered. "I thought that once I got to college, I would have my life together. I'd grow, things would fall into place. But it never did. I just... I went through four years of undergrad like I was just... just floating along with the current! And now I've reached the destination, but it's not at all where I want to be, but I did nothing to paddle to a different destination."

"You can always get back in the water and start paddling. Now or later," Amelia stated, humoring my metaphor.

"I don't know where my destination is though... I haven't found something I want to devote my life to."

"Sometimes it takes time to find your passions."

"I don't have time though! I'm already getting a biology major! I put off applications, but I didn't even want to go to grad school or work in an industry lab! I needed to have figured out my passions four years ago, when I was first picking my major!"

"You always have time to figure it out. You can go back to school, or, you'd be surprised what all you can do with a biology major. Maybe even some day you could go to grad school for something completely unrelated. It can happen, depending on the program. Right now, you have a full-time job lined up. You can just take a breather, relax."

"Maybe I'm just being melodramatic. My first day teaching was pretty good. Maybe I'll find that I really love it, or maybe... maybe if I don't like it, the experience will help me land a job I do like."

"Good, positive thinking."

"Thank you," I said. "Talking to someone is just... helpful. Talking to you is... nice."

Amelia chuckled lightly on the other end of the line. "You can call me whenever you want to, you know that, right? You don't have to text me something stupid like, '*What's up, basic-choir-babe?*' to get my attention. You just have to call and say you need to talk."

"Not my proudest moment," I admitted.

"I like talking to you, Natalie."

"I like talking to you too."

"Feeling better then?"

"I think so."

"Good. So now, about you sitting in the rain..."

"No, no," I stated, shaking my head, even though Amelia couldn't see me. "We need to talk about your caffeine addiction. Just how many cups of coffee do you drink in one day?"

We ended up talking for a really long time. We talked about nothing and everything, personal things, favorite things, childhood pets, boardgames. Eventually my phone started beeping at me about low battery and I realized how tired I really was. I glanced at the time, realizing it was suddenly 5:46 AM. I apologized profusely to Amelia, realizing she had to be up in less than fifteen minutes for work.

Amelia assured me it was okay. "I don't have a coffee addiction for nothing, after all," she mused.

We ended our call and I sat there for a moment, my dying phone in my hands. Slowly, I stood and headed across campus. The sky had cleared, and the sun was rising. The day was going to be a bright one. Groaning, I dragged myself back to my room for about two hours of sleep. It wasn't much, but it was more than Amelia was getting.

When Thursday rolled around, I once again found myself over at Elk Creek. Since my previous struggles, both Amelia and Piper were quick to help me learn the layout of the school. I still got turned around at times, but I was doing much better. The second floor—where Karmen's and Ellie 2.0's classrooms were—remained a mystery to me, but at least I knew where the cafeteria was.

On my way to the cafeteria, I remembered Nicholas wanted me to keep Amelia from going to lunch with them. It unnerved me that they wanted Amelia gone, but I tried to be realistic. They wanted to talk about Amelia with me... that could mean any number of things, and not all of them bad. I wanted to get on the good side of the choir too—Amelia's second family—and I figured that humoring Nicholas would be the first step.

I looped past the cafeteria and towards the choir wing to intercept Amelia. Halfway down the hall I stopped, seeing Amelia heading towards me, Nicholas trotting along beside her, chatting up a storm. Amelia spotted me before I could say anything and sped up, nearly running at me, before she grabbed me in a tight hug. She swung me back and forth, leaving me stumbling over my feet, nearly falling over.

"Woah, calm down!" I exclaimed, regaining my balance. "You aren't strong enough to spin me without toppling me over! I nearly fell!"

"Sorry," Amelia admitted, but she was giggling. "I'm just really excited to see you!"

Nicholas cleared his throat and I glanced down towards him, greeting him. Nicholas acknowledged me, though he gestured wildly at Amelia when she couldn't see him. His message was clear: he wanted me to get rid of her.

"Ready to head to lunch?" Amelia questioned.

I realized I hadn't thought up a legitimate way of getting Amelia out of the cafeteria. I just needed an excuse, and unfortunately, Ellie 2.0 popped into mind.

"Actually, um, I'm glad I ran into you," I stated. "Something kind of popped up."

"See you later," Nicholas butted in, excusing himself. He dashed off towards the cafeteria, leaving Amelia and me alone.

"Is something wrong?" she asked.

"Well... it's just that I was talking to Piper and... well she thinks something is bothering Ellie 2.0. She won't talk about it though, so maybe don't push her. But just, Piper was thinking it might be nice if you all ate lunch together in the teacher's lounge. To raise her spirits, you know."

"Oh, okay," Amelia replied, looking genuinely worried. "I hope she's okay."

"Me too."

"Are you coming then? To the teacher's lounge to eat with us?"

"That's okay. I think... I think it's more of an original friend group situation, if that makes sense. I don't want to butt in and make her uncomfortable if she needs to talk to you guys."

"That's a good point. She can be a bit timid."

"Yeah, so it's all good." I nodded resolutely. "I'll just go eat with the choir kids, get to know them better. I'm sure Nicholas will have plenty to tell me."

"Just... don't listen to *everything* they say," Amelia warned. "Especially anything embarrassing about me. They're elaborate, animated storytellers. They exaggerate a lot."

"Well now I'm going to have to ask about these embarrassing stories they have of you," I stated with a smirk.

Amelia rolled her eyes. "I'm serious!" she exclaimed. "I'll see you after lunch."

I went to the cafeteria on my own, grabbing a tray of food before I headed to table number one. I forgot which table it was exactly, but I recognized Shannon and Nicholas.

Before I even had a chance to sit down, Nicholas gasped, "Did you do it?"

I sat down in the only empty chair, presumably Amelia's seat. Then I turned and addressed Nicholas. "I got her to eat in the teacher's lounge, but I can't promise she'll stay there."

"We should hurry then," Shannon stated. "Tell her now, just in case Ms. Lewis comes back."

"But there's a lot to explain!" Nicholas whined.

"Then stop complaining and tell her!" a boy across the table hush-whispered. "You're wasting valuable time!"

"What do you guys need to tell me?" I questioned, taking a bite of my lunch.

"Listen up, Rose Gold. We need you to be the brains of our operation," a different boy across the table commented. I looked over and found it was one of the twins. His identical brother sat beside him, and I had no means of telling them apart. I knew Amelia told me their names last week, but I had already forgotten.

"Don't call her Rose Gold, that's so stupid," Nicholas complained. "We talked about this, remember? It's just not classy."

"I personally like the code names," Shannon commented. "It makes everything more fun. It feels like official spy work, you know? As opposed to just snooping and meddling."

"Snooping and meddling?" I questioned, growing concerned.

"It's all part of our 'make Ms. Lewis happy' plan," the other twin commented.

"Georgie!" Nicholas hissed at the boy. "I'm in charge of the operation, remember? Stop spilling details."

"Then stop beating around the bush and tell her!" Georgie snapped back.

"Hey, guys, chill," I mediated. "What's this operation you're talking about?"

"Me. Lewis is lonely!" Shannon exclaimed, but she quickly shut up when Nicholas sent her a glare.

"We all love Ms. Lewis with all our hearts," Nicholas said to me. "She has childhood friends, but she's far from home and never gets to see them. She's good friends with some of our other teachers, which is great, but they've got their own lives and families. She always says she's perfectly content, but you can tell she's lonely. Now she has Natalie. I think she needed you more than any of us realized. You coming into her life has made us all aware of just how lonely she was. Like, she *seemed* happy before. But you have no clue just how happy she was when she first mentioned you, Natalie."

"Her eyes just lit up!" Shannon gasped. "We asked her how her break was, and she hardly spent a second telling us about the trip before she was going on and on about *you!*"

"We realized how much happier she could be," Nicholas continued. "And she was crushed at the thought of never seeing you again. That's why we were so desperate to find you and reunite you. We needed to do it to make Ms. Lewis happy. And we did! But there's more to this plan. She's still not perfectly happy."

"She's yet to reach her maximum happiness potential," Georgie commented.

"Okay... so I'm assuming, since you got me back here, that you're now continuing on to the next step of this plan?" I took a stab.

"Yes!" Nicholas nodded enthusiastically. "She's so much happier now that's she's got an amazing best friend, but there are other areas of her life where she's still lonely."

I fiddled with my food. I had a sneaking suspicion where this conversation was heading, and I didn't like it.

Shannon was the one who confirmed my suspicions: "She needs a man in her life!"

"Yes! The next phase of our plan is to get Ms. Lewis a boyfriend!" Nicholas exclaimed. "She's independent, which is fine. Strong, independent women are amazing. But just because she's fine being alone doesn't mean she doesn't dream of the tight, warm embrace of a strong, burly man!"

Georgie rolled his eyes. "Or that's just *your* dream," he said pointedly at Nicholas.

"She hasn't had a single boyfriend in all the years I've known her," Shannon added. "I'm not even sure if she's been on any dates. And that's fine, you know, but we know she loves kids. She wants a family of her own someday. So, she must dream of finding her perfect husband too!"

"And we managed to get you back here for her, so logically the next step is to find her the perfect man!" Nicholas stated.

"Yes, *logically*," I stated sarcastically.

"We want to set her up on a date," Nicholas continued, barely able to sit still at all. "But... we need your help."

"Why?" I asked, genuinely confused.

"Well, we're likely going to end up just making her a dating profile on some apps, start talking to some guys until we find a good match, try and set them up," Nicholas explained, "but that's a lot of work and a huge gamble, especially when we think she has a crush on our history teacher."

I frowned slightly. "That still doesn't explain why you need my help."

"It's just... we don't know for sure if she likes our history teacher or not," Shannon explained.

"Why not just ask her?" I offered.

"We've tried, *many times*, but we can't get a conclusive read. Nicholas and I think she totally has a crush on him, but the other choir members aren't so convinced."

"Shannon asked Ms. Lewis if she likes him, and she just laughed, so she clearly thinks the idea of the crush is laughable," Georgie stated. "That's enough for me to know she doesn't like him."

"She didn't deny it though," Shannon continued.

"She didn't deny it because she was laughing at how absurd it was," Georgie shot back.

Nicholas grabbed my arm to get my attention. "You're older than us. You know her in a different light. She might confide in you if she has feelings. If you could ask her, judge her reaction or confession—"

"There won't be a confession!" Georgie cut in.

"*Anyway*," Nicholas stated hotly. "Natalie, we just want you to get a good read for us. So we can figure out if we need to be dedicating our time to setting them up, or finding her other dates."

I rubbed at my face. All of this would be entirely easier if Amelia was out. If she was out, I could just confess to the choir kids that *I* was the one with the crush on her and avoid all this nonsense with guys. But as it was, I couldn't *say* anything, not even about me liking her, because it would just end up outing Amelia and outing another person was never okay. So instead, what was I supposed to do? Refuse to help the students, knowing they'd wreak havoc on everything, or agree to help and maybe mediate some of that havoc?

"I, um, sure," I muttered out, giving in. "I guess I could ask her. No promises it'll help anything but like, I'll ask."

"Awesome! I knew you'd help us out!" Nicholas squealed, grabbing me in a tight hug.

"Alright," I sighed. "Tell me about this guy—your history teacher. I might as well know what we're getting into.

"It's Mr. Chinipardaz!" Shannon shot out. "He's new this year, fresh out of college, I think."

"He went back for his teaching degree after deciding he didn't want to be a museum curator, so he's not younger than Ms. Lewis. He's a year older," Nicholas added.

"That doesn't matter." Georgie's twin rolled his eyes.

"It does too!" both Shannon and Nicholas gasped, simultaneously appalled.

"Anyway," Georgie muttered, "he teaches sophomore and AP history."

"He's tall, good build... kind of muscular, but he hides it under tight fitting button-downs and slacks. Like a... a sexy librarian!" Shannon swooned.

"Don't mind Shannon, she's basically in love with the man," Nicholas stated, rolling his eyes. "He is though—very good looking—just like she said. Girls are swooning over him all the time. He's like a nerdy, sexy, handsome, pretty man... but he's got brains too."

"Well, I don't see why Ms. Lewis *wouldn't* like him," I offered, though sarcastically. "I've never heard her bring him up before, though."

"*Hmm*," Shannon thought. "Has she said anything about a Dale?"

I thought really hard about it, but I honestly couldn't remember Amelia talking about any guys. "I don't think so," I finally decided.

"Oh, well that's his name: Dale Chinipardaz."

"We just need to figure out if Ms. Lewis likes him, because he's already head-over-heels in love with her," Nicholas rambled.

"How do you know?" I questioned.

"Oh, it's easy," Nicholas stated with a flip of his hand. "He flirts with her *all the time.*"

"Oh, definitely," Shannon agreed. "He brings her flowers all the time. In fact, the bouquet on her desk right now is from him. I bet there's even a note tied to a rose that says something really cheesy."

"And he hides little notes around her classroom for her," Georgie added. "We find them sometimes and bring them to Ms. Lewis. The girls always gush about how he's so sweet and Ms. Lewis has a secret admirer, but she never seems to acknowledge it, so that's why I really don't think she's—"

"Don't forget the antique sheet music for Christmas!" Shannon exclaimed suddenly.

"Oh, yes, his Christmas present for her!" Nicholas added. "He gave her an old Chopin piece for her collection and well, Chopin's just got to be her favorite composer, the way she swooned."

"Has he ever asked her out?" I cut in. "I mean, officially?"

"Not that we know of," Georgie's twin answered with a shrug.

"I doubt he has. He's too much a pansy for that much confrontation. That's why he just leaves notes," Nicholas said.

"He sounds like a wuss," I grumbled, though it wasn't like I had taken any more initiative with Amelia myself.

"That's why *we* have to set them up!" Shannon declared. "I was thinking we could convince them to both chaperon the Spring Fling, and then with some appropriately timed nudges, *bam*, they're dancing together and falling in love!"

Suddenly, Nicholas shot across the table and practically hit Shannon, flailing his arms every which way. He settled back in his seat right as Amelia walked up to us, stopping just behind me.

"You stole my spot," she joked, poking me in the back.

"I thought you were eating in the teacher's lounge," I answered, turning in my seat to look up at her.

"I was, and did," Amelia replied. "We finished eating though, so I thought I'd swing by and say hi."

"Hi!" everyone at the table quickly stated.

Amelia narrowed her eyes. Surely, she knew something was up, but luckily for us, she ignored it. She turned back to me, an air of awkwardness to her demeanor again.

"Do you want to, um, come with me? Back to the choir room? Since it looks like you're done eating?" she asked me.

"*Umm...* sure?" I questioned, glancing between the choir kids. They all gave me expectant looks. Slowly, I stood.

Without another word, Amelia abruptly jerked me out of the cafeteria, leaving me to stumble after her. We were halfway to the choir room before she slowed down her pace. Then finally, she released my hand.

"Is everything okay?" I asked.

"Yep," Amelia answered. "I just..." she stopped then, very abruptly, and I stumbled a step trying to stop as fast as she did. I turned back to face her and found her just staring at me. I opened my mouth to question her, but before I could, she dove on me and grabbed me in a tight hug.

I hugged her back happily, but I was confused. "You're acting weird," I declared, still pulled close to Amelia. "I mean, you're a really huggy person, I get that, but even this is weird for you."

"I just wanted to make sure that you know I care about you," Amelia stated. "We all do. And well... we might have maybe kind of talked about you at lunch, just a tiny bit."

"Okay, well, that's fine," I answered, pulling away from her. "For the record, I care about all of you too."

"We're all going through some rough patches," Amelia admitted, "and because we're friends, we support each other. I just wanted to tell you, personally, that if you ever need anything, anything at all, we're here for you. I'm very serious. I know you're independent and you want to try to figure things out on your own but having some help from time to time never hurt anyone. It's okay to need your friends."

"Thank you, I apricated it. I really do," I replied, nodding. "Now stop being so sappy and come on. Lunch is almost over." This time, I grabbed Amelia's hand and tugged her towards the choir room. Amelia's words had left me on the verge of tears, and I wasn't about to cry in front of her. I needed the conversation to end before I accidently did.

We made it to the choir room a few minutes before the end of lunch. I felt weird. My emotions were whacky, I was stressed, and now I had the added pressure of needing to ask Amelia about Dale. I strolled over to her desk where a bouquet of flowers sat, just like Shannon figured.

"Hey, do you collect... I don't really know what to call it, but like... antique sheet music of classical pieces?" I questioned.

"I don't—well it's not a formal collection," Amelia answered. "But I suppose I do. They aren't originals of course. I couldn't even imagine the price tags. I just... well sometimes I find a really old reprint of a song I like, and it's just nice to have."

"Do you have a lot of Chopin?" I then asked.

Amelia looked up at me, a funny expression on her face. "I have a few Chopin pieces, just like I have a few pieces from a lot of composers. Why? Do you like Chopin?"

"Oh, no, I just..." I felt my face heating up. I struggled to find an explanation that didn't involve Dale. "He's just the only composer I know of off the top of my head."

"Not Beethoven? Or Mozart?" Amelia stated with a smirk. "Chopin is the guy you know?"

"Well, do you have a lot of Rameau?" I questioned hotly. "I know him because you told me about him."

"I do," Amelia replied, nodding, still smiling. "I have a copy of almost everything he wrote. Well, everything except for *Orphée*. I can't find sheet music older than 1982 for it. I feel it's hardly worth collecting if it's not over fifty years old."

"Of course not. How do you find your sheet music?" I asked. "Because, well I'd think you could find just about anything online, but prices might be really high."

"I've gotten stuff through a number of means. Some I've impulse bought online, others have come from consignment stores, some have been gifts. I started my collection buying from some wonderful old ladies selling things from their porches in the south of France."

"France?"

"Sure, and a few other European countries."

"I didn't realize you traveled so much."

"My mother's French," Amelia then said, which clicked together several puzzle pieces in my mind. "Her family is still in France, so we'd visit from time to time."

"You can speak French then, surely," I muttered.

"I told you. I have a weird relationship with French."

"But what does that mean?"

"Anyway, how was lunch? What all did you get to talking about?" Amelia stated abruptly, ending our conversation.

"Just, um, you know, it was lunch," I replied. My fingers had found the little note tied to a rose in the bouquet and I read it. It was nothing but sappy words probably found on the internet, followed by a signed '*D*.'

"Hey, do you know Dale Chinipardaz?" I barked out before I could lose my nerve, tucking the note back into the flowers.

"Sure, he teaches history here," Amelia answered.

"And gives other teachers flowers," I stated.

Amelia glanced over to me and the flowers I was still standing beside. "I didn't realize the flowers were from him, if they are," she said. I strained my ears to figure out if she was lying or not, but she sounded genuine. "Maybe he did get everyone flowers. I didn't think to ask the others."

"Do you know if he has class this period?" I questioned.

"I... don't know. I guess, well I have a schedule around here somewhere. Let me look. Why do you ask?"

"Oh, well, I just... you know, Nicholas was telling me about him. I guess the students like him or something. They thought I should meet him. And I just thought, if he was free now, I could swing by."

"It looks like he's free this period, yes," Amelia replied, procuring a school schedule from her desk. When she said this, the bell rang, signaling the end of lunch. "Are you coming back after you meet him?"

"Probably," I answered, already heading for the door.

"You know, I could just introduce you after school, if you—"

I pulled the choir room door shut behind me so it would close faster. The hall was already full of students hurrying to their lockers and off to class. I didn't know where his room was, but I knew the first floor consisted of the science and math classrooms, so I headed upstairs. I reached the grand central staircase just as the next bell rang, starting the next period.

A few steps into my upstairs journey and I ran into Ellie 2.0. She was sprinting down the hall and nearly ran right into me, but she stopped just in time and looked up at me, surprised.

"Woah, chill, is the building on fire?" I questioned.

"Natalie!" she all but screamed.

"Hi," I responded, nodding. "Where are you off to in such a hurry?"

"Oh, I didn't make enough copies!" she declared, slightly out of breath. "And the copier was out of toner, so I have to grab some from the other copy room."

"Well good luck with that. Don't let the printers best you," I stated with a smirk. I moved to step past Ellie 2.0, but she stopped me.

"Hey, um... how are you doing?" she asked softly.

"*Uhh...* pretty okay," I replied. "Why?"

"Amelia said some stuff at lunch."

"What stuff?"

"Just that you were really stressed out and she doesn't want you to be stressed. She really wants to be there for you, but she doesn't want to step on your toes, you know? She's just a bit worried about you."

"She's worried about me? Huh... well I guess that explains why she was being so clingy."

"Clingy?"

"Yeah, she keeps hugging me."

"Well, she's a very physical person in general," Ellie 2.0 agreed. "That's the thing about Amelia. When she can't find the right words to express how she feels, she relies on her actions... like her hugs, for instance."

"I guess that makes sense."

"Where are you off to anyway? You aren't really ever over on this side of the building. Not that I mind! I just wasn't expecting to see you."

"Oh, I'm trying to find Mr. Chinipardaz's room."

"It's right over there," Ellie 2.0 said, pointing down the hall. "Why do you need to talk to him, if you don't mind me asking? I just didn't know you knew Dale, is all."

"I don't. I'm running some... errands for the choir kids."

"*Hmm...* sounds interesting. Don't let them get you into trouble."

"I'll do my best."

"Right, well, I really need to get these copies."

"Right, right. Catch you later!"

Ellie 2.0 nodded, scurrying off.

I walked up to Dale's room. The door was shut, but the light was on inside and I could see through the little window on the door. I saw him, seated at his desk across from the door, his nose deep in a book. And I just... froze. I just stood there, staring into the classroom at a man not twenty yards from me, a wooden door the only thing standing between us.

He was beautiful. I couldn't think of any other way to describe him. His hair was a burly dark blonde and he was scruffy, glasses resting on his nose. I could tell, just from his shoulders, that he was well built, and he dressed well too. He looked mature, strong, and sensible... smart, but in a humble way. And in that moment, I hated him.

I hated a man I didn't even know because he was beautiful and perfect, just like Amelia. They would be perfect together. They would make beautiful children with each other. They would make the perfect family that all wore matching outfits on their Christmas cards, the family that would host regular dinner parties where Dale would make a casserole and Amelia would make dessert, and their kids would be musical geniuses who would go to Harvard to study law.

Dale looked up from his book, sensing someone staring at him. Our eyes met through the window. He opened his mouth, as if to invite me in, but he never did, because immediately, I turned and fled.

12.

Adults Are Annoying

I slammed open Piper's classroom door, bursting into her room in the middle of class. She must have seen the panic in my eyes, because she immediately stopped what she was saying, told her students there had been a change of plans, and set them up working in groups on some project. I hadn't meant to disrupt her, I just wanted to go back to the joined lab and start setting up. But a few moments later, she joined me back in the lab.

I stopped what I was doing, which was messing around with equipment, and just sat down at one of the lab stations, sighing. Piper sat down across from me, just watching me for a moment, before she finally stated, "You did something fishy at lunch today."

"What are you talking about?"

"You told Amelia that Ellie was feeling down. Amelia brought it up before Ellie got down to lunch, and I had no reason to not believe her. I hadn't talked to Ellie yet. But then Amelia said that *you* told her that Ellie was feeling down and that *you* found out from *me*, so that's when I knew you had lied."

"Sorry," I muttered out. "I wasn't trying to be sneaky or lie or anything, I just... well I needed to keep Amelia out of the cafeteria today."

"Why?"

"The choir kids, Nicholas specifically, wanted her gone for a spell."

"Do I want to know why? They love her, I can't imagine it was anything bad."

"No, they just... well it turns out they've got this plan. They wanted me to snoop around for them."

"I'm not following."

"They're trying to set Amelia up on a date."

"Oh," Piper said, but then she followed it up with a long, drawn out, "*Ohh.*"

"What does that mean?"

"She hasn't seriously dated anyone as long as any of her students have known her. And those kids love to meddle. It's annoying, though I'm positive Amelia fuels it. I could see them trying to set her up," Piper stated resolutely. "Did you tell them you have a crush on her?"

"No!" I gasped. "Why would I tell them that?"

"Because it's true?"

"I can't!" I stated seriously. "I mean, I certainly don't care if the choir gang knows I'm gay. But I can't tell them that I like Amelia, because in a roundabout way, it would out Amelia. That's a horrible thing to do to another person, even if everyone would be completely accepting. I would never do that to her."

"I suppose you have a point."

"Anyway, it doesn't matter, because I think she likes a guy."

"Amelia likes a guy?" Piper asked in full disbelief.

"I think so."

"Who? Chris Hemsworth?"

"No," I scoffed. "I, well, do you know Dale?"

"Dale? Like Dale that works here, the new hire? Dale Chinipardaz?"

"That's the one."

"She likes Dale?"

"Potentially. And regardless, I'm sure he likes her. She's utterly perfect, why wouldn't he?"

"Okay, well, how do you know this?" Piper questioned. "And furthermore, just because Dale likes Amelia, doesn't mean she likes him back."

"Well, no, I know that," I replied. "But the choir kids spent all of lunch telling me about how he always flirts with her and gives her gifts. And Amelia accepts the gifts! Why would she accept them if she didn't like him? She has to know he's flirting with her. She's not that dense. So, if she wasn't interested, she would have just told him to stop already."

"Did you ask her how she feels towards him?"

"No. I couldn't bring myself to. I went over to meet him just now, actually, but... I just couldn't do it. I saw him through the door and I just... they'd be perfect together! He's so put together, good looking, the students adore him just as much as they adore Amelia. They would be the power couple of the century at Elk Creek!"

"Well, that's assuming she likes him back."

"But she must! How could she not?" I exclaimed. "He would be so much better for her than me, really he would be. He could offer her so much more than I ever could."

"But what if she likes you, not him?"

I sighed, resting my head against the tabletop. I couldn't tell if Amelia liked me or not. She very well might, but I was never completely sure. She never flat out said she liked me, so how could I be sure? I needed to ask her, but if she didn't, could I face that humiliation?

"You're being dramatic," Piper flat out stated. "Just because some high schoolers tell you their teachers have crushes on each other, doesn't make it true. High schoolers dream up all sorts of love scenarios in their heads all the time."

"But it could be true—"

"Nope, you've got to stop being so dreary. Look on the bright side of things for once."

I let out a dramatic groan, only further proving Piper's point.

"Head up, now," Piper declared, standing. "You might as well set up for lab. I need to go back and supervise my students."

I nodded, getting to work myself. The lab that week was about photosynthesis. Plants were never my strong suit, but I had learned about photosynthesis in three different classes now, so I was confident I could handle it.

Before I knew it, the afterschool lab had begun. I separated Montrell and Nia right off the bat. The sensors were difficult to get working initially, but one of the boys figured out a trick that got good readings every time. After that, it was smooth sailing.

The students didn't need my help too much, so I was mostly left to my own devices. I tried to not dwell on Amelia and Dale, like Piper had suggested, but without that distraction, my mind fell back to all the stress about my future. Did I enjoy teaching? Did I want to do this for the rest of my life? It was nice, fine, but I somehow didn't feel like I was as passionate about it as my teacher friends.

Eventually I found myself wandering over to Aniyah's lab station. She greeted me, gesturing me over.

"What's new, teach?" she questioned, watching a stopwatch for their experiment.

"Not too much."

"You seem a bit preoccupied."

"Well... I'm stressed about school... and what I'm doing after I graduate, what I'm doing in the long term, is all."

Aniyah, without looking away from the stopwatch, reached out and tapped an empty stool beside her. "Have a seat. We can talk," she stated. "Whenever I get stressed out, my dad always says, '*Have a seat; we'll hash it out.*' So, let's hash."

I took the offered seat, sitting down next to Aniyah. "I just... well I'm not really sure what I want to do for the rest of my life."

"I get that. It's scary figuring that out. And you always gotta have backup plans, because it's all well and good that you dream, but there aren't always opportunities out there, especially for certain people. I would love to become a vet, but what if I can't afford vet school? I can't end up homeless trying to chase a dream. So, I have backup plans. I'm thinking maybe working at a zoo would be fun."

"I think it would be," I agreed.

"I've only ever been to the zoo once in my life and I hardly remember it. But I think it was awesome."

"Why have you only been once?"

"Well... the price, kind of, my family doesn't have a bunch of disposable income. But we could probably go once every few years or so. No, the real reason is because it was my mom's all-time favorite place, so dad doesn't like to go back much anymore."

"Oh, um..." I muttered.

"Her mom died when she was young," one of Aniyah's friends volunteered.

"Yeah, I was really young. I don't remember her," Aniyah confirmed. "My older brother remembers her though. Anyway, dad tried to take us to the zoo on mom's birthday once, to sort of honor her memory, but he couldn't even get out of the car in the parking lot. It was too hard for him. My brother took me in alone, that's the only time I've ever been. I think it should be better now, it's been over a decade, but I don't want to bring it up because I know it's really hard for my dad."

"I bet... and I bet it's not easy raising two kids alone either," I commented.

"Yeah... my brother isn't always the easiest on dad. I think... well I think my dad is watching him make the same mistakes he did as a kid and he doesn't want that for my brother. My dad means the best, you know, but my brother's just sort of an idiot. We don't have a lot of money, and for older boys I guess money is kind of important to them. They need money to fit in, or whatever. But it's hard for him to find work and well... sometimes he gets money in the wrong ways."

"Well, I hope everything works out for him," I said, ignoring what the 'wrong ways to get money' possibly were. "And just because your brother is going down a path in life, doesn't mean that has to be your path too."

"I know. I think happiness is more important than money... I think family is more important too. That's my outlook on education too. I'm not just striving for the highest paying job; I'm looking for a job that makes me happy."

"I don't think my parents get that," I admitted. "They want the best for me, sure, and they want me to have financial security, because that's important, but... my mom, well she found her happiness being a doctor, so I think she projects that onto me. I know I chose a biology major, under her influence, but I couldn't imagine being a doctor. I'd hate it. She nags me about everything I do, every choice I make. And yeah, sometimes I make bad choices, but that's not the point. The point is they're my choices to make and it would just be nice if she supported my decisions."

"Parents should love their kids no matter what and support them always."

"I agree."

"You know, adults are annoying!" Aniyah declared. "I know you're basically an adult, but I mean *adult* adults, parents and stuff, people with full time careers. We all start out as kids with imaginations, hopes and dreams that can't be limited. We show love and compassion wherever we can. But then, when we grow up into adults, everyone just becomes annoying. Suddenly it's all about gain, money, putting yourself first, trampling over others for your own success. Or maybe it's raising kids and projecting on them, living vicariously through them because you hate your life. Everyone's got an opinion about what everyone else should be doing, when really, it's none of their business.

"I don't want to forget about this childhood happiness when I'm grown. I don't want everything I do to be about money. I want to explore and eat candy. I want to wear fun colors to work. I want to spend hours at the park on weekends, not doing yoga with other annoying adults, but exploring, getting dirty, seeing the beauty and awe in life. I just want life to stay fun. I wish all people were like that. I wish adults didn't forget who they were as kids when they grow up. What changes?"

I thought about what Aniyah was saying. I knew plenty of adults that fit into the category of annoying—my parents and professors, to name a few.

I was on the cusp of adulthood, maybe I hadn't yet fallen victim to the void, but I was close. My spring break trip helped me feel alive again, if only temporary. I remembered going to theme parks when I was a kid. It was still magical when I went over spring break, but it was certainly different from my childhood. Something had changed. It was like there was a darkness, a sickening dreariness, that pushed its way into your life as you hit adulthood.

The only adult I could think of that maintained an air of child-like innocence was Amelia. Sure, she could fall into the annoying adult category sometimes too. But there were so many moments where she turned back into a wide-eyed child, the awe of life sparkling in her irises. Things like sugary breakfasts, sweets, and puppies made Amelia giddy like a child all over again. Maybe growing up meant that things stopped being exciting and new, just because you stopped experiencing things for the first time, but surely, just like Amelia who had things that made her excited, there was something for everyone that could turn any adult back into that wide-eyed child.

"Maybe as you grow, you learn more about the world and realize things aren't all fun and games, that there's badness in the world," I stated. "And that badness, well it really weighs a person down. Once you learn those things, you can't really go back to how you were as a child, because you can't just unlearn that... you can't go back to a time where you were ignorant of the evil in the world."

"It shouldn't be that way," Aniyah stated. "Bad things happen all the time. That's just the nature of existence. Bad things happen around my home every day. We learn early that it's not safe to be out at night, that you shouldn't loiter, or look suspicious. But just because it's dangerous doesn't mean we can let it overwhelm us. I'm not going to stop having fun just because life might be scary. I don't want to let the bad ruin my life, so I'm not going to."

I smiled. "If you only ever remember one thing in life, remember that."

"You should remember it too," Aniyah replied.

After lab, I remembered I had totally ditched Amelia. I felt bad and I still wanted to see her, so I meekly made my way over to the choir room, hoping she was still there. Slowly, I opened the choir room door, poking my head in. I found Amelia sitting at her desk and when she looked over to me, I smiled weakly.

"Oh, there you are," she stated. "I assumed you left."

"Yeah, sorry I didn't come back here," I answered, stepping into the room.

"Did you have a nice and long conversation with Dale?"

"No, I, um... well he wasn't in his room. I guess he was busy," I muttered, lying. "I just, I ran into Piper leaving and she thought I better set up the lab. There was a lot of set up. And then, well it was after school, and I just never made my way back over. I'm sorry."

"It's alright. Do you have plans for this evening?"

With a smirk, I walked towards Amelia. "Of course not," I replied. "I cleared all my Thursday evenings so I can spend time with you. I thought we went over this?"

Amelia blushed slightly and smiled in response. She picked up some papers to busy her hands and glanced away from me. "Unfortunately, I have to finalize things for the New York trip. And because I have a bad procrastination habit, that means I'm taking a long night."

"Well, would you like some company?" I asked. "Or would that be too distracting?"

"You're always distracting—"

"Woah now, Amelia. I didn't know my presence was such a struggle for you."

"It's because you're annoying and can't sit still, don't flatter yourself," Amelia stated with pursed lips. "But I'll welcome your company, regardless."

"Cool. I have some homework I need to get done anyway, so hopefully I won't be too much of a bother."

Twenty minutes went by without either of us talking. Amelia turned on some classical tunes that played in the background. Amelia sat behind her desk, and I sat at the front. She was mostly hidden from me, my laptop open in front of me, but I found myself stealing glances to her every now and again. Eventually, my gaze was tugged to the flowers still sitting on her desk. Why would she keep them? I mean, yeah, they were nice flowers, I guess, but it was the principle of thing! I needed to ask Amelia about her feelings, point blank, but I couldn't bring myself to do it. Though I kept thinking about her and Dale.

Thirty minutes in, I finally broke. Well, nearly. I didn't straight up ask her about Dale, but a related topic.

"Do adults get crushes?" I asked, breaking the silence between us.

Amelia stopped flipping through papers and looked up at me. "What kind of question is that?"

"Well... I sometimes think crushes are childish," I began. "I think that usually when you have crushes, it's just sort of a day-dream bliss. You look at the cutie across the room in your class and laugh too hard at all of their really terrible jokes. You never actually really talk to them though. You don't get close to them. The crush can persist *because* you don't get to know them. It starts because you think they're cute, and then the crush becomes this fantasy you make up in your mind. You formulate a character you expect them to be, and it's all this idea in your head. The prospect of actually talking to them, going on a real date, well it would never live up to the expectations you've build up in your head. That realness *crushes* the crush, and the fixation dies.

"I think crushes are just an overwhelming dose of feelings that will always fade in the long run. Crushes aren't something permanent. They're different than if you actually like someone, because if you actually like someone, you like them for who they are. You're willing to talk to them and actually date them, because you want the real them, not some perfect them you made up in your mind. That's the difference, I think.

"So then, back to my question, do adults have crushes, or do they just like and approach people?"

"Crushes *are* childish," Amelia agreed, "but that doesn't mean the logical adult can't get one. So yeah, adults can have crushes. I think crushes are a bit less magical as an adult than say, a middle school crush, but you can still get one. I just, well for me, if I were to get a crush, I wouldn't fixate on it so it would fade quickly. Whereas if I actually liked someone... well that's different."

"So, I'm guessing you don't have a crush on anyone, but... do you like someone?"

"You mean, do I *like*, like someone?" Amelia fake gasped, and I knew she was mocking me. It did sound childish, the way we were talking. But maybe love in general was childish. That didn't make it bad, just because it was childish. Maybe 'childish' just meant loving unconditionally, despite the evil in the world.

"Yes, do you *like*, like someone?" I restated.

Amelia had been smirking at me, but then she dipped her head down. She glanced up at me without tilting her head up, a bashful look to her eyes. "Maybe," she muttered softly.

"Who?" I prompted.

Amelia's demeanor changed. She snapped her head up and sat up straight in her chair just glaring challengingly at me. "I'm not going to tell you," she declared.

"Alright, well *that's* childish," I insisted. "Why not?"

"Because... you'd probably tell everyone."

"You're being ridiculous. We just talked about how adults are supposed to be more mature about their feelings. You said yourself that if you liked someone, you'd act on it. And so, if you did that, they'd already know, and then what would it even matter if I told everyone else?"

"Whatever. I'm still not going to tell you," Amelia huffed stubbornly, crossing her arms in defiance.

"Would you tell your friends? Piper or Eleanor, or any of them?" Amelia shook her head. "Why not?" I questioned. "Isn't that what friends do, share their feelings with each other?"

"If I were going to tell them because they're my friends, I'd tell you too, because you're also my friend."

"*Aww,*" I cooed, smiling. "That's sweet! Why won't you tell your friends though? You know we'll support you no matter what."

"I just... well I'm not quite ready yet, I don't think," Amelia answered. "Anyway, it's whatever."

"True, feelings are gross," I stated, sticking out my tongue. This got Amelia to laugh, which made me laugh as well. "Let's talk about something else, shall we? Let's see... I've got a field trip Friday."

"Oh really?"

"Yeah, though it's going to be boring. I work in one of my professor's labs, right, and they're doing some joint work with Coleman college. It's my turn to head over and do some work, get some results in their lab— they just have some different equipment and stuff."

"How much work do you have to do?"

"It's... a good amount," I admitted. "I can't go over until four anyway, because I have classes, so it'll probably be dark by the time I get out. Maybe closer to nine or something."

"But... Coleman is in the middle of the city..." Amelia said slowly.

"I know. I'm not really looking forward to being downtown in the middle of the night, then driving all the way back to GSU in the dark. But it is what it is. I put off doing my part the last two times. My lab mates are starting to get annoyed with me."

"I basically live right next to Coleman," Amelia stated. "You can crash at my place tomorrow night just so you won't have to drive that late. If you want to, I mean."

"Really?"

"Yeah. I live in a pretty nice apartment complex and it's in a good area. It's gated, so I'll have to give you the code, but for sure. You're absolutely welcome."

"That would be awesome! Seriously! Thank you!"

"No problem," Amelia answered, smiling softly.

Before I left Friday, I knew I needed to tell Lizzie I was going to be gone. I never spent the night away, so if I just up and disappeared for a night, she would definitely report me as a missing person. Which was why, as I was packing an overnight bag just before leaving for Coleman, Lizzie was sitting on my bedroom floor, talking to me.

"Good for you, getting some time away from here," Lizzie declared. "Let me have a little break from you, for once."

"A little rude, but alright."

"Anyway, I can only speculate about what you're doing, since you won't tell me," Lizzie continued. "You don't have any family in town. You aren't that close to anyone else who lives off campus... except your new teacher friends, so I can only assume you're staying with one of them."

"Well, you're not wrong."

"Is that all you're doing then? Just having a good ole fashioned sleepover?"

"No, actually, I have to go over to Coleman for some lab work, so I'm heading into the city. Amelia just happens to live in the city and is willing to let me crash at her place, since I'm going to be working pretty late."

"Wait, Amelia!?" Lizzie shouted. "First of all, *ahh*! You're spending the night with Amelia! Gonna get your sexy on!"

"Stop that!" I huffed. "No one will be getting any sexy on."

"What if Amelia gets her sexy on? Are you going to just shut that down? Because I'm pretty sure you wouldn't be complaining."

"Stop talking."

I left shortly after that and made my trek over to Coleman. I'd been slacking on my lab duties for a couple months now, just because I hated it. I liked science, I really did. I liked biology... but I was more into the fun facts. I liked learning weird little tidbits that I could then share with others. I didn't like research work. It was a lot of setting up, waiting around, running experiments and then running them again when they inevitably didn't work. You had to keep notes of meticulous details, detailing all you did. You had to present your work to the lab, brainstorm ideas, and draft up reports.

And I knew that. I knew all that about research work by the start of my junior year. I knew that with a biology degree, not going to med school, I would be doing research work. I would just be doing more of this work that I hated. But did I switch majors? No. Because doing so would have meant telling my mother, and that prospect was worse than just getting stuck doing research work my entire life.

Now though, I was pretty mad at myself. At least with teaching I could get away from the lab work and move closer to the fact sharing that I much preferred. But was I passionate about it?

Hours later I packed up my bag and trailed out of the Coleman lab, shutting off the lights as I left. Monday, I could bring back my research results so that during our lab meeting we could compile data and figure out our next plan of action. All I knew was that I had fulfilled my Coleman research duties, and I wouldn't have to go back before I graduated. And now, I could enjoy a sleepover with Amelia.

Amelia texted me the gate code, but I couldn't figure out the machine, so she had to come down and help me. When she found me standing outside the locked gate, pouting, she laughed at me. I smiled at her appearance. She looked cute as always, wearing comfy clothes, an oversized shirt, with her hair tied up messily.

"It's really not complicated," she stated. "You just press in the numbers, wait a minute, and then open the gate."

"But there's an enter button!" I declared. "How was I supposed to know that you *didn't* hit the enter button?"

"Because I never told you to in my instructions." Amelia smirked.

I followed Amelia into the building and upstairs. I waited as she opened her door and then stepped inside, waiting in the entry hall, suddenly feeling very shy. Amelia shut the door and moved in around me, throwing her keys down on a nearby table. She flipped on some lights, walked into the living room, and fell back down onto a couch. All the while, I just stood in the entry hall, looking around.

Her apartment was a weird mix of style. It felt very modern—which could have been more the landlord and less Amelia—but the decoration felt homey, almost like a ranch house. Her organization seemed similar to her classroom at Elk Creek. She had some system of organization, clearly, but it looked untidy. The kitchen was pristine, though nothing was straight, and the same could be said for the rest of the space, stacks of disorganized papers on tables, a few things knocked over here or there, but still clean.

"Well, come in and make yourself at home," Amelia stated, watching me closely as I stood awkwardly in the front entry.

I kicked off my shoes, leaving them with Amelia's discarded pair, and dropped my backpack as well. Then I walked to Amelia and plopped down beside her on the couch.

"How was Coleman?" Amelia questioned.

"Fine. I hate research work," I grumbled.

Amelia looked at me with almost a longing, sad expression on her face. "It's really unfortunate when students get pushed into pursuing something that doesn't make them happy," she stated.

"It's not that I don't like biology, I just... well loving biology and doing bench work are two rather different things."

"You need to change your major."

"I'm about to graduate!" I scoffed.

"Then you need to go back to school and study something you actually love."

"Maybe I don't love anything," I huffed hostily. "Maybe I'm just someone who doesn't have any passions in life, and I just float around doing whatever jobs I find until I finally die."

"You're being unreasonably melancholy."

"What's my passion then?"

"I can't tell you. You have to find it yourself."

I fell back against the couch, crossing my arms. After a few minutes of stewing in silence, Amelia pushed herself towards me and leaned her head against my shoulder. My hostility died in an instance, and I found I could barely breathe with her close proximity.

"Are you done being a sour puss?" Amelia questioned. "I want to talk to you."

"We are talking..." I said a bit curiously.

"About how lost you are in life. But dwelling on the current and not searching for answers for the future isn't helping anyone. In the meantime, I want to talk about you." She poked me in the ribs when she said the word 'you.'

"I don't know what you're talking about," I muttered, feeling my cheeks flush. "I'm a boring person. What could there possibly be to talk about?"

"I don't think you're boring at all," Amelia mused. "Not everyone can say their students got into a cat gut throwing contest."

"Hey!"

"Or that they were brave enough to go to Florida all on their own. I don't think you give yourself enough credit. I think you're too busy worrying about what others will think that you aren't seeing what makes you truly happy. Stop thinking about what your mother would want for one second and ask yourself what you want."

"It's just not that easy," I sighed. "I want to go back in time to when I first started college, before I wasted four years of my life, and pick a different major."

"You wish you could just erase the last four years? Nothing good has come from those years, nothing at all?"

"Well... I guess not *nothing*. I met Lizzie. She's a great friend. And I do have a lot of fun memories inside and outside of class. And... and I met you, and the others, and now I have this teaching job."

"Maybe it's not the ideal future you had planned out for yourself when you started college, but maybe it's the future you needed."

"*Hmm*, maybe."

Amelia let out a soft chuckle. She turned, nuzzling her face further into the crook of my neck. Then she whispered, "You're so cute."

"What?" I choked out, her breath hot on my neck, sending chills through my body.

"You're kind of a mess," Amelia then said, laughing again. "Honestly... but you're so adorable."

"You—you think I'm cute? And adorable?" I questioned, my temperature rising.

"Yes," Amelia stated confidently. She slowly pushed herself up so that she could look me in the eyes. "Why? Is that a problem?"

"No, no," I answered quickly. "I mean, I think you're super cute and very adorable too."

Amelia smiled before pulling me into a tight hug. She buried her face into my neck once again. "I'm sleepy," she whimpered.

I glanced towards a clock on the nearby coffee table, noting just how late it was getting. Amelia's sleepiness was surely the cause for her odd behavior, so I chose to not think too much of it.

"Yeah, it is getting pretty late," I agreed. "We should probably get to bed. At least it's a weekend, so we can sleep in."

"I, um, only have one bed," Amelia stated, sitting up and pulling away from me again. "I didn't really think about it when I invited you over. I just wanted to make sure you were safe. It's okay though. I'll sleep on the couch."

I stared at Amelia pointedly. "Why don't you want to share a bed with me?" I questioned. "First it was sharing on the New York trip, and now this. We slept in the same bed in Florida. Why is it different now?"

Amelia colored a bit, her cheeks flushing, and she dipped her head away from me. It sounded like she muttered, "Everything feels different now," under her breath, but I couldn't really hear her.

"We're friends," I declared confidently. "You said so yourself. We should be able to share a bed, and if we can't, we should be able to talk about why not."

"You're right," Amelia admitted, looking over at me again. "I um... well it was nice sharing a bed in Florida. We should do it again."

"It was nice?" I questioned, cocking an eyebrow.

"Don't think about it too much," Amelia answered, standing. She grabbed my hand and pulled me back down a hall towards her bedroom.

We got ready for bed. We changed, brushed our teeth, took off our makeup, fun things like that. Amelia took longer than me, finishing up with some sort of skin care routine while I went back to her bedroom and settled in. I picked a side of the bed, not sure which Amelia preferred, and fiddled with my hands while I waited.

I wore a pair of comfortable cotton shorts and an old T-shirt, my typical bed-wear attire. Lizzie made fun of me for packing it. She said it wasn't 'sexy' enough. I wasn't trying to be sexy though. And I was confident Amelia wasn't *trying* to be sexy either, but well...

When Amelia emerged from the bathroom, she was wearing an outfit very similar to mine: comfortable shorts and a white tank top. She wasn't wearing a bra, and I flushed at my thoughts, looking elsewhere. Bras were very uncomfortable. Who would want to sleep in one? I wasn't wearing one either, though it was less noticeable in my baggy shirt.

Amelia said nothing about the side of the bed where I was, she just slipped wordlessly into bed on the other side. She turned off the lamp on the bedside table and then we were just there in the dark, both lying stiff on our backs, staring up at the ceiling.

It was weird. I found myself barely breathing, worried I would shift the bed and disrupt Amelia, even though there was a foot of space between us. I didn't want to annoy her with my sporadic breaths either though, but if I held my breath, I could hear my pounding heartbeat, and I was afraid Amelia might hear it too. I was extremely uncomfortable and stiff. I hated sleeping on my back, but couldn't will myself to turn onto my side, because I didn't want to jostle the bed.

Even though it was dark, and I wasn't looking at her, I kept picturing Amelia in that white tank top, the short shorts that hugged her figure perfectly. I wanted to fall asleep with that image in my mind, but stupid Dale kept popping up. No matter how hard I tried not to, all I could picture was Dale and Amelia alone in this very bedroom. Dale being allowed to touch her soft waist, Dale pulling the little white tank top off her, Dale slowly lowering her back onto the bed, Dale hovering over her, Dale leaning down to kiss her, Dale, Dale, *Dale.*

"Do you like Dale?" I snapped abruptly, too loud and aggressive for the silent room. Amelia jumped next to me, startled by my outburst.

The bed shifted as Amelia pushed herself up. She sat beside me and looked down at me. "What?" she questioned.

I pushed myself up on my elbows to gain height on Amelia. "The choir kids want to set you up on a date, that's what we were talking about at lunch yesterday. And they specifically want to set you up with Dale. Do you like him?" I asked again, my thoughts more collected, but there was still a bite to my tone.

"I... don't know," Amelia muttered.

"Come on, you have to know!" I said, still hostile. "You either like him or you don't. It's not difficult."

"Well maybe it's not difficult for you, but it is for me!" Amelia then shouted, shoving my arm as she did.

I sat up the rest of the way, directly across from Amelia. "I just want to know if you like him or not, why is that so difficult for you?"

"Because!"

"Because why!?" I snapped.

I saw the fury flash across Amelia's eyes when she broke. "Because I should, but I don't!" she shouted, breathing heavily.

My face folded into a frown. "Wait, what?" I asked, infinitely softer.

Amelia let out a groan, flopping back against the headboard. "He's like... the perfect man," she said, grabbing a pillow and pressing it against her chest. "He's handsome and brilliant, modest, caring. He's romantic and charming, not a bum or a jerk. He's not boring, he's independent. His personality is spot on. He'd fold the world over to give his girl anything and everything. There's absolutely no reason why I *shouldn't* like him! Everyone always tells me how lucky I am that he gives me attention. My students swoon at the thought. I have coworkers bumping into me all the time gushing. Even parents make comments. They don't understand why I'm wasting time. Why, if they were in my place, they would have swooped him up after the first compliment! I *should* like him. Heck, I should love him! I should date him, marry him, carry his children. But... I just don't *want* him!"

"There's nothing wrong with that," I quickly replied. "Just because the whole world finds a man perfect, doesn't mean he's the one for you. I mean, think about all those generic white actors that girls melt over. I can't even tell them apart, and girls gush over them like they're the greatest catch on earth!"

Amelia let out a small laugh, shaking her head slightly. "That's just it though," she muttered. "It's not just that he isn't the man for me. There's more, it's deeper, I just... it's so—so scary. It's scary not liking a man that should be perfect for you."

"Why?"

"Because... because I don't like guys," Amelia whispered. "I like girls."

Amelia's voice sounded small. It was the voice of a near broken woman, someone who had lost countless hours of sleep worrying about such a thing. I knew that voice all too well. I wished I could tell her everything she needed to hear, but I couldn't, so I just did something so characteristically Amelia; I dove on her and pulled her into the tightest of hugs. It was the type of hug that showed all the love and support you have to offer with a single action. I hoped Amelia would understand my message.

Amelia was crying, her head resting against my shoulder, and I just pulled her tighter. I held her as close as I could. I wanted to protect her from the world, take away all her pain and fear. I was excited too, happy she liked girls and so desperate to kiss her... but I couldn't. This was not a love confession; it was a coming-out confession. Right then, Amelia needed me as a friend, and I wasn't about to mess that up. Instead, I just held her as tight as I could, letting her know that I was there for her, and I wasn't going anywhere.

Eventually, Amelia stopped sobbing. She pulled back from me, her eyes puffy and red. She muttered out a soft, "Sorry," as she let go of me.

I gave Amelia a half-grin, reaching up to wipe away a final tear that ran down her cheek. "See? I *knew* you weren't an ugly crier," I said lightly.

Amelia laughed, wiping at her own eyes. "God, you're such a jokester."

"It's okay, you know. Your feelings are valid and you're an amazing woman, Amelia. I mean, Karmen and Eleanor are in love, and we all accept them. We'll accept you and support you too, when you decide to come out to everyone. We'll love you all the same."

"I know, I just... well I'm not sure I'm ready for everyone to know yet," Amelia admitted. "I'm just not ready for everything to change."

"I won't tell anyone, I promise. This is your story to tell."

Amelia smirked. "Aren't you lucky? The first person I ever came out to..."

"I'm honored," I answered, and I truly was.

Amelia looked like she was going to say something else, but she was interrupted by a huge yawn. It caused me to yawn in response, shaking my head at the end as I felt my drowsiness fighting to overcome me.

"We should get some sleep," I stated once I could speak again. Amelia nodded.

We lied back down, a bit robotically, once again on our backs. I stared up at the ceiling. There was still a foot of space between us, but after such a heartfelt confession, the gap felt like a mile wide.

"Thank you, Natalie," I heard Amelia whisper.

"You don't have to thank me," I answered. "I'd do anything to support and comfort you."

Suddenly, I felt Amelia's hand reach over and grab mine, holding it tightly. It seemed like Ellie 2.0 was right: whenever Amelia couldn't find the right words, she showed her emotions through her actions, like hugging and handholding. And if that was how Amelia communicated her feelings, surely then she would understand another person doing the same. It was time to be brave.

"Hey, Amelia?" I questioned softly, a near whisper.

"Yeah?"

"Do you... do you like to cuddle?" I questioned hesitantly.

"I love to cuddle," Amelia answered instantly, which didn't surprise me at all. "I just... well I've been alone for so long, in a bed all to myself, that I guess I've just gotten used to being alone."

My heart constricted at the sadness in Amelia's voice. "I like cuddling too," I declared, because I wasn't sure if Amelia knew. I wasn't good at expressing my feelings. "And you know, I don't get to do it much either.

But I guess, well we aren't alone right now, anymore. So maybe we could—well I guess—if you'd like—maybe we could... cuddle? Together? Just because it's nice and we both haven't in a while..."

It was silent for a moment, and I was terrified I had overstepped a line. But then, Amelia rolled over onto her side, facing me, and I looked to her, our eyes meeting. She held the biggest grin on her face, her eyes shining in the moonlight.

"Big or little spoon?" she voiced.

"*Umm*, I guess big spoon, if you don't mind."

Amelia's smile grew even larger. "Perfect," she gushed. "I prefer being little spoon anyway."

"I guess we're meant to be cuddle buddies then," I chuckled, rolling onto my side so I was facing Amelia. I gave her a slight push, so she'd roll over, then I inched closer to her until her back was flush with my front. I wrapped my arms around her tightly, snuggling against the back of her neck. I heard her sigh contentedly.

"Goodnight, Nats," Amelia hummed.

"Goodnight, Amelia," I breathed in response.

13.

Life Can Change At The Drop Of A Hat

I was abruptly and rudely woken by Amelia leaping on top of me, body slamming me into the mattress. "Oh my god, what's happening?" I gasped, struggling to right myself as I fought against the sheets and my attacker. I blinked aggressively, trying to orientate myself in the bright room.

"Happy one month!" Amelia squealed in my face.

"Happy what?" I questioned, rubbing at my eyes.

"Happy one month!" Amelia repeated. "We've officially known each other for a month now!"

"Wait, really? I can't believe you kept track of that."

"I just, well I looked at my calendar and just remembered the date of our spring break. It isn't anything, really."

I shrugged. "I mean, one month is a pretty big deal. We should probably celebrate, right?"

"Yes! What should we do?"

"Well, I don't know about you, but I think a lazy day in sounds fantastic. Maybe some movies, board games, stuff like that?"

"Can we bake cookies?"

I rolled my eyes. "You and your sweet tooth, I swear. But sure."

"I'm a really good baker," Amelia challenged. "I bet I can bake better cookies than you."

"Is that a challenge?" I questioned, raising an eyebrow.

"*Hmm*, yeah, I guess so!" Amelia nodded emphatically. "Hurry and get up! I'm starving and we still have to make the cookies!"

"Okay, okay!" I giggled, pushing Amelia off the bed so I could get up. "Let me go brush my teeth."

"Yeah, your breath smells awful," Amelia teased. "Oh, and... time starts now!" she suddenly squealed before racing out of the bedroom.

"Wait, this is timed?" I shouted after her. "Not fair!"

Despite the sudden competition, I still went and brushed my teeth, though I remained in my pajamas. When I reached the kitchen, Amelia was already fishing out ingredients. Over her pajamas she wore a red and white plaid apron which made me laugh. I eyed an extra apron hanging up on the wall and grabbed it, tying the garment around me.

Then, as I was pulling up my hair, I stated, "Alright, is there a box mix or a recipe around here somewhere?"

"Oh no, these are from *scratch*," Amelia stated, looking to me incredulously. "You're telling me you don't have even a simple chocolate chip cookie recipe memorized?"

"Look, not all of us bake every day," I stated. "But it's fine. I can improvise."

"If you say so," Amelia stated skeptically. "I set a timer for thirty minutes. That's our time limit."

I had experience making cookies. I made then every year with my mother for the holidays. Chocolate chip cookies were a staple. It's just... we always followed a recipe, one I never thought I'd need to have memorized. I threw together some basics, like flour, sugar, and eggs, but beyond that I didn't know.

Amelia worked furiously at a countertop on the opposite side of the kitchen, hiding her work from me. I casually headed towards her, my mixing bowl of maybe-cookie-dough under my arm, pretending to do something by the sink. As I did, I slowly and inconspicuously looked around Amelia at the ingredients she had added. I realized I missed a lot and was glad I had peeked. My small victory was short lived, however, as Amelia caught me peeping.

"Hey, no cheating!" she exclaimed, shielding her work away from me.

"I don't know what you're talking about," I played dumb, hurrying back to add my missing ingredients.

I was just beginning to form my dough into little balls when Amelia pushed her tray into the oven, setting a different timer for when her cookies would be done. I moved faster, making my cookies into ugly little mounds, but it was the taste that counted, right? Then I quickly shoved mine into the oven as well.

I stood triumphantly, turning to face Amelia. "Alright, what are we going to do while they bake?" I asked.

Amelia was leaning against the counter, her mixing bowl under one arm, her other hand scooping out the remaining cookie dough which she was happily munching on. "Clean up?" she questioned, her mouth half full with cookie dough.

"Here," I stated, handing her my mixing bowl. "You can be the dog and lick the bowls clean. I'll start washing dishes."

"I resent that," Amelia said, eyeing my mixing bowl suspiciously. "How many raw eggs are in this? Probably seven."

"No," I scoffed. "Only two."

"Fine, I guess I'll eat it," she gave in, reaching for my bowl, "but if I get salmonella from this, I'll never forgive you."

I shook my head good naturedly, turning towards the sink to start washing. Amelia never gagged or spit or cringed, so I figured my cookie dough couldn't be all that bad. As I neared the end of our little mess, I noticed a spray nozzle hooked up to the sink. Too bad I hadn't noticed it earlier. It would have been really helpful for cleaning the dishes... or...

I turned quickly and *bam*, sprayed Amelia right in the face with water. She screamed, I laughed, and she brought the mixing bowl up to cover her face like a shield. I stopped spraying water, laughing so hard I nearly fell over.

"Oh, two can play at that game," Amelia stated, grinning evilly. She threw the bowl onto the counter as she made a mad dash for the living room. She grabbed a spray bottle off one of the side tables—I guess she used it to water her plants.

I screamed as I ran out of the kitchen, trying to get away from Amelia as she chased me, spraying me with water. We ran a few laps through the kitchen and living room before I jumped over the back of the couch, giving me a head start as I raced for her bedroom. I couldn't find another spray bottle to retaliate, but I slid to a stop in her bathroom, noticing a damp hand towel.

"I've got you cornered now!" Amelia laughed, stalking me at the entrance of the bathroom. "You've got nowhere to run, you foolish girl, getting yourself trapped in the bathroom. You might as well surrender now!"

"Oh really?" I questioned, grabbing the towel, and spinning on Amelia. "On guard!" I exclaimed, yielding the towel as a whip. I cracked the towel just in front of Amelia and she leapt back.

"You'll never catch me!" she squealed, dashing back out towards the living room.

I chased Amelia around the apartment a few times, never quite getting close enough to hit her with the towel. I wasn't exactly trying too hard.

Getting hit with a wet towel whip really hurt, and I wasn't trying to hurt her, just intimidate her. I did hit her once though. I managed to duck out of sight momentarily, and I snuck up on her from behind. Unable to help myself, with a perfect shot, I whipped out the towel and cracked it right against Amelia's left butt cheek.

Amelia let out a roaring wail, though it was immediately followed by laughter, and then suddenly I was being relentlessly sprayed in the face. I brought the towel up to shield my face so I could get a few breaths in before I dashed away squealing. We continued our back-and-forth game until finally Amelia's timer went off and she called a truce to go retrieve her cookies.

A few minutes later, I pulled my cookies out as well. We sat both trays down on the kitchen table, side by side. As much as I hated to admit it, Amelia's cookies looked way better. They looked professionally made, like something you might buy, whereas my cookies looked like the batch the little kids helped make during the holidays.

"Listen, don't judge," I stated, noticing how Amelia was eyeing my cookies.

Amelia just laughed and got us both a glass of milk for our taste test. I picked out one of my better-looking cookies and took a bite. It was... pretty okay. It certainly tasted like a cookie, and I would definitely eat the rest.

"Well?" Amelia questioned.

"I don't want to toot my own horn, but um... *toot-toot*," I stated with a cheeky grin.

Amelia followed suit, tasting one of her own cookies. The look on her face was one of pure ecstasy, but I figured she was just being a good actor. She pulled the cookie away from her mouth after the first bite, some melted chocolate dripping down onto her lips before she licked it off.

"Well *toot-toot* right back at you," she declared. Then she reached for one of my cookies. "Let's see if these really are as good as you claim. Because they look *awful*."

"I'll admit the presentation is lacking, but the taste is good," I answered, grabbing one of Amelia's cookies to compare.

I watched Amelia try my cookie before I tried hers. She took a bite, chewing it suspiciously, before narrowing her eyes. "It's like... a seven out of ten, at best," she stated with a swallow. "It's good, edible sure, but is it the best? Not at all. Plus, you lose a point because the presentation is so horrid, so really it's a six out of ten."

"Come on, a six? Your cookies can't be that good. I'm thinking a four at the most just looking at them."

"Are you going to taste them or just be bitter that you lost?" Amelia asked pointedly.

I gave in, taking a bite of Amelia's cookie, and I nearly astral projected straight out of my body. It was the best goddamn cookie I had ever tasted. It was like a grandmother's secret recipe, one where even if you followed the recipe, they would never taste the same as when grandma made them, because they carried with them nostalgia and love and memories of better times. I guess my eyes were rolling back into my head in pure bliss, because Amelia started laughing at me.

"Just a four?" she commented smugly.

"Okay, fine, ten out of ten," I begrudgingly admitted. I greedily reached for another of Amelia's cookies, and she didn't stop me. "How did you learn to make these so gosh darn good?"

"My grandmother," Amelia answered softly.

I looked over to Amelia who wore a soft smile on her face. I suddenly felt like Amelia had just shared something deeply personal with me. I knew her grandmother practically raised her and that she loved being with her grandmother. And now I got to taste her cookies, something that kept her grandmother's memory alive. I was touched that Amelia willing shared something so intimate with me.

"They're amazing," I muttered, my mouth still full. "Best breakfast ever."

We finished breakfast, eagerly snarfing down the rest of Amelia's cookies. My cookies weren't as good, but they were still good enough to save. As I packed up my cookies, Amelia slipped out of the kitchen, and when she came back, she was hiding something behind her back.

"Do I want to know what you've got there?" I questioned skeptically.

"I just... well I've been meaning to give this back," Amelia said, pulling out my hoodie from behind her back, the one I loaned her in Florida that she *stole* from me.

"Yeah, my hoodie that you *stole* from me," I stated lightheartedly. "Look, just keep it."

Amelia held the hoodie against her. "It's a really nice hoodie," she stated.

"I know. It's the best one I owned. But I think it likes you better anyway, so you might as well just keep it."

Amelia nodded slowly, still cradling my hoodie in her arms. "Do you want to watch something?"

"Sure, let me just finish packing the cookies up."

"Okay, I'll meet you in the living room."

Once I was done, I came into the living room to find Amelia watching a true crime documentary, cuddling my hoodie—now *her* hoodie—in her arms. She was sitting on the floor, just in front of the couch, so I climbed up on the couch and lied down sideways. Amelia admitted that she liked documentaries, maybe a bit too much, but I thought it was cute in a nerdy sort of way. She talked about a variety of documentaries she had watched in the past, ones that left a lasting impact on her, and I realized there was a lot about the world that I had never stopped to question before.

"We should watch them together sometime," I said. "I mean, if you don't mind re-watching them."

"We should," Amelia replied. "I'd like to talk to someone about them. Here, let's start something from the beginning." She reached for the remote and pulled up a different documentary. It was about women struggling to find their feet in the workplace after the end of World War II in a male dominated industry. It made me realize I had a lot to be grateful for.

We watched another documentary, one that left me uncomfortable and even more aware of my privilege. Amelia had a lot of commentary on the documentaries, said things that made me question even more. I didn't have much to offer in response. I needed to better educate myself about issues so I could talk, really talk, to Amelia about those issues. And I wanted to, someday.

"Would you maybe like to play cards?" Amelia offered, sensing my reserve. She didn't even let me answer, she just fished out a deck of cards form under the coffee table.

"What game?" I asked.

"Poker?" she suggested.

"Okay. Are we making real money bets?

"No. I wouldn't feel right taking money from a broke college kid," Amelia stated, turning to stick her tongue out at me.

"You're so annoying sometimes," I answered, "but fine. We're still keeping track of points though, because where's the fun without some friendly competition?"

"I agree completely," Amelia replied, smirking as I slid off the couch to join her on the floor.

I learned a lot about Amelia that weekend. I learned that she was a master baker who loved documentaries about serious social injustices. But that wasn't all I learned. She might have learned how to sing and bake from her sweet grandmother, but her sleazy older stepbrothers taught her how to cheat at poker.

I was losing horrifically. If we had been betting real money, I would have been in the hole my entire college tuition—for all four years—and Amelia would be walking away a millionaire.

"Okay, you need to chill," I declared, losing yet another hand. "You have to be cheating."

"Well of course," Amelia answered. "If you played poker purely off chance, I would never win this much, statistically."

"I don't think that's allowed. Like I think they ban you from casinos for this."

"You're just being a sore loser."

"I'm not being a sore loser, you're cheating!" I huffed, leaning towards Amelia.

"Sore loser!" she sung, pushing her head towards me.

"Unfair!" I complained.

"Yeah? Well, what are you going to do about it?" she challenged.

Those were fighting words. I dove on Amelia, wrestling her back into the ground. She squealed as I shoved her over and I climbed up onto her hips, sitting on her triumphantly. She tried to push me off, but I grabbed her wrists and pushed her back down, pinning her as I hovered over her.

"Maybe you can pin me down, but you can't stop me from playing dirty," Amelia stated with a wink. Before I could question what that meant, she had reared her knees up, hitting me in the butt, sending me toppling down against her stomach.

"Yeah, and what did that accomplish for you?" I asked, pushing myself up on my elbows. "I've still got you pinned."

There was a devilish glint in Amelia's eyes, but before I could learn what she was thinking, her phone started ringing. I grabbed her phone off the coffee table and handed it to her, though I remained sitting on her.

"It's Eleanor," Amelia sighed, looking at her phone screen. "We can ignore it. She probably just wants to hang out."

The ringing died off to silence for a moment, but then it started ringing again. "I think you should probably answer it," I stated. "She's called twice now. What if it's important?"

"Eleanor's definition of important is rarely my definition of important," Amelia retorted. "Besides, I thought we were having a lazy day in?"

The phone started ringing a third time. "Pick it up," I demanded, sliding off Amelia's lap so she could focus.

Amelia grumbled but did as I said and answered her phone. "What's got your underwear in a knot this time, Eleanor?"

Eleanor must have answered with something serious, because Amelia's face immediately dropped.

"Wait, hang on, I'm grabbing my keys," Amelia stated. "Tell Natalie what's going on. She can fill me in."

Suddenly the cell phone was thrust into my hands, and I scrambled to pull it to my ear. Amelia dashed out of the room, heading back to her bedroom.

"Eleanor?" I asked into the phone. "What's going on?"

Eleanor was crying hysterically on the other end, and I could barely make out what she was saying. Between sobs, I heard her gasp out, "He hit her!"

"Who? Who hit who?" I asked urgently.

"The ER, she's in the ER. They're checking the baby," Eleanor continued to wail. "I don't know what's happening. I have Michael. He doesn't know what's happening and I can't watch him and she's—but then I'm—"

"Okay, woah, woah, calm down," I stated, wracking my brain to try and piece together what was happening. "Amelia and I are on our way. Take a deep breath. Can you try and tell me what happened?"

Amelia ran back into the living room and threw my hoodie at me before chucking my shoes at me too. I put the phone on speaker and set it on the coffee table so I could pull the hoodie on over my pajamas. Amelia ran into the kitchen as I slipped on my shoes.

"Adam hit her! He hit her!" Eleanor wailed. "I'm in the ER. I don't know what to do. I can't keep it together!"

"We'll be there as soon as we can!" Amelia shouted over my shoulder. "We're leaving now. Hang in there." She pulled me into a standing position and shoved the container of my less-good cookies into my arms, taking back her phone in the process. "Hang in there, Eleanor. We'll be there soon," she repeated before hanging up her phone. Then she turned to me, snapping, "We need to go—" dragging me out the door.

I chased after Amelia as we ran down to the parking garage of her apartment complex.

"Adam is Karmen's husband, right?" I questioned, bad at remembering people's names, especially when I had never met them before.

"Yes."

"And he hit her? He hit Karmen?"

"That's what Eleanor said."

"I mean, that's fucked up, don't get me wrong," I replied, "but why is Eleanor freaking out? If he just like, backhanded her, she would be bruised but she should be fine."

"I don't know," Amelia stated, worry evident in her tone.

I simply nodded, unsure of what we were about to walk into.

The last time I was in an ER was when I was eleven. My parents' work overlapped, and the babysitter got sick, so they were unable to find a last-minute replacement. I had to go to work with my mom. I remember the nurses tucked me away in a back office, so I was away from all the commotion. Now, the ER department felt entirely different. I was hyperaware of everything happening around me, all the moans and coughs of people in the waiting room, a patient talking about healthcare coverage to a receptionist, and another person crying into their phone.

"We need to find Eleanor," Amelia stated.

I scanned the waiting room and easily spotted Eleanor. She was the only woman crying unconsolably, a small boy grasped tightly against her. We hurried over and watched as Eleanor fought hard to stop her tears. Michael, the little boy, Karmen's son, wiggled uncomfortably against Eleanor's tight grasp.

"Where's Karmen?" Amelia asked.

"They took her back to a room, I don't know. I can't take Michael back, he can't see, but I can't leave him here alone. I didn't know what to do," Eleanor answered.

I knelt next to Michael, smiling kindly at him. "Come on, Eleanor, you can let go now," I cooed, prying my fingers under Eleanor's until she finally released her death grip on the poor boy.

Now that he was free, Michael turned to face me, studying me intensely. He rubbed at his arm where Eleanor had been holding him, but he said nothing. He was young, around two if I had to guess, but I wasn't too good with kid stuff.

"Alright. Eleanor, we're going to find Karmen," Amelia declared, pulling the shaking Eleanor into a standing position. "Natalie, stay here with Michael." Then the two women were gone before I could say a thing.

Suddenly, *I* felt very alone. Everything felt cold and it was as if everything went silent, a ringing in my ears. It wasn't actually quiet, of course. The typical coughing and moaning of complaining people waiting in agony could still be heard, but their sounds were muffled. I sat down in the seat where Eleanor had been sitting, feeling numb, when I realized that right in front of me was just a small, wide-eyed boy. He looked like Karmen, dark hair and tan skin, but his eyes were a bright green, unlike his mother's. He was clearly too young to comprehend the extent of what was happening, but it was clear to me that he knew something was wrong. He looked like he might cry.

"Who are you?" Michael asked, and I realized the poor kid had been left with a complete stranger. So, thanks, Amelia, that wouldn't be a problem at all. I groaned inwardly.

"I'm um, a good friend of your mom's," I answered. "My name is Natalie."

"Michael," he responded.

"That's a nice name." I looked down in my lap, remembering the container of cookies I had clasped in my hands. "*Umm*, do you like cookies?" I asked. "They're chocolate chip."

Michael nodded furiously so I opened the container and extended a cookie to him. He smiled, happily taking the cookie from me, and shoved it into his mouth.

"Fank foo," he said, mouth full of cookie.

The cookie seemed to be the turning point in his discomfort, because after that, Michael was all questions. He swallowed the last of his cookie and then the flood gate opened.

"Where is mommy?" he asked. "Where is aunty 'Melia and aunt Eleanor?"

I nearly died when Michael pronounced Amelia's name as 'Melia. It was such an adorable nickname; I'd have to file it away for later. But in the meantime, I had to ease Michael's curious and worried young mind.

"Come, sit down next to me," I stated, patting the empty chair beside me. Michael did his best to scramble up onto the chair, but his legs were just a little too short. I helped pull him up, situating him next to me. Then I turned to him, lowering my head so that I was at eye level with him. I stated as confidently as I could, "Everything is fine. You know, sometimes adults are just weird. They do silly things. Do you ever do silly things?"

"Silly things?"

"Yeah, silly things, like..." I glanced around, trying to think of something silly. An idea came to mind, so I puffed my cheeks full of air, made a funny face, then I shoved my hands against my cheeks, blowing a fart noise out of my mouth. Immediately Michael started giggling and quickly tried to imitate me. I laughed in response.

"I might look like an adult, but I still like kid things," I declared. "So, I think we should just play around and have fun until the adults decide to stop being silly. What do you say?"

"Okay!" Michael grinned, making another fart noise, very proud of his newly developed skill.

Somehow, I had managed to avoid a complete child meltdown. I took that as a win.

Nearly an hour passed. Michael and I made fart noises. We played every hand clapping game I could remember or make up on the spot. I even took Michael to the bathroom twice without issue. Thirty minutes into that hour, I texted Amelia for an update, but she never responded. I had no idea what was happening, so I just kept playing with Michael like my life depended on it.

When I ran out of games from my childhood to share, I found some kid friendly games that I downloaded onto my phone for Michael to play. We shared cookies, taking turns munching until only a few crumbs remained. I was starting to wonder if I should ask a nurse for an update— as I still hadn't heard from Amelia—when my phone started ringing. It was Piper.

"Hang on one sec," I said, taking my phone back from Michael. "I've got to talk to Piper."

Michael smiled and cooed, "Aunt Piper?"

"Yep," I answered, nodding. I pulled the phone to my ear. "Piper, what's up?"

"I should be asking you that," Piper replied. "I'm hoping you're more in the loop than we are."

"Oh, yeah I didn't really think to text you. Everything happened so suddenly. Did Eleanor call you too, or did Amelia after we got here?"

"We haven't heard anything from either of them," Piper stated. "No, we found out from *Adam.* I called Karmen—we don't know what's happening—but she didn't answer. I called Eleanor and Amelia too, but nothing. You're the only one who actually picked up. Oh, wait, Ellie's here too. Hang on, I'm putting you on speaker. Okay, there, can you hear me?"

"Hey, Natalie," Ellie 2.0 greeted me.

"Hey," I responded. "Okay, well, what *do* you guys know?"

"Well, twenty minutes ago, Adam just showed up banging on Ellie's door. He seemed pretty mad and kept implying that we were hiding Karmen from him."

"We didn't have any idea what he was talking about," Ellie 2.0 added. "But he was getting a bit hostile, so Cliff told him he needed to leave."

"We couldn't make heads or tails of what he was going on about... something about trouble and Karmen getting hurt and everything kept escalating."

"He was really freaking out," Ellie 2.0 muttered. "He was frantic to find Karmen, really. He tried to shove past Piper and get into the house, but that was when Cliff stepped in. He grabbed a hold of Adam and said that if Adam laid a hand on either of us again, he was going to call the cops."

"Then he ran off," Piper concluded. "But clearly something wasn't right, which was why we started calling everyone, trying to figure out what happened."

"I don't really know much more, all I know is that Adam hit—" I stopped talking abruptly and looked over at Michael who was, to the best of his ability, trying to follow my side of the conversation. "Hey, um, I'm watching Michael, I don't want to say—"

"No, you're right, don't talk," Piper agreed. "We'll piece it together. Did Adam hit Karmen?"

"That's what Eleanor said."

"Where are you, since you're with Michael?" Ellie 2.0 asked.

"The ER."

"Ellie, grab your purse," Piper declared. Then she spoke to me. "Is Karmen okay?"

"I don't know," I admitted. "Amelia and I got here an hour ago. Amelia is back with them, but Amelia won't answer my texts, so I don't know what's happening."

"Okay, listen," Piper stated, "stay put, keep Michael company. I'm calling the cops right now and reporting Adam. Then, Ellie and I are coming to the ER."

"Okay."

"Hang tight, Natalie. We're on our way."

Once I hung up, I looked over at Michael and he seemed worried again.

"Hey, good news, bud," I declared, trying to sound as upbeat as possible. "More friends are coming over. They want to see you and play with you because you're so awesome!"

"Friends?" Michael muttered.

"Aunt Piper and Aunt Ellie?" I tried.

Quickly, a large grin grew across his face, and he started to bounce up and down in his seat. "Yay!" he squealed. "Play games?"

"Absolutely."

I gave Michael back my phone so he could continue playing games. Then, a few minutes later, a nurse approached us.

"Excuse me, are you here with Karmen Caballero?" the nurse asked.

"Yes. Do you have news?" I asked eagerly.

"No, I'm afraid I don't," the nurse admitted. "But they're moving Ms. Caballero back to another wing, and I just, I noticed you have a small child with you. Is he yours?"

I did a double take at the suggestion that he was my son, sputtering out, "Oh, no, um, he's Karmen's son." I wasn't used to people thinking I was old enough to be a mother. Though there were girls younger than me with kids, I personally hardly felt qualified enough to be a mother.

The nurse turned towards Michael and knelt to his height. "Hi there," she smiled. "What's your name?"

"Michael," he answered.

"It's very nice to meet you, Michael. I'm nurse Jackie."

"Hi," Michael muttered bashfully, and the nurse chuckled.

The nurse stood and turned back to me. "Anyway, as I was saying, they're moving Ms. Caballero to another wing, and there's a different waiting room over there that's a bit more child friendly. There are toys and whatnot, so I just thought it might be nicer for you."

"Oh, that would be amazing," I answered, nodding rapidly.

We followed the nurse around to the other waiting room. It was a nicer space, carpeted, with toys covering tables and mounted on walls. The room was divided up into smaller cubicle areas, for privacy, and we were led to an empty space. The nurse explained the lay of the land to me as Michael dove on some toys, letting me know about a complimentary snack room, where the bathroom was, and where a doctor would come out to give us updates when the time came.

I thanked the nurse profusely. Once she left, I sat down on a chair, watching Michael for a moment. Slowly, I leaned my head back, relaxing for a moment, before I glanced around the waiting room. There was a sign hanging above a pair of double doors down the hall that read 'operating rooms.' It made me uneasy, but I tried to reason that those doors could lead anywhere, and just because we were near this wing, didn't mean we were *in* the surgery wing. Besides, Karmen just got smacked around, a little black eye was all. She didn't need an operation.

Then, I spotted a monitor hanging on the wall. The monitor listed patient names, in various colors, and beside each name was the stage of surgery the person was in, like mid-operation, post-op, recovery, things like that. At the bottom of the list, I read that one 'K. Caballero' was in 'pre-surgery prep.'

I pulled out my phone again and texted Amelia, almost frantically, *'Hey, we're in a surgery waiting room now and this monitor says K. Caballero is about to go into surgery. Is that Karmen? What's happening?'*

I didn't get a response. I didn't really expect to, but god did I wish Amelia would answer me. Needing a distraction for myself, I pulled Michael away from the toys so we could grab some complimentary fruit snacks—for the both of us—and then I sat down on the carpet and started playing with Michael. I built tall block towers so he could come in with a toy dinosaur and knock them down. I knew as long as he was laughing, everything was going to be okay.

I lost track of time playing with Michael. My phone never went off. My back was turned to the entrance of our cubicle, but I heard someone approach after a while. I turned when I heard a nurse say, "Here they are." I saw Amelia step into view, my heart racing. The nurse patted Amelia on the back before leaving and Amelia just stood there staring at me as I sat frozen on the floor.

"Play?" Michael questioned, hitting me in the arm with the dinosaur.

"What's happening?" I asked Amelia, finding my voice.

Amelia didn't answer me though. Instead, she walked over and sat down on the floor next to me. Then, she collapsed against me. I wrapped my arms around her, pulling her into a tight hug, watching Michael who was looking to us with question.

I was freaking out. Amelia wasn't talking and I could tell she was trying really hard to keep it together in front of Michael, but I needed to know what was happening. Not knowing was stressing me out.

Michael stood then, walking towards us, his arms hanging at his sides as he dropped the dinosaur toy on the floor. "Aunt 'Melia okay?" he asked.

At the sound of his fragile child voice, Amelia only pushed herself further into me. I figured she didn't want to risk talking because she was afraid she would cry. That meant I had to be the one to diffuse the situation.

"She just... wanted a hug," I answered the boy. "Aunt Amelia likes hugs, and hugs are pretty great. Why don't you hug her too? We can make a hug pile."

"Hug pile?"

"Yeah, we all just hug each other. Come on. It'll be fun."

Michael didn't question me further. He walked over and leaned against Amelia's back, wrapping his tiny arms around her. When he did, I felt Amelia shudder and inhale abruptly. She was already crying but trying to not make any noise so Michael wouldn't know.

We sat like that for a while. Michael got bored before too long and went back to playing on his own. When he did, I rubbed small circles on Amelia's back, her grip on me never loosening. Eventually though, I felt Amelia slowly release my shirt and tip her head up so that she could shakily whisper into my ear, "They're doing an emergency C-Section."

I grabbed Amelia tighter, looking over at Michael. He had found a puzzle somewhere and was intensely working at it, although it was probably a bit above his age group. It would keep him busy in the meantime though.

"Hey, Michael, stay here for a minute, okay?" I said. "Aunty Amelia and I are going to step into the hall and talk about some silly adult things."

"Okay," Michael hummed, clearly busy with the toys and not caring about anything else in that moment.

I stood, pulling Amelia up with me. I led her just a step outside of the cubicle, where we could still see Michael in our peripherals. I looked to Amelia then, her face red and puffy, still on the verge of another sob attack. Internally, I was panicking. It was taking all of my strength and will power to remain cool and collected on the outside.

"Please, you have to tell me what's happening," I urged Amelia, my voice cracking as I said it, the desperation of my words evident. Amelia nodded, taking a few deep breaths to calm herself enough to talk.

"We found Karmen. I saw her. She doesn't look good," Amelia choked out. "She's conscious, at least, and talking. Eleanor calmed down once she could be with Karmen. She told me the brunt of the story, but Karmen filled in some details."

"Okay, good, she's talking, that's good," I muttered, accepting the small victory. "What's the full story though?"

"So, you know Karmen moved out, right? But she was trying to keep things civil, so they were letting Michael stay with his dad and Karmen would just swing by for visits, until the official custody hearing. Karmen went over to pick up a few things and see Michael. Adam went upstairs to grab some stuff for her, and then Michael asked her what a sleazy dyke whore was."

"Oh no... I'm guessing he learned those choice words from his dad..."

Amelia nodded. "Rightfully, Karmen was furious. She left Michael downstairs and went up to confront Adam. She said he could say anything he wanted about her, just not in front of Michael. There was a big fight, lots of yelling, and it kept escalating until Adam hit her."

"How bad?" I immediately asked.

"Just a slap across the face and he instantly and profusely apologized," Amelia explained. "That ended the yelling. Karmen told Adam his behavior was toxic, and she didn't want him around Michael anymore, so she was taking Michael with her. She left the bedroom, Adam started yelling more, a bunch of homophobic stuff, how she was tearing their family apart. He chased her out of the bedroom, grabbed her arm at the top of the stairs. He tried to pull her back to keep her from leaving, but she jerked free, lost her balance, and fell down the stairs."

I wasn't breathing. That would explain the emergency C-Section. There was no way Karmen could have fallen down a flight of stairs and not hit her belly on anything. All the trauma to the unborn child could be catastrophic. Heck, depending on what hit where and how hard, that fall could be catastrophic to Karmen. No wonder Eleanor and Amelia were crying.

"Karmen made it very clear that it was her fault she fell, that Adam didn't shove her or anything. Evidently, he ran right down to check on her, tried to call an ambulance, but Karmen was so furious she just shoved him away. She grabbed Michael and left before he could get help."

"Did she go straight to the hospital?" I asked. "Please tell me she did."

"No, she went to Eleanor. And she might lose the baby *because* she didn't go straight to the hospital."

"Fuck," I muttered under my breath, pulling at my hair as I looked up at the ceiling. "Shit."

"Once Karmen told Eleanor what happened, Eleanor immediately rushed them to the hospital. On the car ride, Karmen started bleeding vaginally, heavily, and the staff here rushed her right in. It isn't good."

"The... the baby's still alive though? They're trying to save her?"

"Yes. Karmen's dreadfully pale. She looks terrible. The doctors have to get the child out and treat any injuries, though they're worried Karmen's bleeding internally. They need to address that and then, well, if the baby makes it through the procedure, she'll need to be in intensive care."

"God, this is awful. It's so much worse than I thought."

"The doctors are letting Eleanor stay with Karmen during the C-Section, but trust me, Eleanor isn't fairing too well either."

"I bet not."

"How's Michael doing?" Amelia questioned.

"He seems fine," I answered. "I don't think he really understands what's happening though. He's well behaved, but he's going to get bored of being in the hospital eventually. I mean, we already ate all the cookies."

"Karmen's definitely going to be admitted for overnight, and I'm sure Eleanor will want to stay with her," Amelia explained. "We might have to watch Michael overnight. Maybe we can stay with him at Eleanor's place, they have more kid things—oh. I mean, I will. You can go back to school."

"What? Seriously? Hell no," I stated. "I'm your guys' friend. I'm not going to abandon any of you in your time of need. And speaking of which, Piper called me while you were back with Eleanor and Karmen."

"Oh, god, we should have called her," Amelia muttered. "Did Eleanor call her too?"

"Actually, no. Apparently Adam went over to Ellie 2.0's place and got a little hostile with them over hiding Karmen. I think Cliff chased him off, but like, they were really confused. They tried to call Karmen first, of course, then Eleanor and you, but none of you answered. Then she called me, though lord knows how she knew I'd be around."

"Oh, um, I might have told them all that you were spending the night with me. But that's not important right now."

I shook my head, a bit surprised, but it was the least of my worries. "Anyway, so I talked to Piper and explained all I knew, which wasn't much at the time. They said they were going to call the police and report Adam for hitting Karmen, and then they'd come over here."

"I should probably call and give them an update..." Amelia muttered, "but I don't have the energy. Let's just wait with Michael until they get here."

"Okay," I agreed. "I'll just text them and let them know what waiting room we're in."

We went back into the cubicle and sat down on the floor with Michael. He had since abandoned the difficult puzzle for a robot toy, but he soon decided dinosaur verses city was far more exciting. Happy to have another playmate at his disposal, Michael set Amelia and me to work building a city he could then plow over.

Time ticked by slowly. I forced myself to stop watching the clock so time would seem to move faster. The monitor on the wall updated and told us Karmen was in surgery, but more than that we didn't know. Our focus in the meantime was on Michael and keeping him entertained.

Michael loved Amelia. I knew she wasn't technically his aunt, but she was certainly the *favorite* fake aunt. Amelia had a youthful soul. I could play pretend with a toddler, sure, but there was something more about how Amelia interacted with Michael. She poured her entire heart and soul into the boy, as if he were her own son, and he in turn was bursting with love for her.

Amelia would make a great mother.

I mentally cursed myself. I shouldn't be thinking such things, not now, not when Karmen and her child were fighting for their lives. My thoughts were only confusing me. When did my object of desire turn from unapproachable bad boys that treated girls like shit, to gorgeous older women that had their lives together and would make great mothers? Is that what growing up felt like? Was I going to forgo my dreams of exploration and rebellion to settle for a white picket fence and a 401(k)?

Amelia was so occupied playing with Michael, and I was so occupied daydreaming about domestication, that neither of us noticed when Piper and Ellie 2.0 walked up. Piper greeted us, startling us both.

Before Amelia or I could react to Piper, Michael leapt up and ran over, shouting her name with glee. He wrapped his arms around Piper's legs, hugging her tightly. Piper patted him on the back, then let go of him so he could run to Ellie 2.0 and do the same. Ellie 2.0 smiled, picking Michael up, and tickled him, his childish laughter the brightest thing in that wing of the hospital.

"I see you came back out to the waiting room, Amelia," Piper commented. "I presume you have news?"

Amelia looked towards me for moral support, taking a deep breath. Then, she nodded, standing. "Let Natalie watch Michael. I'll tell you guys what I know."

I stood, taking Michael out of Ellie 2.0's arms, but he wiggled against me until I sat him down on the floor. The three women stepped back out into the hall and Michael saw them, instantly distressed. He reached out for them, trying to run after them, but I held him back.

"They have to talk about silly adult stuff first," I stated. "Remember silly stuff?"

"Silly stuff!" Michael exclaimed, proudly making a fart noise.

"Exactly. They'll be right back, I promise. Why don't we keep playing dinosaur until they get back?" I offered.

Luckily, Michael agreed, and true to my word, the others returned in only a matter of minutes. As soon as he could, Michael pulled both Piper and Ellie 2.0 over to play with him, beckoning Amelia over as well. Clearly, I had been replaced by his favorites.

I sat down on one of the chairs, closing my eyes for a few minutes. I was still nervous but having the others with me made me feel like a load had been lifted off my shoulders. That was what friends were for. Sure, I could have handled Michael all day, but it was nice getting the extra help and comfort. As I relaxed, I realized I was downright starving.

"Anyone else hungry?" I commented, sitting forward and opening my eyes.

Immediately, Amelia exclaimed, "I am!"

"We should have brought you food," Piper stated. "We easily could have picked something up; we were just so worried about getting over here as fast as we could..."

"No worries, I'll just swing by the cafeteria," I declared, standing. "Michael, do you like... hot dogs?"

"Yeah!" the boy exclaimed.

"PB and J as backup?" I questioned. "He's not allergic to peanuts, is he?"

"Either would be fine," Amelia answered. "Here." She threw her purse at me.

"What's this for?" I asked.

"You don't have your wallet, so unless you were planning on stealing," Amelia stated with a smirk. "My wallet's in there. Spend as much as you want."

"Woah," I muttered. "Never thought I'd have a sugar momma," I added with a wink.

"Hey!" Amelia snapped, her cheeks reddening.

Piper glared at me for my comment, but I didn't care. I slipped out of the cubicle and swung Amelia's purse up over my shoulder. It was a pastel blue—matching Amelia's personality well, in my opinion—and inside I fished out a matching wallet. I realized, looking in Amelia's wallet, that I no longer felt so weird about her success. I was just happy for her. I knew she came from old money, but I also knew she had a lot of issues with her family, and I knew she worked hard for every cent she earned. I understood that now.

I followed some signs around to the cafeteria and picked out food I thought we'd like. As I waited in line, I looked around at all the people in the cafeteria. Some were alone, some were in big groups. Some were in pairs, either partners, friends, or family members. Everyone was there for different reasons, yet our lives had worked out so that we were all in that hospital at the same time.

Domestication was scary. Settling down, buying a house, getting married, and starting a family were freaky things to a confused college kid like myself. There were mothers younger than me, kids younger than me already more successful, making a name for themselves in the world, but I still felt like a lost child. I was growing up. I paid taxes and went to college, drove, got my own groceries, cooked for myself, yet there was a part of me that felt trapped back in middle school. Would that feeling ever go away? Would I ever feel older, ready for a career, ready for marriage, ready to be a mother? Those thoughts terrified me, yet even so, I couldn't stop thinking about Amelia playing with Michael, making him laugh and giggle... I was willing to face all my fears about my future head on if it meant having Amelia by my side.

Fuck me. I had never had such intense feelings of love towards someone before. Amelia was going to *ruin* me. We hadn't even kissed! I shouldn't be picturing my future with her. I needed to focus on the things at hand, like Karmen. She was having a baby and hopefully both her and her child would be okay. Happy thoughts, friendly thoughts.

I made my way back to the surgery waiting room. As I passed the monitor, I noted that 'K. Caballero' was in... 'recovery!' Karmen was out of surgery! I spun the corner of our cubicle, exclaiming, "Karmen's in recovery!"

The others gasped and then a collective sigh of relief spread through the group. We didn't know the fate of the baby or how Karmen was fairing, but she was out of surgery and that meant we'd hear an update soon.

I set out the food I'd gotten, though I found Amelia seated on the floor with Michael passed out, fast asleep in her lap. I handed her a hamburger and sat down beside her, digging into my food as well. No doctors came out to notify us about Karmen. We figured they just updated Eleanor who didn't want to leave Karmen's side to update us. I mean, she could have texted us, but I tried to not judge. I think if the woman I loved had just gone through something so traumatic, I wouldn't be too inclined to spend time distracted by my phone.

Ellie 2.0 started talking about a project she was having her class do, to keep the mood light, and after that Piper talked about some science fair. Michael continued to sleep, curled up in Amelia's arms. Eventually, I started feeling pretty tired too. I leaned over, resting my head on Amelia's shoulder. In turn, Amelia leaned her head against mine, and we settled against each other. I noticed Piper watching us with a slight smirk, but I just ignored her, closing my eyes.

I dozed off, but I woke up when I heard some commotion. Blinking rapidly, sitting up more, I tried to orientate myself against the kink in my neck. Gaining sense of my surroundings, I noticed Eleanor was sitting down next to Piper.

Eleanor took a deep breath. "The baby's here," she stated. "Karmen named her Isabella Alexandria."

"That's a beautiful name," Ellie 2.0 said, smiling.

"How are they?" Piper questioned.

"Isabella's in the NICU," Eleanor answered. "The doctors know there was internal bleeding, but they think it was all from Karmen—her uterus—not the baby. So, they think Isabella's fine. She's been through a lot of trauma though, so they want to watch her, and she is a bit premature too, so there's that. Karmen's um, resting. They stopped the bleeding but there's going to be a lot of scar tissue and well... they don't think she'll ever be able to have another child. They... they told me that, not Karmen yet. I think she'll be crushed. You know how much she wants a big family."

"But she's alive and she's going to recover," Piper said firmly. "She's going to be okay."

"I know. I'm so grateful," Eleanor whispered, clenching her fists tightly, her eyes glistening with tears she refused to let fall.

Piper reached out a comforting hand. "Are you staying with Karmen overnight?" Eleanor nodded. "Alright, Ellie and I will take Michael then. Karmen can focus on recovering and you can help with the new baby."

"Thank you," Eleanor replied.

"We should get going. It's getting rather late for Michael," Piper stated, standing.

Everyone stood, exchanging hugs with Eleanor, giving her hand squeezes of comfort. Everything was going to be okay. The worst of the day was over, and we were going to survive.

Amelia stood slower, Michael still asleep in her arms. They debated passing him over to Piper, but in the end decided Amelia should just carry him down to their car. Eleanor gave us her car keys so we could get Michael's car seat out and move it to Ellie 2.0's car.

When we reached the outside world, the sky was dark and the air hot. The breeze was nice, however, and the fresh air smelled fantastic. I helped Ellie 2.0 move the car seat, and Amelia carefully slid Michael into his seat, buckling him in. Then Amelia and I bid Piper and Ellie 2.0 farewell, watching them drive away.

"We parked on the other side of the lot," Amelia said, drawing me out of my trance. I nodded, and we slowly made our way across the parking lot. "I'm glad they're okay," Amelia said as we walked. "I mean, recovery is still iffy, of course, very scary, but they both made it through the initial crisis, so that's got to mean a lot, right?"

"I'm glad they're okay too, and they're going to continue being okay," I replied. "Karmen's a fighter and I'll be dammed if her daughter isn't a fighter too."

"I'm impressed with you also," Amelia then said.

"What? Why?"

"You handled Michael so well. You were brilliant. I just... I'm really glad you were here today, Natalie. I don't think you realize how much it means to me. If I had been alone, juggling Eleanor, Karmen, *and* Michael? I couldn't have done it. So, thank you. Thank you so much for being here today."

"You don't have to thank me for that," I said as we stopped at Amelia's car. "I would drop anything if any of you needed me, seriously."

Amelia looked at me and just sort of stared for a moment. Then she said, a bit abruptly, "Spend the night again."

"I mean... yeah, okay."

Amelia cracked a small grin. "Would you like to cuddle again tonight?" she questioned softly.

"Yes, I'd love to."

"I think we could both use some cuddles after today."

"Definitely."

Back at Amelia's apartment, all I wanted to do was dive into bed with Amelia, nuzzle my face into her neck, and sleep for an eternity. But alas, my attempt was thwarted by Amelia, who threw a pillow at me.

"Go brush your teeth and change your clothes," she stated. "I don't need my bed smelling like a hospital."

I relented, heading towards the bathroom. Since I was still in my pajamas, Amelia loaned me an old T-shirt and some shorts to sleep in. Alone in the bathroom I bushed my teeth and splashed some water on my face. I stripped out of my clothes, standing in only my underwear, holding Amelia's clothes against me. I breathed in her scent, pressing her shirt against my nose, my head spinning. It was the greatest smell in the world.

I was startled by my phone going off. I glanced to the counter, noting that Lizzie was trying to video call me. I was going to just ignore her when I realized she probably thought Amelia murdered me or something when I hadn't returned home.

"Hey, Lizzie," I stated nonchalantly, answering the call. "Sorry, I'm changing."

"Well thank god you're not *dead!*" Lizzie exclaimed. "Where the heck *are* you?"

"Amelia's," I answered.

"Oh my god, you're spending the night again?" Lizzie squealed. "O-M-G, did you two have sex!?"

I struggled to quickly grasp my phone, turning down the volume, praying Amelia hadn't heard that. "Good lord, can you chill!?" I snapped. "I don't know how you bridged that gap, but no! We had a very stressful day and just lost track of time."

"*Ahh...* a stressful day," Lizzie stated. "Do you know what's a good way to get rid of unwanted stress?"

"Lizzie, I swear to god if you say se—"

"Sex!" Lizzie shouted over me.

"Alright, I'm hanging up."

"No, I'm sorry!" Lizzie quickly gasped. "But like, also, have sex."

"Hanging up now."

"When do I get to meet her?"

"Never!" I answered, ending the call.

14.

The Past Sets The Future In Motion

Sunday afternoon I woke up, wrapped in Amelia's sheets. Amelia was sitting up in bed, already drinking coffee, absorbed in her phone. I got lost for a moment just observing her, but then the extent of yesterday crashed down on me. Immediately I asked Amelia if there had been any updates. Eleanor texted periodically, but everyone was just recovering as expected, which was fantastic news.

Amelia and I spent the day just lounging around. We distracted ourselves with some television, some more documentaries. We ended up watching one about childhood cancer, but when one of the little boys died, Amelia abruptly turned off the TV. We knew, just by seeing the glistening of each other's eyes, that we couldn't do it. It was too soon.

Begrudgingly, around five, I had to leave. I had homework due Monday which I hadn't touched at all. Amelia bid me farewell, promising to keep me updated about everything. When I got home, Lizzie bombarded me with questions, but after I explained the Karmen situation, she grew quiet.

"I'm sorry, I didn't know. Are they okay?" Lizzie questioned.

"Yeah, they're recovering well. I'm just... pretty drained. I think... I think I just need some alone time in my room, you know?"

"Totally," Lizzie stated, nodding. "Just let me know if you need anything."

"Thanks."

In my room I situated some things, getting ready to do my homework. I opened my backpack and fished out some papers, pushing things over on my desk to make room. When I did, the seal toy Amelia had gotten for me in Florida tumbled onto the floor. I bent over, retrieving it, and held it in my hands, just looking at it.

It was honestly so ugly. And it looked like a rhino. Maybe it was actually supposed to be a narwhal, not a seal. At least that would explain the weird protrusion on its head. But it was sparkly, with huge eyes, and definitely not realistic. But it reminded me of Amelia—it was *from* Amelia. Suddenly, it felt like there was a softball lodged in my throat.

I fell back onto my bed, cuddling the seal toy against my chest. My chest felt tight and constricted and before I knew it, I was crying. It had to have just been built up emotions from the weekend, emotions I had to suppress for Michael's sake finally surfacing. I curled myself around the ugly little seal. God, how I wished it was Amelia I was cuddled up against and not just a stuffed critter.

I wished it was five years in the future. I wished I had figured out what I was doing with my life, that I was content with my choices. I wished I was happy, doing something I enjoyed and loved. I wished I had financial security, or at least something closer to that than I had currently. I wished I could just skip over the not knowing and figuring it out, skip to the already having done that where I could just enjoy the life I had made for myself.

Wednesday, after my classes, I headed over to the hospital to visit Karmen. I had been chatting with Amelia over text, staying in the loop as much as possible. Eleanor took Monday and Tuesday off to stay with Karmen, but went back to work Wednesday, meaning it was Karmen's first morning at the hospital alone. Hopefully she would get discharged soon, but in the meantime, I figured she could use a visitor. I got to the hospital around two, figuring Eleanor would be right back over once school let out.

Not wanting to show up empty handed, I swung by the store on the way to the hospital. I grabbed some flowers for Karmen and a baby blanket for Isabella. I nearly got the child a toy, but I realized she was too small, so I figured the baby blanket would be a better gift.

I found my way up to Karmen's room, her door propped open. I knocked softly on the door, sticking my head into the room. Karmen stirred in the bed, pushing herself up slightly.

"Oh, hi, Natalie," Karmen stated sleepily. "Come in. How are you?"

"Sorry, did I wake you up?" I questioned as I stepped into the room, sitting the flowers down on a table.

"No, no, I was just resting my eyes," Karmen assured me. "Thank you for the flowers. They're quite lovely."

I handed the baby blanket over to Karmen. "This is for Isabella. I figured you could use a blanket more than some toys right now."

"Thanks," Karmen stated, smiling. "She's still in the NICU, but hopefully she'll be strong enough to be back with me by this evening. Thanks for visiting too. I know you're busy with school."

"Oh, it's not a problem. I've got some free time today," I answered, taking a seat on a bedside chair. "How are you?"

"I'm doing better," Karmen answered. "I'm still pretty bedridden, resting and recovering, but I certainly feel a lot better today. I mean, I hurt, but it's better... more manageable."

"That's good. I'm glad things are looking up."

"And Eleanor finally went back to work today, which is *such* a step in the right direction."

I looked to Karmen quizzically. "Was... something wrong?" I questioned. "Was she bothering you?"

Karmen shook her head. "Of course not. I greatly appreciate her company. But Eleanor needs work, something to focus on and distract her. If she doesn't have something positive to focus on, things get a little rough for her."

I frowned, thinking about Eleanor's destructive alcohol tendency when we were in Florida. "She... wasn't drinking, was she?" I muttered, not quite able to believe she would.

"No, but she's self-destructive in other ways," Karmen replied. "She gets in her head too much... depression sets in."

"Oh... I had no idea."

"Eleanor's faced a lot of hardships in her life."

"I heard about the neighborhood she grew up in," I answered. "I guess some stuff went down with her parents, but her grandmother really seemed to save her."

"That's the brunt of it," Karmen commented, "but the parts Eleanor omits? Those are the parts that haunt her the most."

"I'd ask you to elaborate, but I guess that's really something Eleanor has to tell me."

"You're right. It's her past to tell you, not mine."

"Well, we should take a break from talking about Eleanor's past then—" I grinned— "but before we forget about her altogether, I want to hear how your great love affair is going. How are things now that you don't have to see Eleanor in secret? How are the divorces going?"

Karmen let out a sharp laugh before tightening her face in pain. "Oh geez, don't make me laugh. My abdomen is beyond sore," she groaned. Then she added, "If you want to know how the divorce is going, my husband pushed me down a flight of stairs."

"I thought he didn't push you, just stopped you and you jerked away?"

Karmen let out a deep sigh, her face pinching together in pain again. Then she looked over at me seriously. "I never wanted a husband, Natalie. I only ever wanted kids. And I'll be dammed if Adam takes my kids."

"So...?"

"I'm not pressing charges, and I don't want to lie," Karmen stated, "but maybe I just won't admit the entire truth, you know?"

"I'm not going to judge you," I declared. "I don't... well I'm not sure Piper would love to hear that, but—"

"Yeah, well Piper can handle her divorce how she wants, and I'll handle mine how I want," Karmen scoffed. "Piper's got a lot of opinions about what's right and what's not, but just because she lives by the most annoyingly strong moral compass of all time, doesn't mean we all do."

"I don't mean to pry, but well... I was getting this weird vibe back in Florida that there was tension between Eleanor and Piper. I guess I just don't really understand it. Sometimes Piper acts like the motherly figure of the group, but sometimes she seems to grind your gears as bad as Eleanor can. I just don't understand."

"There's plenty of tension between Eleanor and Piper... plenty of tension between Piper and me, even," Karmen answered. "I mean, how would you feel if you were just trying to do your best, but your friend was always breathing down your back about how you could be a better person, or how you did something mean and it was wrong."

"I didn't realize. Surely Piper is just trying to look out for you guys."

"Of course she is, but there's a time and a place to belittle people about their bad choices, and Piper has pretty horrid timing."

We fell silent for a minute as I reflected on what Karmen said. Piper helped me in a lot of ways. She got me my job at Elk Creek, pushed me to figure out my feelings for Amelia, and she always seemed to be trying to get me to see how much potential I had. But if I had a real problem, would I go to Piper? When I felt hopeless and like a failure, it wasn't Piper I went to. It was the same reason I wouldn't go to my parents, because I was afraid they would judge me. I was afraid Piper would be disappointed in me.

"How, um, how's Eleanor taking things?" I asked, pulling myself out of my thoughts. "I know you said she's going through some stuff, but like, how's her divorce going?"

"Matthew's taking their divorce better," Karmen said, but then she stopped. "Sorry, Matthew is Eleanor's husband, I don't know who all you've been introduced to."

"Yeah, I'm finally starting to piece together everyone's names."

"Eleanor's and Matthew's relationship has always been... different. They kind of remind me of an arranged marriage, one where they got along fine but just were never in love with each other. They still talk regularly, as friends, very civilly. I think it's good they can still be friends. It makes things easier with Vanessa, their daughter."

"I'd love to meet all your kids someday," I spoke up. "Michael is very sweet and adorable, and I can't wait to see Isabella grow up. I'd love to meet Vanessa sometime too."

"I have a picture of Vanessa with Michael on my phone," Karmen stated. She pointed to her phone, which was sitting on a table near me, and I handed it over to her so she could find the picture. "Vanessa is precious. I hope things go well with her custody so she can be a part of our lives. Here you go."

Karmen passed her phone back to me. In the picture, Michael had his back turned to the camera, playing with some toys—I'd recognize his messy brown hair just about anywhere. To the side of the frame was a little girl, Vanessa. Her skin was a light tan, though her nose was unmistakably Eleanor's. Her hair was super curly, just as curly as her mother's, but it was a light blonde, tied up into little buns on each side of her head. Her eyes shinned too, bright like Eleanor's. She was smiling up a storm, grinning contagiously at whoever was taking the picture.

"She's adorable," I cooed.

Karmen pulled her phone back and sat admiring the photo herself. She smiled, sighing wistfully. "I dream about Eleanor and me, married, together as a family. Michael and Vanessa could play in the backyard, and now Isabella... cuddled up asleep in Eleanor's arms..."

"Hey," I stated softly, reaching over, and resting a comforting hand on Karmen's arm. "Divorces are rough and take time, but things will look up after that. You and Eleanor are meant for each other. It's all going to work out, I promise."

Karmen nodded, tucking her phone away. Then, she looked over at me, cracking a grin. "Speaking of couples, how are you and Amelia?" she questioned. I stiffened, visibly, at her remark, but my reaction didn't faze her. "Come on, Natalie. Amelia's visited me and she talked more about you than she asked how I was doing."

"We've, um, been talking more," I muttered. "There's this whole big to do with the choir kids that I got roped into and well, I guess Dale—from Elk Creek—has a crush on Amelia. And look, I won't lie, it kind of made me jealous."

"Of course Dale likes Amelia," Karmen stated, rolling her eyes. "I could tell just sitting in on our start of the year meeting that he had heart eyes for her. He's a blundering idiot though. I think it took him nearly seven months just to gain the courage to tell her 'good morning.' Did he finally grow a backbone and ask her out? *Ooo*, did she turn him down?"

"I um, well no, I don't think *he* specifically asked her," I answered. "But she did say some stuff about him, and well, she told me some stuff too but well, I promised I wouldn't tell anyone. It's not my secret to tell, so I can't."

"Did she come out to you?"

My eyes widened slightly, surprised Karmen had so easily guessed what had happened. I quickly tried to reign in my reaction so Karmen wouldn't realize she was right. "Why... would you say that?" I questioned as calmly as I could force myself, but my voice cracked midway through.

Karmen chuckled lightly, holding her side as she bit through the pain. "I can't think of any other secrets Amelia would have. She's been denying her feelings for a while now, but we all know she likes women. We've just been waiting for her to feel comfortable enough to tell us. Should have known she'd confide in you first."

"Don't let her know that you know!" I snapped accusingly, pointing threateningly at Karmen. "This is serious! I promised her!"

"I won't say a word and when she tells me, I'll act just as surprised as ever. Promise."

"Good."

"But so, does this mean she confessed her feelings for you?"

"What feelings?"

Karmen groaned, rolling her eyes. "I think I understand Eleanor's and Piper's frustration with you two. Just sleep with her already. I saw the picture of you pinning her up against the wall. The sexual tension between you two could be cut with a knife."

"Okay, maybe there are feelings of attraction, but all other feelings are still trying to be figured out, so can we talk about something else?" I snapped, a bit agitated.

Karmen shrugged. "I heard you don't want to be a biologist."

"Who told you that?" I gasped.

"Amelia, when she was rambling on about you endlessly." Karmen smirked. "Is it true though?"

"I like biology, I do, I just... I don't want to work in the sciences," I stated. "I'm not a fan of the academic research world. If you work for a college, you have to do all this dumb work for tenure, and getting grant money, and what else. If I ended up working for a company, I'd have to look into things they cared about, which I might not even be interested in. I don't want to be stuck doing research and writing papers for the rest of my life. So, no, I don't want to be a biologist. But I went to school for four years to get a stupid degree in biology, so what am I supposed to do now?"

Karmen smiled softly. She reached out gently, trying to touch my arm, but her IV line restricted her movement. I reached my hand towards her as well and met her halfway, resting our arms against the bedside.

"Piper might be sad to hear it, but well, Amelia's been saying for a week now that you weren't happy with biology. It's not too surprising. Eleanor and I figured you'd make some changes here soon enough."

I groaned, pulling my arm back so I could burry my face in my hands. "That's the problem though," I muttered, sitting up straight. "I don't know what I want to do. So, what, I've closed the door on biology. That still leaves like a hundred doors open. How am I supposed to know what I want to dedicate my life to? And... and what about this dumb biology degree I'm getting? I wouldn't even be qualified for other stuff unless I went back to school."

"You need to stop stressing," Karmen declared. "Life has a way of working things out. Just keep your mind and heart open, and you'll find something."

"Thanks," I said halfheartedly. I didn't want motivational poster advice, I wanted actual helpful advice. I was starting to think adulthood was just stumbling around pretending until something actually worked. But that wasn't comforting to hear. I wanted answers now.

Karmen pulled me out of my stupor easily and we ended up talking for longer than I initially intended. I realized that over the past month, I had built a rather solid friendship with Karmen and Eleanor. I looked up to them a lot. Sure, I had helped them back in Florida, and maybe there were things about them I still didn't know, but I liked to think of them as my cool gay aunts.

They teased me, relentlessly. It was annoying at times, but also comforting. It was nice having people that genuinely cared about me, even if they showed their affection through memes that had been dead for over a year.

I realized, as I watched Karmen tell me stories about her son, or something embarrassing Eleanor had done in the past, that it wasn't just Amelia I had fallen in love with. I loved Karmen and Eleanor too. And I loved Piper and Ellie 2.0. I found a new family with them.

We ended up talking about Ellie 2.0. I felt bad because out of all the high school teachers, I spoke to her the least.

"I just never seem to have the chance to talk to her," I lamented. "Her classroom is the furthest from the lab, and I always seem to end up eating lunch in the cafeteria. Ellie 2.0's busy outside of school too. She hardly answers my texts just because she's so busy. I just feel kind of bad. I want to be closer to her."

"Ellie 2.0's a hard nut to crack," Karmen explained. "We haven't known her as long and you're right, she's a real workaholic. She doesn't like to fight, doesn't like our drama in the friend group. She's always mediating. I think it's because her parents fought a lot. They had an arranged marriage and sometimes that works out great, but I think there was always tension in her family."

"We should all go to brunch one weekend," I stated. "It would be nice to just hangout and talk with everyone, outside of work and school."

"As soon as I get out of here, we'll mark something on the calendar," Karmen stated with a wink.

Talking about Ellie 2.0 and her family led us down a path talking about our own pasts. Karmen knew the brunt of my childhood, but I added more details about my extended family that came in on holidays. From there, I talked about my family's holiday traditions, like Aunt Jean's potato salad on Easter, or opening up one present on Christmas Eve. Karmen thought it was hilarious and quickly told me to stop talking because laughing hurt too much.

"Yeah, well I don't see why having brisket at Christmas, turkey on Thanksgiving, and ham on Easter is so hilarious," I huffed.

"Because, Natalie, it's all so very *white-middle-class-American*," Karmen said, smirking. "You haven't lived until you've experienced a Latin-American celebration. You have, what, four uncles and aunts and about ten cousins showing up on holidays? If we only invited that many, we'd miss three-fourths of the family, and invited or not, they're showing up. Plus, brisket, turkey, and ham? No, no, *no!* Tamales, enchiladas, and slaving over Pozole with your abeula, madre, and tías! White people don't understand sabor, Natalie, flavor!"

"Well, I mean, no one asked me, but I'd eat tamales over brisket any day," I answered.

"Do you all gather around the piano at Christmas and sing carols too? Go around the neighborhood spreading Christmas joy?"

"Of course not. I don't think *anyone* carols anymore."

"If there was ever a family get together that my tío Juan didn't sing *La Bamba* after three shots of tequila, I'd think I was celebrating with the wrong family."

"It just sounds like your family is more jubilant than mine. Some people just aren't partiers."

"No, chiquita, gringos just don't know how to party." I narrowed my eyes at Karmen, trying to decipher what she was trying to tell me. She sighed. "I don't mean anything against you, of course. It's just that, well, the world was so full of vivid and rich cultures, and then the white man tranced in, raping our land and culture, just to replace it with their boring, stale, week-old lifestyle."

"Your culture's still alive and well," I answered with a shrug. "I mean, every Spanish class I've ever taken, we've talked about the culture in South America and Spain."

"Not everything's as perfect as it looks in a textbook. Things are different here in the states too. And maybe I'm overprotective of my roots now, but that's just because I spent a good chunk of my childhood resenting the fact that I wasn't white. I tried to whitewash myself, tried to distance myself from my culture and family in the name of fitting in at school. My parents had my older sister when they were still in high school. Their parents helped support them while they finished their education, and in the meantime, they lived with my grandparents in the Latin-American suburbs of California. Finally, my dad landed a really good job in Boston, so we moved.

"I was young before we moved. I hardly remembered what it was like living in California where our culture was more prevalent. And I didn't remember a time when we relied on our family to help make ends meet. What I knew was growing up in the white suburbs with a cushion of wealth. My parents found their success in rich social circles, but there was a caveat to that life. Privileged suburban life, country club weekend golfing, and yacht club get-togethers? Those were things for rich *white* folks. My dad figured out pretty early on he could pass as white and that granted him more opportunities. He started going by 'Bobby Richardson,' after his favorite baseball player." Karmen stopped and scoffed. "He didn't *have* a favorite baseball player, he just pretended he did. Just another façade to that fake life he built. But anyway, I was young then and very impressionable.

"I saw the way my parents acted and all the opportunities they got, and I saw my older sister getting picked on at school... microaggressions to full on bullying. I thought that in order to find peace and get what you wanted, you had to be white. So, I did what my dad was doing and tried to whitewash myself. I pushed myself to fit into the rich lifestyle we were living, to fit in with the popular kids. I thought girls had to just act dumb and go shopping with daddy's credit card.

"My sister really hated me in high school. She couldn't understand what I had become. She was too closely connected to our family back in California and was never happy in Boston with our parents. She used to fight with them all the time, called them posers and liars, threatened to expose them—and me.

"My abuela eventually moved in with us. She wasn't well enough to live on her own anymore. My sister spent all her time with our abuela, cooking and singing in the kitchen. I didn't want any of that though. I looked down at our culture, at who we really were. I snuck out of the house, searching for boys from school. I wanted to be at parties, out on yachts or in huge mansions, draped over some dumb boy, known for my tits. Maybe I wasn't happy, but at least they weren't calling me slurs, isolating me from their world like I was trash. My parents were immune to it. They did the same things I did! But my abuela was particularly upset at my behavior. I remember when our family came to visit that I would yell slurs at them just like the kids at school would. I pretended I wasn't one of them, that we weren't related. Isn't that horrific?"

"What... changed?" I muttered.

"I met Adam at church," Karmen whispered. Then she laughed, but sharply cursed against the stab of pain. "God, I have to stop laughing," she groaned. "Anyway, despite everything, I was raised a devote Catholic. Every Sunday, my mother dragged us to mass, and as I grew up, I found it increasingly ironic. I knew all the lies my mother told and the sinful things my father did. How did any of that follow the teachings of the church? They thought just going to mass every Sunday made them good people, but then the other six days of the week they went against everything they had prayed. I wanted to leave the church for good, but my abuela fought hard against me. She made a deal with me that I had to go to the kitchen with her and volunteer one Saturday, with other youth group members at our church. And then after that, if I really hated it, I could leave. I figured giving up one Saturday would be worth getting every Sunday free.

"So, I went to the soup kitchen with her and other youth group members. I complained the whole time, about how the hair net would ruin my hair, and I would get food under my fresh acrylic nails. But then, I saw him, dishing out peas... the most handsome boy to occupy my thoughts. I caught him on break, cornered him in a backroom. I did everything I normally did to seduce a guy.

"But Adam turned me down. I was shocked. Guys never turned me down. I wanted to know why he did. He said I was very cute, and probably quite nice, but that I needed to learn how to love myself. I didn't understand. I wanted to know more, so I started hanging out with him as often as I could. But because Adam was so religious, he would only hang out with girls at youth group. So, I joined youth group, kept going to church, and Adam really... helped me turn my life around.

"He taught me that I was smart, and I didn't need to act dumb and helpless for guys to like me. He helped me realize how disgusting my behavior was towards my family, helped me apologize to my abuela. Once I apologized, we started talking more and she taught me all about my heritage. My sister told me stories from back in California that made me miss a home I didn't really remember. And because Adam helped me so much, my abuela and sister welcomed him with open arms.

"It was so easy to fall for him. He was the first guy that saw a beauty in me that wasn't purely physical. He pushed me to apply myself and follow my passions. He didn't belittle me for just wanting to be a teacher and a mother. He liked that fact a little too much, maybe. He liked that I was smart and could hold good conversation, but that I wouldn't step on his toes as man of the house. A red flag but... I was too far gone at that point."

"I think I get it," I stated, nodding. "I wasn't sure how a conservative church man fit into your narrative, but I think I understand now. Not sure how you managed to survive that whole 'no sex before marriage' thing, though."

"It was tortuous," Karmen answered truthfully. "Once I was old enough to gain the eye of boys, all I wanted to do was sleep around. Part of that was a need for attention, sure, but a lot of it was just that I love the experience of sex. I love the back-and-forth, the foreplay, the ecstasy. When I first met Adam, it wasn't so bad. I was discovering myself and learning about my family. When we moved here from Boston though, and we both started working, I didn't have my family as a distraction, or my goals either. It was just the antagonizing wait until marriage when we could finally work on starting a family. I mean, some people can go their entire lives without having or wanting sex. Some people can calm the urges to once a week or less. But not me."

I puzzled over what Karmen was saying. I shouldn't have asked, but I was horrifically curious and couldn't stop myself. "Did you sleep with Eleanor because you were starved for sex and she offered, or because you liked her?" I questioned genuinely.

Karmen looked towards the ceiling, taking in my question, and contemplated her answer. After a moment, she responded, "I'd be a liar if I said I never once contemplated my feelings for Eleanor. She... was so different from Adam. I always gravitated towards her. Her energy is infectious. She made me feel alive in ways Adam never could, just as friends, even. But well, I accepted her offer that first night because I needed to get laid. I think if anyone had offered at that point, I would have taken them up on the offer."

"When did you fall in love with Eleanor then?"

"When we were lying in bed together after that first night."

My eyes widened in shock, very surprised. From what Eleanor told me in Florida, she didn't catch feelings that fast. I figured it was the same for Karmen, with all the weird back and forth they had, but here she was confessing to me that right after they first slept together, she fell for Eleanor.

"Why did you go through with your wedding then?" I questioned softly. "I mean, because that was right before your wedding, right? Why didn't you call it off?"

Karmen sighed. "I could sit here and lie to your face, give you a million excuses as to why I did. I could tell you that I did love Adam, despite what I did, or that at the end of the day all I longed for was a family with a normal husband. But the truth of it is, I was afraid. I was afraid of the strength of my feelings for Eleanor after such little time. I was afraid of the consequences of loving another woman. I was afraid of having to face Adam and my family. Out of fear, I chose to marry Adam."

I was silent. My mouth felt dry. I reach out a comforting hand to Karmen. "You know, you don't have to cower in shame. It's okay," I stated.

"I know that now," Karmen answered. "I've done a lot of growing since then. I'm much stronger now than the young, naïve girl that married Adam. I love Eleanor and I want to be with her. I know that now. Maybe things would have been easier had I chosen her in the first place, but I don't regret the choices I've made. If I hadn't married Adam, we wouldn't have Michael and Isabella, and if I hadn't pushed Eleanor to marry Matthew, we wouldn't have Vanessa either."

"Wait, you *pushed* Eleanor to marry Matthew?"

Karmen bit her lip. She looked ashamed of what she was about to confess. "I, um, was the one who suggested we sleep together before her wedding. I used 'tradition' as an excuse—total bullshit—I really just missed her. I longed for her. After we did, she wanted to call off her wedding. She was never as afraid as I was, but I was terrified, so I refused to let her. I... maybe sometimes wish I hadn't, but like I said, I don't *regret* the things I've done."

"And you shouldn't live in regret," I agreed. "The past is in the past. You can't change it."

Before Karmen could continue, there was a soft knock on the open door. I turned to see who it was and saw Eleanor standing in the doorway, holding a pillow.

"Look what I found," Eleanor said, her eyes locked on Karmen like I wasn't even in the room. "It's the pillow I gave you when you had Michael. You know, the one that you chucked at my head when we had our biggest fight?"

"Well yeah, because you were being an ass," Karmen replied, smiling. She extended her arms out like a child wanting to be picked up, and Eleanor walked to the bedside. She sat the pillow next to Karmen before she leaned down and gave Karmen a kiss.

I watched them in their embrace, my heart swelling. They weren't perhaps the perfect model lesbian couple, but it was still nice seeing two women in love and able to show it openly. It gave me hope for my future. I thought about all my sleepless nights of crying, thinking I was broken and alone, as if my love was dirty. It was possible to be happy, though. I could see the happiness between Eleanor and Karmen, flowing between and all around them.

I cleared my throat, muttering out, "I'm here too," when I noticed their kiss deepening. "And I'm pretty sure Karmen has to recover more before you two start doing stuff again, so hands off each other."

Karmen chuckled lightly as Eleanor reluctantly pulled away from her. "Yes, doctor," she mocked.

"Hey, Short Stack," Eleanor stated, turning to greet me. She reached over to ruffle my hair, but I dodged, shoving my chair back so I was out of Eleanor's reach.

"Oh no, you don't," I warned.

Eleanor laughed, moving a few pillows around on the bed before she climbed up next to Karmen. Karmen shifted, giving Eleanor more room, and the two adjusted so that Eleanor could wrap her arms around Karmen. Karmen leaned back in Eleanor's lap, her eyes closed, smiling contentedly.

"What all did I miss?" Eleanor questioned.

"We were just talking about the past... about our feelings," Karmen stated wistfully.

"*Eww*, sounds gay," Eleanor mocked, sticking out her tongue.

Karmen reached back and slapped around until she made light contact with Eleanor's cheek. "Yes, it's *very* gay, you dork," she stated. "And frankly—oh wait." She sat up a bit, looking around. "You left your meds here, Eleanor. They're over on that table."

"Oh, Natalie, toss them to me?" Eleanor asked.

"*Uhh*, sure," I answered, leaning over and grabbing an orange prescription pill bottle near me. I tossed it back to Eleanor who managed to catch it, despite how poorly I threw it.

"Not much of a sports person, huh?" Eleanor teased me. She looked at me and must have seen the curiosity in my eyes, because she stated, "Antidepressants and ADHD medicine." I nodded, my curiosity quelled, despite it being none of my business.

"We were talking about our pasts before you got here," Karmen stated. "Natalie's curious about yours."

"*Mmm*, my turn to share then, is it?"

"You don't have to tell me," I quickly said. "It's your past, your life, and you can choose if, when, and who you want to share it with. I won't be upset if you don't want to tell me."

"No, it's okay," Eleanor sighed. "You're my friend, Natalie; I'm not trying to keep secrets from you. Besides, my therapist says I should be more open about talking about what happened to me."

"Well, if you want to, I've got time."

"Okay, here goes. My mom was a disaster. I grew up in a bad neighborhood and bounced around foster care in bad neighborhoods. Everyone has their own idea about what a 'bad neighborhood' looks like. Not all their ideas are true. But I can safely say I grew up in a bad area. The buildings were old, and their owners couldn't afford upkeep, so they were all falling down and unsafe. A lot of buildings were abandoned and filled with the homeless and meth labs. That was how most people got their income: drugs. People would shoot up in the streets, meth labs would explode regularly. There were fires, things were just trashed. There was debris everywhere, liter, broken glass, needles. There were bars on the windows of every run-down gas station. Robberies were common.

"My mom hung out there a lot. She was rebellious and problematic. She got into alcohol a lot as a pre-teen and teen, that was how it all started. My grandparents got her help and she cleaned up a little, got into college. That was where she met my dad. My dad was a pretty lucky dude. He was black, but he got adopted into a nice family. He was really smart, studying to go to law school. They met up, fell in love, and everything was pretty good. He was good for my mom, that's what my grandmother always told me. He was well mannered with good morals... a good influence on my mom. They were going to get married. I think, personally, my mom got pregnant with me and that was why they were suddenly so insistent on getting married, but I'll never really know. Anyway, they went to meet my mom's parents and tell them they were engaged.

"My grandfather was extremely racist. He saw my dad, a black guy, and just immediately thought he was a drug dealer who was going to pull my mom down a bad road again. He told my dad to get out, to stay away from his daughter. My mom fought against this, but my grandfather was serious. I think he chased my dad out of the house with a shotgun. It was bad.

"Anyway, after that, my mom got really upset. She ran away, got kicked out of school, and turned back to old bad habits... drinking and getting addicted to ever escalating drugs. That was when I was born, at some point. She was staying in some crack house in that shit neighborhood when she had me. I came out the womb addicted to god knows what. My mom didn't know how to raise a kid, and frankly, she didn't care. My dad though... my dad cared.

"He knew he had a kid and spent a lot of time trying to track down my mom. He was going to get me and take me away from her. I read his obituary years later. I think he found my mom, tried to take me, but she was drugged up out of her mind. She called the cops on him. And well, you know, to the cops, they just saw a black guy trying to take a woman's child. They shot him. I read the police report too. It was all bullshit. I... I never knew my dad, but he was in law school! He wasn't stupid! He wasn't the issue; my mom was!" Eleanor snapped and I could tell she was getting angry, probably out of pain.

"Hey, breathe," Karmen stated, rubbing her hand along Eleanor's leg to calm her.

Eleanor took a deep breath, taking a minute to regain her composure. "You're right, I'm sorry," she muttered. "I just, well the police investigated my mom more after that and realized she was drugged out of her mind and there was just an infant with her. I got pulled into foster care so fast. My mom ended up in jail years later for selling drugs to minors, ended up dead in prison a month later. I was just an orphan bouncing around in foster care never knowing my parents.

"And foster care was just... so awful. Everything was miserable. I bounced between several homes, but the one I remember the most was a family that was only in it for the money. There were four other kids with me, and we were all shoved into a tiny attic space. I was struggling with the adjustment. I was miserable. My foster parents didn't give a damn about me though, so long as I stayed alive and got them a check every month. They didn't like my behavior, nothing I did was ever good. It resulted in a lot of abuse... They yelled in my face, told me I was worthless, locked me in a cupboard for crying, told me I was a waste of space and food. I still have nightmares about that place.

"I went to Byram for a year while I was living with that family. I hated everything. I was scared of everything. School should have been my escape, but the place was run-down. I wasn't motivated to do anything. I thought my life was hopeless. I didn't think I'd make it to eighteen to escape foster care.

"But then, one day, child services showed up claiming they located a family member willing to take me in. That was my grandmother, on my mom's side. My racist grandfather had passed by then; I never met him. Overnight, I went from the most inhumane living conditions with constant physical and mental abuse to a cushioned white suburban mansion with a loving grandmother. She thought the world of me, even though she didn't know me. She told me stories about my parents, about how she didn't know about me and once she did, she never stopped looking for me. I was her only grandchild, and she was so happy to have me.

"The transition wasn't easy. I was scared of everything, even scared of my grandmother. She never hurt me, I just had all this trauma and didn't know how to trust people. My grandma wanted the world for me, though. She gave me everything. She was always there when I woke up crying from a nightmare. At first, I'd recoil, because I had been punished for crying in the past, but she never hurt me or forced me to do anything. She let me learn to trust her at my own pace.

"The school in the district where my grandma lived was much nicer than the other schools I'd been to. I started having fun learning and progressing because I could go home and tell my grandma what I accomplished. She was always so proud. But at sixteen, I hit a rough patch.

"Before that point, I didn't really understand what racism was. My foster families were all white, and maybe my skin color did dictate my abuse, but I never put two and two together. I had such a bad education growing up, I didn't learn about racial issues or the civil rights movement until I was older. But I was a mixed kid from the slums who came to an all-white school in the suburbs. When I was sixteen, I learned all that the hard way. I learned to drive, got my license, and my grandmother got me a car as a present to celebrate all the progress I had made. I thought my life was finally perfect.

"The kids at the school where my grandmother sent me were all rich, privileged, white kids. Their parents had a lot of not nice things to say about me going to that school, especially knowing my mom's history. They had a lot of not nice things to say about my grandmother too. The kids I went to school with heard what their parents were saying, about how I didn't deserve to go to school there, how I was filth, how my mom was a good for nothing drug addict that slept around with niggers. Teenagers are mean. They'd come to school and tell me to my face exactly what they heard their parents gossiping about behind our backs.

"They told me I was half-black, that I was contaminating their pure school. They told me I should go back to the ghetto where people like me deserved to be. I might have been healing, but my mind still wasn't in a good place. I didn't know how to cope with that. Over time I just... agreed.

"One night, I took my new car and I drove to the neighborhood where my dad was shot, where my mom had me. I didn't know where I was going, or why, or what I was going to do. I was just outcasted by my current life, I felt like I had to, that the streets were where I belonged. I stopped at a corner to talk to some guys and one of them grabbed me, pulled me out of the car window and held a knife to my throat while his buddies ransacked my car. They took off with it, ended up getting rid of it before the police caught them. But luckily, they let me go when they took the car.

"I felt entirely isolated and unwanted. The white kids didn't want me, they thought I was disgusting, but the black kids didn't view me as kin, they had just robbed me! I was too white for the black neighborhoods and too black for the white ones. I was defeated.

"I couldn't stand to face my grandmother after what had just happened, knowing I would finally disappoint her. I went home, played it off. She wouldn't know the car was missing until tomorrow morning, and I wasn't planning on being around to deal with the fall out. That night, while she was sleeping, I took a bunch of alcohol from her cabinets and a razor from her sewing kit. I locked myself in the bathroom. I wasn't planning on ever walking back out of that room. But luckily, my grandma had to pee like seven times throughout the night, and she found me before I could do anything.

"I switched schools again, this time to a private school: Elk Creek. At the time, Elk Creek was still predominantly white, but their no-tolerance policy towards bullying made it better. Therapy and meds helped get my life back in check, helped me focus and excel in school. And well, I guess the rest is history. I've come a long way from where I started, and I was really lucky that my grandmother saved me. I still have demons I have to battle every day. No matter how far away from my past I get, I will never be able to fully escape it. The medicine keeps me sane and functioning, and my friends keep me grounded. But yeah, I guess that's my past in a nutshell," Eleanor concluded.

"I... don't know what to say," I muttered.

"You don't have to say anything. You were curious, now you know."

"Well, thank you for sharing."

"Anyway, so have you and Amelia kissed yet?" Eleanor questioned, smirking.

"Oh my gosh!" I groaned.

That evening, I sat in bed, unable to sleep. My thoughts were consumed by Eleanor and Karmen and all the hardships they faced in life. Life was hard for them. I realized in comparison, my life was pretty cushy. I grew up privileged and went to mostly white schools. We were taught about racism like it was a thing of the past, something long extinct like covered wagons and nighttime streetlamp lighters. We conquered racism with the civil rights, done and done. But... it wasn't.

Clearly, Eleanor struggled with racism at the white school she ended up at. There were horrific stereotypes that remained, like black people are murderers and drug addicts, less than full people. Eleanor had a real shit life. She easily could have grown up to be a drug addict just like her mom. But her mom was white. Anyone could be a drug addict, or a drug dealer, or a murderer. White people were just always getting excused. He was just a troubled youth. She didn't mean it. He's just a kid. I have never heard those words used to excuse the behavior of a black kid though. Was that racism, still alive and well today?

There were harmful stereotypes about Latin-Americans too that Karmen faced. I had never even stopped to consider that before. I only ever learned about the Civil Rights era, predominantly black led, or so we were told. I knew people had a lot of negative things to say about Jews, because we learned *all* about World War II and Hitler, but what about everyone else who wasn't white? Were Asians persecuted? What about Italians, or Irish, those immigrants we learned about coming to America during the industrial revolution? Weren't they smashed into small apartments, struggling in inhumane living conditions? I was taught it was like that because America was facing such a boom in population, but was that actually racism? Were white British immigrants shoved into tiny apartments too? Was the separation just money based? That didn't make any sense. Every country had rich and poor people. But was racial separation rooted in economic differences?

I felt lied to a horrifically sheltered. America was supposed to be the land of the free, but it was starting to feel like the only free people were rich and white, so they could pay their way out of jail. The world was still bad and horrifically unfair. I wanted the world to change for Karmen's and Eleanor's kids, but would it even be possible to change the world so drastically before they grew up? Would Michael get called slurs at school? Would kids call Vanessa the N-word, thinking it was funny, but she'd take it to heart because she would *know*... she would know the history behind that word and all the feelings, the years of abuse and struggle? Would

Isabella get good job opportunities, or would her peers think she was just a maid, no matter what she accomplished? I didn't want that life for them.

Their mothers needed to win the custody hearings. Their fathers were white; they'd never understand. They were liable to excuse the bad and racist behavior of their kids' peers because they were raised to believe that was normal. I mean, that's how I was raised. I laughed at racist jokes before, thinking they were harmless, because it wasn't like a physical and violent attack, just words, just jokes. But they weren't. They were harmful too. Those kids needed their moms. They needed to understand the struggles their mothers faced so they could build the skill set to fight back and be confident in who they were. They needed someone who would fight for their equal rights, not erase their heritage.

I pictured Michael in my mind, his cute, sweet, innocent, little face. I would protect that child with my life. He was so adorable calling Amelia 'Melia. What an adorable nickname. Racism wasn't an innate part of human life; that child knew no such hatred. No child was ever born with that hatred, it was instilled in them as they grew up. People brainwashed their kids to be racist assholes, just like Eleanor was saying. The kids that bullied her only repeated what they heard their parents saying. We had a bigger impact on children than we realized. How careful I would have to be going forward so I could be a proper role model to those kids. And not just Karmen's and Eleanor's kids, but to my students as well.

The following day I headed into Elk Creek. Barely two steps out of the main office and I was swarmed by four choir kids—Nicholas, Shannon, and the twins. They grabbed me and pulled me off to the side where a few couches were.

"It's lunch time, what're you guys doing over here?" I questioned.

"Did you ask Ms. Lewis about Mr. Chinipardaz?" Nicholas demanded.

Oh, right. It felt like it had been ages since last week, and I had practically forgotten. "Yes," I answered with a nod.

"And?"

"And I don't think she's interested."

"You don't think, or you know?" Nicholas questioned.

"I know she's not interested," I corrected resolutely.

"How do you know? Did she say so?" Shannon asked.

"Yeah, what exactly did she say?" Nicholas added.

"I, well, just... trust me, you guys," I stammered, stumbling over my words. "Dale isn't exactly her type."

"Well darn," Shannon stated. "That would have been just perfect."

"We'll just have to find some guys that look exactly opposite of Mr. Chinipardaz... like guys that look like dads," one of the red-headed twins suggested.

"I guess, to the dating app?"

"To the dating app!" Nicholas exclaimed, racing off down the hall, holding his phone up in the air. The others quickly chased after him, leaving me standing alone in the hall.

This... could be bad. If Amelia wasn't going to come out to her choir, she needed to come up with an imaginary boyfriend ASAP, or there were going to be a lot of awkward introductions to random men in her future.

That week's lab was about pill bugs. You know, roly-poly, isopods, the little bugs you find under dead brush that can roll up into a little ball? We were dealing with stimuli and the senses, seeing what smells the bugs liked, what type of environment they preferred, and if you could control their movement.

Since the disaster of the first lab I led, I had learned a few tricks of the trade. I kept everyone occupied to avoid unnecessary distractions, separated kids before problems evolved, and talked to them to get to know them better, build a level of trust among us.

I didn't want to pursue a career in research, that much I was confident of. But I still found biology to be interesting and liked explaining things to the students. I did enjoy the teaching aspect of the job and I started to understand Amelia's passion, even if I didn't feel it quite as intensely.

It was wholesome interacting with students. We would never be as close as Amelia was with her choir kids, but by the third week, I learned most of their names and I was learning about their lives and hobbies. None of my students were white and they all came from a pretty rough neighborhood, just like Eleanor had. I wasn't an expert on such things, but I noticed some of the same behaviors Eleanor exhibited in the students in my lab. They had low levels of self-confidence, were quick to snap on the defensive, and most had trouble accepting praise and compliments. It made me want to help them in any way I could. I decided maybe I could be their source of compassion, taking Amelia as my inspiration.

I cared for all my students greatly and worried about their well-being at home, but I found myself specifically more and more invested in Aniyah. She was easy to talk to; we related on many things. I found myself growing protective of her. That sounded like something that would get me in trouble someday, but I couldn't help it.

"How's life?" I asked Aniyah, swinging over to her lab station towards the end of class.

"It's fine," she answered, "same old, same old."

"It's getting closer to summer. Are you excited?"

"Not really."

"Why not?" I asked, a bit surprised.

Aniyah shrugged. "When it's summer, I don't have school to run off to for most of the day. There's not much for me to do, I guess. What about you? Looking forward to summer?"

"Yeah, I mean, I guess," I replied, realizing that I actually wasn't that excited. "I'm graduating, I guess, so I've got that whole mess at the end of the school year to look forward to. Then I'm supposed to help Ms. Kegan with summer school. Maybe you could do some summer school? Or volunteer and help out?"

"Yeah, that could be fun."

"I'll talk to Ms. Kegan and ask her, but I'm sure it wouldn't be a problem."

"Cool. Thanks!"

After lab, I left through Piper's room and caught her just before she left. I asked her about Aniyah helping out and she was all for it. I was excited to tell Aniyah next week.

"See you later, Natalie," Piper said as I headed for the door. "And have fun in New York. I think you're a fool for volunteering to go on a weeklong trip with the choir, but have fun."

"It's not a week; it's five days," I answered. "But thanks, Piper."

"A week, five days, same difference when it's that lot," Piper stated, smirking.

When I reached the choir room, I knocked on the propped open door to alert Amelia to my presence. She was sitting at her desk, looking through some papers, probably a few last-minute checks before the trip. When she heard my knock, she looked up at me with a smile.

"Hey, Natalie," she said.

"How are things looking, capt'n?" I asked, walking up to her desk.

"Good, good. I think everything's in order. Hopefully it is. Are you sure you still want to come with us?"

"Still trying to get rid of me, huh?" I questioned.

"No, I'm just worried about your sanity. Choir nerds are... weird. We're extra high maintenance, just as a warning. And I'm not saying that you aren't all those things too, but well, you aren't a choir nerd in your own right, so you're liable to get overwhelmed."

"I think you're just worried that I'll lead all your students into a fantastically fun disaster, which true, I very well might. I make no promises," I said with a wink.

"God, you would," Amelia groaned. "Try not to get yourself or any of my students arrested, okay?"

"*Aww*, where's the fun in that?"

"The fun is me not getting fired, m'kay?"

Feeling a bit ballsy, I walked around behind Amelia and draped my arms over her shoulders, leaning my chin down next to her head. "Believe it or not, I am a semi-mature adult and I know when to be serious. Trust me, I'll do nothing to reflect badly on you or Elk Creek and I will protect your students' lives with my own, guaranteed. This is going to be an amazing trip."

"I'm certainly excited about it. New York is a great city... it can't be all fun and games though. We do have Nationals to worry about."

"Yeah, because you assured me you guys could get to Worlds, so, pressure's on!"

"The top three schools get invited to Worlds. It's not difficult."

"Okay, yeah, sure, and how many schools are competing at Nationals?"

"Over the course of the week? I think there's about one-hundred... three get invited from each state but they can't all afford to go."

"Top three out of one-hundred... sure. A three percent chance isn't difficult at all," I teased.

"It would be three percent if we all had an equal chance of winning, but skill comes into play too. I took math classes back in the day, don't be smart with me."

"Oh, I didn't know you were a math major!" I faked gasped.

Amelia smacked at me, but it was half-hearted and only spurred me to laugh in her ear, hugging her tighter.

15.

The Night Before The Trip Barn Shindig

The choir was leaving Friday after school, which gave me plenty of time to mull around and pack. I was being lazy, however, and only half packing that Thursday evening. Lizzie was gone, likely out getting laid, knowing her. I had the place to myself, just listening to some music, rocking in my desk chair.

My phone rang, disconnecting from my blue tooth speaker, cutting off my music. I reached for my phone, realizing it was an unknown number, likely just a telemarketer or a scammer. I contemplated ignoring it, but sometimes scam calls could be entertaining, so I answered it.

"You have a car, right?" the person on the other line stated right away. It sounded like a kid, maybe a little girl, I couldn't quite tell.

Before I could answer, I heard another person—muffled in the background—reply with, "Of course she's got a car; she gets to school somehow, doesn't she?"

"Right, dumb question," the person calling me declared. Their voice sounded so familiar, but I couldn't place it. "Look, I'm texting you an address, be there in fifteen minutes."

"I'm sorry, who is this?" I finally asked. "I think you have the wrong number."

I received a very loud scoff. "Take a guess, Rose Gold."

"I don't—wait—Nicholas?" I questioned.

"*Ding, ding, ding*! And we have a winner!" Nicholas exclaimed. "Did you get my text with the address? Be there in fifteen. Oh, and bring your ID."

"Hang on," I muttered, pulling my phone away from my ear, putting Nicholas on speaker so I could look at my text messages. "How did you get my phone number? And yeah, I got the text."

"We got it from Ms. Lewis, obviously. Look, meet us there in fifteen. You got any alcohol?"

"I'm sorry, what?" I snapped. "What's happening?"

"We're pre-gaming the National's trip. It's an annual tradition," Nicholas declared. "Are you on your way yet? The meet up point is ten minutes from GSU, so you better get going."

I was so beside myself I could barely find the words to express how I was feelings. "I can't be an accessory to getting you guys alcohol!" I finally managed to gasp out.

"So you don't have booze, whatever," Nicholas sighed and I could practically hear his eyes rolling. "Just bring your ID if you can, and anyway, Shannon has a fake so it's not like we're depending on you for the alcohol. No, we're inviting you out. Come on."

"Nicholas, I can't condone—"

The line clicked dead. I stared at my phone for a minute before I opened the text Nicholas sent me. I couldn't believe Amelia gave her students my phone number, for one, and for another, I couldn't believe they expected me to go party with them! Maybe I was still in school and only running the afterschool lab, but I was still employed by Elk Creek! I was pretty sure going out with students and drinking was a strict no-no.

But then I thought about my experiences with alcohol. I remembered back in high school when I went to my first house party as a freshman. I didn't know what I was doing, so I just downed drink after drink to look cool around the upperclassmen. Next thing I knew, I was puking my guts up in the bathroom, alone and scared, until a senior came in and found me. She was so sweet—I never learned her name—but she held my hair out of my face and told me she'd drive me home and make sure I was okay.

From then on, I went to many house parties, but I never drank. I spent my time wandering around, keeping a close eye on all the freshmen. I turned into the senior girl who helped me out. I let them know that it was okay to not drink if they didn't want to, by setting an example, and I let them know it was okay to leave if they felt uncomfortable. I took away keys from anyone who tried to drive and sat in the bathroom, holding girls' hair as they vomited.

I had to go and watch the choir kids. I had a moral obligation to make sure they were safe. I promised myself I would always be there for Amelia and all those she loved, including her choir. So, I grabbed my car keys and raced outside, prepared to be the adult guardian of the situation.

When I reached the address Nicholas sent me, I was confused, and I thought I was in the wrong place. I parked beside a field across from a gas station. The only other building was a beat-up looking grocery store next to the gas station. I looked down at my phone to text Nicholas about my confusion, when suddenly four individuals jumped my car.

I screamed, startled by their presence as they pounded on my windows. But then I realized it was just the choir kids, so I unlocked my doors. Nicholas and the read-headed twins hopped into the backseat, and suddenly Shannon was beside me in the passenger's seat, extending a bag of alcohol in my direction.

"Jesus," I groaned, shoving the alcohol into the backseat. "What's up with this place? Why are you guys out here in the middle of nowhere?"

"It's the only place that doesn't card," Shannon stated. "I have a fake, but you know, it doesn't always work."

"Thanks for coming!" Nicholas then declared, reaching forward to press his hand into my upper arm. "We're going to have a blast! This is the biggest party of the year, seriously!"

"Okay let's lay down some ground rules real quick," I stated, turning in my seat so I could better see the boys. "First, I'm not condoning the drinking, but I know I'm not going to be able to stop you, so I'm not going to try. But I draw the line at Nicholas. He's, what, twelve? You can't be drinking, bud."

"He knows. We already told him," Shannon stated.

"I'm well aware," Nicholas said, nodding in agreement.

"Okay, well, good," I answered. "Also, what time is it? Nine? I'm getting you all home by midnight."

"Kill joy," Nicholas huffed.

"One?" one of the twins tried.

"No," I stated, refusing to budge.

"Twelve-thirty?" the other twin tried.

"Okay, fine, maybe twelve-thirty if you don't go too crazy."

"Deal!" Shannon exclaimed. "Now come on, drive! We have to get to the rest of the party!"

"Rest of the party?" I questioned.

"Well yeah, it's not just us, silly," Nicholas laughed. "We're pre-gaming the trip. Everyone in honors choir is going to be there!"

"Oh, yeah, silly me," I said, putting my car into drive. "I'm guessing your parents don't know about this, but does Ms. Lewis know? Is she going to be there?"

"Of course not!" Nicholas gasped. "Do you really think she'd let us go out partying the night before we leave?"

"On a *school night*," one of the twins added dramatically.

"She'd get fired so quick if they found out she let us have alcohol," Shannon stated. "Even if she wasn't providing, you know. We would never do that to her."

"Oh, but you'll do it to me?" I scoffed.

"We aren't going to get caught," Nicholas said. "And besides, we're going to share stories about Ms. Lewis."

I smirked. "Yeah, okay. Where to, Shannon?"

I had no idea where we were. We drove further into the countryside and ended up driving down a dirt road for what felt like an hour. Then suddenly, out of nowhere, there was a barn in front of us. I could see lights on inside the barn, colorful lights and strobe lights going off, and I could hear music pounding. I parked near some other cars as the choir kids leapt from my car. Nicholas grabbed my hand, and we all went running straight for the barn.

The twins pulled the barn doors open and Shannon stepped inside, yelling, "Your president has brought the alcohol!" holding up the bottles above her head.

Then, Nicholas pulled me inside next to Shannon and shouted just as loudly, "We've got Natalie too!"

The entire barn erupted into cheers and suddenly we were swarmed. A group of kids grabbed Nicholas and hoisted him up into the air, because he was certainly small enough to be carried, and another mob pulled Shannon and the alcohol over to a table of snacks and punch. The twins grabbed me and pulled me over to what I assumed was a dance floor.

I didn't know what was happening half the time I was there. I was bounced between dancing and kids that kept trying to get me to sing karaoke, but I refused. Everything was so loud in the barn; I could barely hear. I grew increasingly aware of just how 'weird' choir nerds were. They had a bunch of inside jokes and traditions. We kept dancing and singing—

chanting something, even—until Nicholas appeared on the upper loft and the music ended for good. The lights died back to just a soft hue.

"My choir, it's time," he stated, "for our campfire stories. Grab some food, grab some booze, grab a buddy. Meet out at the campfire!"

I went along with the twins as everyone filed outside. The light from the barn was dimmed, making it easy to see the glow of a fire not far off. The choir members huddled around the fire, laughing as they made smores. I sat down on a log between Nicholas and Shannon—as directed—and the twins sat down nearby. Shannon pulled out another bottle of alcohol and took a swig before passing it along. I watched as the bottle traveled around the group, each student taking a small sip before passing it on.

"We have a guest of honor with us here tonight," Nicholas said, poking me. "Natalie's coming on the trip with us, so it was only right we invited her out here tonight. We have a lot of traditions in our choir and they're all important because they link us close like family. Personally, this is one of my favorite traditions. I like the bonding, all huddled together, sharing stories to keep the memory of our past and present members alive. So, who has a story they'd like to share?"

"Can it be about anything?" someone asked, likely a freshman.

"It should be about choir, or someone in choir," Nicholas answered. "Like maybe someone could share a story about our Nationals trip last year, so the freshmen can hear about it."

"I can tell everyone about last year's Nationals," some boy stated, "as long as you let me also share the story about the time Audrey snorted milk out of her nose."

"Hey!" I heard a girl protest. "Fine! But if you're telling that, I get to tell them about the time you wet your pants backstage!"

I laughed along with the choir, listening to their tales of mischief and fun. Some students shared stories they had heard at this same event when they were younger, about students that had since graduated. They were passing on the best stories to the generations to come.

"And that, my friends, is the story of how George Arnold, my freshmen year, was nearly used in a satanic sacrifice, all because he was trying to have sex with twin sisters and their step-mom," one of the boys finished off his tale.

"Do you remember George swore off sex for like the next five years after that!?" someone else added.

"Well wouldn't you too after some girls tried to pour candle wax on your penis while chanting to Satan!?"

"But the real question is, did he *actually* get to do it with the step-mom?"

Everyone was laughing, although some people were cringing. Once Nicholas composed himself enough, he choked out, "Alright, um, who's next? Katie? What have you got for us?"

"Oh, well, I hardly think it'll stand up against *that* story," Katie chuckled, "but I was going to tell the story of when Ms. Lewis nearly died."

"You'll have to be more specific than that!" Shannon scoffed. "I can think of *at least* twenty instances where she thought she was going to die."

"I was thinking the snapping story?"

"*Ooo*, I approve!" Nicholas declared, nodding. "Go on, Katie."

"Okay, well, let's see. I guess this happened my sophomore year," Katie began. "We were learning a new song and Ms. Lewis was parsing out the rhythm for us by snapping. We'd been at it for a while and she was really getting into it, as she does. But well, she ended up snapping so much she rubbed the skin off her finger in a spot and it started bleeding. Except she didn't notice at first, and blood started running down her arm.

"Well, we were doing our best to alert her to what was happening, but you know, we couldn't just stop singing because that would be breaking rule number seven, and we weren't about to do that! But finally, Ben Ashton had enough of it, and he just yelled out, 'Ms. Lewis, your arm!' So, she stops and looks at her hand, which by now her whole arm is covered in blood and it's dripping off onto the floor—"

"Nuh uh, it wasn't that bad," someone cut in.

"Was too! I was there!" another defended.

"Shush, let me tell the story!" Katie declared. "So, she's bleeding all over the place, right, and she starts screaming because she doesn't know what's going on. She turns to run out of the room to grab a paper towel or something and she just runs right smack into the door frame. We just see her smack the door and then just fall straight to the ground. So, we all run over there, because we don't know if she's okay, and she's just practically unconscious. Some of us are trying to get her up and others were using the intercom to call down to the office, because what else are you supposed to do when your teacher knocks herself unconscious in the middle of class!? But anyway, Ms. Lewis came to, and Mrs. Lucas showed up all freaked out, but it was fine. Ms. Lewis didn't even have a concussion and her finger healed quite quick."

The rest of the choir burst out in conversation—as they did after each story—throwing in their own extra little tidbits and scoffs of disbelief.

"She did *too* have a concussion, remember, we heard her talking to Ms. Taylor about it!"

"She wasn't hardly bleeding at all, I'm serious, guys! Joe was in class that year and he faints at the sight of really any blood, but he didn't pass out, so obviously there wasn't that much blood!"

"I thought she ran into the piano, not the door..."

"No, you're imagining that."

"No, I thought it was the piano too."

"Wait, I remember her running into the piano, but wasn't Ann in class then? Ann had definitely already graduated by the time Joe was in choir."

"Wait, did Ms. Lewis run into two different things and knock herself out *twice*!?"

"Oh my gosh, I think you're right!"

"Okay, okay, everyone, bring it in!" Nicholas shouted over everyone. "Let's make sure everyone gets a chance to share. Okay, Katie just went, so let's see... Luke! What have you got for us?"

"Well, you know, I thought I'd continue this tale of all the ridiculous things Ms. Lewis has done and tell the story of the time she nearly killed Dan."

"Oh, that one's a riot!" Shannon exclaimed.

"This was one nice spring day," Luke began his story. "We were all having a good time relaxing. It was the last day of school, and it was just a real nice day out. Ms. Lewis opened all the windows in the choir room, and actually, that was the same day Abraham ordered pizza in Spanish and had it delivered in through the window because Mrs. Gare wouldn't let him leave the classroom. But anyway, we were all just dancing around, because why not, when a grasshopper landed on Ms. Lewis' head.

"I don't think she noticed at first, but someone pointed it out to her. Except they didn't say grasshopper, they just said bug, and Ms. Lewis really doesn't like bugs, especially when they're on her. So, she starts screaming and jumping around in a frenzy. Well, the grasshopper got off pretty quick, because who'd want to hang around on top of a crazy lady? But it just so happened what while Ms. Lewis was flailing around, she knocked loose this cobweb that was hanging in the air, and this *huge* spider fell right on top of her!

"Lots of people screamed when they saw this, because a spider is a much bigger deal than a grasshopper. So now Ms. Lewis is jumping around in near hysterics, begging us to help get it off her, so that's when Dan pops up. Dan sees the spider sort of just hanging out on her shoulder, probably disoriented from all the flailing she's doing. So, Dan walks up and reaches out to swat the spider off, but at the last second, she jerks and elbows him right in the jaw.

"Dan falls to the ground in the middle of this massive commotion. Someone's shouting to smash the spider and the next thing we know, Chelsey hands Ms. Lewis her physics textbook to smash the spider with. And poor Dan, Ms. Lewis didn't even notice she'd knocked him out. But she turns, and the spider *jumps*! And she sees it and panics, just flinging the textbook, and that massive book falls right down, smashing into Dan's face!

"So, Dan goes down again, and he's seeing stars at this point, moaning and groaning. Now Ms. Lewis sees him, and she's profusely apologizing, trying to make sure he's okay. But then, the spider crawls back up on her arm, so then Ms. Lewis is up all over again, jumping around and screaming about the dang spider. We help Dan to his feet, and I guess Ms. Lewis finally knocks the spider off, because someone else stomped on it. Anyway, after that, we always keep the windows closed in the choir room to avoid unwanted buggy visitors."

"Such an amazing end to a school year," Shannon laughed. "Though poor Dan! And poor Ms. Lewis too. She's such a disaster."

I shook my head, laughing along with the rest of the choir. Finally, Nicholas shushed us again.

"Okay, okay, simmer down," Nicholas stated. He stood up on the log he had been sitting on as if he could no longer contain himself. "It's my turn and I want to tell the story of how Ms. Lewis met her best friend!"

"Who's that?" I questioned.

"You, you idiot," Shannon giggled, bumping against me.

"It was just this spring," Nicholas began, sounding as if he was telling a campfire ghost story. "Our teachers decided to take a much-needed vacation... a trip out of state. Little did our choir director know that on that vacation, she would meet someone who would forever change her life."

"And our lives," someone else added. "We like Natalie too, you know."

"*Ahh*, sheesh, guys, thanks," I muttered.

"It was on that fateful spring day that our Ms. Lewis and Natalie locked eyes waiting in line for a ride. From there, it was fate throwing them together! Two complete strangers, stuck in a land unfamiliar to them, being pulled together time and time again. Despite any efforts she might have put up, Ms. Lewis was helpless to the pink haired girl."

"You're making it sound like a love story," one of the twins declared, and I felt my cheeks heating up. I turned a little, suddenly very interested in the grass beneath my feet.

"You weren't even there," another person declared. "Let Natalie tell the story. She was there, after all."

"Fine," Nicholas huffed, turning to me, "but you better embellish it like your life depends on it. I'm not here for a boring story."

"I, um... well it's a bit complicated," I stated, slowly looking up. "I mean, yes, we ran into each other in line, but I met Ms. Kegan and Ms. Caballero before that. I didn't know they all knew each other at the time, but that's how it worked out. And I mean, we saw each other in line, but then we parted ways and—"

"You're a horrid storyteller... no offense!" someone shouted.

"Yeah, I said embellish it!" Nicholas huffed. "What were you doing when you crossed paths? What was your first impression of Ms. Lewis? We've never met any of her friends outside of Elk Creek, this is very exciting for us!"

"Fine, fine, I... well..." I paused, reflecting on when we'd first met. "I was, um, eavesdropping on their conversation," I began, and was followed with several *ooo's* and *ahh's*. "I don't really remember what all was said, just that it was a warm day and I think maybe Ms. Lewis was tired of her friends in that moment. There was something bothering them that they wouldn't drop."

"The affair."

I stopped and looked up fully, trying to see who had just said that. "I... you guys know?" I questioned.

"If you're talking about Ms. Taylor's and Ms. Caballero's affair, then yes, we know," Nicholas replied. "If it's a different one, then I don't know. Anyone heard of any other affairs lately?"

"Between Tom's mom and Rachel's dad."

"Hey! I told you not to talk about that!"

"No, no, I mean, yes, I'm talking about Ms. Taylor and Ms. Caballero," I clarified. "But listen, you didn't hear any of this from me."

"It's kind of old news, no offense to them," Nicholas answered. "We're glad they left their husbands. We were always rooting for them, you know?"

"Can we get back to Ms. Lewis?" Shannon asked impatiently. "I want to know Natalie's first impression of her!"

"Wait, wait!" Nicholas shouted, scrambling to pull out his phone. "This is just the most perfect opportunity to set up her dating profile. I'm sure Natalie can do a great job describing her!"

"Are you guys seriously trying to set her up?" I questioned.

"Of course!" Shannon declared. "You know how happy she can be. So, just think how much happier she would finally be with a man in her life!"

"Here, look at the pictures we picked out for her. See if you approve," Nicholas said, handing me his phone.

I took a minute to look at the pictures, the choir getting distracted by a story about Tom's mom and Rachel's dad. I heard them gossiping, and at one point, Nicholas even leapt up and ran over to someone, but I was focused on my own little world: a handful of pictures of Amelia on Nicholas' phone.

They were all beautiful, just stunning pictures. Amelia had a radiant beauty to her that was easily captured in candid photos. The first picture was her outside a city building, possibly in New York even. The next showed her in a café, a cup of coffee between her hands, smiling and laughing with her hair partially covering her face. There was a picture of her gracefully running alongside several of her choir students, though where they were running to, I'd never know. There was also a picture of her with both of Ellie 2.0's rescue dogs.

"So, what do you think?" Nicholas startled me, plopping down beside me once more.

"I think they're nice pictures," I replied, passing back his phone.

"I think we should list her hobbies," Nicholas stated, the twins gathering closer to him. "Singing definitely needs to be on there. Anything else?"

"Baking," I answered subconsciously. Then I laughed to myself. "And cheating at poker."

When I looked up, I saw dozens of eyes just staring at me. I looked between the choir students before I muttered out, "*Umm... what?*"

"We didn't know she liked to bake," Nicholas said, staring at me as well. "Or that she could play poker for that matter."

"Oh, well... yeah," I muttered, trying to play it off.

"I knew you'd be good help," Shannon declared. "You're her best friend, so you've got to know all the ins and outs about her, right?"

"Yeah, but Natalie's only known her for like a month," Nicholas huffed under his breath. "We've known her for *years*."

"I'm sorry, I didn't—" I muttered, upset at his hostility.

"You're fine. Don't worry about it," Shannon assured me.

"You need to make this more appealing... more romantic," one of the twins commented, pointing at Nicholas' phone.

"Natalie, give us some inspiration," the other twin added.

"Yeah, tell us your first impression of her," Shannon pushed.

"I, well, I was more invested in Ms. Taylor's conversation that I was Ms. Lewis, really," I stated. "Ms. Lewis was standing back in the shadows. I couldn't really see her. I guess there was an air of mystery to her, but then when we got onto the ride, she was very open and friendly. I... I mean... well this is beside the point, but it's a dating profile, so I just... well she carries herself well. Her body language sort of pulls you in. I could listen to her talk for hours, I—her voice is so sweet, and her singing, I don't know. She's sassy and sweet in all the right amounts and she's just perfect that way."

I looked up again, blinking, realizing I had once against lost myself thinking about Amelia. I was afraid I might have said something too revealing, so I glanced around cautiously, but everyone was preoccupied. Nicholas typed away furiously on his phone. After a minute, one of the twins asked Nicholas what he had down so far.

"Amelia Lewis," Nicholas declared, "twenty-seven, high school choir director, enjoys singing—obviously—as well as baking and poker—"

"Well, cheating at poker," someone commented.

"I can't say cheating at poker on a dating profile!" Nicholas whined. "Fine, I'll put card games. That sounds better anyway. Let's see, outgoing, always looking for funny guys, needs someone who's down for adventure. Looking for a fun time but open to the possibility of something more."

I thought about Nicholas' phrasing of 'funny guys' and how distressed Amelia had been over not liking Dale. She doesn't want funny guys, I wanted shout, she wants funny girls... like me... but of course I couldn't say that. I couldn't out Amelia and frankly, I didn't want them making her a dating profile for women any more than I wanted them making one for men.

"You okay?" Shannon questioned. "You look a little upset, Natalie."

"I... I don't know if you should be doing this," I spoke up. "Ms. Lewis is perfectly capable of finding herself a date, so maybe she has a reason for still being single and we should respect that."

"Well sure, she *thinks* she's fine," Nicholas said. "But just imagine how happy she'll be. She doesn't know it yet, but it'll be just the perfect next step in her life. Trust us, Natalie. We thought she was happy until we discovered just how much *happier* she could be. After spring break, she was like a totally different person, and all because she met you!"

"I can't stop you, clearly," I huffed, "but let it be known that I want no part in this whatsoever."

"That's what you said about this party, yet here you are," one of the twins pointed out.

"I mean it about this though," I said more forcefully.

"Let's um, table this for now," Shannon offered, pushing Nicholas's phone down as she sensed the growing tension. "Let's see, whose turns is it to tell a story? Oh... Natalie... I guess it's your turn."

"Oh, I don't have any stories," I answered. "I'm not in the choir anyway."

"But you know Ms. Lewis pretty dang well," someone stated.

"Yeah, tell us an outside of school story about Ms. Lewis!"

"Tell us about her cheating at poker!"

"No, I want to know about the baking!"

"I think a story about spring break would be pretty cool."

"Ms. Lewis already told us everything that happened over break."

I scoffed. "I find it pretty hard to believe that she told you *everything*. I mean, did she tell you that I can totally do a flip into a swimming pool?"

"She said you 'tried,'" someone air quoted. "And she was making fun of you, so you pulled her into the pool for revenge."

"Huh, okay, well, what about the competition we did?"

"Taking pictures with characters? Heard it."

"And the ice-cream afterwards?" I questioned. Everyone was silent, a few heads shook. "Okay, perfect then. I'll tell you about the time I learned Ms. Lewis has a ridiculous sweet tooth," I began.

"That's common knowledge," someone complained.

"*Shh*, let her talk!" Shannon declared.

"We had this competition, which you all heard about, and the prize for winning was that the losing team had to buy the winners ice-cream. I was with Ms. Lewis and Ms. Caballero on a team, and we were totally going to win, but our friends decided to abandon us so they wouldn't have to buy us ice-cream. But Ms. Lewis, for the past several hours, had been going on and on about how desperately she wanted some Rocky Road in a waffle cone. When she realized she wasn't going to get any, she just looked so sad. I couldn't stand it. So, I offered to buy her ice-cream.

"She picked out so much ice-cream with so many toppings. It was outrageously expensive, like almost fifty dollars, no joke. Never buy ice-cream at an amusement park if you can avoid it. The price is hardly worth it. But well... it was worth it to me in that moment because of how Amelia's eyes lit up. She was so excited, her eyes just shining as she looked over all the flavors. And when she realized I was buying her a Rocky Road waffle cone, without even asking, this look came over her like I was the greatest person on earth, and she hugged me. It was so abrupt, so sudden, and she let go just as quickly as she did, but I loved it." I swallowed hard. "I experienced my first ever Amelia hug in an ice-cream parlor... it was perfect."

I stopped talking, lost in my own thoughts as I relived our Florida trip. The rest of the choir broke off into their own conversations, but I was hardly listening. After a few moments, I looked up and my eyes met with Nicholas. Unlike his typical bubbly self, who would usually be shouting out his own comments, he was just staring at me with a confused and questioning look. It felt like he was seeing me in a different light, and he wasn't sure what to make of it yet. I was deathly afraid I had said too much.

"*Geez*, look at the time, guys," I stated suddenly, very loudly. "I said I'd have you all home by now, so I guess it's time to break up this party. You all have school tomorrow, as do I."

"But I haven't gotten to share my story yet!" Shannon protested.

"I haven't either!" a chorus followed.

"Ugh, well, I suppose maybe we can have... three more stories," I lamented.

"Fabulous! Because I've been dying to tell the story about the time we did a photoshoot in New York and nearly got arrested... twice!" Shannon exclaimed.

I leaned back slightly on the log, listening in on Shannon's story. There was a guy involved who seemed to have rather liked Ms. Lewis, and after the story someone complained, "You know, I wish things would have worked out with Mr. Chinipardaz. I still think they'd make a great couple."

"Yeah, I mean he went out of his way to get her sheet music for her collection. That's true love!"

"He bought her that piece by her favorite composer, right?"

"Yeah, a piece by Chopin," Nicholas declared. "I just think it's positively ridiculous that a man could get Ms. Lewis sheet music from her favorite composer for her personal collection, and she didn't just drop her panties on sight!"

I couldn't help myself. I scoffed, loudly, grumbling out, "Well that's because Chopin isn't her favorite composer."

"What?" Nicholas deadpanned, staring straight at me. "Chopin is definitely her favorite. She's said so multiple times."

"Yeah, sorry, Natalie, but you're wrong on that one."

"Now hang on," Shannon said. "Natalie knew about the baking and poker, so maybe we should hear her out."

"Who's her favorite composer then, if it's not Chopin?" one of the twins asked.

"Oh, god, it's that one French dude I'd never heard of before..." I muttered, trying to remember. "It's none of the common ones, like Beethoven or Mozart..."

"Well, no, neither of them are French," Nicholas stated, rolling his eyes.

"Wait, actually, I think I vaguely remember Ms. Lewis mentioning this once," Shannon stated, furrowing her brow in thought. "It was when we helped her organize the sheet music closet in the band room." She turned to Nicholas. "Remember? You found that older copy in the back corner and asked her about it?"

"Oh, wait, I *do*!" Nicholas suddenly exclaimed. "She got so wistful, and she said all dreamy, 'Oh, it's a piece by... it's a piece from... from... Rameau!'"

"Yes, Rameau, that's it!" I gasped.

"I'm starting to think I don't really know Ms. Lewis at all," Nicholas grumbled out dejectedly.

"No, that's not right!" I protested. "You guys all know Ms. Lewis so well! You know so many things about her that I could only hope to know."

"Sure, we *know* her, but there are clearly much more personal things about her life that she doesn't share with us."

"Well, I mean, isn't everyone like that though?" I said. "You share a certain amount of yourself with others when you get to know them, but there are a select few things you hold very close that you only share with really special people."

"*Hmm*, yeah, special people..." Nicholas said, his stare locked on me.

"Well, we should just be glad we've got Natalie on our side now so she can share all these details about Ms. Lewis with us!" Shannon mediated.

"Does she have a favorite piece by Rameau?" someone questioned.

"Oh, um... she's been hunting for an old copy of... Orphie?" I muttered, unconvinced with my memory.

"Do you mean *Orphée*?" Nicholas pronounced far better than I had.

"Yeah."

"We should get her that piece by Rameau," Shannon declared suddenly. "You know, as her end-of-the-year gift, like we get her every year, as thanks."

"Yeah, fuck Mr. Chinipardaz and his Chopin!" someone shouted aggressively. "We loved her before he even knew her! We can prove to her that we're better than him and that we can be trusted so she'll open up to us more!"

"Guys, I don't really think—" I tried to rectify the situation I had created, but it was quickly spiraling out of control.

"Yeah! Let's do it!"

Part 3.

Old Pasts & New Beginnings

16.

Parents Know Best, But They're Projecting

I hadn't been on a bus since high school, which I was grateful for, as my experiences with buses were less than fun. My high school had those typical all-American yellow buses, all worn down, not at all comfortable, and a little gross. Elk Creek, however, being a private school, didn't have to share buses with the city's school system and instead rented two huge charter buses for the New York trip. They would make the eleven-hour trip much more bearable, especially since we'd be on the bus from three PM until two AM that Friday.

My professors were all lenient with the school I'd be missing Monday and Tuesday. They were used to seniors missing class for various reasons—job interviews, school interviews, taking standardized entrance exams, and even just senioritis. After class Friday, I arrived at Elk Creek pulling a small carryon sized suitcase, and I met the buses in the parking lot. I found Nicholas at the head of the commotion, directing everyone.

I walked up to Nicholas, careful to control my laughter. "You in charge of this operation?" I asked, but a small giggle escaped.

"This is no times for jokes, Natalie!" Nicholas scolded. "We're singing for Nationals in—" he glanced down at his watch— "sixty-seven hours, forty-two minutes, and ten, nine, eight seconds... well you get the picture. We don't have time for jokes."

"Alright, alright," I answered. "Where do I put my bag?"

"*Ohmygosh*," Nicholas spat out in an exasperated huff. "Suitcases under the bus, backpacks and personal items in your seat. Haven't you been listening?"

"I just got here!" I defended myself. "And thanks."

Before I could stumble off, Nicholas handed me a packet of the trip's itinerary. Then he shoved me off and I went in search of Amelia. Last night had made me oddly longing towards her, living through memories of her and her adorable goofiness when she wasn't actually there beside me. I found her around the bus, loading suitcases with the bus driver, and I stopped to help.

The commotion continued around me. I always heard Nicholas shouting commands. Students were running every which way, chaperons were reviewing the itinerary, parents were hugging their kids goodbye. But then I heard a very loud, very aggressive shout that I couldn't ignore.

"Nicholas Alexander Su, what the hell are you doing!?"

I looked around the bus curiously and saw a man, dressed in a full suit, sprinting across the parking lot. The man screamed again for Nicholas, demanding the boy come to him. When Nicholas heard this, he turned to bolt, but Amelia dove out from around the bus and grabbed him.

"Nicholas!" Amelia snapped, grasping the boy firmly by the upper arms. "Please tell me you didn't forge your father's signature on the permission slip."

"He wasn't going to let me go!" Nicholas wailed, nearly in tears.

By this point, Nicholas' father reached his son and grabbed him, flat out jerking Nicholas away from Amelia. He shouted in her face, "Keep your hands off my son! How dare you try and steal him away to New York!"

At this point, a small crowd of students had gathered to watch the commotion. "Hey, everyone, on the bus!" I commanded, sending them off. Once the crowd was ushered away, I turned back and stood up as straight as I could, mustering courage I didn't quite feel.

"I'm not stealing your son," Amelia said calmly. I looked at Nicholas—whose father had a death grip on his arm—tears now streaming down his face. "I was under the impression he had permission to come on this trip," Amelia continued. "Someone signed the permission slip. Perhaps if it wasn't you, it was your wife who gave him permission."

"Don't you dare pin my wife against me!" Mr. Su continued to yell. "We are in agreement that Nicholas has far more important things to be focusing on this weekend instead of chasing silly dreams. He does not have permission to leave with you, and trust me, the school board will be hearing of this incident. Nicholas, come," his father snapped, jerking Nicholas to the side as he turned to leave.

"Ms. Lewis, please!" Nicholas wailed, fighting against his father's pull.

"I can't take you against your father's wishes," Amelia sadly replied.

"But you guys need me!" Nicholas cried. "I have a solo and—and—it's tradition!"

I boldly stepped forward, blocking Mr. Su's path. "Hey, let's just take a deep breath," I stated. The man just ignored me, moving to step around me, but I stepped forward and blocked his path again. "Look, your son has been working very hard and training for this competition for a long time. It would be a real shame if he didn't get to go."

"Who are you?" Mr. Su snapped at me. "A student here? I thought Elk Creek had higher dress code standards than to let girls run around with pink hair. Singing is disgraceful. Your parents ought to be ashamed of you too, pouring so much energy into a meaningless hobby. We have high expectations for Nicholas, none of which include wasting time singing."

"Listen, Nicholas happens to be a friend of mind. I care about him a lot. Can't you see that you're causing him distress? A father should put his son's happiness above all else," I retorted, choosing to ignore his wrong assumptions about me.

"What's your name? I'll have you suspended for trying to coerce Ms. Lewis into kidnapping my child!"

"Natalie, stop," Amelia stated, practically pleading.

"No," I declared, standing taller. "I refuse to be bossed around by a rich old man who thinks he owns the world. I don't care if you don't think singing is an acceptable path for your son to pursue. I don't care if you think being a doctor or a lawyer are the only acceptable careers worthy of your son. The fact is, singing in this choir makes Nicholas happy, and there are far worse passions he could have. I refuse to just stand here and let you crush Nicholas' dreams because he's an ambitious, hardworking, amazing boy, and he deserves better than that. Any parent should be so proud of him for everything he's achieved and will achieve, including his singing. I know I sure am proud of him."

"How dare you question my motives as a parent!? No son of mine will be a singer. I won't have our family name being tarnished by some faggot sport!"

Anger flared within me. It was fueled by my love for Nicholas, by my desire to protect him at all costs. It was fueled by the pain I had experienced in my own coming out. It was fueled by the fear Karmen had, afraid of loving another woman. All of my passionate anger was fueled by love... just wanting to love freely... wanting to love the person you cared most about, to love those that mattered most, to do what you loved and were passionate about.

I grabbed Nicholas' free arm and, with all my might, pulled the boy away from his father, pushing the kid behind my back, separating him from his dad. "No one will hurt my friends in my presence," I growled. "Not even their own father."

"Natalie!" Amelia shouted. She ran to my side and tried to pull me out of the middle, but I wouldn't budge. "Natalie, move! You can't stand between a parent and their child!"

"He's not a child. He's our friend," I corrected. "And this man is no parent, he's an abusive monster."

"Is this how you handle your students? You aren't fit to teach!" Mr. Su declared, pointing at Amelia. "You shouldn't be allowed to fill kids' minds with such filth. Elk Creek is meant to be an academically prestigious school. Math and science should always come before recreational singing, yet you're having these kids miss school? You should be ashamed of yourself for ruining their chances of success."

"Listen up, *Jack*," I stated, mimicking Mr. Su and pointing an aggressive finger right back at him. "Yes, math and science are important subjects, but so are history, literature, writing, *and* the fine arts. Singing is important to these students because it gives them happiness. Life is meaningless without happiness. Do you know why Nicholas was willing to go behind your back and sneak away on this trip? Huh? Do you?" I paused but didn't give Mr. Su enough time to reply. "Nicholas was willing to go behind your back, willing to face your wrath when you found out, because this choir is the only happiness he's got. I mean, he sure isn't experiencing love and happiness at home with *you*, that's for sure!"

"Natalie, *please* stop," Amelia begged, still pulling at my arm. Nicholas was still behind me, clutching my shirt, trembling. I didn't budge though. I stood my ground, staring down Mr. Su.

Finally, Mr. Su cleared this throat. "Nicholas?" he questioned. I felt Nicholas squeeze tighter against me. "We will discuss this topic further at home... when you return from New York."

"What?" Nicholas asked meekly, peeking out from around me. I turned to Amelia, just as shocked.

"I think this is a foolish path to pursue," Mr. Su continued, "but if this trip really means that much to you... then go."

Nicholas wiped away his tears and stood at attention before his father. "Thank you, father," he stated. Mr. Su nodded slowly, as if contemplating saying more, but he just turned and walked back out to his car. None of us moved until he pulled out of the school lot.

Suddenly, I was engulfed in a hug from Nicholas. He sniffled against me, squeezing me as tight as he could. "Thank you," he mumbled. "Thank you for standing up for me like that. You and Ms. Lewis... you're the only people who have ever stood up for me."

I waited until Nicholas pulled back, looking up at me with glistening eyes. "Hey, it's what friends do, right?" I answered, ruffling his hair the same way Eleanor always ruffled mine.

"Hey, Nicholas?" Amelia asked softly. "Get on the bus and finalize our headcount, then check in with Shannon, alright?" Nicholas nodded, wiping at his eyes once more before bounding off.

I turned to Amelia and before she could say anything, I barked out, "I'm sorry."

"As you should be," she answered. "You're a foolish idiot."

"I know, I know. You told me several times to stop, and I should have. It wasn't my place, and I could have made things way worse. But I just... I'm so sick of parents forcing their kids to do things because it's what the parents want. I'm sick of adults thinking they know what's best for everyone when it's none of their damn business. I'm sick of people not being able to love who they want and not being able to pursue a passion they love. Everyone's got opinions about everyone's business and it's so annoying."

Amelia let out a long sigh. "Nicholas' home life reminds me of my life growing up. His parents don't approve of his passion for singing and actively try to prevent him from succeeding at it. You didn't have to stand up for him like that though. Nicholas would have understood. He knows his parents are peculiar and that he's still a minor under their control."

"But if I wasn't going to stand up for him, who would have?" I questioned. "Why should I stay quiet when I could make a difference? I... I'd happily put any parent in their place for their child's well-being. I'm not joking. I'll tell your parents off too if they give you trouble."

"Okay, calm down tiger," Amelia stated. "But... thank you. On Nicholas' behalf, on the choir's behalf, and also on my behalf. It means a lot knowing you're so willing to stand up for us... for me."

"That's just what friends are for. No need to thank me."

"Alright, well, we need to get going. We're on bus number one with Nicholas, in case you missed the seating chart in the itinerary."

"Sure you don't want me on bus two with Shannon? So there's an Elk Creek teacher on both buses?" I waggled my eyebrows when I said this, since I still didn't technically consider myself to be an Elk Creek teacher, even though technically, I supposed I was.

"*Hmm*, nope," Amelia answered, popping the 'p' of 'nope.' She tugged me towards the bus we were riding on, stopping at the front steps to push me forward. "I need to make sure Shannon's okay, but I'll be right back and then we can roll out."

"Alright," I replied, nodding, stepping onto the bus.

On the bus, the students were all spread out, so each person had an entire row to themselves. Nicholas popped his head up from the second row on the left. "Sit across from me?" he questioned, pointing to an empty row.

"Sure," I answered, sliding into my seat.

"Nicholas!" someone called from a few rows back. "Remember to change the location settings to New York and start getting matches on the drive!"

"Oh, right," Nicholas declared, pulling out his phone.

"What are you up to?" I asked.

"Just the dating app," Nicholas replied. "We figured we might as well try to hook Ms. Lewis up with a New York hottie."

"Why though? She won't be able to have any sort of meaningful relationship since we're leaving in five days. What's the most she'd get out of it? A one-night stand?"

"Sure." Nicholas shrugged. "And I mean, I don't know. She's from New York. Maybe she'll fall in love and move back to the city. We'd hate to see her go, but she does seem to love New York."

Amelia got on the bus then and Nicholas abruptly shushed me. He stood, pointing to the empty row ahead of me. "You can sit up here, Ms. Lewis," he stated, shielding his phone away from her. I sat back away from Nicholas, leaning against the wall of the bus, and propped my feet up on the seat beside me.

Amelia spoke to the bus driver, telling him we were ready to leave, then she glanced over at me. She walked past the seat Nicholas designated for her and right up to me, then she reached down and picked up with legs without a word. She swung my legs out and dumped them onto the floor, sitting down in the seat she cleared for herself.

"Hey, I was relaxing there?" I questioned with fake annoyance. "How am I supposed to lie down and sleep if you're sitting next to me?"

"I can offer you something better," Amelia answered, "good company."

"Good company doesn't get me my beauty rest," I replied.

"Good company and a shoulder to lean on?" Amelia offered.

I narrowed my eyes suspiciously. "Your shoulder's boney. Make it your lap and I guess I'll let you stay."

"Sure, I don't mind," Amelia answered. "That is, assuming you fall asleep before me, otherwise I'm staking claim to *your* lap."

I grinned at Amelia's teasing and gave her a wink. As the bus started to roll forward, I caught a glimpse of Nicholas out of the corner of my eye. He was staring at us intensely, once again with a look of confused contemplation, just as he had been looking at me while we sat around the campfire. I tried to not dwell on it. He was sort of a weird kid anyway.

I woke to the sound of muffled whispering, but it wasn't enough to make me fully open my eyes. I remained where I was, just listening. I heard the sound of a camera shutter, presumably from a phone that wasn't silenced. Immediately, this was followed with the harsh whispering of, "Put your phone on silent! You're going to wake them!"

I finally opened my eyes, trying to figure out what was going on. I was leaning against the wall of the bus, facing the row where Nicholas was. He was on his knees, facing one of the twins that was sitting behind him, shoving his phone down. Did they just... take a picture of me? Why?

I dropped my eyes from the boys, noticing a weight pressing down against my center. There, I found Amelia curled up against me. We started out just dozing, leaning against each other's shoulders, but at some point, I must have turned, and Amelia curled up against me, her head resting on my collar bone. I wasn't complaining, but I could see how our position was photogenic.

Suddenly, someone in the back of the bus sung out, "It's New York!"

"We've been in New York for a while now," someone else commented.

"No, not the state, the *city*!"

I turned slightly, careful to not disrupt Amelia, and glanced out the window at the brilliantly lit city. Grinning, I turned back and gently shook Amelia. She let out a whimper and tried to shield her face from me, but I shook her again.

"We're here," I whispered to her.

Amelia groaned, pulling herself up into a sitting position, stretching and yawning. "Oh god," she groaned. "I have the worst kink in my neck."

"That's what happens when you sleep on a bus," I commented.

From there it didn't take long to reach our hotel. I was amazed by the luxury and quality of the five-star establishment. I floated between Nicholas and Amelia, helping everyone get their bags and their room assignments while chaperons helped everyone get upstairs. I waited to make sure we didn't lose any students, and then Amelia and I headed up to our room, eager to sleep in a real bed.

When Amelia opened the door to our room, I froze in the entry. I wasn't expecting a suite, especially not a luxury suite, king-sized bed and all, alone with Amelia. I grabbed my suitcase and moved it from where the bellhop had left it. Amelia was already on the other side of the room, setting up her things. I stopped and smirked at her.

"I bet you five dollars that you take up the entire bed," I stated, patting the bedspread.

"What are you talking about?" Amelia questioned, turning to face me. "It's a king-sized bed. You could probably fit four people in that bed. We could be sleeping comfortable, with plenty of space, and there'd still be three feet between us."

"Yes, we *could*," I answered, "but you're totally going to seek out heat in your sleep and end up leaving me with six inches of bed space. If you don't think it'll happen, the bet is five dollars."

Amelia looked between me and the bed. "That's not a bet I'm willing to make," she replied, quite to my surprise.

"Are you kidding? I can't believe you'd accept defeat so easily!"

"I'm not admitting defeat, it's just that well... I was actually going to ask if you, um, if you wanted to—well if you wanted—" Amelia stumbled over her words, her face growing redder with each passing syllable.

"Ask if I wanted to what?"

"If you wanted to cuddle," she muttered out, dipping her head as if she were embarrassed. "It's just, well it was nice, in my apartment." She looked up slowly, catching my eyes. "If you want to, though, I mean, we don't have to."

I grinned, leaping onto the bed before diving onto Amelia, using the bed as a springboard. Once I grabbed her, I pulled her into a tight hug.

Amelia stumbled back a few steps to account for my impact. "Of course I want to cuddle," I stated, nuzzling against her. "You don't have to ask me twice."

By two o'clock the following afternoon, I was already exhausted. Breakfast barely seemed to fuel me and after that, Amelia dragged the clan all over New York City. I had a ton of fun, to be honest. We hit the big tourist locations within walking distance, but Amelia also knew a lot of really spectacular little local places. Amelia made it even nicer because I could tell she was enjoying sharing this part of her with all of us. Her energy was never ending. Me, on the other hand... I was running low.

After lunch at a cute local place, we went back to the hotel. The hotel had a large dining hall with a stage, perfect for a rehearsal spot. I hung around to support the students, even though I was in desperate need of a nap. I applauded when I felt the time was right and shouted words of encouragement whenever I could.

After two hours of practice, Amelia dismissed Nicholas so he could rest his voice after properly rehearsing his solo and duet. Amelia stood front and center in the auditorium, directing, and Nicholas came back to sit beside me. He pulled out his phone and started messing around while I watched Amelia's back with interest.

Nicholas tapped on my shoulder and when I turned to him, he held out his phone. There was a picture of a guy on it, one who I would describe as a 'teddy bear' type... or maybe a 'hipster lumberjack.'

"What do you think?" Nicholas asked me.

"About what?"

"The guy."

"Oh, um, he's good looking, I guess."

"He's not like Mr. Chinipardaz, quite the opposite, actually, so I thought he might be her type," Nicholas explained, pulling back his phone. "Maybe you could ask her what her type is, just in case. Georgie and I have been taking turn messaging guys for her, but guys on dating apps kind of suck. I think I might start just introducing her to good looking guys we bump into."

"I told you I don't want any part in this."

"It's really not a big deal, you know, getting a guy to ask her out. Or even going to dinner with a nice gentleman."

I tried to ignore Nicholas. I didn't think Amelia would agree to go out with a guy just for a quick lay, since she wasn't into men. But there was a little voice of doubt in the back of my mind. It kept popping up, saying things like, *'A fuck is a fuck, penis or not,'* or, *'She'll go just to humor the kids.'* And heck, she hadn't really dated in the past ten years, maybe she was just desperate to get laid, I didn't know! It wasn't like we ever talked about sex, certainly not casually.

"Are you excited for tonight?" Nicholas questioned, not looking up from his phone.

"What's happening tonight?"

"Oh my god," Nicholas groaned. "Didn't you read the itinerary?"

"I mean, I saw what time breakfast was. Otherwise, I've just been going along with the flow. I haven't missed anything yet."

"We're seeing a musical on Broadway."

I turned and looked at Nicholas skeptically. "Wait, really?"

"Yeah, it's part of our educational experience. We sing and act all the time, might as well go and observe the pros, you know?"

"Musicals are... fun. I haven't been to many, but I never *didn't* enjoy them."

"Well, you better get excited, because we're seeing one of Ms. Lewis' favorites, and she's going to be bouncing off the walls."

"*Hmm*, I can't wait."

I stood in front of the mirror hanging beside the dresser, hooking a necklace on, and fluffing my hair a bit. Amelia was in the bathroom getting ready herself, the bathroom door left open. I could hear her humming, presumably a tune from the musical we were about to see. The musical was a formal event, so we were expected to dress nicely. I brought some good clothing options, but according to the twins—who drilled me extensively on my wardrobe—nothing I owned was quite 'evening' enough. Shannon graciously lent me her prom dress from last year, which was a nude ballgown. It fit me pretty well, but most importantly it didn't clash with my hair, which the twins said was *very* important.

I fished my eyeliner out to go back over my makeup, just to refresh. I leaned forward, getting closer to the mirror so I could see what I was doing.

From the bathroom, Amelia stated, "You know, I *love* musicals."

At the sultry sound of her saying the word 'love,' I jumped, stabbing myself in the eye. I yelped and cursed under my breath, holding my eye in pain.

"Are you okay?" Amelia asked from the bathroom. When I looked up, I found she was leaning out of the bathroom, clearly concerned. I looked back to mirror, my eye tearing up, and found my makeup was smudged. I frowned, grabbing a tissue to fix it.

"Yeah, I'm fine, just stabbed myself in the eye," I answered. The formalness of the event was making me jittery. "Musicals are um, pretty great," I stated.

"I like singing and performances in general," Amelia continued, dipping back into the bathroom. "But together, it's a whole new level. There's the singing, that perfect, relentless pitch, and the wonderful acting with splendid characters that pull at your heart strings... all the drama. You know I'm a slut for good drama."

I swallowed tickly. "So you've said."

"Oh, and the dancing. There's just something about a big dance number where everyone moves perfectly. It just gets my heart *pounding*! It sends chills down my spine!"

I felt my nerves light up. Why did everything suddenly feel and sound so sexual? Was it because I'd been wondering about Amelia's sex life all afternoon? Or was there just a sexiness to stage performance that Amelia loved so utterly, it was being mimicked in her tone?

Amelia tossed her makeup bag onto the dresser next to me, startling me. I jumped slightly, looking over at her. My breath caught in my throat as I took in her appearance. She was wearing a deep red ballgown, her lips an equally deep red, and I felt myself blushing as I began to imagine lipstick marks ending up all over my neck.

I cleared my throat. "Is it, um, is it time to get going?" I questioned, dragging my eyes away from Amelia.

"Yep, let's go gather the crew!"

We arrived early, and to add to the educational aspect of the trip, got a history tour of the theater beforehand. We were led to our seats after that, the students squealing and taking all sorts of pictures with the stage in the background. I saw Amelia take a spin for a student, her dress flowing our gracefully. This was her, in her natural element, and she was beautiful in every way possible.

"Please, dear god, I can't sit by her... not if she's going to be like this the entire time," I whimpered silently. I couldn't handle it. I was getting giddy just standing there watching her, thinking about her. I suddenly felt extremely hot, and I fanned myself with a program, taking slow and deliberate deep breaths.

Eventually the students filed into their seats, and along with the chaperons, they took up a good chunk of a section. I saw Amelia beckoning for me, so I slowly went over to her, only for her to grasp my hand, the biggest smile on her face. She pulled me into a row behind the rest of the choir, just the two of us, and I stumbled over my feet, but Amelia held tight until I regained my balance.

"It's um, just the two of us back here?" I questioned meekly as Amelia sat down.

"Yep. I was up a row before, but when I added another ticket, I didn't want you to have to sit back here by yourself, so I moved my seat."

"Oh, um, cool."

There wasn't much to do before the show started. Some of the students went off in search of a bathroom or to buy merch. Amelia messed around on her phone beside me, so I pulled out my own phone to occupy myself. Periodically, I'd glance towards her. Eventually, she started going through the playbill and bored of my phone myself, I started looking around the theater.

The ceilings were high and adorned with gold. There were countless carved details all over; I could look around for hours and still miss things. I dropped my head down and made awkward direct eye contact with a guy several rows ahead of us. I glanced away and pulled out my phone again.

Before long, I was back to looking around the theater. I accidentally made eye contact with the same guy again. He was turned around in his seat staring back at me. I frowned, giving him a look of question, trying to ask if he needed something. He was younger, though probably closer to Amelia's age than mine, and well kept. He had a dark demeanor about him, complimented with his dark hair and dark suit. After a moment, the man glanced away, and I went back to my phone.

I didn't think much of this, except that same exchange happened two more times in the span of fifteen minutes. I would get bored of looking at my phone, look up, and that man would just be staring at me again. I turned in my seat, looking behind me to see if anything weird was going on back there, but nothing. I looked back at the man, then behind me again, and back once more.

"What are you doing?" Amelia questioned, noticing my movement.

I looked to Amelia, then turned back to the man once more and it finally hit me. He wasn't looking at me or something behind me, he was staring at Amelia!

"Do you know that guy?" I asked. "Down there, three rows and like... six columns over."

"What guy?" Amelia questioned, scanning the crowd.

"He's been staring at you. He'll turn around again, I'm sure, just—there!" I exclaimed, pointing when the man turned around again. This time he saw me pointing and caught and held Amelia's gaze. He raised one eyebrow with a smirk and then winked.

Amelia didn't answer me, so I looked back at her and saw she was frowning, her brows furrowed down.

"Are you okay?" I questioned.

"Yeah, um, he just—" Amelia muttered, but then the man stood up and she cut off abruptly. He looked like he was heading towards us. I looked back to Amelia to question further, but she suddenly jumped up too. "I... need to run to the restroom," she barked out, immediately turning and straight *running* out of the theater.

I was too confused to move. I was just starting to come back to my senses, planning on following after Amelia to make sure she was okay, when the man was suddenly standing in the row behind me, towering over me. I gulped. He was much more intimidating up close.

"*Umm...* hi," I muttered, turning in my seat to better position myself.

"Do correct me if I'm wrong, but please, is there a Ms. Amelia Lewis sitting here beside you?" the man asked, no introduction, no greeting.

"Sorry, come again?" I questioned, choosing to play dumb.

"Amelia Lewis."

"No, uh, um, nope, never heard that name before. I'm here with my friend, if that's the woman you're referring to. Her name is, um, Anna," I stated, cringing at how bad my lying was.

It was clear the man didn't believe me, but he gave in, apparently not in the mood to argue with a stranger. "*Ahh,* my apologies then," he stated, turning to leave.

"But, um, wait!" I gasped. "Maybe my friend *does* know you. What's your name? I can ask her when she returns."

"Wolfgang." Then he left without further elaboration. I expected him to go back to his seat, but I realized he was instead headed to the back of the theater in the direction Amelia went.

I didn't know what was happening, but Amelia's reaction made me uncomfortable. I shot her a text that Wolfgang was heading her way—was that a first name? A last name?—and then I bolted for the back of the theater myself.

I didn't know where I was going. I dodged between people, trying not to trip over the dress I was wearing. I asked an usher where the bathroom was and they pointed, so I headed off in that direction. Before I got there, however, I rounded the corner and saw both Amelia and Wolfgang standing off to the side of the hall. I slowed, noticing that Wolfgang had a tight grip on Amelia's arm, holding her uncomfortably close to him. She wasn't struggling against him though. They were talking. I stood back behind a marble pillar, close enough to hear them over the light murmur of conversation in the hall, close enough to intervene if I needed, but not close enough that they'd know I was there.

"How horrid of you to come back into town and not let me know," Wolfgang stated, his voice deep and rough, though I supposed charming.

"I didn't come for personal reasons; I came for work," Amelia answered. "Besides, it's not like I owe you an update every week. You aren't in my life anymore, in case you forgot."

"She's got bite now," Wolfgang stated, smirking. "You're looking pretty well off for working a low-class job. Unless you finally came to your senses and went to work for your father."

"My job is far more important than you could ever hope yours is."

"What, teaching? Singing recreationally?" Wolfgang scoffed. "Grow up, Amelia. In case you didn't notice, you're not the one about to be on stage. You're an audience member. Pretty big failure for someone so set on stardom."

"Teaching wasn't a last resort. I chose it, willingly and happily, because I'm passionate about it. It's certainly more wholesome than what you do... paying politicians under the table to suit yourself, tax evasion, the works."

Wolfgang laughed. It was deep and eerie and made me immediately uncomfortable. "Oh, Amelia, darling, you've turned out just fine despite a couple bumps in the road along the way," he continued. "I always did admire the gall you had to go against your father's wishes. It's nice to see you've developed such a strong backbone. I could certainly use a girl like you on my arm at galas."

Amelia snorted, finally taking a step back. She tried to pull away from Wolfgang, but he held her arm tight and wouldn't let her go. "You're an idiot," she huffed. "Let go of me. This conversation's over."

"Oh, but it's only just beginning. We have so much to catch up on."

"I left this life behind when I chose to pursue singing. You're part of this life I abandoned. I want nothing to do with this, or you. So now, if you'll excuse me..." She made to jerk away again, but Wolfgang still wouldn't let her. I was starting to see the panic rise in her eyes. Quickly, I moved to intervene.

"You're gorgeous, Amelia. I find you irresistible still," Wolfgang murmured. "Do you have some time later, maybe tomorrow? We can go back to my penthouse and—"

"Jolly seeing you again!" I stated, harshly slapping my hand down on Wolfgang's arm. I left it there, squeezing his arm as hard as I could, hoping it was threatening. "Amelia, thank goodness I stumbled into you! The show's about the start, so we better get back to our seats!"

"Oh yes, we can't miss the opening!" Amelia stated, nodding. She moved back a step again and I harshly shoved against Wolfgang's arm, doing my best to stand tall and threatening.

"What are you? Her little guard dog?" Wolfgang huffed, begrudgingly releasing Amelia. "Pathetic."

"Come on," I said to Amelia, and I pushed into her, pulling her off in the direction of our seats.

We fell back into our seats just as the lights dimmed and a spotlight shone on stage. I looked to Amelia with concern, but she wouldn't look at me, her attention on the stage. I let out a sigh and relaxed back into my seat. As long as she was beside me, I knew Wolfgang wasn't bothering her, and that was enough for the time being.

I found myself mesmerized by the show. I forgot how entertaining musicals were, though I'd never consider myself a huge theater fanatic. Still, I thought the performance was fantastic, breathtaking at times even.

Before I even registered that the curtain was closing for intermission, Amelia grabbed me, ducking her head down and burying her face against my shoulder.

"Are you okay?" I questioned. The lights came back on in the theater and a mob of people flooded forth from their seats.

"I just... well if Wolfgang doesn't see me, maybe he won't come over and—"

I nodded, having almost entirely forgotten about the man through the course of the show. I pulled out my playbill and held it open in front of us, shielding Amelia from Wolfgang's line of sight as nonchalantly as possible.

"So, you clearly know him," I said.

"Yes."

"Care to elaborate?"

"We... dated... I guess. In the past," Amelia mumbled.

"*Ahh,* an ex. I'm guessing it didn't end so well."

"I don't want to talk about it," Amelia answered curtly. I just nodded, respecting her boundaries.

After a bit, a warning for guests to return to their seats was broadcasted with a flicker of the lights. Amelia shifted, turning her head to look at me while keeping it rested against my shoulder. I glanced down at her, meeting her kind brown eyes.

"Thank you," she said.

"For what?"

"For covering me... for not pushing things... for coming to find me when he went after me."

"Of course. You don't have to thank me for that."

"No, really, thank you. You don't understand how much it means to me," she insisted.

"If you say so."

When the lights dimmed and the show resumed, Amelia returned to sitting normally. However, as the next act began, I felt Amelia reach over and tightly grasp my hand. I looked to her in question, and she met my gaze. She shot me the kindest grin in the whole world. I felt my insides melt at the sight. Then Amelia turned her attention back to the show and I did too, our hands still tightly clasped.

Once again, I found myself engrossed in the show. I rooted for the characters, heavily invested in the plot. I felt as though I was experiencing a side to musical theater that I had never experienced before: the artistic side of the performance. I watched the actors' movements like an intricate dance, the inflections of their voices like an orchestra. There was a beauty in the performance... the art.

Suddenly, my attention on the stage was broken. I glanced towards Amelia. She still held my hand, squeezing it harder. She had shifted in her seat so that she was now perched on the edge, leaning forward as if trying to get closer to the show. I saw her mouthing the lines of the actors, word for word. Another song began, and she squeezed my hand tighter. To the beat of the song, she would rock forward, her lips still mouthing the words, but now, quiet, vocal, gasps and moans escaped her lips. She didn't hardly blink, as if in a trance, just staring at the stage. Her attention was locked, her body reacting in ways she probably didn't even realize.

My heart was pounding, thudding so loudly in my chest and ears that it almost drowned out the music. My core felt like it was on fire, burning me alive, and all I could think about was how to put out the burn. Air was but a distant thought. Getting closer to Amelia was at the forefront of my mind. I felt chills run up my spine when Amelia rolled her hips forward again, and I couldn't breathe.

A loud crash of a beat in the song startled me. I jumped, then froze, suddenly aware of how badly I couldn't breathe, how desperately I needed to get out of there. With no regard for anything around me, I shot straight up, jerking my hand free from Amelia. In a panic, I clambered over her and the other guests in our row before escaping to the aisle. Once free of the seats, I ran straight to the back of the theater, breaking free into the deserted lobby. I heaved air back into my lungs, spun, and then bolted to the nearest bathroom.

I slammed open the women's restroom door, startling a poor woman who was inside. I apologized and she ducked out as quickly as she could. Alone in the bathroom, I stood at the sinks, staring at my reflection in the mirror, watching my chest heave. I tried with all my might to calm down, but the back of the eyelids flashed with vivid images of the way Amelia's body moved, and I groaned in frustration. I wanted to splash cold water on my face, but it would ruin my makeup and I didn't need nosey little Nicholas asking me what was wrong. Instead, I just rested my head in my hands, leaning against the cool marble of the sinks, and focused on my slowly steadying heartbeat.

Next thing I knew, there was commotion all around me. I looked up at the flood of women entering the bathroom and realized sheepishly that the musical must be over—that dramatic musical piece must have been the finale. I didn't feel entirely put together, but I knew the choir would be leaving soon and I needed to get back to them. With a final deep breath, I stood up straight and exited the bathroom, heading back towards our seats.

I spotted Amelia over the flood of people leaving the theater—almost as if my eyes were instinctively drawn to her. I was about to head over to her when I noticed Shannon, the twins, and Nicholas, who were, to my horrid disgust, talking with Wolfgang.

"She's your teacher, you say?" I heard Wolfgang question as I stormed up.

"Yes," Nicholas answered. "She's very lovely."

"So I've gathered from all that you've told me," Wolfgang stated, smirking. "She's quite the beautiful and lovely young woman."

"Well, it's just marvelous that you mentioned it," Shannon commented.

"Yes, because actually, we think she might rather like you," Nicholas continued, looking Wolfgang up and down. "I think you're just her type…"

"Oh, really, now?" Wolfgang chuckled.

"She's free tomorrow at six for dinner," Nicholas cut straight to the point.

"That sounds lovely. Shall I speak with her to discuss the details of this date?"

"What are you doing?" I snapped hostility, finally reaching them.

"We're getting Ms. Lewis a date, obviously," Nicholas answered, shrugging and rolling his eyes.

"No need," Shannon commented to Wolfgang, ignoring me. "We're staying in a hotel off Times Square. You two can have dinner at the restaurant there. It's called—"

"Wait, no, don't tell him that!" I exclaimed, grabbing for Shannon.

Wolfgang took a step back as Shannon stumbled away from me. He looked at me, a judgmental look plastered on his face. "Why, the guard dog returns," he stated lowly.

"Look, don't' listen to them. They're just being, um, silly kids!" I barked out. "You know how kids can be. So, um, anyway, this date situation? Not happening."

"Um, yes it is!" Nicholas glowered.

"I hardly think this matter is your choice to make," Wolfgang stated. "It should be up to the lady if she wishes to attend a date with me, and I can be *quite* persuasive."

"She doesn't, trust me," I growled.

"Don't listen to her!" Nicholas exclaimed, jumping in front of me. "She's just got Ms. Lewis' best interest in mind. We all do! But you're entirely right. Ms. Lewis can decide if she wants to stay and have dinner with you or not."

"Just be here at six tomorrow evening," Shannon commented, putting a piece of paper into Wolfgang's hand. "I assure you, Ms. Lewis will be there. Charm her, and we're sure she'll stay."

I shoved Nicholas' head down, so he was out of the way. "Don't show your face anywhere near her tomorrow!" I huffed defensively.

The twins stepped in then, blocking me. "Just an empty threat!" one of them offered.

"I'll keep it in mind," Wolfgang stated with a smirk. "Now, if you'll excuse me." Then he turned and left the theater.

Before I could turn and yell at the stupid kids, Nicholas yelled at me first. "What are you doing!?" he practically screamed, his fists tight at his sides. "We're trying to get Ms. Lewis a hot date! Didn't you see how gorgeous that man was?!"

"Not him!" I hissed. "I... I don't like him!"

"Why not? He's gorgeous and frankly, he's got to have money," Nicholas counter argued. "Ms. Lewis would be all over him!"

"I don't think she'd be at all interested in whatever economic conquers he's accomplished!" I snapped.

"She *needs* to relax before the competition, and honestly, I think he could really help her out," Shannon cut in, practically swooning.

"*Eww!*" I huffed. "You guys need to stop meddling in her personal life. Seriously! She's not going to be interested in Wolfgang because—"

"Come along. We need to get back to the buses," Amelia suddenly cut us all off, startling me so bad I nearly jumped into the twins' arms. I spun to look at Amelia—who had come up behind me—and immediately Nicholas harshly jabbed his elbow into my gut to keep me quiet. I groaned, stepping away from him, while Shannon and the twins smiled innocently.

"Yes, Ms. Lewis," they all chanted in unison before bounding off.

I shook my head, leveling my anger. Nicholas would be furious with me, but there was no way I was going to let Amelia blindly walk into a date with Wolfgang. I turned to tell her then and there what her students were brewing, but she suddenly grabbed my hand and intertwined our fingers. I gulped, a calm sweeping over my body. I looked to Amelia and suddenly nothing else mattered, but her and me, and me and her.

"Are you okay?" Amelia asked as we trailed towards the exit. "You dashed out of the last scene rather abruptly. I was going to follow, but I needed to make sure I didn't lose any of the students, and then—"

"I'm fine," I answered quickly. "Just um, a sudden stomach pain. It's passed now though, probably nothing. I'm fine now."

"Okay, good to know," Amelia stated, smirking as she dragged me to the bus.

It was pretty late when we reached the hotel. A few students lingered in the lobby to grab snacks, but most headed straight up to their rooms along with the chaperons. Amelia and I waited in the lobby for the last of the students, making sure everyone made it upstairs.

"That's the last of them," Amelia stated. "Shall we head up to our room now?"

I looked to Amelia and found she was staring intensely at me. "Sure," I answered. When I did, Amelia grabbed my hand again, grasping it tightly as we headed for the elevators.

There was a lull in guests flocking to their rooms at that time, so we ended up in an elevator alone. The second the elevator doors shut, I realized how close Amelia was to me. She was pressed nearly flush against me, our hands still tightly interlocked. I gulped.

"Did you, um, enjoy the show?" I asked, feelings my body temperature rising, my head slightly spinning.

"I loved it," Amelia answered, grinning, biting her lip. "Live theater is just... fantastic."

"I'm glad you had a good time," I replied. "I enjoyed myself too."

The elevator dinged on our floor and the doors pulled open. "So, what do you want to do when we get back to the room?" Amelia questioned.

I quickly stepped out of the elevator, fighting to get some air between us so I could breathe normally again. "What do you mean?" I asked. I headed towards our room, practically pulling Amelia along. "I figured we'd just go to bed."

"We could, but it's not *that* late," Amelia answered, even though it really was. "We could stay up and talk, or maybe... play some poker?"

I laughed. "Yeah, no, I don't think so," I stated, pulling out my keycard. "You're too good at poker... cheaty, actually."

"If I promise not to cheat, can we play?" Amelia pleaded with puppy-dog eyes.

I was entirely susceptible to her puppy-dog eyes and knew I couldn't refuse, but I couldn't give in so easily. "I don't know..." I said, opening the door. "Poker can get kind of boring if you aren't betting anything... and I'm not about to bet real money with you, even if you don't cheat." The door shut behind us and I continued into the room, my back turned to Amelia, who had released my hand at the door.

"What about strip poker, then?"

I tripped over my own feet in shock and fell face first onto the bed. I pushed myself up, turning to sit down where I had landed. I looked over to Amelia, who was still hovering near the door.

"Did you just say strip poker?" I questioned.

"Sure," Amelia answered with a shrug. "What? Do you have cold feet about a little strip poker game?" There was a glint in Amelia's eyes that spelt trouble and she looked downright predatory. That look alone sent heat straight to my core.

I *really* should have said no. It was not an appropriate time for strip poker, partly because we were chaperons on a school trip, and partly because we needed to be up early tomorrow, but also partly because I had feelings for Amelia that would only further complicate things. Despite all that, though, there was a larger part of me that just wanted to see Amelia topless.

I know it was my hormones and not my logic that answered, but I sent Amelia a challenging look and stated, "You're on."

Amelia went to her bag and pulled out a deck of cards, stalking over to the bed. She sat down across from me, pulling out and expertly shuffling the deck. "This is going to be a fast game," she stated. "We're both in dresses, so that's an article or two less of clothing than usual."

"Well, this is poorly planned," I answered. "Feel free to pussy out whenever it gets to be too much for you."

"The same goes for you," Amelia replied. She extended the shuffled deck to me. "You can cut the deck to make sure I'm not cheating."

"You'll still find a way," I stated, but I cut the deck anyway.

As we played, I could tell Amelia genuinely wasn't cheating because she wasn't sweeping the floor with me like the last time we played. She was still better than me, but we remained mostly even through the rounds. Shoes came off first, then Amelia lost the sweater she had pulled over her shoulders. When I lost the next round, I thought I was going to have to remove my dress, but thinking ingeniously, I proudly pulled a hairpin out of my hair. Amelia complained that wasn't fair and I stuck out my tongue at her.

"It's still something I'm wearing," I countered.

"How many more hairpins do you have?"

"Three."

Amelia grinned. "I have ten. Better start winning more frequently."

Perhaps she could see the frustration and sheer determination in my eyes, because by some miracle I got her down to two hairpins before I lost again, but then I lost three times in a row and suddenly I was out of hairpins. Another loss meant my dress was coming off. I should have known Amelia wouldn't let me win so easily. The next round, I lost again.

"Dress, off, now," Amelia demanded, and her words sent a jolt through my body. The command in her voice in combination with the hungry look in her eyes was more than enough to make me quiver with want. I took a deep breath. I wasn't shy, but the thought of being exposed in front of Amelia was... exciting me... exciting me in ways I wasn't sure Amelia realized.

"Are you forfeiting?" Amelia challenged when I didn't move to take off my dress.

"You wish," I scoffed. "I just... need some help getting it off," I answered smugly, standing up from the bed and looking to Amelia expectantly.

I could tell I caught Amelia by surprise, because her eyes widened momentarily, but she regained her composure quickly. She stood, walking over to my side of the bed, and stood right behind me. I felt her unzip my dress. Then, she ran her hands up my sides, touching the fabric on my shoulders before slowly running her hands back down my arms, pulling the dress off as she went. Shivers exploded throughout my entire body, and I bit my lip, trying to contain myself.

"You're doing this to win a game," I cursed to myself, though I hardly believed it.

The heat of Amelia's body being so close to my back suddenly disappeared as my dress fell, pooling at my feet. I realized my eyes had fluttered shut at the earlier sensations, so I opened them slowly. The cool breeze that surrounded me reminded me, abruptly, that I was standing before Amelia in only my underwear.

I heard a hum of satisfaction behind me and turned quickly, just in time to catch Amelia's eyes shooting up to meet mine. "You ass looks very nice in that underwear," Amelia stated, this time catching *me* off guard.

I blinked repeatedly, too shocked to reply. I watched as Amelia's eyes moved, checking out the rest of my body. I suddenly felt a bit self-conscious, so I stood up straighter and sucked in my gut more. I stood there, nearly squirming under Amelia's gaze. I watched her eyes, the subtle movements in her body, the rise and fall of every breath she took. And suddenly I thought, maybe I wasn't the only one so turned on. Maybe... maybe there was something...

"Come on," I stated, breaking the trance. "We've got a few more rounds to go still."

"I thought you'd chicken out by now," Amelia answered, returning to her spot. "If you lose again, the bra comes off, and then..."

"I know. I'll be naked," I said, passing out cards, thinking there were certainly worse things. "You only have to lose two more rounds as well though, and we'll be in the same boat."

"I didn't know you were such a risk taker," Amelia teased, reaching for her cards.

That round, I realized Amelia was much more distracted, her gaze locked on me the entire time. My confidence was growing. Not so much about winning the game but making a move. I wanted Amelia, badly. She seemed keenly interested in me as well.

I used her distraction to my advantage and two rounds later I reigned victorious after beating Amelia twice. Now, she had to remove her dress. I quickly offered to help, as she had done for me. Amelia looked at me before she stood and turned, waiting patiently for my assistance.

I stood. Amelia's gaze locked on me from over her shoulder. I walked around behind her and reached out, grabbing her zipper. I subconsciously stepped closer to her, able to smell her perfume. It was the same vanilla scent that drove me crazy in Florida, now filling my nostrils once again. The heat inside my body grew as I pulled the zipper down.

I parted her dress at the now opened zipper, exposing her back, her smooth skin, and defined shoulder blades. I gave in, letting my hand wander, grazing my fingertips across her exposed skin. I heard Amelia's breath hitch, her entire body shuddering. The intense burn I felt in my core seemed to steady itself into a constant warmth. It morphed into an intense need to be nearer to her. I stepped closer until our bodies were practically flush. My hands traced up her skin just inside the open zipper, running my palms over her shoulder blades before reaching her shoulders. Slowly, I pushed the fabric off her upper body. When the skin on her shoulders was fully exposed, my chin found its way to her shoulder, and I rested my head there. Instinctively, I tilted my lips towards her neck. I wanted to kiss her, desperately, but not yet. Still, I felt Amelia shiver under the feeling of my warm breath on her neck.

Distantly, I heard her dress hit the floor, but my mind was elsewhere. I focused on our bare skin, flush against each other. Her skin was so soft and warm. I fought the urge to wrap my arms around her. The heat in my body pooled into my core. I didn't know what my hands were doing. They were somewhere near Amelia's sides, maybe lower, just hovering. They twitched, wanting desperately to reach up. I brushed against Amelia's skin. She jerked, shoving her butt back into my pelvis, and a groan escaped my lips.

"Amelia," I muttered, breathlessly, needily, all too aware of the wetness between my legs.

Suddenly, everything was cold.

I blinked, standing up straight, and opened my eyes. Across from me Amelia stood, her arms crossed over her front protectively, her eyes wide with panic. I opened my mouth to say something, anything, apologize, but before I could, Amelia had grabbed her pajamas from the night before, jerked them back on, and bolted straight for the door.

"Amelia, wait!" I forced out just before the door closed, but then she was gone.

I was horrified. The very thing I didn't want to happen, to drive a wedge between Amelia and me, was exactly what I had done. I let my feelings get in the way of our friendship, and now I had ruined everything! Now furious, I turned and knocked all the cards onto the floor, kicking at Amelia's dress, bunching it up into a pile. Then I collapsed onto the floor, fought off tears furiously, before I just laid there.

I didn't follow her. I could tell just from her expression that she didn't want me to. I hoped she'd come back soon though. In the meantime, I busied myself with picking up the cards. I picked up our dresses too, got into my own pajamas, and sat down at the desk. I was startled by my phone chiming and went to see who had just texted me.

It was a text from Amelia. *'Sorry, I must have got that weird stomach bug you had at the theater. Hopefully it's nothing. I'll be fine.'*

I didn't believe her at all—clearly, we had a bathroom connected to our room, so that wouldn't have been any reason to bolt—though I didn't think she had expected me to. I responded with, *'Come back to the room, please. It's getting late. You don't have anywhere else to sleep.'* I waited for a second, but then hurried to add, *'I'm sorry, I went too far. Please come back.'*

'No, I'm sorry,' was the reply. *'You're fine, I swear. It must have been something I ate. Stomach issues, you know?'*

She was being dismissive. I didn't have an option though. I needed her to come back. *'Okay,'* I gave in.

'I'll come back up in a few minutes.'

I glanced at the time. It was nearly two in the morning. I waited for what felt like ages until finally, the door opened. Amelia walked in, her head down. She looked tired and dejected.

"I'll sleep on the couch," I stated immediately.

Amelia shook her head. "No, that's ridiculous," she answered. "Hotel couches are probably filthy anyway. We can both sleep in the bed again."

"Are you sure?"

"Like I said, I'm fine," Amelia muttered. "My stomach is... better, so it's all good."

"Right, your stomach..."

"Let's just get some sleep."

I lied down in bed, watching Amelia as she navigated the room, getting ready for bed herself. Then, she climbed into bed and we both lied on our backs, staring up at the ceiling, a couple feet of space between us. It felt like we had taken five steps backwards in our relationship, our friendship. And it was all my fault. I was mad, furious. I balled my hands into fists.

And then, suddenly, Amelia flipped on her side and slid towards me, cuddling her head into the crook of my neck. Slowly, I reached up and rested my hands on her, hugging her close to me.

After a few moments of silence, in which I contemplated what happened and how Amelia might be feeling, I whispered, "Amelia?"

"*Hmm*?"

"We should... talk about what happened."

Amelia pulled herself closer into me. "I'm sorry, you're right. We should. I just... I think I panic sometimes... when I'm feeling overwhelmed and I just... need to get away."

"I understand that. I get overwhelmed too," I answered, thinking back to the theater.

"And I just... seeing Wolfgang again made me remember some things and it makes me feel... well he always made me feel... I don't know, I just..."

I furrowed my brown in slight confusion, pulling Amelia ever closer to me. "Do you want to... talk about that?" I questioned.

"Yes, someday, but not now," Amelia answered. "We need sleep now."

"Okay," I gave in. "Goodnight, Amelia."

"Goodnight, Nats."

17.

It's Showtime

The following day went much the same, minus the Broadway musical. We got up at an ungodly hour, ate breakfast at the hotel, then explored the city more. Before I knew it, we were back at the hotel for practice. Since the competition was tomorrow and the students needed all the energy they could muster, Amelia didn't work them as hard as she had the day prior. I watched them from the audience, consumed in my thoughts.

Nicholas and Shannon were definitely upset with me. They kept sending me death glares from across the room, and at one point, Nicholas got snapped at for not smiling appropriately. I didn't care though. I knew more than they did about Wolfgang and the sooner I could tell them, the better it would be.

At just past 5:30, Nicholas raised his hand and interrupted practice.

"Yes, Nicholas?" Amelia called on him.

"It's past 5:30 and personally, I think we should call it here," he stated bravely, or bossily, depending on how you took it. "We have a big day tomorrow and there will still be time to work during warmups... besides, I'm positively starving. We should stop now so we can eat and have time to relax, ready ourselves for tomorrow."

Nicholas was never one to suggest they stop singing, so I could tell Amelia was a bit suspicious. She took his words to heart though and seemed to agree.

"Perhaps that's not such a bad idea..." she admitted. "I'll let you all go for the evening. Go relax, have a bit of fun, and don't get into any trouble, alright?"

I watched as everyone except Nicholas, Shannon, and the twins gathered their things and left the auditorium, the chaperons following after. The remaining four students gathered together not far from me,

Nicholas shooting me dagger glares should I try and intervene. He only... mildly intimidated me. I decide to stay back, listen to what they had to say, and only intervene when I felt it necessary. I watched as Amelia finished packing up her things and headed over to her collective favorites.

"What are your plans?" she asked the group. She moved past them, heading in my direction, and her students followed along beside her.

"We want to get dinner," one of the twins answered.

"We were thinking the hotel restaurant," the other twin added.

"That sounds good. Their breakfasts are amazing, so I'd imagine their dinners are probably marvelous as well," Amelia replied.

"We'd love for you to join us," Nicholas added.

"Sure," Amelia answered instantly. She neared me then and reached out towards me. "Up for dinner, Natalie?"

I glanced towards Nicholas instead of immediately answering. His eyes widened with realization. It was clear I wasn't going to lie my way out of going to dinner, meaning I'd third wheel crash the date, and if I *did* lie my way out, Amelia would bail as well. Unable to sort this out quickly enough, he turned towards Shannon, silently pleading for help.

"Actually, Natalie and I already have plans," Shannon shot out. I looked to her and raised an eyebrow skeptically. "We're going to this um, really cool event next door."

"Oh really? I didn't know that," Amelia said, turning back to me. "What's the event?"

"Glass blowing!" Shannon practically yelled. Nicholas looked very displeased with her choice, and I fought to hold in a laugh.

"That sounds fun," Amelia answered, none-the-wiser. "Why don't we all go to the glass blowing event, and then we can get dinner together afterwards?"

"Because we really want dinner now!" one of the twins shouted.

"Now, because we have to go to bed early anyway," the other twin tried to help.

Nicholas was practically fuming, very unhappy with how poorly things were going. He took a deep breath and stated, ever the definition of poise, "Actually, the event is invite only. Shannon got an invite and a plus one and chose to take Natalie." He turned and glared at Shannon.

"Yeah, um, Natalie said it sounded interesting and I just thought it would be fun to get to know her better. We could... gossip about college stuff, you know," Shannon added.

"Oh..." Amelia stated, turning to me with a look of confusion on her face.

I was actually getting kick out of their horrid display of lies, so I decided to play into it, just a little, just to make their lives more difficult. It was karma, you nosey little brats!

"Actually, Shannon, I don't think it's the best idea," I stated. "It sounds like fun, but it runs pretty late, and you have a competition tomorrow. I think we better just cancel."

"Okay, then we can all go to dinner!" Amelia declared contentedly.

"No, because, um, Natalie has to hang out with me!" one of the twins shouted abruptly, desperately trying to save things. It didn't make any sense, however, and Amelia was starting to sense something was up. Nicholas was fuming.

"You brat!" Nicholas shouted at me. "Why do you have to be so—so—obstinate!?"

"Nicholas!" Amelia scolded. "What's going on?"

Shannon and the twins were silent. Nicholas clenched his jaw and squeezed his fists together. I just sighed.

"They set you up on a date," I spilled, turning to Amelia.

"What?" she questioned.

"I did say they were trying," I offered with a small shrug.

"Well, yes, but... we don't even live in New York," Amelia stated, turning back to her students. "I appreciate you guys looking out for me and trying to help but... there was no way this could have developed into anything."

"For quick companionship then, not long term," Shannon quickly offered.

Amelia visibly shrunk back upon hearing that. She tensed, looking sickly. I quickly stepped to her side and grabbed her arm to steady her. Then I reached up and took hold of her head so I could turn her and look into her eyes.

"Are you okay?" I asked, searching her brown eyes.

Amelia let out a shaky breath, her color returning. She gave a small smile, leaning into my hand for a moment before pulling away and turning back to her students.

"I'm just... not comfortable with the idea of you setting me up," Amelia admitted.

"Oh..." the twins muttered, shying away.

"I know you were just trying to help. It's okay," Amelia reassured them.

"Are you sure you don't want to at least see a picture of the guy?" Shannon offered. "You know, before you make up your mind for sure?"

"I'm not interested," Amelia admitted defeatedly. "Excuse me, I need to head back to my room." And with that, Amelia turned and left the auditorium.

I watched Amelia go with great concern, and grabbed for my stuff, about to follow her out. I expected Nicholas to try and stop me, but it was actually Shannon who complained.

"If you would have just played along, we could have gotten her downstairs and she might have stayed once she was down there!" Shannon huffed. "We told you; she just needs that first push!"

I turned towards Shannon to argue, but before I could, Nicholas reached out and pushed his arm strongly against Shannon to get her to stop talking.

"No, let it go, Shannon," he said, his voice low and tired sounding. He stared at me, his brows furrowed. "We've misread the situation."

"What are you talking about?" Shannon questioned, but Nicholas refused to say more.

In that moment, I cared more about Amelia's wellbeing than figuring out what Nicholas was talking about, so I just left and headed up to our room. When I got there, Amelia was lying on her stomach on the bed, her phone in her hands, looking at something online. I flopped down next to her, leaning against her, watching over her shoulder as she scrolled through social media. We sat in silence for a moment, just leaning against each other, until I finally spoke.

"Hey, are you okay?" I questioned. It felt like such a dumb question once it was out of my mouth.

Amelia let out a sigh. "I didn't think they'd go so far as to actually set up a date for me."

I shifted so I could rub circles on her back. "Well... they're pretty strong willed, if you haven't noticed. And I think that's your fault, for teaching them that."

"Maybe you're right."

"And for the record, I think it's totally acceptable that you think it's weird and you don't want to get set up by them," I added.

Amelia let out a light chuckle. "It *is* weird," she agreed. "But they also have no idea what my type is."

"Wait a second..." I said, narrowing my eyes. "Are you saying that if they set you up with someone your type, you'd go on the date?"

Amelia started laughing before she turned, rolling over onto her back. My hand, which had been on her back, ended up against her lower stomach. She rested her hand on mine, so I left it there. She smiled up at me and I smiled back.

"I'd be more willing to consider it, but no," she replied.

"Well why not?" I joked. "They're doing all the boring work for you."

"I'm just not interested," she answered. "I have... other things that I'm currently focusing on in my life."

I felt Amelia's stomach rumble under my hand. "You hungry?" I questioned. Amelia nodded. "Want to grab food?"

"Definitely."

"Okay, let me just grab—wait. What time is it?"

"Like six," Amelia answered, looking at her phone.

"We can't leave," I said quickly.

"Why?"

"Because your um, blind date will be downstairs, and we don't want to run into him."

"So? Even if we see him and he sees me, surely he wouldn't chase me down. Blind dates aren't that bold."

Maybe not a blind date... but Wolfgang? "No, we can't," I declared.

"Why?"

"Because. I told you."

"Come on. You're being ridiculous."

"I'm serious!"

"So am I! Now come on, let's go get food."

"No!"

"Natalie, stop being ridiculous. Come on!"

"We can't!"

"Why? Give me a good reason!"

"Because... because..." Oh, goddammit, Amelia, why couldn't you just trust me!? I huffed. "Because your students set you up on a date with Wolfgang," I confessed in frustration.

"What?" Amelia asked, more confused, and she fell back onto the bed.

"I'm sorry," I said quickly. "I absolutely wasn't going to let you go on that date, knowing it was Wolfgang, and that's the same reason I'm not going to let you go downstairs right now. I didn't like the way he was manhandling you yesterday and I just... well I know you two are exes and you have a history, but I'm just not comfortable with him being able to confront you. I mean, unless you want to talk to him, in which case I won't stop you, but I will be going downstairs with you. Because I care about you and he... he creeps me out."

"I don't want to see him," Amelia stated, and I let out a sigh of relief.

I sat back down on the bed next to Amelia, rubbing at her arm comfortingly. "Let's just order room service and we can... watch a documentary. I'll just grab the remote and—" I leaned over towards the nightstand, grabbing the remote, but Amelia reached over and rested her hand on my thigh, stopping me.

"Wolfgang is not a nice man," she stated, her voice quiet, but unwavering. "He's exactly like my father. He comes from the same stock, so to say. All he cares about in life is money and power. He doesn't know how to love, doesn't know what compassion is, and would never put anyone else before himself. He always made me feel so worthless."

"I'm sorry," I muttered, reaching out to hold Amelia's other hand. We were close enough that she leaned into me, sighing.

"We dated because my father pushed us together. He was real buddy-buddy with Wolfgang's father. There was always pyramid stuff happening behind my back, advances, grooming, all that. I was young, still in the grasp of my parents, still impressionable, and Wolfgang was older, more manipulative, less kind.

"I didn't mind at the time, didn't really see all the red flags. I was just excited that a boy was interested in me for the first time. I just sort of assumed that was what love was like. But there was, well, always an obstacle standing between us."

"Yeah, your sexuality."

Amelia frowned. "M—maybe... I... well I didn't know I was into women back then, I hadn't really questioned it yet. I just... I don't know. I... liked Wolfgang back then. I was... attracted to him, I guess. But he was just so pushy all the time. Even though he would respect when I said no, he always acted like there was something wrong with me, and he was just pushier the next time.

"I felt so pressured every time I was with him, but I think my mom kind of thought he'd be that way, since he was older. She questioned everything Wolfgang did. She wouldn't let us be alone together. I mean, we could have found time to be alone, of course, but I didn't want to, so we never did. But Wolfgang... he wanted to be alone, all the time. And even though I liked him—even though I thought I was in love with him—I never felt that same drive he did. And he just started saying there was something wrong with me.

"Why didn't I want to sleep with him? I was a teenager, I was supposed to want that, right? While we were dating, I could avoid it, but if we got married, then what? I was dreading what our wedding night might hold while all my friends were dreaming about sex just as much as Wolfgang was.

"Clearly, it didn't work out with Wolfgang. I finally got up the courage to break up with him around the time I decided I wanted to pursue singing. He was really mad. Something about being with me for so long and him patiently waiting, that I was being a tease, dragging him along, that I *owed* him something. He also had a lot of nasty things to say about my career choices, like my parents.

"The whole experience kind of ruined me on dating," Amelia muttered. "I had a horrid falling out with my family and was working my ass off, so it's not like I had a lot of free time or mental capacity for dating anyway. And I just felt, I don't know. It's hard to explain. My friends were going off, having sex, telling me about their first times and I was just there, not wanting any of that."

"Look, I get it," I replied with a shrug. "We're born to be attracted to whoever we're attracted to, and Wolfgang just isn't it for you. Boys in general aren't, and that's cool."

"Anyway, I'm not interested in seeing him... certainly not interested in catching up," Amelia concluded. "Of all the men in New York, they found Wolfgang to set me up with. What irony."

"Yeah, really," I chuckled.

"Anyway, I'm starving. Let's order room service, shall we?"

"Sounds good to me."

I leaned back on the bed while Amelia rifled through the menu, listening to her list various foods. I was... curious. From what Amelia told me, it didn't sound like she had seriously dated anyone since Wolfgang, which would line up well with Amelia not dating anyone for over a decade. Wolfgang was pushy, but it also sounded like he never managed to take full advantage of her. I was grateful for that, of course. But was... Amelia a virgin?

It didn't matter, obviously. Virginity was a construct anyway. It didn't matter. I could care less who Amelia had or hadn't slept with. But it was just kind of interesting.

I excused myself to the bathroom while Amelia called in our room service order. I thought about asking Amelia—as a joke, but also to quell my curiosity. I didn't figure it was a good time though, what with all the Wolfgang stuff, and the set-up dates, and the competition. I pulled out my phone, thinking about the time Piper first told me Amelia hadn't dated anyone in years.

'Hey, is Amelia a virgin?' I texted Piper.

'Weird text to get from you on a Sunday evening,' Piper responded.

'I know. But is she?'

'No. What even prompted you to ask?'

'You said she hasn't dated anyone in ten years. And maybe I'm wrong, but she doesn't seem like the casual sex type.'

'No, you're right. But she slept with her first boyfriend back when she was seventeen or something.'

'Was his name Wolfgang?'

'I think so. It sounds familiar.'

'I don't think they ever slept together.'

'Oh...' Piper replied. And then, after a moment, she added, *'Amelia might be a virgin then.'*

The morning of the competition, everything was hectic. Jonas lost his voice and Shannon nearly had a conniption because he was her duet partner. Amelia sprayed some horrible smelling stuff into his throat though, and fifteen minutes later, he was good as new. Tom accidently stained his costume, but I drew over it with a sharpie and we just pretended it was a decorative pin. Scott nearly had a meltdown because he forgot his dress shoes, but I guess the twins are shoe fanatics, because they brought like ten extra pairs. Chelsey started crying because she couldn't get her hair to look right, but Avery helped her get it just right, and then everything was fine.

We flew out of the hotel doors with minimal time to spare, but we made it to the venue alright. Amelia handled last-minute registration details while I went with the choir to a back room that would serve as our home base. I helped finish off some makeup while others warmed up and practiced.

I hardly saw Amelia. Sometimes she would be in the home room, helping with things or giving out reminders, but she often ran out to the auditorium to watch the performances. I stayed out of the way as best I could and offered myself up to help with anything I could.

Towards the early afternoon, after the event hosts dropped off a catered lunch, I received a text from Eleanor. It read: *'Has anyone texted you or Amelia recently? Namely Piper?'*

'I texted Piper last night,' I answered. *'Not sure about Amelia. I've hardly talked to her. Though I bet she's been too busy to check her phone. Why?'*

'Piper got some really devastating news this morning.'

My heart hammered in my rib cage while my mind shot through every worse-case scenario. *'Do you know what happened?'* I asked.

'No. I just know she got a phone call this morning, looked bad all morning, and she left work at lunch. I texted her, but she won't answer me.'

'But like, she's okay? So, the baby's okay?'

'I think so. It might be related to Christian. That's what Karmen thinks.'

'Do you want me to try and get ahold of her?'

'You can try. Karmen and I are going over to Ellie 2.0's house after school to check on her. I'll keep you updated.'

'Okay. I'll let you know if I figure anything out,' I answered.

I texted Piper and tried calling her, but she didn't answer, and the phone call went straight to voicemail. I knew she and her soon to be ex-husband had a really shitty falling out, but as far as I knew, her divorce was going better than, say, Karmen's. I realized though that Piper didn't talk about her personal life very much. I always took that as everything was fine, but maybe she was just hiding stuff. Worrying about Piper was stressing me out.

And, speaking of stress, the closer we neared the end of the singing competition, the more I worried about the students. How was their singing going? Could they really make it to Worlds? I was worried that their incessant need to set Amelia up on a date had distracted them from their work.

Around two o'clock, Amelia came and found me in the home room.

"It's time for the group numbers," she said. "We're fourth in the order, and I have to direct, but I thought maybe you'd want to come out and watch?"

"Sure," I answered, standing and following Amelia. "Have you checked your phone at all today?"

"Oh? No. I've been too busy. I've hardly stopped moving!" Amelia laughed. "Why though?"

"Oh, um, Eleanor just had a question. She texted me though, so don't worry about it," I said. I didn't want to worry Amelia and distract her. She could worry about Piper after the competition.

I waited with Amelia in the auditorium through the first three group numbers. The judges were seated in two lines, front and center, all dressed like court judges in an execution case. I thought the first three performances were outstanding. I couldn't figure how the judges could pick a winner, since they all seemed flawless to me. And next was Elk Creek. I knew they would do great. I had heard them countless times. There wasn't a single thing they could improve. They were flawless too.

And they were, as far as I was concerned. I did spend most of their performance just watching Amelia, gazing at her directing. I wasn't sure if she helped them much. Maybe she kept them on pace, maybe she helped their entrances, but in the very least, she helped them feel calm. They were just there with their teacher, their mentor, their friend... and they were there with all their other adopted choir family members. In the end, it didn't matter if they won the competition or not, because they had already won. They won each other and that would forever be more than enough.

After our group performance, it was back to waiting. The choir returned to the home room, and Amelia and I watched the rest of the group performances. I thought they all did great, but Amelia had a lot more constructive criticism, which helped calm her students' nerves. Then it was time for the awards ceremony.

We all filed into the auditorium and sat in our designated seats. Despite Amelia saying they had it in the bag multiple times, she was still clearly nervous. She couldn't sit still beside me, fidgeting and biting at her fingers. I reached over and grabbed her hand to calm her.

As like most award ceremonies, this one was unnecessarily drawn out. There were words of thanks and speeches, and before each and every name was announced, there was a long and drawn-out drumroll, AKA, feet stomping.

Soloist awards were given out first. Of our five soloists, Shannon placed third and unsurprisingly, Nicholas won first place. He deserved it. He had been practicing that solo relentlessly for ages.

Duet awards came next. Shannon and Jonas got fifth, which was sad, but Nicholas and his partner got second, which was really good! Nicholas was huffy, of course, but I could tell it was just dramatics. He was still beaming with happiness. And then, something utterly fantastic happened: I finally learned Georgie's twin's name!

"And finally, for our first-place duet division winners... we have... Georgie and Wesley Evans from Elk Creek College Preparatory!"

We all screamed and applauded, very excited for the twins who evidently had never placed at Nationals before. I still couldn't tell them apart, but at least I knew both of their names.

And last, we were down to the group category. Amelia wasn't even sitting at that point, just hovering over her seat, energy buzzing all around her. We had to listen to the top ten, which took a really long time. When the announcer reached fourth place, I started listening more closely.

"And now... in fourth place... the runner up of this year's National Choral Competition, we have... drumroll!" I squeezed Amelia's hand harder as feet started stomping. "Sea Coast High!"

I was breathing heavily. I wanted to be relieved, believe that Elk Creek had made the top three and would definitely be making it to Worlds, but what if they didn't place at all?

"Now, for the remaining three places, we'd like to invite the top three schools, in random order, to join us up on stage," the announcer said. "From there, we'll announce the winners. Please hold your applause until all three schools are called. Would the following three schools please come up on stage: Fortuna Conservatory, Pleasant Hill School of the Fine Arts, and... Elk Creek College Preparatory!"

I heard Amelia squeak out a sound of relief, which sounded almost like choking before bursting into happy tears, but she held it together. Clearly, she was quite excited, as was the rest of the screaming choir. I was equally excited and relieved.

"You're going to Worlds!" I stated, a huge grin on my face.

Our students headed up on stage while Amelia and I stayed back in our seats with the chaperons. The choir members of all three schools piled onto the stage, cramming together. And then, the announcer began the ranking.

"In third place, for this year's National Choral Competition, we have... drumroll... Fortuna Conservatory!"

Amelia sighed again. I turned to her with a smile.

"And now..." the announcer cut back in, "for the winner of this year's National Choral Competition, drumroll please..."

I looked to Amelia. Her eyes were tightly shut, her hand clasped around mine. She stomped her feet on the ground, her other hand up in the air, fingers crossed.

"And the winner is..." the announcer continued, "Elk Creek College Preparatory!"

I knew he said the full Elk Creek name, but I didn't hear the end because the auditorium erupted into such screaming, everything was overpowered. I felt, and saw, Amelia fall, stunned and excited, before she stood, screaming in glee, and pulled me up into a tight, bouncing hug.

"We won!" she chanted, jumping up and down. "We won! We're going to Worlds!"

Excitement buzzed all over the auditorium. The announcer thanked everyone and dismissed us, Amelia grabbing me, and we raced, hand in hand, towards the stage. With grace, Amelia leapt up onto the stage, immediately tackled by all her students. I climbed up more slowly, watching them leaping and jumping around while screaming. Nicholas held in his arms a huge trophy that had been presented to Elk Creek.

Before I could properly congratulate everyone, Amelia wiggled her way out of the students and tackled me in another hug. And then, all the students promptly followed her, tackling me all the way to the floor, laughing.

When we returned to the hotel that evening, we found that Amelia had catered a banquet to welcome us back from the competition. It was perhaps a bit presumptuous, but there were good odds that at least one of the performances would place. We celebrated in the banquet hall, eating more food than was healthy, and the students had some extra fun on the makeshift dancefloor, equipped with karaoke.

Karaoke is a fun past time for most high school and college aged kids, but the choir nerds took it to a whole new level. They even managed to talk Amelia into getting up and singing a few songs. I could listen to her sing song after song for the rest of my life. I'd never tire of hearing her voice. Eventually though, Amelia pulled away from her students and returned to the table where I was sitting, flopping down beside me with a laugh.

"I know they did good at the competition—they're all amazing singers," I said to Amelia, "but in my book, you're always going to be the best singer."

"Oh, please," Amelia scoffed. "That's karaoke! It's not supposed to be good!"

"Then why did it sound so good?" I questioned with a smirk.

"So, what was Eleanor asking you about earlier?" Amelia asked passively, taking a swig of her water.

"Oh, that, yeah, I just, um... I didn't want to worry you and distract you from the competition—"

"What happened?"

"Apparently something with Piper, I'm not sure of any details, really."

And speaking of: my phone buzzed in my pocket, so I pulled it out, realizing Piper had texted me. I unlocked my phone, opening the conversation, but before I could read her text, someone tapped me on the shoulder. I turned around and saw it was Nicholas.

"Hey," he said to both Amelia and me. "Do you mind if I pull Natalie away for a few moments? There's something I want to talk to her about."

"Go right ahead," Amelia stated, waving her hand. "I'm going to raid the dessert table again. I need a few more of those delicious cookies."

"Sure," I answered, sitting down my phone on the table before standing and following Nicholas.

Nicholas led me over to the far corner of the room where we were mostly hidden by the karaoke stage.

"Hey," he stated.

"*Umm...* hey," I answered. "What did you want to talk about?"

"Look, it's not really any of my business, I guess, but... well, I wanted to apologize about Shannon, and about my actions too."

"What are you talking about?"

"It was wrong of us to try and set Ms. Lewis up on a date."

"Yeah..." I agreed, "but you should be apologizing to Ms. Lewis about that, not me."

"Yes, and I will, but I wanted to first apologize to you, because I didn't know. I didn't think that you and Ms. Lewis—"

"Nicholas!" one of the twins screamed, finding us in the corner. "Sing a song with me!"

"I'm trying to talk to Natalie—"

"Please!"

"Go on," I urged. "Go celebrate with you classmates. You deserve it. We can finish talking later, okay?"

"Okay," Nicholas gave in, heading off.

"Congrats again on your first-place win!" I shouted after him.

I shook my head, wondering just what Nicholas could have been getting at. Ah well, it couldn't have been that important, otherwise he would have fought harder to tell me. He was an obstinate guy. I walked back over to the table, content to sit with Amelia for as long as I could before another student inevitably pulled her away again.

I sat down next to Amelia, laughing slightly, shaking my head. "Those kids," I muttered fondly. "Anyway, I thought you said you were going for more desserts...?" I looked over to Amelia, questioning why she was still there, dessert-less, and I realized she was holding my phone. She was looking at it, frowning, reading... Remembering that it had been Piper who texted me, I remembered Eleanor's urgent text from earlier, and I worried that it must be something pretty bad.

"What are you doing?" I questioned, standing to try and see what Piper wrote. When I did, I saw that she was reading my text conversation with Piper, though nothing recent. Instead, she was looking at our conversation from the night before.

Suddenly, Amelia leapt up and grabbed my wrist. "Hey, Natalie?" she stated calmly, but I could hear the anger and even hurt evident in her voice. "Let's go outside and talk for a second, okay?" I opened my mouth to maybe protest, but she cut me off. "Now." She jerked my wrist, getting me to turn, before she released me and stormed off, my cell phone still in her hands.

I followed Amelia—what choice did I have—out of the banquet hall, through the lobby, outside the hotel, and over to a dark alley that looked kind of sketchy but was not inherently dangerous. I could tell Amelia was unhappy, and yeah, it was kind of dickish that I asked Piper if she was a virgin, but did it really matter?

Amelia stopped walking and turned back to face me. She looked up at me as if she were about to cry and I realized very quickly that this was a lot more serious than I originally thought.

"Why, on earth—" she fought to keep her voice level— "would you go to Piper to discuss my sexual history?"

"Because I'm an idiot," I answered, and I felt like that was true. I clearly upset her, and I never meant to do that.

"Why wouldn't you just ask me!?" Amelia snapped. "I've never lied to you! I would have told you! But instead, you had to go behind my back and *speculate* about my life!"

"I didn't want to ask you because you had just told me about your shitty history with Wolfgang, and I wanted to just be supportive in that moment!" I answered. "You can't honestly tell me that you would have been one-hundred percent okay, in that moment, with me bringing it up!"

"Well probably not! That part of my past was really traumatizing! I spent years in utter turmoil! But you could have just kept your stupid mouth shut and just asked me the next day if it's really that important to you!"

"Look, I'm sorry I asked Piper!" I yelled. "It's just stupid. I don't need to know. I just... I wanted to know because I'm a nosey idiot and I didn't want to ask you because I'm a chicken, so I just asked Piper. But it was stupid and childish, and I shouldn't have done it."

"You're right! You shouldn't have! Piper doesn't even know!" Amelia shouted again. "It's personal, you know, and I don't just go around telling everyone!"

I stopped shouting and just stared at Amelia, her eyes glistening with tears that were threatening to fall. I knew Amelia was upset but I didn't understand why. If Amelia had gone behind my back and asked Lizzie if I was a virgin, I wouldn't have cared at all! Why did it matter so much?

"What?" Amelia snapped. "Are you going to say something, or just stare at me like an idiot?"

"Well, are you?" I asked defiantly, not breaking my stare.

"Am I what?"

"Are you a virgin?"

Those were the four words that broke the dam, setting free the waterworks that were Amelia, now bawling, struggling to stand. Immediately I moved to hold her, to comfort her, but she pulled back from me.

"No, maybe, I..." Amelia struggled to say. "I don't know."

I stood, scrunching my face in confusion. "I don't understand," I nearly whispered. "What does that mean?"

In defiance, Amelia sniffled, looking up to the sky to will her tears to stop. I gave her as much time as she needed. Finally, when she was calm enough to talk again, she said, "I just... this is really hard for me to talk about. I've... done things, but not like, all the way, I mean..." Amelia let out a noise of pure frustration. "Natalie, it's so hard for me to find the words to express how I feel. I've always had a weird and complicated relationship with my sexuality."

"I know that," I answered, shrugging.

"No, it's not just about me liking women," she continued. "It's just... well there has to be something wrong with me. There are times when I feel like it's something I want, so desperately, and I'd go all the way, then and there. I'd love it because I'd be totally there, mind and body, fully interested and invested. But there are other times, really, a majority of the time, where the thought almost... repulses me. It's like the act, the thought of it, means nothing to me. I'm there, and I can go through the motions, but there's no enjoyment... but there's no dislike either, I mean... god. I don't even know what I mean anymore. It's more than just an attraction to girls and a lack of attraction to guys. It can happen with girls too, even the same person. I could be loving every minute, but then a second later, be completely uninterested in... *that.* I must just have a sickeningly low sex drive. I've always thought about it. Wolfgang told me I should see a doctor. Maybe I should..."

I stared at Amelia, taking in her words. I could tell she felt vulnerable and scared... maybe scared of rejection, or just that I'd agree and tell her that she wasn't normal, that something was wrong with her, that she was messed up. But I didn't feel that way at all. In fact, what she said kind of reminded me of some things I had read online.

"Or maybe you're just asexual," I stated with a slight shrug.

Amelia frowned. "What does that mean?"

"It means, roughly, that you aren't interested in sex," I answered. "It's a spectrum though, just like all things related to sexuality. You can be asexual and still have sex, or you can be asexual and still masturbate. It's just, well what you were saying... it reminds me of asexuality. I don't know, of course, but maybe... you could read up on it. It might help. And there's nothing wrong with you, of course. Sex is... overrated, in my opinion. I know Karmen and Eleanor would probably argue—I think they rank sex as just as important as eating and sleeping—but at the end of the day, it's an activity. Just like sports, or painting, or watching TV. Some people love it, some people hate it, and some people are indifferent towards it. And all of those views are valid."

Amelia made a choked sound, her hand rising until she bit on her knuckle. I could see tears running down her cheeks. After a moment, I heard her mutter, "I wish everyone was as nice as you."

Clearly, Amelia had been beating herself up about this for quite a while now. Wolfgang was a huge jerk to her about it, made her feel like she was broken. She felt isolated by her horny friends growing up because she didn't feel the same things they felt. Of course she'd get so uncomfortable when Eleanor brought up her sexuality; Eleanor was doing the same thing all those other people always did, making Amelia feel broken because she couldn't relate.

"Amelia, like I said, there's absolutely nothing wrong with you," I continued. "I will always care about you, no matter what, and this isn't going to make me look at you any differently. It doesn't matter to me one bit if you had sex in the past or if you have sex in the future. You should do what's comfortable to you and if anyone tells you otherwise, they can take a hike."

Finally, Amelia half-smiled at me, and I knew it was going to be okay. "Thank you," she whispered. "You... you don't understand how badly I needed to hear that..."

"No need to thank me," I answered softly in return.

She extended her arm, offering me back my phone. "I'm sorry I snooped through your phone. I just... after what you were saying about Piper, and when I saw she had texted you, I got anxious, but then I scrolled and... well that wasn't very nice of me either."

I shook my head slightly, reaching out, but instead of grabbing my phone, I grabbed her wrist. I tugged her a few steps forward, catching her in my arms when she stumbled towards me. I wrapped my arms around her, and she did the same to me.

"Snoop," I mimicked her, pushing my nose against her neck. It made her giggle.

"Stop it," she laughed. "My neck's ticklish."

"Oh, you mean, stop this?" I questioned, lightly grazing my nose across her skin again. She tensed, laughing again, but I squeezed her tighter so she couldn't escape.

"Natalie!" she scolded, but it came out soft since she was still laughing.

"Are you going to be okay?" I questioned seriously, pulling back from her neck so I could look into her eyes.

"Yeah, I'm okay," Amelia replied. "I just, um... well I've been meaning to talk to you about the other night... the poker game—"

"I'm so sorry about that. I didn't—"

"No, listen, there's something I've been meaning to tell you."

I looked into Amelia's eyes and was mesmerized almost instantly, finding it difficult to focus with her face so close to mine.

"Um, sure," I stuttered. "What is it?"

"Well, I, um..." Amelia licked her lips, the movement tugging my eyes down to her lips. When I looked back up to meet her eyes, I noticed Amelia's eyes dart to my lips as well. Her eyes returned to mine, my heart beating in overdrive.

Suddenly, everything clicked.

Amelia being flirtatious but getting uncomfortable when things went too far. Amelia's reluctancy to sleep in a bed with me until I proved nothing more was going to happen. Amelia needing to take things slow. Amelia panicking when I removed her dress during a game of strip poker and fleeing. She *did* like me, but she was uncomfortable with the idea of sex.

Amelia whispered, "I think it would be easier if I just showed you." Then her eyes darted back down to my lips, and she leaned towards me.

My eyes fluttered shut on instinct and I felt the ever so light, fleeting touch of warmth on my lips. However, the near instant our lips touched, I heard someone shout out, "Ms. Lewis! Natalie! Where are you guys!?" The second we both heard this, Amelia straight *shoved* me away from her. I stumbled backwards, landing on my butt, unable to catch myself before I fell.

Confused, I glanced back towards the hotel's entrance only to see Shannon and the twins running up to us. I looked back to Amelia. Her face was bright red, and she was rubbing at her eyes—to wipe away tears and makeup smudges. She looked embarrassed and panicked. I pulled myself up and brushed off my pants.

"What are you guys doing out here in the alley?" Shannon questioned.

"Yeah, we want you to show the freshmen your breakdancing moves!" one of the twins exclaimed to Amelia.

"Breakdancing moves?" I questioned, butting into the conversation. "I think *I* need to see these moves."

Amelia looked to me, silently apologizing, but I just rolled my eyes in response.

"Come on!" I declared, grabbing Amelia's hand.

We didn't talk about the almost-kiss. When we got back to the room, Amelia got ready for bed and I took a particularly long shower, just thinking about what had happened. I knew I wanted to kiss her again, properly, and I wanted her to be comfortable enough to at least come out to her friends—maybe the honors choir if she was feeling particularly ballsy. But Amelia still needed to figure out her sexuality. She liked girls, that was a start, but it was clear there was more in store for her in her journey of self-discovery.

When I finally stepped out of the shower and pulled on my pajamas, Amelia was ready for bed, sitting under the covers, looking at stuff on her phone. I crawled into bed beside her, pushing myself up against her,

"What're you looking at?" I questioned. "Anything good?"

"I'm reading about asexuality," Amelia answered. "It's... well you're right. It's been very enlightening, and I do feel that way, I think."

"Do you want to talk about it?"

"I just... well this site's really nice," Amelia hummed, tilting her phone so I could see. "Look, there's a whole section about how asexuality is what someone feels, not what they do. Asexual people can still have sex, be married, and fall in love. You don't need sexual attraction to do those things. And romantic attraction is different too. Asexual individuals can still experience romantic attraction which... I do. I always thought the two went hand in hand, so I never would have... well... it's all just very enlightening and... validating. It's nice to see that others feel the same way I do."

"That's a big step in figuring out your sexuality," I said. "Learning that you aren't alone... I remember how alone I felt when I first realized I liked girls, but then I started learning more and meeting others and you're right. It's very validating."

"Can I... ask you something? Just... a random question?"

"Of course."

"Would you ever date an asexual person?"

I sat up straighter, looking to Amelia, my expression very serious. I wanted to shout, *"Yes, Amelia, yes! I'm in love with you, of course I want to date you!"* but I didn't know if she was asking me because she liked me, or if she thought being asexual meant no one who wasn't asexual would ever want to date her.

"It wouldn't bother me in the slightest, so of course I would, if I liked the person," I answered. "I told you, I think sex is kind of overrated."

"But... do you think you could go the rest of your life never having sex again?" Amelia asked. "Would anyone who's not asexual really be able to do that and still be entirely happy?"

I pushed myself up on my knees, looking at Amelia as seriously as I could. "I like a lot of things," I stated. "I like enchiladas, binging TV shows online, traveling, leading biology labs, and of course, cranberries—" at that, Amelia chuckled— "but if the right woman came along, and I mean, I really thought she was the one—I wanted to spend the rest of my life with her and only her—then I would give up any of those things for the rest of my life to be with her. The same goes for sex. If I really loved her and she didn't want to ever have sex, I would respect her wishes and I would never look back."

Amelia's eyes were glistening again. Without a word, she turned and buried herself into my lap.

18.

The Lawyer And The Child

I wasn't sure where Amelia and I stood. Part of me was afraid to ask, but another part of me was just preoccupied. We had to make sure an entire choir got home safely, and besides, Amelia had a lot to think about and reflect on. The last thing I wanted to do was pressure her towards anything, so I was extra careful what I said around her. This was her time to explore and discover, not my time to dictate.

We returned home Tuesday after a full day of travel. I bid Amelia—and the choir kids—farewell in the Elk Creek parking lot. Half of them acted like they'd never see me again, even though I'd be back Thursday. Amelia caught the odd look on my face when five students grabbed me in a hug, practically sobbing.

"I told you, choir nerds are excessive and weird," Amelia chuckled.

"Stop being so dramatic," I stated, shoving the students off me. They looked up at me, lips quivering for a moment, before they all burst out laughing.

Wednesday, on my way into Elk Creek, I swung by Piper's classroom first. I still didn't know what was going on with her, nor did the others. When I found her in her room, just after last period ended, right before lunch, she looked tired and stressed, but not unusually so.

"Oh, hello, Natalie," Piper said, glancing up at me. "How was the trip? I heard the choir placed first."

"They did. It was fun," I answered. "Say, how are you doing?"

"Fine, though I've been better," Piper admitted.

"Eleanor texted me Monday. She said she thought you'd gotten some bad news. I hadn't heard anything else though."

Piper's face went a little funny at the mention of this. "I... was planning on discussing this with the others," she admitted. "After the afterschool activities today, would you be willing to meet with us up in Karmen's room?"

"Sure."

"Alright. Well, I better head to lunch."

"Okay. I think I'll go find Amelia," I answered.

Piper nodded and trailed out of her room. I wasn't sure what to make of that. She certainly wasn't as chipper as normal, but she didn't exactly seem sad, or angry, or anything.

Regardless, I headed down towards the choir room. On my way, I heard someone shout out my name. I looked up, glancing down a hallway, only to spot Nicholas. He ran towards me, waving his arms in the air, calling for me to wait.

"Hey," I greeted him as he reached me.

"Come with me," he declared, grabbing my hand, and tugging me along. "I need to get something out of my locker, but I also need to talk to you."

"What are you doing over here and not at lunch?" I questioned as I allowed Nicholas to lead me.

"I had to make up an exam."

"Gotchu," I answered. "Is this going to take long? I was kind of hoping to talk to Ms. Lewis before lunch ends."

"It won't take long," Nicholas replied. "Look, here's my locker." Nicholas released my hand to get into his locker.

I leaned against the wall beside him. "What did you need to tell me?"

"I didn't know you liked Ms. Lewis."

"What?" I scoffed. "Come on! You're the one always saying we're best friends! Why would you think I didn't like her?"

"No, I mean—" Nicholas turned out from his locker to look straight at me— "you're totally in love with her."

I choked on air, coughing violently. How did he know? He wasn't in the alley, otherwise I would have figured he'd seen the almost-kiss. I tried to play off his accusations, but I could tell he wasn't buying it.

"Look, it's not a big deal," Nicholas stated with a shrug, turning back to whatever he was doing in his locker. "I mean, she's clearly head-over-heels for you as well."

"Really?" I asked, a smile on my lips, but I quickly came to my senses. "I mean, no she isn't. Why would you think that?"

"Oh my god, stop," Nicholas whined. "You two are totally in love with each other. And it's very obvious. I mean, be realistic. Who would meet

320

a new friend on vacation and be that *obsessed* with her if there weren't any feelings involved? I can't believe I didn't see it sooner. Anyway, you two are in love with each other, but it's pretty clear something's standing between you two. I think it's because Ms. Lewis isn't out yet, which is fine, she can do that on her own terms. I won't tell anyone. Outing others isn't cool. I literally just wanted to apologize for trying to set Ms. Lewis up with guys when she A, clearly doesn't like men, and B, *you* like her. It was insensitive."

I gave a soft smile. "It's not your fault. You guys didn't know, and you were only trying to help."

"I know, but I should have figured it out sooner!" Nicholas declared. "You two *literally* flirt *all the time*. It's kind of gross."

"Um, rude," I stated.

"Anyway, if it's any consolation, I think you two are super cute together," Nicholas added. "I can text you the picture we took of Ms. Lewis cuddled up on your lap on the bus. It's a *really* cute picture." He winked. "And obviously we've stopped the whole 'set Ms. Lewis up' thing, since she's uncomfortable with it—for very obvious reasons, now. But I just, well... does she know?"

"Know what?"

"Well, you were like completely oblivious that Ms. Lewis likes you, so I can only assume you haven't told her that you like her. I was just wondering if my hunch was correct."

"I—we—well stuff has been said but not so..."

"Specifically?"

"Yeah..."

"As I figured," Nicholas stated, nodding. "Anyway, I wanted your opinion on this. We got it for Ms. Lewis, to give to her at the end of the school year."

"What is it?" I questioned, looking down at what Nicholas was holding. It looked a bit like a plastic file folder, though that didn't clear anything up.

Nicholas held up the file, opening it so I could see the contents. It was sheet music, that much I could tell, and it looked decently old. I tried to read the title, which had a subtitle in a language other than English. I did, however, recognize the word '*Orphée.*'

"It's Rameau," Nicholas stated. "An old copy... the oldest we could find. We think it might be a re-write of the original, but we couldn't get it appraised."

"And you guys are giving it to Amelia?" I questioned, but then I quickly groaned, "Fuck, I mean Ms. Lewis."

Nicholas stifled a laugh. "Yes. I just wanted your opinion on it. Do you think she'll like it?"

"I mean, I don't know anything about classical composers or sheet music, but I know it's her favorite composer and I know she said that's the last of his work that she still didn't have an antique copy of."

"Fabulous then," Nicholas said, tucking away the file folder. "Anyway, you need to talk to Ms. Lewis about your feelings. I said we'd stop trying to set Ms. Lewis up, but since I *know*, I'm definitely going to be pushy here."

"Well... I'm planning on it, hopefully."

"Then good luck!" Nicholas squealed, shooting me two thumbs up. "I'm rooting for you two! Seriously! You're both adorable! *Ahh*, I'm so excited!"

I just rolled my eyes and left, heading towards the choir wing.

When I reached the choir room, Amelia was inside, as I suspected. I took a deep breath and stuck my head in through the open choir room door.

"Hey, 'Melia," I cooed.

Amelia looked up at me from her desk. "Hey, Nats," she responded with a soft smile.

"Did you eat anything?" I questioned.

Amelia nodded. "I just finished early. I swung by the teacher's longue, actually, because I'm kind of worried about Piper. She wasn't there though."

"That's probably my fault. I was talking to her in her classroom."

"Is she okay?"

"No? I can tell there's definitely something bothering her. She said she was going to tell everyone what had happened after all the afterschool programs."

"That's what Eleanor said. We're meeting up in Karmen's room."

"Yeah. How's Karmen doing, by the way? She's not back, is she? Surely not?"

"No. She'll probably be out the rest of the year," Amelia answered. "She might come back for finals and to prep for summer, but not yet."

"Okay, good. When Piper said we were meeting in her classroom, I thought she might be back, and I was like, that's way too soon."

"No, yeah. The janitors will clean her room while the afterschool programs run, and lock up, but I know Eleanor has a key to Karmen's classroom."

"Okay, cool. She's doing well though? Resting up?"

"Yeah. I think she's getting a little stir crazy at home, but she's healing well."

"Glad to hear it. And I really hope Piper's okay too."

"I do too," Amelia said. "I guess we'll find out after school."

For the remainder of the day, and the lab, I felt my mind getting pulled in many directions. At the forefront of my mind was Piper. I was worried about what could have happened, about that phone call, about why she left work early. I also thought about what Nicholas said, how he knew. He was likely to confront Amelia about it when he apologized to her, and even though I didn't think I had been subtle in letting Amelia know I liked her, if she didn't know I did, I didn't really want her finding out through Nicholas. That meant I needed to tell her myself, and soon.

I didn't want to pressure her though. She was still figuring things out, and like it or not, confessing would definitely put strain on our friendship, even if I made it clear that I didn't expect anything. I didn't know what to do.

The lab that week was really simple. We just ran a simulation of natural selection using spoons and colored candies. The students enjoyed it, especially because they got to eat the candy. The math was hard at first, but once they got the hang of it, it was easy going. I noticed that Aniyah seemed a bit distant, but I didn't hardly have time to say hi, as I was too busy running around and directing changes in the environments.

After lab, on my way up to Karmen's classroom, I ran into Amelia on the grand central stairs. She caught my eye and smiled, reaching out for me like she might take my hand, but then she thought better of herself and folded her arms together.

"Ready to go figure out what happened?" I questioned.

"I hope it's all a guise to surprise us with good news," Amelia muttered.

When we shoved open Karmen's door, we walked in on a particularly interesting scene. Ellie 2.0 was sitting at a student desk, Piper was standing, leaning against Karmen's desk, fighting back a blush, and Eleanor—sitting on a student desk across from Piper—leaned forward, gasping, "Oh my god, she did *not!*"

"What's, uh, happening?" I questioned, sitting down at another one of the desks.

"My, um... lawyer quit on me," Piper stated, refusing to look anyone in the eyes. Instead, she was glancing around the classroom, still blushing, her hand up against her cheek as if to further hide.

"That's terrible," I stated. "Can you get another one?"

"No, no, tell them *why* she quit," Eleanor continued, a shit eating grin on her face.

"Listen, s—stop that!" Piper scolded. "It's not funny."

"Here, look," Ellie 2.0 declared, holding up her phone. "This lawyer looks perfectly nice and competent. I bet she'd be a great replacement—"

"What is happening?" Amelia questioned, more forcefully.

"Piper's lawyer fell in love with her and told her she can't keep representing her," Eleanor stated, hiding a smirk behind her hand.

"You're kidding," I declared.

"It's rather embarrassing," Piper muttered. "And a fair bit problematic, because she's really good—"

"In bed," Eleanor coughed under her breath.

Ellie 2.0 elbowed Eleanor as Piper gasped out, "She's a good lawyer! That's *it*."

"Now hang on, hang on, hang on," I stated, waving my hands. "There's no way this just came up out of the blue. I feel like I'm missing some crucial backstory here."

"Agreed," Amelia said, nodding.

"Well, there, um, might have been signs," Piper said, still fighting back her blush and refusing to look at any of us. "But it was just... nice having a companion outside of you all. And I never meant for it to go so far, I just... it's all been rather abrupt and stressful."

"What'd she say? What'd you tell her?" I asked.

"We went out to dinner Sunday evening—to discuss the case!" Piper stated harshly, glaring at Eleanor who was making a teasing face. "And we'd been to dinner before, to discuss things. And yes, maybe I did notice that she was being flirtatious, but... it was nice! You know, I'd been with Christian since high school. I haven't gotten out much, without him, and after the whole issue, well... but she told me she wasn't sure she'd be able to keep representlanting me. And when I asked why... she said it was because she had caught feelings for me. So, I, um, left."

"You *left*?" Eleanor asked incredulously.

"Well, what was I supposed to do? I mean, it rather blindsided me, and then I realized how she must have been seeing things, and I just... needed to leave."

"So, the phone call?"

"She told me she was giving my case to her coworker, and that she needed to see me."

"*Ooo*," Eleanor cooed.

"She wanted to pursue things, that's why she gave my case up, but I told her I couldn't. I don't... I don't think I like women like that. There's nothing wrong with that, of course, but just personally, I don't think. And well anyway, it doesn't matter, because I don't want to be in a relationship. I don't want to ever date another person so long as I live."

"*Ahh*, how lame," Eleanor huffed. "You should have given it a go and seen how things went."

"But I don't like—"

"It's perfectly valid to be honest with her," Ellie 2.0 cut in. "You can't help if you don't like women like that—despite us being greatly outnumbered in this room—" she said, rolling her eyes at Eleanor— "and it's perfectly reasonable that currently you wouldn't want to pursue another relationship. Christian really hurt you."

"I can't believe you're blushing so bad," Eleanor howled, finally breaking and laughing fully. "Hasn't anyone ever had a crush on you before? Besides Christian, obviously."

"Well, sure," Piper muttered. "But I just... well I know she was my lawyer, but, well I thought we were building a steady sort of friendship and now, well, I've ruined that."

"I hardly think *you* ruined it," Ellie 2.0 said.

"We talked every day," Piper finally declared. "Of course, about the case, and Christian, and the baby, but... but we still *talked*. And now, I haven't heard from her since Monday—"

"Wait, do you miss her?" Amelia asked, smirking.

My grin grew as Piper's blush grew brighter. "Oh my gosh, call her!" I declared. "Tell her you want to meet up!"

"No!" Piper protested.

"She shouldn't lead her on," Ellie 2.0 stated, being logical. "If she's got feelings, distance is the best thing at this current moment in time."

"But if they're going to remain friends—" Eleanor started, but Ellie 2.0 cut her off.

"Then after a break, they can mend their friendship, but as of right now, space."

"Ellie 2.0's probably right," Amelia admitted. "As much as I'd like to see the outcome of this, you don't want to lead her on. It'll only hurt her more in the long run."

"I can't believe you didn't tell us your lawyer was hot on you," I stated.

"I only just realized!" Piper protested. "I mean, hindsight is twenty/twenty, so I should have known, but..."

"Is she cute?" Amelia prodded.

Piper blushed harder and turned away from us, mumbling, "Perhaps."

"What's her name?" I asked.

"Veronica," Piper continued mumbling.

"Cute name," Amelia commented.

"How's the new lawyer?" Ellie 2.0 asked.

"She's... decent, competent," Piper replied, glancing back at us. "Veronica wouldn't have left me with someone who was bad. But she's just... different."

"I'm sure she'll do a great job and help you wonderfully," Ellie 2.0 added.

A cellphone started ringing, and Piper reached into the pocket of her dress to fish out her phone. She looked at the screen, biting her lip.

"Oh my gosh, is that her!?" I gasped excitedly.

"Is it!?" Eleanor gasped with equal excitement.

"N—no!" Piper stated, but her blush gave her away.

Eleanor leapt up and dashed around the desk, grabbing at Piper's phone. "Answer it!" Eleanor declared. Piper dipped away from her, trying to dodge, but Amelia, feeling playful as well, joined in.

"Yes, answer it!" I stated, getting up as well.

Between the three of us, Piper couldn't very well dodge us all. Eleanor managed to catch the phone and tug it from Piper's hand.

"Eleanor, give me back my phone!" Piper scolded.

Eleanor answered the call instead of listening. "Hello? Veronica?" she questioned. "Uh-huh, no, yeah, she's right here." Eleanor pulled the phone down and held it against her chest, whisper-mouthing, "It's your boo-thang, Piper."

"Give that to me!" Piper protested, diving after Eleanor, but Amelia held her back.

Eleanor pulled the phone back up to ear. "Yeah, she's actually been meaning to call you. Yeah, she really misses—"

"Give me that!" Piper hissed, struggling free of Karmen to dash at Eleanor.

I turned back to Ellie 2.0, shaking my head. "How crazy," I declared fondly.

"Eleanor!"

"I think it's kind of cute," Ellie 2.0 replied, shrugging. "I've never seen Piper so flustered before. I mean, regardless of what'll happen between them, I hope they at least stay friends."

"Yeah, I'd like to meet her. Surely she's—" I began, but my words cut off abruptly as my attention was suddenly, and very ungracefully, snapped away from Ellie 2.0 upon hearing the following two sounds in quick succession: first, the sound of a splatter of water—weird—and then immediately, Amelia screaming, "Oh my god, did your water just break!?"

I spun around to find Piper, one hand bracing herself against Karmen's desk, her other hand on her stomach, her face pale white, eyes wide. Amelia had a hold of her shoulder and looked just as panicked. Eleanor was mid-jumping to grab Piper was well.

"But... I'm—I'm not due yet..." Piper meekly squeaked out.

"She'll call you back," Eleanor said into Piper's phone, hanging up the call abruptly.

"I'm not an expert or anything," I stated, eyes wide, "but doesn't that mean you're in labor? Like, a baby is coming out of you... soon?"

Piper looked up across the room at me, her brows furrowed in worry. We were all just frozen in place, afraid and totally shocked. Finally, Ellie 2.0 spoke up.

"Well, I guess we should take you to the hospital," she offered.

"Right, right," Eleanor replied. "*Umm...* keys—" She started slapping at her pockets. "Who's driving?"

"I will!" Amelia answered, producing her car keys from her pocket. "Can you walk?" she asked Piper.

"Of course I can walk!" Piper snapped. "I'm giving birth, not dying!"

"Okay, Ms. Know-It-All," Amelia replied. "You just poured a gallon of body fluids onto the floor. How was I supposed to know?"

As we ushered Piper out of the classroom, Eleanor let out a delighted squeal. "I can't believe we're getting two new babies in the same month! That's so exciting! Oh my god, I have to text Karmen. She'll be ecstatic!"

"I'm going to grab a janitor on the way out," I stated. "Let them know about the, uh, situation in there."

"Good thinking," Ellie 2.0 agreed.

"Let's go deliver a baby!" Amelia shouted in glee, leaping up and giving Eleanor a high five.

Once I found a janitor, I chased after my friends, practically tripping over my feet as I burst out the front doors of the school. I spotted them hurrying towards Amelia's car and I ran after them, hardly paying attention to anything other than my friends. But I slowed and stopped just a few strides into the parking lot, glancing back over my shoulder.

Sure enough, sitting on the sidewalk was Aniyah, her head down and resting on her knees. I glanced down at my phone, checking the time. It was nearly an hour after lab had ended, why was she still here? I looked back to my friends, then back to Aniyah.

"Hey, don't wait up for me!" I shouted out to my friends. "I'll meet you at the hospital!"

I turned back and walked up to Aniyah, sitting down beside her.

"Hey, what's up?" I questioned.

Aniyah raised her head, looking at me. "Oh, hi, Natalie," she answered.

"What're you doing?" I asked. "Did you miss your carpool?"

"No, well... my brother was supposed to pick me up, but he got arrested the other day, and my dad couldn't get off work early. I was going to walk, but I just... I don't know. I don't really want to walk all that way alone. I was thinking maybe I could just wait until my dad gets off work and call him."

I watched as Amelia's car pulled out of the parking lot. Piper was giving birth and that was a monumental moment, but she wouldn't be alone. She had Amelia, Eleanor, and Ellie 2.0—plus, Karmen, even. Besides, they'd probably be better company in the delivery room than I would be. Piper would be okay. In that moment, Aniyah needed me more.

"I can drive you home," I offered.

"Oh, I couldn't ask you to do that," Aniyah replied.

"You're not asking. I'm offering," I answered.

"Well... I guess so," she gave in.

The drive was short enough. It was only a couple of miles. The drive felt long for me, however, because of how uncomfortable I became. It wasn't that I was uncomfortable being with Aniyah, quite the opposite, in fact. We had a lovely conversation at the start of the drive. I told her about our trip to New York, and she talked about all the places she hoped to one day travel to. We also talked a bit about her at home life, her brother, and her father. She didn't mention much about why her brother went to jail, and she said her father was sick. I didn't push and question, just nodded in response.

No, it wasn't Aniyah that made me uncomfortable. The closer we got to her house, the slower I drove. Not consciously, but my attention was drawn to the outside world, and I started to realize just how sheltered I had been. I had never been in a neighborhood like this one before. My mother had always been very conscious about where we went and where she let me go, and in college, that had manifested itself in me. I *thought* I had been in rough neighborhoods before, but my perception was clearly skewed.

First, I noticed the roads. What was once smooth pavement became jagged and full of potholes. The houses went from nice, to old, to falling apart. The number of smashed in windows increased. I started to become more aware of the people around us too, people sitting on front porches smoking and drinking, people walking between parked cars, people just walking up and down the street, shouting and calling out to others.

As I drove, I realized this was one of those neighborhoods my mother told me to avoid. This was the side of town that my white family warned me of, the type of area with drugs, and gangs, and gun shots—the most dangerous place. This was a place where, as you drove through, you locked your doors and windows and sped up to get out of as fast as possible. Despite this, I was going to have to stop, unlock my car, and open the door to drop Aniyah off.

Uncomfortable was an understatement. Each person I saw set off alarms in my head. Fear bubbled inside me, a fear that had been ingrained into my very soul since birth into privileged white society: the black man is an animalistic killer, a criminal, a rapist, and in the ghetto they hunt white girls like wolves hunt rabbits.

I stopped at a stoplight, my skin prickling, the grip on my steering wheel causing my knuckles to turn white. I watched every person I saw like a hawk, my foot twitching and ready to floor it should one so much as step towards my car.

"Hey, are you okay?" Aniyah's voice broke me from my dangerous head space.

I blinked a few times, taking a deep breath. I was ashamed of my thoughts. Aniyah was right beside me, a girl of pure compassion and ambition. She was human, just like me. And she lived in this neighborhood.

"You're scared of the area," Aniyah observed. "You probably grew up sheltered and in a white-centric area, huh? I get it. I see how the media paints an image of us. To you, a black guy walking down the sidewalk

329

probably looks like a criminal. To me—" she pointed out the car window at a man walking down the sidewalk, carrying a soda— "he looks like my uncle, just on his way home from a day of hard and honest work at the car shop. He goes to church every Sunday—just like his momma taught him— and he's got two daughters at home, five and ten. He took up an extra shift this week because his eldest's birthday is coming up and she wants a fancy toy that all the girls at school have. Too bad she'll never get it though, because your people saw him the day before, as a monster, and shot him dead in the street just for walking home with a soda. He's never owned a gun in his life, never even so much as raised his voice, but somehow that's still enough to shoot in 'self-defense.'"

The car behind me honked and I realized that the light had turned green without me knowing. I didn't know if that had actually happened to her uncle, or if it was just a generalization, but it didn't matter either way. The fact was, I was racist. Despite growing up being told racism was bad, the very people who taught me that had also taught me to be racist, hidden under a veil of false pretenses and lies.

"I'm... sorry..." was all I could think to say as I started driving again.

"It's just life," Aniyah muttered. "Some people get everything handed to them and still take it all for granted, some of us have to fight a thousand times harder for just a fraction of that and die trying. Anyway, that's my house there."

I pulled to a stop in front of a semi-falling down house right behind a barred-up gas station. There was litter everywhere, including broken bottles lining the broken-down street. I thought about it compared to the neighborhood where I had grown up. Was it the person who made the neighborhood, or the neighborhood that made the person? Was it coincidence this falling down street was occupied by mainly black people, or circumstantial? Did they have a choice? Why would someone choose to live in poverty unless it was their only option?

"Want to come inside for a few minutes?" Aniyah asked. "I made cookies yesterday. We probably still have some."

"*Umm...* sure," I answered. I fought against my discomfort, telling myself that I was fine. Racism wasn't birthed in fact. It came from certain groups wanting control over other groups. It was entitlement. It was gross. These people were no different than me. They had feelings, emotions, and dreams. They lived and felt, were happy and sad, loved and gave, just as they faced disappointment and sorrow. Who was to say what I deserved over what they deserved? We were all people.

Aniyah led me inside for a tour. Right inside, we walked upstairs to reach the upper unit, which they likely rented. They had a few folding chairs and on old looking TV sitting on the floor of their living room. The kitchen was baren, save for their plastic dishes. Aniyah brought me to her room and found the box of cookies she had made. She only had a small mattress on the floor, just with one pillow and a single blanket. Her schoolbooks were stacked in the corner next to a plastic bin where she stored her clothes. That was it.

Based on how Aniyah carried herself in lab, I never would have guessed the impoverished conditions in which she lived. In fact, although I knew what the word 'poverty' meant, I never truly understood it. I thought about Eleanor's upbringing and her life in foster care. Did she live in conditions like these? I couldn't even fathom living with such little. I was so privileged, and I took it all for granted. I could give up half of what I owned, and still live comfortably with more than Aniyah and her family had. It wasn't fair. How could I be so much better off than Aniyah? Was it just the money my family had? Because my mom was a doctor? What about my grandparents? Was it the education that got us where we were? Could we only get all of that because we were white?

"Here, they're good ole chocolate chip," Aniyah declared, handing me a cookie. "Consider it thanks for driving me home."

I took the cookie a bit into it reluctantly. I felt like Aniyah needed it more than me, but I didn't want to be rude. I bit into the cookie and smiled. It tasted, maybe, better than Amelia's.

"This is good... *really* good," I declared. "And you made this yourself?"

"Yup."

"I have a friend who makes *killer* cookies, but I think this cookie could give her a run for her money."

"I'm a pretty decent baker."

"Yeah, no kidding. You're pretty talented, you know?"

"Thanks. And thanks for driving me home."

"Of course," I answered. Aniyah walked me back down to the front door. Before I left, I turned back to her and said, "Listen, if you ever need a ride home again, just let me know, okay? It's not a big deal driving you home."

"Alright, I'll remember that. Thanks."

I found Ellie 2.0 in the waiting room when I got to the hospital. She was staying out of the delivery room because she didn't think she could stomach a live birth. I was inclined to agree with her, so I stayed out there with her. Eleanor stayed in the delivery room with Piper, and Karmen showed up, after finding a babysitter, to stay by Piper's side as well. They were both already mothers; they knew the routine. Amelia floated between the delivery room and the waiting room, a little too squeamish for the blood, but too curious to remain outside.

"What are you thinking about?" Ellie 2.0 questioned, pulling me out of my thoughts and onto her.

"Oh, um, just Piper," I lied.

"Okay, and?"

"And?"

"And what else?" she clarified. "You look like someone kicked your puppy."

I looked over at Ellie 2.0. She was so... nice. I felt like she would never judge anybody. I knew she wasn't white, and she at least came from a religious family. Was her life experience entirely different from mine? Did she have a complicated backstory just like Eleanor, and Karmen, and Amelia? I mean, surely everyone did. We were all unique individuals. But did I have a complicated backstory? I was pretty boring. I grew up with a loving family, good friends, a good education, and good opportunities. I went to college. I was going to graduate, granted into a field I didn't like, but still. And I was raised racist, which I was only just realizing at age twenty-two.

"Earth to Natalie," Ellie 2.0 declared. "What's going on in that head of yours?"

"I'm a racist," I stated.

Ellie 2.0's eyes widened, but then her expression softened. "What makes you say that?" she asked.

"I... do you know who Aniyah Smith is? She's in my afterschool biology lab, one of the students from Byram."

"Yeah, I've met her," Ellie 2.0 said. "She took Eleanor's physics lab last year and I ran into her one afternoon. I think Eleanor and she are rather close."

"I drove her home today. That's why I was late getting over here. She didn't have a ride home, so I thought, why not, you know? But then I saw her neighborhood and I started having all these feelings... like I was scared to be there. I was raised being told that was what bad neighborhoods were like, and that people who live there are bad guys. But it's just black people living in poverty. They aren't bad people—well I mean, no one *attacked* us or anything. And Aniyah *lives* there, every day! That's her home! Those feelings I was having were entirely unjustified, but they exist because I was raised racist—by people who told me racism was bad! Like just because you don't outright lynch black people, doesn't mean you aren't still racist!"

I sighed, rubbing at my eyes. "I grew up so sheltered... and so privileged. I never even questioned racism until I heard about Eleanor's past, and all the problems with Byram, everything originating with race and economic differences... and it's just like, why should I live such a comfy life with all these amazing opportunities while other people are struggling so horribly? I mean, god, I'm graduating with a degree I don't even *want!* I took my upper-level education for granted. Aniyah deserves a college biology degree more than I do!"

"That's a lot to digest," Ellie 2.0 stated, nodding. "Race is a really complicated issue in America. And yeah, a lot of problems arise from white people kicking down people of color. You and I were born into a system set up years and years ago, and when something's been around for so long, with generation after generation growing up thinking that's the norm, it's really hard to break out of that cycle. I mean, people of color face the discrimination firsthand. We learn to either shut-up and deal with it or speak up and face repercussions. And white people are raised thinking they're the best, that everyone else deserves their fate for this reason or another, and when you get everything handed to you, why would *you* want to break that system? It's benefitting you."

"Of course I'm benefitting from it," I muttered. "And that makes me feel so shitty. I'm not that great of a person. Why should I get this life over someone who actually deserves it?"

"Deserves... doesn't deserve... we're all born, handed a role in life, and we can only change so much of that. I think it's more what you chose to *do* with it. Since you have so much privilege, why not use it to help minorities out?"

"Yeah, but how?"

"Start by educating yourself," Ellie 2.0 said. "Step one is admitting the world is flawed and you benefit from it based on your skin color—and other things, like being cis-gendered and raised Christian. Then, educate yourself on all the injustices in the world. Listen to others. Learn their life stories, their feelings, their struggles. And get angry about it. Then fight for change. Educate others like you educated yourself."

"Is that why you like teaching? To help educate others?"

Ellie 2.0 shrugged. "I like teaching for a number of reasons. Am I open and honest to all of my students? Do we have discussions about issues raised in the books we read? Of course. I expose them to what I can, but at the end of the day, it's up to them to open their eyes and really *ingest* it all. I also just really care about the impact a good education can have. I know America isn't great, but it can provide a lot of great opportunities to those who are lucky. My students are lucky. I want them to realize that, and maybe someday they'll fight to give others the same opportunities they had."

"When did you realize you were so passionate about all this?" I asked. "I'm still trying to figure out what I'm passionate about. Sometimes I think I could be passionate about teaching, but I just don't know if it's a good fit for me."

"*Hmm,* where to start..." Ellie 2.0 pondered. "I guess when I was in grade-school I realized how blessed I was. I immigrated to America with my parents and siblings when I was about four. I hardly remember our home country in the Middle East. I don't have any memories of it, personally, but I remember 9-11 plenty well, and how America reacted. I just remember all the attacks back home, my parents crying over it, not knowing if our family back home was dead or alive, or how long they'd live. I remember my dad losing his job, being victim to hate crimes... The world looked at us like we were monsters, automatic bad guys. But we're just people, you know? I have parents, and siblings, and dogs... there's no respect for our culture, just because it's different. People are afraid of our native languages, but it's all from assumptions! Just negative stereotypes! We pray like they do, we love like they do... I just think that education can eliminate ignorance. Ignorance can breed hate, but if you educate, people realize that we're not so different, you know?"

I frowned, thinking about how my own parents reacted to 9-11. I was young when it happened; I didn't really remember it. But I remembered hearing my uncles talk about it, how all the attacks in the Middle East were good and needed. What about all the innocent civilians that were killed in the crossfire though? They had families... they had lives... they were *people.* Just because they spoke a different language, or worshiped different gods, or ate different food, didn't mean they deserved to *die.* The same could be said for those who died in the towers, but why did civilian American lives mean more than civilian Middle Eastern lives? Why were they worth more? They weren't.

"Excuse me, do you know if there's a Piper Kegan back here?"

I looked up at a tall and imposing woman. She was beautiful and clearly concerned. And she had just asked where Piper was.

"Yes, she's in a delivery room. We're her friends," Ellie 2.0 answered the woman. "And you are...?"

"My name's Veronica Reeves," the woman replied, reaching out and shaking Ellie 2.0's hand. "I'm sorry, I just, I got word that she'd gone into labor, and I know she isn't due for—"

"*You're* Veronica?" I gasped unceremoniously, cutting her off.

"*Umm,* yes..."

I exchanged a glance with Ellie 2.0, sitting up straighter. "Yeah, I don't know if you should go back into the delivery room. Three of our friends are back there already, so it might get a little crowded. But you're free to wait here with us. You could probably see her afterwards."

Veronica nodded, taking a seat beside me. Ellie 2.0 tapped me and gestured questioningly. I just shrugged slightly and shook my head. I was just as surprised as Ellie 2.0 to see Veronica. She must have been very concerned, overhearing what she did on the phone, but I still didn't expect her to come to the hospital. She clearly cared for Piper greatly.

Suddenly, Amelia burst out into the waiting room, gasping, "I almost threw up!" She rushed over to us, panting. "But she's here! The baby's here! I really didn't want to see as much as I did, but she's here!"

"That's fantastic!" Ellie 2.0 gasped.

"Yes!" I agreed.

Next to me, Veronica leapt up out of her seat. "How's she doing?" she asked. "Is Piper okay?"

Amelia looked to Veronica funnily. "*Umm...* I don't believe we've met...?"

"Oh, um, terribly sorry, I'm—"

"This is *Veronica*," I cut in.

"Ver—Oh!" Amelia answered, eyes wide. She turned back to the woman, grasping her hand in a firm shake. "It's so nice to meet you, Veronica! Yes, Piper's doing quite well. And I assume the baby is too—I heard her scream—although as I said, they shoved me out of the delivery room because I was going to throw up and possibly faint." She turned back to Ellie 2.0 and me. "Eleanor and Karmen said they'd come out shortly with a more informative update."

We all sat back down again and waited for that more informative update. It was a bit awkward. Veronica sat ramrod straight, her eyes fixed on the door leading back into the delivery room. Ellie 2.0 seemed mostly calm, relieved. Amelia, above all, clearly wanted to ask Veronica questions, as did I.

Eventually Amelia broke. "I think I'd like some water. Are you thirsty, Natalie?"

"Yeah, I could use a drink," I replied.

Instantly, the two of us leapt up and dashed down the hall, around the corner.

"Veronica!?" Amelia gasped to me. "She's very... attractive."

"I know. Stunning, really."

"And she showed up at the hospital, just after overhearing us yelling about Piper's water breaking?"

"Yeah, I guess so," I answered. "She must like... really care about Piper."

"I can't believe it."

"Me either."

After taking a little time to compose ourselves and calm our excitement, we returned to our seats. Ellie 2.0 had engaged Veronica in pleasant conversation, so we joined in easily. We learned more about her past, why she chose to become a lawyer. Amelia tried to naturally bring up what had happened between her and Piper, but Veronica got flustered and refused to comment further.

Eventually, we were allowed to go back and visit Piper and the new baby. When the nurse brought us back to the room, Piper was practically unconscious with exhaustion, lying in bed. Karmen was sitting in one of the chairs, cuddling and rocking the baby as if it were her own child, Eleanor sitting right beside her. The baby was really small, connected to oxygen and a few wires, but she was still big enough that Karmen could hold her without the doctors throwing a fit.

Amelia, Ellie 2.0, and I had entered the room first. We walked towards Karmen and Eleanor to see the baby.

"Did she name her yet?" Amelia asked in a whisper.

"Katrina Loella," Eleanor answered.

"She's premature and tiny, but the doctors are confident she'll grow up healthy and strong," Karmen replied.

"*Aww*, Katrina," Amelia stated, smiling. She reached out, gently holding one of Katrina's tiny hands between her fingers. "Welcome to the world, beautiful."

"Who the fuck is that?" Eleanor barked out suddenly.

I turned, noting that Eleanor was looking at Veronica, who had avoided the cluster of us in favor of walking over to the bedside. Her attention was entirely focused on Piper. She reached out slowly and gently to tuck some unruly strands of Piper's hair back behind her ear.

"That's *Veronica*," Amelia stated.

"*Veronica?*" Eleanor repeated.

Veronica, hearing her name, turned back towards us. "How's she doing?" she asked.

"She's exhausted. She's resting," Karmen replied.

Veronica nodded, looking back longingly at Piper. "I um, I don't want to overstay my welcome," she said. "I just... I wanted to make sure she's okay."

"You could stay until she wakes up," Karmen offered. "It might be tomorrow, but—"

"No, no, I... I don't know if she'd want me around. I just couldn't *not* come check on her, after the panic, and I... I'm going to go." Veronica stood for a moment, still looking at Piper, before she turned and headed towards the door. "It was, um, nice to meet all of you. Piper's said many fantastic things about her friends. I'm sorry we couldn't meet under different circumstances—"

"Do you want us to tell Piper you were here?" Karmen asked.

Veronica bit at her lip. "I... don't want to upset her," she muttered. "I'm sorry." Then she hurried out of the room.

I watched her go before turning back to my friends. "I feel sorry for her," Amelia said. "She clearly *really* cares about Piper."

"It sucks falling for a straight girl," I answered.

"She seems nice though," Amelia replied. "Maybe they can be friends."

"Maybe."

I left the hospital not long after that. That many overnight guests weren't allowed, and besides, I had school the next day. Piper was going to have to stay through the weekend, because Katrina was premature. And so, as soon as the weekend rolled around, I was right back over at the hospital to properly visit my friend. I found Karmen in the room with Piper when I arrived. Eleanor was back home watching the kids, giving

Karmen a reprieve from the house, and she was more than happy to come help Piper with the new baby.

I couldn't relate with them on any of their mom experiences, but it was fun to listen to them. Most of the time, Karmen just teased Piper about the trials and tribulations of parenthood.

"Giving birth was hard enough!" Piper exclaimed. "You're supposed to tell me the hard part is over!"

"I *wish* labor was the hardest part," Karmen scoffed. "Just wait until she learns the word 'no.' Then you'll know pain."

"How was it really?" I asked meekly. "I know you were terrified of giving birth. Hopefully it wasn't *that* bad."

"Horrid, miserable, makes me want to do unspeakable things to Christian," Piper forced out. She glanced over to the room's crib, where Katrina was peacefully sleeping. "But worth it entirely. I'm... really glad I decided to have the child and fight to keep her."

"She's got your eyes," Karmen stated.

"I have no desire whatsoever to go through with that ever again, however," Piper continued. "I never wished for this, never wanted it, frankly. I'm not upset how things ended up though, I suppose. I just don't think I could ever give birth to another, or raise another, or trust someone enough to date again—"

"Yeah, speaking of which, how's the situation going with Veronica?" Karmen questioned, wiggling an eyebrow.

"There is no situation," Piper answered, coloring slightly in the cheeks. "I haven't heard from her since—since well... I know she called before I went into labor, but she never called back after that, and I'm not sure I—"

"You didn't tell her, then?" I asked Karmen.

"Tell me what?" Piper questioned suspiciously.

"Veronica stopped by the hospital to check up on you," Karmen lamented easily. "She asked that we didn't tell you she was here, but I don't think there's any harm in you knowing."

"She... came here? To check on me?"

"She's got it bad for you."

"I wish I could give her what she wants..." Piper muttered dejectedly.

"Speaking of struggling couples, how are you and Amelia doing, Natalie?" Karmen questioned, turning towards me and smirking.

"We aren't struggling," I declared.

"How was that trip? I heard from Amelia you had to share a bed."

"We did, not that it means anything," I answered. "I think... well I think I learned a lot about Amelia on our trip. We didn't exactly talk directly about our feelings for each other, but after we almost kissed, I kind of think we probably should talk about it—"

"Wait, you kissed!?" Karmen gasped.

"No, we *almost* kissed," I clarified. "Like, we were going to, I think, but then we got interrupted. And I do really want to tell her how I feel, just be completely open and honest with her. I'm just looking for the right time."

"If it's meant to be, any time is the right time."

"Yes, well, I kind of thought Piper giving birth to her first and only child was a little more important than confessing to Amelia."

"Yes, thank you!" Piper agreed.

We were drawn away from each other by a knock on the door. I turned, expecting another nurse, but instead I saw a husky blonde guy making a curtsey in the doorway, a bouquet of flowers in his hand.

"Hi there, Cliff," Karmen greeted him.

Cliff, Ellie 2.0's fiancé, stood and walked into the room, presenting the flowers to Piper before leaning down and giving her a kiss on each cheek in greeting. "Looking brilliant as always," he declared to Piper before he turned and greeted the rest of us. "And hello, ladies. Is this the beautiful young lady that's going to be gracing our house?" he questioned, turning to the sleeping Katrina.

"The one and only," Piper replied.

"Absolutely beautiful, just like her mother," Cliff stated, nodding. "Congratulations are in order." He turned back around then, and his attention settled on me. "And you, you must be Natalie, because I don't think these gals know more than one college kid with pink hair."

"That would be me. The hair does give away my identity rather often."

"Is Ellie with you, or did you ditch her somewhere?" Piper questioned.

"She's working late, prepping a poetry slam. If she gets done early though, she might come visit."

"Tell her that's not necessary. She'll see me Sunday when they release me."

"I forgot the poetry slam's coming up," Karmen commented. "I'm surprised you didn't have your students join," she stated, pointing accusingly at Cliff.

"I didn't manage to get a team together before the registration deadline," Cliff lamented. "But I plan on taking notes on Ellie's form, and then we'll come out swinging next year and take her down."

"Very chivalrous of you," Piper stated.

"I know. I'm fantastic. But enough about me! I want to know about this girly right here—" he pointed to me— "that's got our Amelia all tongue tied!"

"*Umm...* I'm going to opt out of this conversation," I stated.

"Oh right, you mentioned the denial," Cliff said, glancing back over his shoulder at Piper. He shrugged. "Can't win them all, I guess."

"I'm not in denial," I defended. "I'm... I'm working on it. I don't know how all your relationships went down, but I kind of don't think you met, fell in love, and made out all in the same day. Just give me some time!"

"I know real life takes time. I just think it's a little bit funny. I never really pegged Amelia as the queer type."

"That's because you're oblivious to the world," Karmen scoffed, while Piper simultaneously said, "Yeah, because you're dense as a rock."

Cliff glanced between them skeptically. "You guys were at Philly's on St. Patrick's Day a year ago, weren't you? A couple of drinks in and Amelia seemed pretty good at flirting with men to me. I don't think her liking women was *that* obvious."

"That's because guys always think that if a girl is just being nice to them, she's flirting," Karmen replied. "If you told Amelia to purposefully flirt with a guy, she'd probably step on his foot and think that was how it's done."

"She's done theater, I hardly think she'd be *that* bad of an actor," I defended Amelia.

"Adorable, standing up for your girlfriend," Cliff said, smirking at me.

I felt my cheeks color at his statement. I grumbled out, "You fit right into this friend group, huh?"

"She didn't deny it!" Karmen practically squealed.

"What? I mean, no! She's not my girlfriend!" I barked out. "Come on, guys!"

The group laughed at me, only furthering my blush.

Suddenly, I found myself outrageously stressed. Piper's sudden and early delivery meant an early maternity leave. Though I was always running the afterschool labs alone, Piper helped organize materials and decide *what* was being done for lab. So, without her around, I had to start doing all of that myself. And, I had to grade the labs without any help from Piper.

Adding to the stress of my now doubled workload, it was also the last month of school. The last round of exams were coming up, followed by final projects and final exams. I knew I was going to be staying in the city over summer, and through at least the next school year because of my job at Elk Creek. What I didn't know was where I was going to live or what I was going to do after that. My job, though legitimate, was not a real teaching job. The principal expressed to me that all teachers there are required to have, at minimum, a master's degree. Like Ellie 2.0, they offered—should things continue to go well through the summer and next fall—that I could take night classes to get my master's and become, someday, a fully hired full time teacher at Elk Creek.

But did I want that?

Two weeks later, the afterschool lab went just about as horribly as my first lab. The kids were extra rambunctious, eager for the end of school, and I was so busy dashing between lab stations that I didn't even notice Aniyah was absent. In fact, I didn't realize she wasn't there until I was cleaning up and sorting through everyone's lab packets. Her absence set off alarm bells in my head. I tried to be rational. She was likely just sick, and next week she'd be back, happy, and chipper, and ready to learn.

Amidst my stress from work and school and worrying about what I was going to do with my future, there was also that lingering thought in the back of my mind about how I was going to confess to Amelia. I could do it now. But the end of school was fast approaching. I was busy; Amelia was busy. And I really needed to focus on passing my classes so that I'd actually graduate. I didn't need any distractions. If I confessed and she rejected me, it would cause a lot of pain right before finals, and well, if she accepted me, it would be super distracting. Either way, I decided I needed to wait for the time being and not lose focus on my schoolwork.

I couldn't just slip out Thursday unnoticed, though. Amelia and I always met up after lab, even if we only talked for a few minutes, so it wouldn't be right to leave without seeing her. I trailed over to the choir room just as her last student was leaving their private voice lesson.

"Hey, Natalie," Amelia greeted me, whooshing past me as she carried a stack of files. "Sorry about the mess in here. I'm getting a head start on packing up my classroom for summer."

"Sounds like a lot of work," I commented, strolling over to her desk.

I looked down and recognized the file folder on her desk. It was the same plastic file folder Nicholas showed me, the one that had the old Rameau sheet music. The honors choir must have finally given it to her.

Amelia noticed me staring at her gift and she came up, picking up the folder. "Look," she said, opening up the folder. "It's a Rameau piece. The honors choir gave it to me as an end of the school year gift. Isn't that sweet?"

"Very," I replied.

"It is very nice, that they were willing to go out of their way and hunt something like this down," Amelia hummed. "Really though, I should be thanking you."

"What? Why?" I questioned, confused.

"If you didn't have any role in this, I'm sure this would be a Chopin piece."

"Maybe they just couldn't find any Chopin," I suggested.

"Natalie, it's *Orphée*... You're the only person I've shared my love for Rameau with, especially about *Orphée*." Amelia softened. "I shared this with you because it's something really special to me. It's easy for me to tell people I like Chopin. And I do. I think his music is fun and beautiful. But Rameau... it's not easy for me to tell people I love Rameau. It's silly. They're just composers. But Rameau means something extra special to me. My mother used to play his music for me all the time as a child. It reminds me of some of the only pleasant memories I have of my mother."

"I didn't realize it was so special. I mean, not like that. I knew it was important, just not the extent. I wouldn't have told the choir if you were trying to keep it a secret. I'm sorry," I apologized.

"I'm not mad at you," Amelia corrected. "It means a lot to me that you remembered such a silly little tidbit about my life. And it means even more that you were willing to tell the students, so their gift would be even more heartfelt."

"I'm just glad you like it... that it means so much to you."

"It's how I feel about French."

"Pardon?"

"French, you know, how I always say I have a complicated relationship with the language?"

"Oh... yeah."

"When I was really little, my mother used to speak French all the time, and we would travel to France to visit family. But then my father, he started getting into shadier and shadier business practices, started getting more manipulative, and well, he didn't speak French, so he told my mother she couldn't. When I think about French, I think about a time when my mother was freer... happier... when she still loved openly and when my father loved openly as well. And then I remember how much things have changed and it... hurts... It makes me sad."

"That sucks. I'm sorry."

"No, it's just, maybe I put too much value into silly things," Amelia stated.

"I don't think you do. I think it's good to be sentimental. I think it's... well I think it's nice."

Amelia nodded, smiling. "Would you like to do something this evening?" she asked, changing the subject.

"I would love to, but I have a bunch of finals coming up next week and I kind of need to focus on studying."

"Oh, of course, absolutely."

"I'm going to head out, but I promise I'll keep in touch via text, so you won't think I just fell off the face of the earth."

Amelia laughed. "You need to be focusing on studying, not texting."

"Well, everyone needs to take study breaks," I replied, heading out the door. "Bye, Amelia. I'll see you later."

"Later, Natalie," she called after me.

I headed towards the door, already regretting the onslaught of mindless studying I would be enduring. Before I could reach the doors, however, I ran into Ellie 2.0 as she was leaving work.

"Hey, Natalie," she called. "Wait, before you leave, are you doing anything this Saturday?"

"Oh, um, no, just finals are coming up, so I'll probably be spending the weekend studying," I replied.

"Oh," Ellie 2.0 answered, her face kind of falling. "I figured you might be busy."

"Well, why do you ask? I can make time, if need be," I countered.

"It's Elk Creek's annual end of the year charity gala," she explained. "Every year, we put on a formal gala and invite parents and alumni. There are speeches about the school's achievements, lots of conversating, bidding games to get donations, stuff like that. I just wanted to invite you. You're basically a teacher here now, though maybe not officially, but also, it would just mean a lot if you showed up to support our endeavors. I'm sure your company would be a nice break from the endless flood of parents."

"I mean, I would love to go," I answered earnestly. "I'm just not sure if I can afford to. My grades are a bit lower than I hoped they would be, so I really need good scores on my finals. Any free time I have to study is really important."

"As a teacher, I completely understand," Ellie 2.0 replied. "Please, don't feel like you have to come, especially if you need to study. I just wanted to invite you. Here, have an invitation just in case." She pulled off her shoulder bag and fished out an invitation, handing it to me.

"Thank you," I said, taking the luxurious invitation—gold print on sturdy cardstock. The invitation alone was enough to tell me it was going to be one extra fancy gala. "I'll think about it."

19.

Alcohol, Hor D'oeuvres, And Broken Hearts

The next day, Friday evening, I sat in my room listening to music as I hit the books *hard*. I did my best to focus on learning—well, cramming—but I was too easily distracted and kept wiggling in my seat. I was almost ready to cave and text Amelia for a much-needed break when Lizzie burst into my room.

"Hey, lame-oh nerd," she stated, jerking an earbud out of my ear.

"Hey, I'm trying to study here!" I complained.

"I know, and it's such a drag!" Lizzie exclaimed. "Listen, omega-alpha-pi-sixty-nine-four-twenty-blazie-it-what-the-fuck-ever frat is throwing an end of the year party *tonight* and we're going."

"Nope," I stated, shaking my head. "You know I don't do college parties, Lizzie."

"Which is why you're totally the lamest nerd ever!" Lizzie stated. "You can't go your entire college career and not go to a *single* party! Therefore, you have to come with me to this party!"

I looked back at Lizzie incredulously. "Lizzie, we have tests next week. I can't just waste an entire evening at a party."

"One evening isn't going to ruin your entire studying. Besides, you're going to come to this party because Josh is throwing it."

I stared at Lizzie blankly. "Is Josh supposed to be some party throwing god or something? Because I don't care."

"Nat-e-oh!" Lizzie stated matter-of-factly. "At the end of every year, Josh does a betting contest with senior girls—"

"Sounds creepy—"

"And if you match him Jell-O shot for Jell-O shot, he'll give you a hundred dollars."

I continued to just stare at Lizzie.

"Oh, come on, please!" Lizzie begged. "Wouldn't you love to end your college career off with a banger of a party *and* be a hundred dollars richer?"

"That would imply that I even *could* match him shot for shot..."

"It'll be so much fun!"

I let out a heavy sigh, slamming my textbook shut. "Fine. Let's get this miserable experience over with," I declared, standing. Lizzie let out a squeal.

Josh's end of the year party extravaganza was not my first real college party experience, but it *was* my first time being completed wasted at a frat house. And by first time, I also mean last time. It wasn't an entirely miserable experience; I was just used to being the sober one at parties and I was feeling pretty out of my element.

I vaguely remembered the Jell-O shots, lined up next to Josh and surrounded by Greek Life kids chanting, "Shots, shots, shots!" Lizzie was right there too, shouting just as loud. I didn't win the shot contest, rather, Lizzie did. And then she insisted we had to stay around and celebrate further. Somehow, a beer found its way into my hand, and I drank it, and then I had another one. There was music blasting in the frat house loud enough to break your eardrums, and even in the dim lighting I could see people grinding on each other as they danced. There were beer pong games everywhere, and even though I was drunk, a lot of people were way more drunk than I was, barfing in the corner, falling over, and staggering between people.

Some people I didn't know offered me more alcohol, and I politely declined. I was verging on feeling too dizzy to walk, and I didn't like that. I tried to find my way out of the house, but then my stomach churned. I gasped, dashing clumsily for the nearest bathroom before emptying my stomach contents into the toilet. I slid down onto the floor, leaning back against the sink, groaning.

"I should have just stayed home and studied," I grumbled. "Even that would be better than this hell hole."

"Fitting thing for a nerd to say," someone beside me said. I looked over and found Lizzie sitting on the bathroom floor next to me.

"Didn't expect to see you here," I commented. "I thought you were trying to hook up with that one guy—what was his name? Abe?"

"I think his name's like... Alex..." Lizzie answered. "*Ehh*, doesn't matter. I found him upstairs shagging another girl."

"Sorry about that."

"Doesn't matter. I'm done with sex," Lizzie stated. "At least until after finals."

"Sounds reasonable." I groaned. "God, why do people enjoy getting drunk? My head is spinning, my stomach hurts, and most importantly, I'm *not* having fun."

"I'll share the money I won with you, how's about that?"

"Appreciated."

"What are you gonna spend it on?"

I shrugged. "I don't know. Maybe I'll buy something nice for Amelia."

"Amelia... she's the one you're tryna get with, yeah?" Lizzie questioned.

"Flattering way to put it," I scoffed. "But yes."

"How's that going? I'm guessing you haven't slept with her yet, 'cause you'd tell me if you did, right?"

"No, I haven't. I'm just trying to date her anyway. *If* I could ever date her. Sometimes I think the universe doesn't want us together. Whenever I think I've worked up the courage to tell her, something happens, or something pops up, but it's always *something.*"

"Nonsense. The universe ain't got a say in your love life. Look, you just gotta learn the right way about things. Just sleep with her. That's what I'd do. I do it all the time, actually. It's a great conversation starter. It's like, 'Oh hey, I remember you. We hooked up at Josh's party last Friday, remember? Good times. Let's grab lunch and catch up.' Then boom, you're dating."

"I don't think even *you've* managed to pull that off," I stated. "Besides, that would be so awkward. Like we'd have sex and then what? I'd see her at work and be like, 'Oh, come here often?' What shit advice."

"Fine, maybe it *is* shit advice, but don't you dare try and deny that you don't want to sleep with her, because I know you do."

"She's not the type, honestly."

"Not the type to have sex?" Lizzie questioned. "That's hard pressed to find, but I'm sure it happens. Some people must just not like it. Not me though. I like sex, couldn't live without it, I don't think."

"I don't mind, honestly," I said. "I mean, I never really considered *not* having sex, but it's been, what, a year since I last slept with somebody? It's not like I'm dying or anything."

"That's a pretty big decision though, wouldn't you say? To go without it forever?"

"I don't think so. I think sex is overrated."

"It probably is. Imma still do it though."

"I don't think I'd mind, as long as I have her."

"Probably better that way anyway, 'cause you two could relate on other levels that are probs deeper. And it'd be good for the STDs too, I guess."

"I think they're called STIs now."

"Point is, doesn't matter. If it makes her happy and it makes you happy, then good on both of you."

"Thanks."

"So, you tryna date her then?"

"Yeah, hopefully," I answered. "I mean, if I ever get around to confessing my feelings for her, and hopefully she feels the same for me."

"Feelings... like how you totally love her, yeah?"

I bit my lip. "I mean... yeah."

"Best not drunk call her and confess then. Could you imagine how awkward that'd be?"

"Good thing I'm not drunk enough to do that then, huh?" I agreed.

"You should give me your phone, just to be sure."

"*Haa*, not going to happen!" I declared. "Knowing you, *you'd* drunk call her and confess *for me*! Trust me, the phone is much safer in my hands."

"Why haven't you told her yet?"

"I don't know... I guess I'm kind of afraid. I mean, she's new on her journey navigating her sexual orientation, and she isn't exactly out to anyone yet. I guess maybe I'm afraid that if I did confess my feelings, she wouldn't express her own just because she's afraid and not ready. I'm afraid she'd rather be single and alone, but keep her life as it is, than take that leap of faith with me, a dumb college kid who doesn't even know what I want out of life yet."

"What a fat load of bologna," Lizzie scoffed. "Don't you know that love always wins?"

"Not in real life."

"Look, fuck real life then. If you can't be happy in real life, what's the point?"

"Let's not get all philosophical while we're drunk."

"You're right. We should be on drugs to do that. Want me to find some weed for us? I could use some of the money I won to get some."

"You just won the cash from a junkie, you don't need to give it right back to him."

"Fair point. Wanna get out of here, then? We could go home and gorge ourselves on junk food."

"Now that's something I could get into!" I declared.

I woke up to my phone ringing and my head absolutely pounding. I rolled over, groaning, and grabbed my phone to see who it was. It was my mother. Unfortunately, I knew I had to answer.

"Hey, mom," I stated, trying to pull myself up and out of bed.

"Nice to finally hear from you. I feel like you never call anymore."

"Sorry, I've just been really busy with work and school stuff. Finals are coming up."

"Yes, and then graduation. You know, we never did get any more information about graduation. Have you picked up your cap and gown yet?"

"No."

"Surely they have them in by now. Don't you think you better check into that? And does the family need to RSVP for graduation; do you know how that works?"

"It'll be fine mom. I told you the date already and I'll check in about the cap and gown. They might give them to us like the day before, so we don't mess them up."

"Well, when I was in college—"

"I know, things were much better organized. Anyway, I need to—"

"And how's that job of yours working out?" my mother continued. "You know, I'm very proud of you for finding a job like that, because the lack of effort you were putting in towards job hunting was atrocious. But I do think you really need to consider continuing your education. A bachelor's in biology isn't going to get you—"

"I'm working on it, mom. I really need to get going."

"Okay, well I still think—"

"Bye, mom. Love you." Then I hung up.

"Are you studying or snoozing?"

I startled, ungracefully tumbling out of my desk chair, crashing onto the floor with a thud. Slowly, I sat up, holding my head.

"*Oww*," I whined, glancing over to see that Lizzie was the cause of my rude awakening.

"I'm sorry," Lizzie declared, trying not to laugh. "I didn't mean to startle you, it's just that you gave me clear instructions to make sure you studied *all day*, and sleeping is not studying, so I had to wake you up."

"Gosh, what time is it?"

"Nearly six."

I stretched, rubbing at a kink that had developed in my neck. "Well, I guess I'm not making it to the charity gala, even if I wanted to," I said out loud to myself. "Too much studying to get done."

"Wait, a charity gala?" Lizzie questioned.

"Yeah, at Elk Creek," I said dismissively.

"You're telling me that you're passing up the opportunity to go to a high-end event with snobbish rich people that is definitely going to have fantastic free food that you could smuggle back to me? And they're probably going to have free booze too! And you're passing up this opportunity because, what, you have to sleep on your textbook?"

"I accidently fell asleep!" I defended. "I'm actually trying to study, I swear!"

"Natalie! Free food and alcohol!" Lizzie shouted, grabbing my shoulders and shaking me. "You're telling me you're going to sit here, bored, retaining nothing, instead of going and... I don't know... networking for your future!?"

I glanced over to the textbook sitting on my desk. "You do have a point about not retaining anything..." I muttered.

"See? You need a break from studying."

"I don't know... I already went to that party with you and lost a lot of valuable study time, so I really shouldn't."

"What about um... Amelia! She's going to be there, right?"

"Yeah." I shrugged. "So?"

"So!?" Lizzie gasped in my face. "Amelia is going to be there in a form fitting ballgown just *longing* to see you tonight."

I felt my face flush and my breath hitch ever so slightly.

"Fuck it, fine," I exclaimed in frustration, giving in.

"When's the gala?"

"Like 7:30."

"You got a ballgown to wear?"

"Yeah, I just casually have my ballgown collection here at college with me," I stated sarcastically. "No, Lizzie, I don't have a ballgown."

"Well lucky for you, your roommate is in a sorority, and I happen to have a myriad of gowns," Lizzie replied. "Come on, let's get you dolled up!"

The next thirty or so minutes of my life consisted of trying on multiple dresses, letting Lizzie pick and prod at my hair, and do my makeup in what she considered to be a very evening look. The only thing I couldn't do was borrow Lizzie's shoes, as she wore about two sizes too big for me. Instead, I had to just wear some tennis shoes and hope they didn't show from under the gown.

Finally, I stood before the floor length mirror in Lizzie's room, admiring myself. In Lizzie's closet, we managed to find a sleeveless gown, grey on top, pastel pink on the bottom, but covered in a grey lace so it had a sort of smokey effect to it. It matched my hair, so it was absolutely perfect. I noticed in the mirror that my hair was growing out, revealing my natural ashy brown color. Was this going to be the end of an era? Would young Natalie with pink hair finally move on to adult Natalie with a natural hair color? Did pink even fit me anymore?

Lizzie drove me to Elk Creek, declaring that I needed a designated driver because I was going to get totally wasted. I didn't feel like fighting her on it. And hey, maybe she was right anyway. The frat party wasn't my style, but a more snooty, mature, gala might be. But I wasn't going to get drunk again. I told her I'd text her when I was ready to go and that I wasn't going to stay for too long because I did have a lot of studying to do.

"Yeah, and if I never get a text from you, I'll just assume you got too swept up with Amelia, if you catch my drift," Lizzie stated with a wink.

"I'm not," I answered firmly. "We have finals Monday, remember?"

"Amelia can help you study... the art of love making."

"Not what my final is over."

"*Fineee.* Just steal me some food on your way out, alright?"

"Alright, see you later."

As I was walking up to the doors of Elk Creek, amidst other straggling guests flocking in at the last minute, I realized I was stressed. I felt anxious, like I was wasting precious time that could be better spent. And I realized just how many other things I needed to figure out. I needed to figure out where I was going to live this summer. I needed to figure out if I wanted to go back to school, or just focus on working. Did I want to become a teacher? Was that the career I wanted? What all did I need to do for graduation? If I went back to school, would I continue studying biology? I felt like I wasn't really going to enjoy the event, considering all the things I had been procrastinating on. The more I avoided my issues, the more stressed I became.

Inside the school, I found Ellie 2.0 standing at a table in charge of the guest list. I waited behind a few couples before it was my turn to check in, but as soon as Ellie 2.0 saw me, she squealed.

"Natalie!" she exclaimed, immediately running around from behind the table to grab me in a tight hug. "I didn't think you were going to make it!"

"Honestly, I didn't either," I admitted. "But I needed a break from studying, so I figured why not come over?"

"Wow, you look fantastic. I love your dress. Amelia is going to be so happy when she sees you. She was super sad when she thought you weren't going to be able to come. It'll be such a great surprise when she finally sees you!"

"Won't she be kind of, I don't know, too busy mingling to spend much time talking to me?"

"Well, sure, she has to mingle. But she'll make time for you, I'm sure! Anyway, everyone's gathering in the main gym, if you want to head in. I'll be in once things actually get started."

"Sounds good."

Inside the gym, it felt like I was at a very formally themed prom. The gym floor was lined with a black tarp and there were gold decorations everywhere. The quality of the décor stood out dramatically as well. There were standing tables all over, and at the front of the gym was a raised stage with a microphone. They also had somehow managed to hang a chandelier from the central scoreboard.

I scanned the room looking for my teacher friends, but my eyes landed on a server carrying a tray of hors d'oeuvres. My stomach rumbled. I realized I had barely eaten all day, being too preoccupied with studying. And then, behind the server, I also spotted a bar equipped with a bar tender. I should have known Lizzie would be right about the alcohol.

That little voice in the back of my head made itself known again, and I felt my stomach tensing with anxiety. *"You should be home studying, so you don't fail. You've hardly done any studying. You're going to fail your finals, and then you'll flunk out of school and never graduate because you're a big fat loser."* I frowned with annoyance. I wanted to relax. I wanted to stop worrying, stop stressing. I just... I just needed something to take the edge off my stress.

I walked straight over to the bar and ordered a drink. Once I had my drink. I made my way over to the side of the gym, hunting down servers to grab food from. I sipped my drink, noting that it was strong, and happily took another sip.

Not long after, the event officially began. The principal got up on stage and talked for a while, followed by other speeches, and breaks for mingling, with music and time for dancing. I spent my time going from the bar to walking around the perimeter collecting hors d'oeuvres. I was avoiding the center of the gym like the plague. I didn't want to have to make small talk with parents, to explain my position, or god forbid, my hair color. Because of this, it took a while before I ran into any of my friends. On my third lap around the place, I bumped into Karmen, who was mid-ending a conversation with a nice-looking couple.

"Giving birth won't keep me from the annual charity gala!" Karmen laughed to them. "Thank you again. It was nice seeing you."

The couple turned to leave and Karmen turned too, right into me.

"Natalie!" Karmen gasped.

"Hey," I replied. "I wasn't sure you were going to be here, since you're on maternity leave and all."

"Oh, sure, but working all day in a classroom is much different than a single night out. That's what babysitters are for!"

"Piper's not here though, right?"

"Oh no, it's far too early. She's in a much worse spot. But it's also her first child, you know, I've had two now. It gets easier the more you do it."

"So I've heard."

"I am surprised to see you here though. Don't you have finals soon?" Karmen asked.

"Yeah, just taking a little break from studying."

"Have you talked to Amelia yet?"

"No, I haven't run into her."

"She does know you're here though, right?"

"*Umm...* no?" I questioned. "I mean, I didn't think I was going to come until last minute, and I never told her, so unless Ellie 2.0 has—"

"You really should go talk to her. And, you know, let her know how good she looks in her gown. You know." Karmen nudged and winked at me.

"Yeah, if I run into her, I will."

"Good," Karmen replied. "I have to go mingle some more, but it was nice running into you."

Alone again, I continued in search of more food, and to also maybe steal some back for Lizzie. I started to get lost in my thoughts, however. What was I going to do with the rest of my life?

That was a really big and intimidating question. I didn't mind teaching at Elk Creek, but I was only doing it once a week with a small class. Actual teaching would be much different. It was nice that Elk Creek would provide me job security while I went back to school for a master's, but then to be stuck in a contract with Elk Creek? It would be nice working with my friends, but if I hated the job, I'd just be miserable regardless.

I could just go back to school and continue pursuing biology. I'd probably need to find a job in a lab or else just join a Ph.D. program and be in a lab from there. But that came back to the fact that I didn't like lab work, that I hated drafting up papers, and that I had no real research ambition. Some people loved searching for things and discovering things. I didn't though, not really.

But what other options did I have? I was graduating with a bachelor's in biology. It was either continue with biology or go back to school for something else and have just wasted four years of expensive education.

Thinking about school got me thinking about finals again and how I really should be studying, not galivanting around a gala. I didn't feel confident in what I knew, and to fail finals your last semester, I'd be such a failure! Would I even still be allowed to teach at Elk Creek if I didn't graduate? Wasn't I just on a trial basis until I officially got a degree? And what about the afterschool lab and Aniyah? Was she okay? She wasn't at lab, and I couldn't help but worry about her... and her family... and neighborhood... and racism... and the horrid state of our country—!

"I thought you couldn't come."

I spun, caught off guard, and found Amelia. When I glanced up at her, I found my mind completely blank, if only for a moment. She was wearing a black gown, flowy with sequins on the shoulders. The cut was low, showing cleavage that I couldn't help noticing. The contrast between the dark of her gown and the light pale of her skin on the swell of her breasts— it was almost like she was glowing, like the moon, or the sparkle of light across dark water. Her hair was tied up as well, in a way I loved, and the dark of her eye makeup brought out the twinkle in her eyes.

"Natalie?" she questioned.

"*Umm*, sorry," I muttered. "My mind's kind of all over the place right now. I have a lot going on."

"I know, which is why I didn't think you'd be here. Are you sure you shouldn't be, well, studying?"

"I should be, yes, but I mean, breaks are important too, right?"

"Of course." Amelia smiled softly. "I'm glad you're here. You look really... nice. Your dress matches your hair."

"Yeah, it's a real coincidence. It's actually my roommate's," I answered. "I wasn't planning on coming, so I had to find something last minute. I've just been so focused on other things, like my finals."

"Would you like to come over to our table, we're—"

"I mean, I want to finish this semester off on a good note, because I'd like my final GPA to be nice. And anyway, I still need to graduate!"

"Of course."

"But now what, you know? That's the worst of it all. I don't know where I'm heading next. And I really should figure that out soon."

"Right. We could grab some drinks and go talk—"

"Also, Aniyah wasn't at lab the other day, which is really weird and I'm kind of worried about her," I muttered. "I mean, it's probably nothing. I shouldn't be assuming the worst. It's just that her home life is rough, and I wish I could help. I think I never really understood poverty, you know. Like I knew it existed, but not that it was so *bad*, you know?"

"It's terrible," Amelia agreed. "We have this fundraiser for a reason—to get money for the school but also so we can donate it to neighborhoods in need. I don't have to mingle with donors all night though. I can spend time with you too. We could get some food, maybe dance—"

"And I have to figure out where I'm going to live over summer!" I sighed. "I live on campus with Lizzie, but once I graduate, I can't, and so I have to figure out how to rent an apartment and—"

"Hey, Natalie," Amelia almost snapped. "Would you like to dance? This song is—"

"And my job at Elk Creek! I mean, do I even want to keep teaching or—"

"Look at that," Amelia stated. "I have to go, um, talk to those parents. Bye." Then before I could say anything, Amelia was gone in an instance.

Huh... that was weird. She sounded annoyed and a bit tired, but I figured mingling would do that to a person. If I had to talk to parent after parent, I would probably get annoyed with it too.

I glanced down at my glass and noted it was verging on empty, which meant it was time for another trip over to the bar. I was feeling a little... floaty. And maybe a bit loose. I probably shouldn't indulge in another drink, but they were free...

On my way to the bar, my path was intersected by Eleanor.

"Short Stack!" she exclaimed. "I haven't had *one* drink all night! Isn't that just great!?"

I paused, staring at Eleanor, trying to comprehend why her words were nice but her tone was angry. "Why are you yelling so aggressively?" I asked.

"Because I'm trying to stay positive and not yell at a parent, which is *really difficult* without alcohol!"

"*Ahh*, that makes sense. But good for you, for not drinking."

"I see *you* haven't stayed clear of the bar," Eleanor commented.

"Well, no," I admitted.

"That's fine. If Karmen wasn't here breathing down my neck and keeping me busy, I'd have a few drinks myself. Oh, and speaking of, Karmen's gesturing to me. Looks like she's got a couple that wants to talk to me. Well, I'll catch you later."

"Later," I said, waving Eleanor off.

I looked back to the bar once Eleanor was gone, thinking that maybe I really *shouldn't* have any more to drink. At the bar, I saw Amelia. I watched her slam down not one, not two, but three amber colored shots, one after the other. I thought it seemed a little odd for such a formal event, but the parents were probably getting to her too. Just then, a server passed by with a particularly good-looking tray of food, and I quickly hurried after, my stomach still rumbling.

I wasn't planning on staying the entire night, but before I knew it, all the speeches and celebrations were over, and the guests were leaving by the handfuls. It was down to just a few lingering guests before I fully realized.

I had more to drink than I planned, but thankfully Lizzie was going to pick me up. I thought about what Lizzie said though, about me going home with Amelia. I mean, I wasn't going to. I needed to study, and my notes weren't at Amelia's apartment. And even if I wanted to, she'd never let me because she wanted me to succeed and she knew the importance of studying. But maybe... well would it really be such a bad time to tell her that I was hopelessly in love with her?

Well, that I liked her. Let's start small and not be too dramatic.

I glanced around the gym at the remaining teachers and didn't see Amelia anywhere. I did spot Karmen and Eleanor, however, standing close at a table alone. I thought about asking them, but I didn't want to interrupt their little love fest. I looked around more until I found Ellie 2.0 tidying up some tables.

"Hey," I stated, coming up to her. "Have you seen Amelia around?"

"Oh, um, hey, Natalie," Ellie 2.0 commented, turning to face me. "I—have you been drinking?"

"What? Yeah, I mean, a bit."

"Oh, well, um, sorry. I think I saw Amelia heading out towards the classrooms with Dale. I think they might have been dropping some stuff off in the classrooms."

"Thanks," I answered, heading towards the halls.

It didn't really hit me until then that I was tipsy, like very tipsy, verging on being drunk. My head was spinning enough that I felt unstable, but not necessarily enough that I was going to fall over. I also felt kind of giggly. Maybe doing this now wasn't such a good idea, considering I was intoxicated, but also, maybe that was good. The alcohol was keeping me from overthinking, which was nice.

I heard voices as I went down the hall, giggly voices of people who had been drinking. One of the voices was certainly Amelia, but the other voice was masculine. And then it hit me that Ellie 2.0 had said Amelia went out into the hall with Dale. Why on earth would she be talking with Dale? I turned the corner, curious to discover what Amelia was doing.

I stopped, frozen, my alcohol soggy brain taking a minute to process what I was looking at. I saw Amelia, wrapped up in the embrace of *fucking Dale Chinipardaz*. And then I saw, without a doubt, Amelia lean forward and kiss Dale—hard.

I turned, hit with a wave of equal pain and nausea, and just ran. She told me she liked women! Why would she kiss a man? Not him kissing her, but her kissing him! I burst out of a side door, glad I was wearing tennis shoes and not dumb heels. I grabbed the rail of the stairs, clutching my stomach before doubling over and puking. I stumbled down two stairs, collapsing onto the concrete, before I pulled my phone out and called Lizzie, begging her to come get me.

Once I hung up, I started bawling uncontrollably. My head was pounding, my world was spinning. I no longer cared about anything. I didn't care about finals, my grades, graduating, work, my future, nothing. I wanted to just curl up and cry forever.

When Lizzie picked me up, I refused to tell her anything. I rubbed away the tears, smearing my makeup all over my face. I knew I looked horrible. I didn't care. When we got back to our apartment, I promptly dumped my stuff on my bed, kicking off my dumb sneakers, and locked myself in the bathroom.

Lizzie knocked on the bathroom door and called, "Are... are you sure you're okay, Nats?"

"Just... leave me alone," I wailed. And she did.

The ballgown was uncomfortable and I hated it. I wanted to rip it up. But it was Lizzie's, so I couldn't. With a shaky sigh, I tugged down the zipper and let the dress pool at my ankles. Then, I collapsed onto the floor, lying on the ballgown, wearing nothing but my underwear, and cried myself to sleep.

20.

What Goes Around Comes Around

When I woke up, my head was pounding. I couldn't breathe. My sinuses were congested from crying and I felt nauseous. I was hungover. My eyes were swollen and puffy from crying and sleeping in my makeup. Someone was pounding on the bathroom door, but I couldn't bring myself to care.

"What?" I dejectedly muttered out in response.

It was Lizzie. "I was just going to let you stay in there until you felt better and came out on your own," Lizzie called through the door, "but well, your phone keeps going off and I think it might be important. Maybe you should answer it."

"Who's calling?" I questioned with no energy.

"*Uhh...* Someone named Eleanor? She's called upwards of seven times now, relentlessly."

I let out a struggled sigh. "Fine," I groaned. "One second."

I stood, very slowly, my head absolutely pounding, and looked at myself in the mirror. I looked barely alive. Wonderful. I was also still in my underwear, but I couldn't be bothered to care. Bending down to pick the ball gown up off the floor, I slowly opened the bathroom door and dragged myself to my room. When I entered, I found Lizzie looking at me with concern-filled eyes.

"I'm... fine," I stated.

"You look like shit," Lizzie observed.

"Yeah, I mean, you're right," I answered. I dumped Lizzie's dress on my bed and rooted around for an oversized hoodie, which I pulled on for comfort and to cover my near naked body. Just as I finished pulling the hoodie over my head, my phone started ringing again. I looked over and it was indeed Eleanor calling for an eighth time.

"I'll give you some privacy," Lizzie said, sliding out of my room and shutting the door behind her.

"Thanks," I called out. I sat down on my bed then and answered my phone, slowly bringing it up to my ear. "Hey," I muttered out.

"Finally! What in the *fuck* did you do last night!?" Eleanor literally screamed at me. Her yelling was not at all helping my pounding head and I quickly jerked my phone back away from my ear. "I swear to god, Natalie, I will kick your ass!" she continued to yell.

"Hey, um, can you stop yelling?" I groaned. "My head is killing me."

"Not until you give me some answers!" Eleanor snapped. "What were you thinking last night!?"

"Look, I don't know what you want me to say," I grumbled. "Amelia really hurt me last night and I don't super feel like talking about it right now."

"What do you mean, Amelia hurt *you*? You hurt *her*! She's been over here crying her eyes out since last night. Literally, she kept all of us up all night and let me tell you, two screaming toddlers and a screaming child on top of a bawling Amelia means that no one in this house got an ounce of sleep last night!"

"Why has Amelia been crying? She's the one who broke my heart, not the other way around."

"What are you talking about?"

"She kissed Dale."

Eleanor scoffed. "Yeah, okay, after you utterly rejected her."

"What? I would never," I answered.

"Did... you really not notice?" Eleanor then asked, her voice softer and kinder than it had been.

"Notice what?" I questioned honestly.

"Amelia really, *really* wanted you to ask her out to the gala."

"... What? You mean... ask her out like you'd ask someone to prom or something?" I asked. "I didn't even know that was a thing that could happen... a thing I could do..."

"Well, I'm starting to understand your obliviousness a little better... you're just an idiot."

"Hey!"

"Listen, Amelia thought you couldn't go to the gala because of finals, so she got over it. But then you did show up, so she was hurt you didn't ask her. That's why Ellie 2.0 told you to talk to her, and Karmen said she told you too."

"*Ohh...*" I muttered, starting to piece things together.

"And Amelia said she tried really hard to get your attention," Eleanor continued. "Because she realized you came last minute, but she thought she could, well you know... make a move."

"When?" I asked incredulously. "I think I would have noticed if she was... trying..." I trailed off, thinking about yesterday. I was so caught up with all the shit I had to deal with, I had totally blown off Amelia and all attempts at spending time with her.

"She said she got mad because you kept ignoring her, but I'm pretty sure she was just hurt," Eleanor added, confirming my thoughts. "Which is unfortunate, because next thing I knew, she was getting utterly wasted. And Amelia is mature enough to not do something like that at an event with parents unless she's *really* hurt."

"I feel like such an idiot... I'm guessing she kissed Dale then because she was drunk and mad at me?"

"Wow, you aren't nearly as dense as I thought you were," Eleanor mocked. "She hated the kiss, for the record, if you're concerned. She immediately started crying once they kissed and then she promptly proceeded to gag and throw up. That's how Karmen and I found her, actually. Dale came and told us he was worried about Amelia, said she threw up on his shoes, and we found her in the bathroom still puking her guts up."

"Is she okay?"

"She's heartbroken, you idiot."

"I know, and it's all my fault. It was just a huge, stupid, misunderstanding. I... I have to talk to her," I concluded. "I have to explain what happened. I have to let her know that I care."

"Good, I'm glad that you've finally come to your senses."

"Right, um, I'll just get cleaned up a bit, then I'll come over and tell her—"

Suddenly, Karmen cut in. "Oh no, that's not happening," she declared. "Amelia is a chronic mess—she certainly doesn't want you to see her like this—and furthermore, you have finals. As your friends and as teachers, we're here to make sure you graduate. You have to study."

"But I hurt Amelia," I whined. "Do you have any idea how awful that makes me feel?"

"She's a big girl, as are you. She'll be okay. In the meantime, pass your finals, alright?"

"But, Karmen—"

"No buts."

"Fine," I begrudgingly gave in.

When Piper found out what happened—because she inevitably was going to—she took Amelia's phone away and threatened the others that I was not to be distracted while I was studying. The intension was nice, perhaps, in that she wanted me to succeed and knew I would get distracted easily, but it didn't matter. I couldn't stop thinking about Amelia at all. How was I supposed to study when I thought I had ruined everything with Amelia, and couldn't even talk to her about it? I knew I needed to get good grades and pass my classes and graduate, but it was so difficult to stay motivated.

Monday came and went, as did two of my finals. Tuesday passed, along with more finals. And then I came home to Lizzie twirling around the apartment in her graduation cap and gown.

"Grab yours. Let's go take pictures!" Lizzie declared.

"I haven't got my cap and gown yet," I answered.

"Didn't you go to the bookstore and pick it up?"

"No."

"Oh my gosh, Natalie. Today's pick-up day! If you don't go and grab it now, I don't know how you'll get it. Come on."

Lizzie shed her cap and gown so we could run across campus and catch the bookstore workers before they closed. It was close, but we managed. I gave them my name and student ID number, and the worker disappeared into the back to retrieve my things.

A few minutes later he popped his head back out. "You said 'Natalie Benton,' right? With a B?"

"Yeah, Benton, B-E-N-T-O-N," I confirmed.

He went back into the back. Moments later he came back out, grabbed his boss, and they went back to the back with more whispering. Finally, it was the boss who returned.

"We don't seem to have anything for a 'Natalie Benton,'" she stated. "Are you sure that's the name on your student account?"

"Most definitely."

"And you're sure you applied to graduate?"

I blinked once, twice. I looked back at Lizzie. "We had to... apply to graduate?" I questioned.

"Are you serious?" Lizzie asked. "Yes, we had to apply to graduate! Like months ago!"

"Well shit."

I lied in bed, just frustrated. How could I have forgotten to apply to graduate? How on earth was I going to tell my mother that? She had the entire family excited, all lined up and ready to fly in for the ceremony, and I was the idiot who didn't apply to graduate and who was, therefore, not graduating. I wasn't sure if my school offered summer graduation, which meant I might have to wait until next fall. And would I still have to take classes so they wouldn't kick me out until I managed to graduate? How could I work full time at Elk Creek for a year while still being stuck in school for another semester?

I needed advice. Amelia was definitely off limits, as Piper had confiscated her phone. The others were also not supposed to answer me, but I figured I could probably get away with it. I swept through my contacts looking for who would be most likely to challenge Piper's threats. I brought my phone to my ear as I called.

"Woah, kid. If Piper finds out you're calling people, she's gonna show up at GSU and *make* you study," Eleanor laughed as she picked up.

"Yeah, um, funny story, I'm not graduating," I answered.

"Shit, what?"

"I'm sorry. I just needed someone to talk to, and I can't call Amelia and—"

"You don't have to apologize for calling me, Natalie. Are you okay? What happened?"

"I never applied to graduate, which means I can't graduate and I'm not getting my diploma," I explained. "I don't really know what to do. I don't know how to tell my parents, or what it means for the upcoming semesters."

"Okay, first of all, breathe," Eleanor instructed. "Forgetting to apply to graduate is definitely not the end of the world. Just, relax until you can apply to graduate again. Work at Elk Creek in the meantime. It can't be that bad."

"I'm worried that they'll make me take more classes... that they wouldn't give me my diploma if I wasn't an active student."

"Then just take some bullshit filler classes next semester and graduate then. You meet all the requirements already, right?"

"I think so."

"Then yeah, just take like pottery or something, get your base twelve credit hours."

"I just—I'm so sick of biology and academia. I was so excited to be getting out for a while. I can't believe I didn't apply to graduate. I'm such an idiot."

"It's a bit funny," Eleanor declared. "But, well, I didn't realize you were so sick of biology. I mean, I knew you were looking to do something else, but you accepted a job teaching biology."

"And it's fine. I like teaching at Elk Creek and all. But it's just... well I see the passion you have for teaching, and I just don't think I've got that same spark, you know?"

"Well now you've got a perfect opportunity to take some random classes in whatever you're interested in, since you're stuck in school for another semester."

"*Huh*, I guess you're right."

"Of course I'm right."

"Thanks," I stated, rolling my eyes. "You don't suppose Piper would let me talk to Amelia early, would you?"

"Only if you told her you're not graduating."

"Right, well, maybe I'll just wait on that then..."

"Look, don't worry. I know it's not what you were planning on, but it's not the end of the world, and it might even be good for you."

"Thanks for letting me talk to you."

"No problem, Natalie. You can always call."

"I'll talk to you later."

"Later, Short Stack."

Wednesday was increasingly difficult for me. Finishing my last final was bittersweet. It was supposed to be my last final in all of undergrad, but it wasn't, so it was far less enjoyable. I still wasn't sure how I was going to break the news to my parents, though I needed to do so soon. But no, the real reason Wednesday was so hard for me was because I was going on four full days, in a row, of not talking to Amelia at all and I *really* missed her. I wanted to text her or call her, anything. But Piper was keeping Amelia's phone until Thursday, forcing our next conversation to be face-to-face. But I was dying.

Just after five that evening, I broke.

I had to see her. I had to talk to her. I couldn't wait until Thursday. I thought Amelia finished her afterschool rehearsals at six, which meant it was the perfect time to run over to Elk Creek and catch her. I needed her to know that I was sorry and that I really did care about her, so I didn't want to show up empty handed, but I also didn't have time to run to the store and grab something.

I rooted through my desk drawers, pulling out a notebook from one of my biology classes. I turned to a random page and cut out a heart, right from the center. Trying to link the weird biology notes to the heart, I wrote in thick black letters a science pun: *"Are you a charged atom? 'Cause I've got my ion you."* It was stupid, but kind of funny. Maybe Amelia would laugh at it. That was all I really wanted to do, just make her laugh, to know that everything was going to be okay.

I still didn't think it was a very good peace offering gift, though. I remembered that outside, a bunch of fresh spring tulips had sprouted in the university's garden beds, and I knew exactly where some pink ones were that would be perfect. Without a second thought, I grabbed some scissors and my car keys, racing out of the apartment.

Outside, I cut the nicest pink tulip I could find and held it up next to my slightly lopsided heart, giving a weak smile. It would have to do. I hoped I hadn't messed things up too badly. I checked the time, realizing it was suddenly nearly six. Quickly, I raced for my car and sped to Elk Creek, hoping to get there before Amelia left.

At the high school, I barely got my car in park before I leapt out, frantically grabbing my gift. I ran for the main doors and tried to unlock it with my key card, but it didn't work. It was after hours, and the building had been locked up.

Unwilling to give up so soon, I ran to the side of the building—towards the fine arts wing—and tried to open the side doors, but they were locked too. I pressed my face to the glass, peering inside. I looked all around for Amelia, but I didn't see a single person inside.

I sighed. I was too late.

It wouldn't be the end of the world if I had to wait until tomorrow. I just really missed Amelia and wanted to see her. It was okay though. In less than twenty-four hours I would be back over at Elk Creek, talking to her for real, and hopefully making up. I headed back around the building, dragging my feet.

As I rounded the building towards the parking lot, I glanced up and noticed, to my immediate delight, Amelia, just as she was reaching her car to leave. Realizing that she was about to get in her car and drive off, I panicked, and ran towards her. The lot was big though and I wasn't that fast.

"Amelia!" I screamed. "Amelia, wait!" To further gain her attention, I started jumping up and waving my arms in the air as I clumsily skipped and stubbled towards her.

Thankfully, Amelia heard me. She turned back to face me, looking towards me with confusion. "Natalie?" she questioned stepping away from her car as I ran up.

"I'm—I'm sorry," I heaved, bending over, and leaning on my knees as I fought to catch my breath. "I didn't—I'm not—I just—I'm not very good at recognizing other people's feelings. I didn't catch all the hints everyone kept dropping—including you. I let myself get too worked up about my future and I'm sorry I hurt you. That was never my intention." I stood up fully, taking a deep breath. "I just, well, I like you Amelia... a lot. And I'm scared about the future and what I'm going to do, but well, I really hope that no matter what my future has in store for me, that you'll be there. Because I can't imagine not having you in my life. In fact, it's been really difficult not talking to you these past few days. I just can't take it anymore."

I stopped talking and extended my arms. The tulip was bent and missing a petal from me waving it around while running, and the writing on the heart was a bit smeared. I looked at them and just laughed, but I held them out to Amelia anyway.

"These are, um, for you," I muttered.

Amelia stepped forward, taking the tulip and paper heart from my hands. She looked at the paper and read it. "Did you... cut this out of your school notes?" she questioned, inspecting it.

"*Ahh*, yeah, I couldn't find any other paper." I laughed kind of awkwardly.

Amelia cracked a grin, looking up at me. "Really? A science pun? This is really stupid."

"I know. I was going to get you like an actual proper bouquet of flowers and a real card, but I just decided I couldn't spare another minute without you, so I ran right over here. I hope you don't mind. I mean, I can get you something better later, I just—"

Amelia shook her head, cutting me off. "They're perfect," she practically whispered, and it was then that I realized she was struggling to keep herself from crying.

"I'm sorry, I didn't—"

Amelia stepped up to me and pressed her finger into my lips, cutting me off again. She shook her head more firmly. "No, they're perfect. Stop talking," she declared. Then she immediately grabbed me and pulled me into a tight hug. She wrapped her arms tight around me and up my back, holding onto my shoulders from behind, pulling me in extra close. I wrapped my arms around her too and I felt relief flood through me.

Before I could say anything else, I felt and heard Amelia's stomach rumble against me.

"Are you perchance hungry?" I questioned with mirth. I moved to pull back from Amelia to look her in the eyes, but she just squeezed me harder and nuzzled her face closer against my neck.

"Maybe," she muttered. "I haven't eaten since this morning."

"Why haven't you eaten all day?" I gasped.

"I don't have an appetite when I'm sad," she confessed. "And I really missed you..."

"Well, we have to rectify this situation," I decided. "How about we go grab some pancakes?"

Upon hearing that, Amelia jerked back from me, smiling into my eyes like a happy child on Christmas morning. "Pancakes?" she squealed.

"Yes, pancakes," I stated, nodding. "You can even get yours with tons of syrup and nasty whipped cream," I added, sticking out my tongue.

"That's the best way to eat pancakes, thank you very much!" Amelia stated, bopping my nose. "Now come on. I'm starving!"

Sitting across from Amelia in that twenty-four-hour diner reminded me of our time spent in Florida, back when we were free, unburdened, and falling in love. Well... maybe I was getting ahead of myself. I hadn't confessed to her or anything, we had just reunited our friendship. In that moment I was just glad to have her back. A conversation about our feelings would come in due time.

We spent the evening just laughing. I'd make fun of Amelia whenever she got whipped cream on her nose, and she made fun of me when I got syrup on my sleeve. When we finished our pancakes, we got milkshakes and stayed at the diner longer, just talking.

"Are you done with finals then?" Amelia asked between sips. "Excited for graduation?"

"Oh, well, about that," I muttered. "I kind of forgot to apply for graduation."

"You what?"

"So apparently there's this thing where you have to apply to graduate, otherwise you can't, and the university doesn't give you a degree. And I forgot to do that. So, I can't graduate."

"That's terrible. Can't you protest?"

"I tried, but I kind of missed the deadline by like a few months? I have to just wait until next semester to apply and graduate. But I think the school's going to make me take at least twelve-credit hours to remain an active student. It could be good, taking other classes, since I don't think I want to keep up with biology, but I'm worried about Elk Creek... Pretty sure the expectation was that I'd have an actual degree before I started teaching."

"Yeah, that's probably not flexible..." Amelia admitted.

"But I wasn't really thinking teaching was for me anyway. Maybe this is a blessing... it'll give me another semester to think and figure out what I want to do with my life. I still have to break the news to my parents though."

"I know you butt heads with your mother, but surely she'll be understanding."

"My mom's going to be furious," I answered. "She had some big plans set up revolving around my graduation. But she'll simmer down, I assume. What about you? Do you talk to you parents much? I assume they live in New York or France or something."

"Yeah, I don't see them much, but we video call every once in a while. My father made it very clear that I wasn't his daughter anymore because of the path I chose to follow, so I've been essentially on my own since college. We only call because of my mom, really. I think she at least still cared, maybe enough to keep me in their will still, but after Monday, I doubt I'll be anymore."

"What do you mean?"

"I called them Monday. I just... wanted to tell them something. It didn't matter, because like I said, I hardly ever talk to them, and I rarely ever see them. But I just... well I wanted them to know, I suppose."

"Know what?"

"I came out to them," Amelia stated.

"I'm so proud of you!" I immediately gasped. I grinned and reached out across the table to hold her hand. She had come so far since we first met.

"They aren't happy," Amelia admitted, squeezing my hand. "I expected it, but I just... well I don't know. I mean, nothing's different since I'm on my own and living miles from them, but it just... kind of sucks to think about."

"I'm still really proud of you and I'll be here for you always even if your family isn't."

"Thank you."

"No problem." I smiled kindly. "How's school going, now that you're in the last few weeks of classes?"

"My regular choirs are basically finished," Amelia explained. "We had our end of the year recitals today, actually, so they're done. Now I can focus more heavily on getting my honors kids ready for Worlds. Which, speaking of, you're invited to."

"I'm invited to Worlds?" I questioned. "Isn't it in Europe?"

Amelia nodded. "Paris, to be specific."

"I... wow. I mean, I would love to go, I just—"

"I'll pay for your plane ticket," Amelia added.

"I mean, I really want to go," I answered. "It's just that I don't know what I'm going to be doing over summer anymore."

"Oh... right..."

"Because I was going to just get an off-campus apartment, but I *haven't* yet and they're going to kick us out of the on-campus apartments here pretty soon. But if I lose my job at Elk Creek because I didn't graduate, I won't have any income to pay rent, and why would I be staying in the city anyway?"

"Are you going to have to move back home then?"

"Maybe."

"You could stay with me."

"Amelia, I... don't know," I muttered. I wanted to, absolutely, but we were in a weird limbo between more than friends but not quite lovers, and it would feel like rushing things if we moved in together.

"You're right. Too soon," Amelia declared, mimicking my thoughts. "Maybe I could convince Eleanor and Karmen to let you stay with them. I mean, they did just get a house together. They have space."

"I couldn't ask them to go out of their way for me like that."

"Nonsense, might as well ask," Amelia said.

"Maybe..." I stated. I glanced at Amelia's now empty milkshake glass. "We should probably head out, so our poor waiter doesn't have to keep checking up on us."

Amelia nodded. "We're kind of close to downtown. Would you maybe like to spend the night at my place?"

"I, um, I don't want to impose."

"You're not imposing. I just invited you," Amelia laughed.

"Then I would love to."

"Great!" Amelia grinned. "I could honestly use some cuddles after that conversation with my parents."

"Sounds perfect."

Back at Amelia's apartment, we participated in what was quickly becoming a common activity for us, which was watching a documentary and having a healthy debate afterwards. Both Amelia and I were particularly opinionated people, though Amelia more educated in issues than I was, so it was fun and rewarding to bounce ideas back and forth. I usually went into issues thinking I had a strong stance, but left usually swayed by Amelia, who had a more well-rounded perspective.

Over our time knowing each other, we dove into many controversial topics, including—but not limited to—racism, transgender children, free range parenting, the health care system, and our own community: LGBTQ+ rights. We had a long drawn out, rather depressing, conversation about the death penalty once. I figured they were criminals, that they deserved their punishment. But Amelia made me realize that for one, innocent people got convicted, and for two, what gives some humans the power to decide who lives and who dies when killing is still killing? That lead into another documentary about prisons though, and I realized I actually hated the system as a whole.

That was neither here nor there, however, as that evening, we watched a documentary on the American school system. I knew the whole system was a disaster. I'd lived through public school, and I heard everything

Eleanor had to say about school districts, and poor areas, and lemons. The documentary rounded things off, made me really sick that so many kids were struggling and getting poor educations just because of where they were born. Adults didn't have control over stuff—like ending up homeless or in poverty, especially when race came into play—but I knew people argued they did. Like if they just worked harder, they wouldn't be poor. But I didn't think anyone could argue that it was a kid's fault for being stuck in such situations, and if education was the key to success, and success the key to a good job with good pay and good benefits, how were those kids ever supposed to reach that with a terrible education?

I realized that in the past few months, I had learned so much, and my perspectives on things had changed so drastically. I also knew I was privileged and that I grew up with a cushioned life, but similar to how I always knew about poverty but never really *understood* it until I was standing in Aniyah's house. I never really *understood* my privilege until I started learning about it face-on. And frankly, I had my teacher friends to thank for that. Learning about where they came from and how they learned about privilege and the injustices in the world helped me reflect and critically analyze my own life. Watching documentaries with Amelia and then having conversations that branched into more education helped too. And working with the afterschool program at Elk Creek, doing something actively to help close the gap between bad and good education in America, made me realize things as well.

"I feel like I want to just camp out in Washington D.C. on the steps of government buildings, protesting every day," I declared. "Wait, *eww*. I never thought about this before, but I guess that if I wanted to make a huge difference in the world, I'd have to get a job in politics, because that's how laws get made and changed." I pulled a disgruntled face. "That's disgusting."

Amelia laughed at me. "Politicians are the face of change, sure," she stated, "but the people that are actually making a difference in the world are the ones on the home front, working in soup kitchens and heading fundraisers, starting non-profits and donating their time."

"You're right," I added hopefully. "I think I'd utterly hate working in politics. Could you imagine me running for office?"

"You don't really seem the type, no," Amelia agreed.

I couldn't hope that America would change overnight... maybe not even during my lifetime entirely. But it was possible that I could maybe make a difference in the lives of a few kids, and maybe if more and more people started doing that all over the country, it would be enough to get a wave rolling that *would* lead to nationwide change. I wanted to volunteer my time and help as much as I could. I wanted to have more serious conversations about these issues and raise more awareness.

"It's getting late," Amelia commented, turning off the TV. "We should probably get to bed. Are you doing anything tomorrow?"

"Not really. I'm done with finals."

"Do you want to come into work with me then?" she asked. "You have to be there for lab anyway, and you could just crash classes and hang out. Most classes aren't doing much anymore, just watching movies anyway."

I shrugged. "Sure, I don't see why not. It sounds fun."

Before I knew it, we were snuggled down in Amelia's bed, the covers pulled close around us. We were spooning, my face nuzzled into the back of her neck. Maybe I was excessively stressed about my future, and still upset about missing graduation, but Amelia was a miracle worker when it came to calming me down.

There was no way around it anymore. We needed to talk about our feelings.

21.

Some Jokes Are Hurtful, So Maybe Just Stop

Amelia and I pulled into Elk Creek about thirty minutes before school officially started. A few students were there, mainly freshmen that couldn't drive yet with parents who needed to be at work early, but the school was mostly desolate. We walked in through the main entrance by the office and immediately ran into Eleanor, who was walking down the hall. She waved to greet us but quickly stopped dead in her tracks.

"Oh my gosh!" Eleanor stated, her jaw slack.

"*Umm*, good morning, Eleanor..." Amelia commented.

Eleanor ran up to us. "Karmen and Piper are going to be so upset when they find out they missed seeing the two of you walk into work together!" she stated jubilantly. "Oh my gosh! Natalie's wearing your clothes!"

"Very observant of you, Sherlock," I commented, unimpressed. I hadn't planned on spending the night with Amelia, and she was gracious enough to let me borrow something to wear, so I wouldn't have to wear the same thing I wore yesterday.

"You two spent the night together!" Eleanor said accusingly. "I can't believe it! This is so exciting! Wait a second." She moved, pulling out her phone, and quickly took a picture of Amelia and me.

"What was that for?" Amelia questioned.

"I have to send it to the group," Eleanor explained, rooting through her phone.

A second later and Eleanor could no longer contain herself, holding out her phone for us to see. On her phone was a picture of the two of us with the caption: *'Look what the cat dragged in.'*

Before we could say anything, another message came into Eleanor's phone, this time a message from Karmen: *'Isn't that Amelia's shirt Nats is wearing?'*

"Jesus Christ," Amelia huffed out. "Are you done? I need to go organize a few things before school starts."

"Have fun," Eleanor declared as Amelia headed off. I moved to follow her, but Eleanor grabbed my arm. "I thought I'd help you set up for lab this week. I know you've been overworked since Piper had a kid."

"*Umm*, okay, sure, thanks," I answered.

I should have known Eleanor wasn't just interested in helping me without any other agenda. She managed to keep it together until the bell rang, signaling the start of class. I glanced over to see if she was going to leave, but she didn't.

"I guess you don't have a class first period?" I questioned.

"Usually, but the seniors don't have class this week," Eleanor answered.

"Oh... did they already have graduation?"

"No, graduation's Saturday. They had finals at the start of this week and then they get a few days off for graduation practice and whatnot. You can come to graduation if you want. We can save you a seat."

"Yeah, sure. I mean, I guess I should. There're several seniors from choir that I know pretty well, so it would be nice to see them off."

"I'm sure Amelia can fill you in on the details..." Eleanor trailed off, so I looked up at her, pausing my set-up process. She was grinning at me devilishly. I braced myself for the inevitable. "Speaking of Amelia," she said, "how was last night?"

My eye twitched in irritation. "It was just dandy," I answered evenly.

"Piper was going to give Amelia her phone back tonight, but clearly you two didn't listen. What happened? Did she break into Ellie 2.0's house and steal her phone back?" Eleanor asked with a playful grin.

"Funny," I stated sarcastically. "I know where Amelia both lives and works, so it's not like Piper could really keep us apart. I just showed up here yesterday and caught her after class before she left."

"It's kind of funny what happened, if you think about it. You being an oblivious fool... Amelia kissing a guy and puking on his shoes. But I take it you worked things out, in more ways than one."

I narrowed my eyes. "What do you mean?"

"You worked it out *and* you got your work out in the bedroom, obviously," Eleanor stated, never one for subtlety.

"We didn't—" I tried to protest, but Eleanor cut me off.

"You came into work together this morning *and* you're wearing her clothes."

I let out a long and loud sigh. "I understand what it looks like, but trust me, we didn't. I have no reason to lie to you about that. Piper I *might* lie to about it, just because she can be a bit judgmental at times, but I have no reason to lie to you."

"Piper would definitely lecture you about hooking up before you were supposed to be talking again," Eleanor agreed, "but she'd also be ecstatic, because it's about damn time."

"Okay, but also we *didn't*," I reiterated.

I think Eleanor actually believed me that time, because she shouted out exasperatedly, "Why not!?"

"That's just not how our evening went down."

"How could it not—okay, fine. Tell me what *did* happen, then."

"I came over here, gave her a flower and a paper heart. I told her I was sorry, that I missed her, and then we just hugged it out."

"*Eww*, what?" Eleanor huffed. "You mean you didn't even kiss?"

"No..." I stopped for a minute, thinking. Prior to Eleanor's reaction, I never really considered our lack of kissing to be a big deal. I knew Amelia was likely asexual and contemplating the extents of that. I knew she was comfortable with hugs and cuddles, though maybe nothing else. And I was fine with that. I had an amazing time with Amelia yesterday, even without a kiss, and I decided Eleanor needed to know that.

"We just hugged and then we went out and got pancakes and milkshakes," I declared. "Then we went back to her place and just hung out."

"But you kissed after you got food?"

"No."

"When you got back to Amelia's place?"

"Nope."

"Before you went to bed?"

"Nada."

"When you woke up!?"

"Not at all."

"When you got here this morning!?" Eleanor was now practically yelling, her voice raising with each declaration.

"We did not," I stated.

"You didn't kiss at all!?" Eleanor hissed in frustration.

"I can confirm that we did not kiss at all."

Eleanor just stared at me for a while, kind of like she thought I was crazy. After a moment she found her voice again and questioned, more calmly, "Well what all did you guys talk about then?"

"Um, I don't know, food, me missing graduation, family..."

"Your love life?"

"Didn't come up."

"Oh... my god," Eleanor stated. "Five minutes ago, I literally thought you two finally slept together, but it kind of sounds like nothing happened."

"Not *nothing*," I replied. "We made up after getting upset at each other and not talking to each other."

"The whole point of us keeping you apart and Piper keeping you from talking was so that when you saw each other again, you'd make up, make out, and ship off!" Eleanor exclaimed exasperatedly. "But you didn't kiss, you didn't talk about your feelings, you didn't even talk about the fact that you two have massive lady boners for each other!"

"It didn't come up!" I shouted in response.

"You're a helpless case!" Eleanor snapped. "Honestly, both of you are. What are you then? Just friends that get off to the thought of each other? Natalie, we're talking about Amelia here! Do you want to bang her or not!?"

I felt my face flush. The room felt hot. I pulled at the collar of Amelia's shirt uncomfortably. "Can we... can we not talk about Amelia like that?" I stuttered out.

Eleanor covered her face with her hands and let out a scream that was muffled from her position. When she pulled her hands away, she stated, "Are we going to have to lock the two of you in a room until you finally give in and just hump one out?"

"Eleanor, please, can we not—"

"Can we not *what*, Natalie? Not talk about sex?" Eleanor questioned, her tone harsh. "You wouldn't be so red if you didn't want to sleep with Amelia. You can't deny it. I just don't understand why you won't just do it!"

I was getting annoyed. I pinched the bridge of my nose. "I know this might be difficult for you to grasp, but not everything revolves around sex, Eleanor."

Eleanor looked at me skeptically. "I mean, maybe not. But I still think if you two just slept together, the whole world would be happier. I know at least I would stop pulling out my hair trying to deal with you two."

"I don't think Amelia wants to dive into a relationship like that, and honestly, I don't either."

"Look, Amelia might not have had sex in a few years, but that's just all the more reason to do it," Eleanor said, shrugging. "Natalie... she needs to get laid. And honestly, well... when did you last have sex?"

"That's not the point, I—"

"Yeah, you need to get laid too," Eleanor concluded.

Finding my patience at the end of its rope, I yelled out, "Eleanor, I don't want to fuck her, I want to date her!"

Eleanor pursed her lips. "Oh honey... did no one tell you that those things aren't mutually exclusive? In fact, usually they come as a package deal."

"You're not listening to me!" I shouted, shaking my fists in frustration. "It might have worked out for you and Karmen to sleep together first, figure out feelings later, but it's different for Amelia and me. We have... a lot riding on this. Amelia has a lot of feelings, and you know what, so do I, and we need to figure out our feelings first, ask questions now, and see where that leads."

Eleanor stared at me until my breathing slowed and evened out. Then she stated, "How boring," quite dismissively, and I wanted to strangle her. She must have seen the anger in my eyes, because she quickly added, "I'm joking! *Geez*, relax! See? This is why I said you need to get laid. You're so uptight."

"You just don't understand. Amelia isn't like that. She doesn't just jump into bed with people."

"Yeah, because she's been trying to play straight for the last how many years, when it's really women she's lusting after. But trust me, she's been waiting to sleep with a woman for like, her whole life."

"You're wrong," I stated strongly.

Eleanor frowned. "Natalie, I really don't think I'm wrong. I've known Amelia for a long time. I know she hasn't technically come out, but she likes women. You and I both know that, seriously."

"I know she likes women, I'm talking about sex," I grumbled. "Look, I shouldn't be telling you this. I'm done setting up in here, so I'm going to go find Amelia and hang out with her."

"Woah, woah, woah," Eleanor barked, leaping around a desk to block my exit. "You can't just drop some hint about Amelia and then expect to run away. If there's a serious reason why you and Amelia haven't slept together, you should share."

"I understand that friends are relentlessly nosey about their friends' lives, especially sex lives," I declared, "but this is none of your business. Neither Amelia nor I are sleeping with you, so it ends here."

Eleanor grabbed me by the upper arms, holding me in place. "Natalie, do you not want to have sex with Amelia? Or well, does Amelia not want to sleep with you?"

"I—I mean it doesn't matter if we do or don't, that's what I'm saying," I stuttered.

"You always stutter when you're stressed and trying to hide something," Eleanor accused. "Sit," she commanded, pulling out a chair. I sat down at a desk and Eleanor sat atop it, staring down at me. "I promise that whatever secret you're hiding will never leave my lips. I won't even tell Karmen. But something is clearly on your mind, and I know you. You need to talk to someone to help you sort it out. So, spill."

"Eleanor, I can't—"

"Bullshit. Open your mouth and talk."

"I—fuck, fine," I growled. "It's just that well... we haven't talked about it, not fully, so I'm not trying to jump to any conclusions, but there's a good chance Amelia might not want to sleep with me... ever... or even kiss me for that matter."

"That's ridiculous," Eleanor nearly laughed. "She's enamored by you, can't you tell? She's miserable when she can't be with you and absolutely glowing whenever you're around."

"I'm not saying she's not," I answered, flushing slightly at just how strongly Amelia might care about me. "I just... she told me something while we were in New York. I don't want to say that it complicated things, because it didn't, but it's just something else we need to talk about."

"What did she tell you?"

"I shouldn't tell you."

"Natalie..." Eleanor warned.

"This is peer pressure," I protested.

"I just want you and Amelia to be happy, and if this thing is keeping you from being happy together, then I want to help you in any way I can. So, if you need to talk about it, I'm here for you."

I was struggling greatly. It wasn't my place to say anything to Eleanor, but I didn't have anyone to talk to about it. And maybe if Eleanor knew, then she wouldn't keep making jokes around Amelia, so Amelia would be more comfortable, and then it would all work out in the long run.

"Amelia might be... asexual," I muttered out.

There was a beat where Eleanor just stared at me, processing. I waited patiently for her denial, or any questions she would have. Instead, however, a look of dawning realization overcame her, and she stood abruptly, pacing back and forth in front of me.

"Shit..." Eleanor mumbled. "Fuck."

"*Umm*, you good?" I questioned.

"I'm just thinking about all the jokes we've made around Amelia, how much we've teased her. I didn't even think that she could be—well, I feel awful. Why didn't she say something to us?"

"I don't think she knew?" I answered honestly. "I mean, she knew how she felt, but I don't think she had the words to describe it. She didn't know what asexuality was when I told her, but she did some research and she said she related to it a lot."

Eleanor fell onto a desk chair across from me. "It explains so much, actually. I just never thought to question it. I thought she was always weird around men because she liked women, but well... I get it now. I get why you two have been taking things ridiculously slow. It's because that's what she's comfortable with. *Ahh*, it makes so much sense now."

"Right, so anyway, if you could maybe take it easy on the sex stuff, that would be great."

"Are you okay?"

"What do you mean?" I questioned.

"I mean, are you cool with Amelia being asexual, if she really is?"

"Of course, Eleanor, I... I love her," I choked out. It felt odd saying such a thing, but the truth of my words felt comfortable. I *did* love Amelia for exactly who she was.

Eleanor smiled genuinely at me but maintained her composure. "Are you asexual too?" she questioned.

"No."

"Then are you really okay with never having sex with her? I mean, if you commit your entire life to her, that's it, no more sex, ever. And what if she doesn't want to kiss you? Will you really be okay with that?"

"That's a serious question," I stated, nodding. "And I realize that you and Karmen are sex fanatics, so it might be difficult for you to imagine, but it really doesn't bother me. I mean, sex is fun and cool and stuff, but at the end of the day, it's just some activity. Lots of activities are fun, but I would give up anything—in a heartbeat—to be with Amelia."

"Wow... you really love her, huh?"

"I do."

"But what about the intimacy of sex? How will you guys ever reach such a level of intimacy in your relationship without sex?"

"There are tons of ways to be intimate with another person," I answered. "I mean, I think sharing your biggest fears and insecurities with someone who could potential judge you is way more intimate than sex. People have one night stands all the time, but how many people will they confess their true feelings to?"

"I... guess that's true."

"It's up to Amelia what all she's comfortable with. I'm willing to take whatever she's willing to give and nothing more. I just... I can't imagine my life without her. I need her... in whatever way she's willing to share herself with me."

Eleanor shook her head, growing quiet. "I used to joke and make fun of you two so much," she muttered. "I thought you were just two chickens that were too scared of your feelings. But it turns out, you actually have a very strong, deep, and meaningful relationship already, and you haven't even kissed once. You're turning my idea of a relationship on its head..."

"There are lots of ways to have meaningful relationships. The way you and Karmen did things, well that worked out for you, but it's not what's going to work for Amelia and me. We're doing things our own way, so I just... can you respect that?"

"Of course. I'm sorry."

"You're fine," I declared, reaching out and patting Eleanor on the back. "We aren't born knowing everything about everyone and we can't be faulted for being ignorant. We should always try to learn though and grow as individuals. That's what I've learned this semester, with everything you guys have helped expose me to."

"Shit, kid, when did you get so wise?" Eleanor laughed.

Suddenly, someone started pounding on the classroom door and Eleanor and I both jumped straight up. I spun and my pulse skyrocketed when I saw it was Amelia knocking at the door. Eleanor darted over and opened the door for her.

"Clear your calendars!" Amelia exclaimed, happy and seemingly oblivious to everything Eleanor and I had just been talking about. "Piper got a babysitter for tonight and I'm taking you all out for dinner!"

"Woah, what's the special occasion?" Eleanor questioned.

"We need to hang out more as a friend group!" Amelia declared. "And also, I have some news I want to share with you all! Anyway, catch you later. I've got to go tell Ellie 2.0 the news. Toodaloo!" Then as quickly as she came, Amelia skipped off.

Eleanor turned back to me, a small smirk on her face. "Wonder what her news is? Hopefully she didn't get a different girlfriend in the past hour."

"Shut up," I stated, shoving at Eleanor's shoulder.

Within ten minutes of lab that afternoon, I noticed that Aniyah wasn't there again. Two absences in a row meant she wasn't sick, no way. There had to be another reason and I was growing concerned. So concerned, in fact, that I ended lab a little early and called Piper.

I was greeted not so nicely by Piper going, "I *just* got Katrina down for a nap, and this phone call nearly woke her up, so this better be super important."

"Parenthood's made you a little bitter," I declared.

"Hilarious, Natalie. I haven't gotten a solid three hours of sleep since I gave birth."

"I'm sure it's not easy. I'm just giving you a hard time."

"Seriously, why did you call? Is something wrong at school?"

"Aniyah was gone again this week," I stated.

"She missed the last lab of the year?" Piper asked, and I could tell Piper was a bit concerned as well.

"Yes. I'm worried about her," I admitted.

"Well, that's certainly unusual for Aniyah."

"Her at home life is kind of rough, I just... what if something bad happened?"

"I could try contacting Byram. They might have an excuse for her absence."

"What if school doesn't know?"

"We'll just have to hope they do."

"I, um... I know where she lives," I stated. "I could go—"

"Natalie, for the love of god, do *not* do that," Piper warned.

"But if Aniyah is in trouble, I—"

"Do not need to be banging on their door, especially in that neighborhood. You getting gravely hurt isn't going to solve any problems."

"But, Piper, I—"

"No, Natalie, I'm putting my foot down. I'll call Byram and let you know what they say. Otherwise, you're staying put."

"Fine," I gave in half-heartedly.

"I'm very serious," Piper continued. "This is not the time."

"You're right," I sighed. "I'm just... really worried."

"Me too," Piper admitted, "but hopefully all is well, and she just got busy with some other activity."

That evening, Amelia took us out to the diner where her and I had been just the day before. I teased her about it, saying the poor staff would be sick of us, but she insisted she needed the comfort of the hole-in-the-wall diner. I wasn't the only one who teased her though.

"Damn, Amelia, you're paying, *and* you chose the cheapest place in town," Eleanor laughed as we walked inside.

"Oh, shush!" Amelia barked. "This place has great food and really, I'm going to need a milkshake after this, so..."

The hostess led us over to a table once everyone arrived and Amelia grabbed my arm, tugging me back a step behind the others. She squeezed my arm unnecessarily hard, and I looked towards her curiously.

"Sit by me? Please?" she practically begged.

I looked at her oddly. "Of course," I responded. I planned to sit next to her anyway... surely, she knew I would.

We settled into our table, looking through the menu. Everyone was caught up in conversation as I glanced around the table. It felt almost like we were back in Florida, just chatting with no real concern. Things were different now, of course: there were two new babies and three whole divorces, not to mention my on-going woes. But we ordered our food and it felt like nothing had changed.

Once the waiter left to put in our order, Eleanor grabbed everyone's attention, turning towards Amelia. "So, Amelia," she stated, "what's that thing you wanted to tell all of us?"

Amelia shifted uncomfortably in her seat, worrying her hands, and she stumbled over her words. We were all waiting patiently, but Amelia glanced to me, a look of panic, a desperate cry for help plastered on her face. I didn't know what she was wanting to say, but I figured she needed more time to compose herself, so I did what I could to distract everyone, blurting out the first thing that came to mind.

"I'm not graduating," I declared, though I immediately cringed, figuring how Piper would react. Oh well, I had to tell her eventually.

"Really?" Ellie 2.0 asked quizzically.

"Why not!?" Piper snapped. "What did you do?"

"*Ahh*, well, um..." I muttered. "You see... I might have kind of maybe forgot to apply to graduate? And apparently you *can't* graduate if you don't do that."

"Natalie!" Piper practically shouted. "How could you forget to do something so important?"

"I know, I know, but I mean, it's not like anyone explicitly *told* me!" I defended. "I mean, I might have deleted an email or two from my advisor without reading them, but that's not the point! The point is, I didn't do it, so now I have to hang around and take another semester before I can officially graduate. Which sucks, but it has to happen."

"I told her it would be good for her to take some cross-disciplinary classes," Eleanor commented. "Since she doesn't want to stick with biology, she can take other things and see if they strike her fancy."

"You knew!?" Piper snapped at Eleanor.

"Piper, can you blame her for not wanting to tell you?" Karmen said softly. "You're reacting just as badly as her parents will."

"Speaking of which, I still need to tell my parents," I muttered. "But I think Eleanor's right. I think it will be nice to take some other non-biology focused classes and just... take the summer to contemplate my future, since I'm not sure Elk Creek will let me keep the position without a degree..."

"You're right, they won't," Piper declared, clearly still upset and disappointed in me. She crossed her arms, but after a moment, sighed. "I wasn't sure how you'd adjust to teaching in all honesty. I'm surprised you held it through the semester. I can tell your heart just isn't in it."

"Well, I'm not a quitter," I scoffed. "But you're right. I don't think teaching is my calling..."

"I'm sure you'll figure out what you want to do this summer," Ellie 2.0 commented. "Summer is the perfect time to do some soul searching."

"And speaking of summer," Amelia cut in, looking towards Eleanor and Karmen, "Natalie needs some place to stay this summer..."

Eleanor and Karmen glanced to each other before Eleanor turned pointedly to Amelia. "Hell no, make your girlfriend stay at your place," she huffed.

Karmen playfully smacked Eleanor but was unsuccessful in hiding her own laugh. "Eleanor, they're not dating," she snickered. "Unless that's what Amelia gathered us here to talk about..."

"No, I..." Amelia's face turned a shade of red. "Natalie can't stay with me, it would be—"

"Presumptuous," I concluded. "But I'm not trying to impose on you guys either. I guess if I'm out of a job, I can't exactly pay rent on a place. I guess I'll just have to live at home this summer. It'll be fine."

"Home?" Ellie 2.0 questioned. "You mean in North Carolina?"

"Yeah."

Eleanor and Karmen glanced back at each other before Eleanor broke. "You can't do that," she declared, looking back to me. "We could barely handle Amelia when you were gone for a week, we'd never survive it if you were gone for three months!"

"Absolutely, you have to stay in town," Karmen agreed. "We'll have to move around some stuff, but it's not like we don't have the space in the new house."

"Guys, I can't impose—"

"Nonsense. When are you moving off campus?" Eleanor asked.

"What am I supposed to tell my parents?" I declared. "That not only am I not graduating, but that I'm spending the summer living with two older women and their kids? I haven't even told them about you guys. They're going to have so many questions!" I slammed my head down on the table, grabbing at my hair, and groaned dramatically.

"Looks like your two adoptive gay aunts are just going to have to come help you with move out and meet your parents then," Karmen stated cheerfully.

"It'll be fine," Eleanor added dismissively. "We deal with obnoxious parents all the time. We're pros."

"Alright, fine, but I'm going to find a part time job this summer and help pay for some expenses," I stated. "I am not a mooch."

"You really don't have to—" Karmen began.

"Yeah, you can pay us with babysitting duties. That's your part time job now," Eleanor added, grinning widely.

"See? I knew it would all work out," Amelia stated, smiling.

Eleanor swiveled on Amelia. "Yeah, don't act like you're off the hook. That was most definitely not the big news you wanted to tell us, so don't even act like it was."

"Oh, um, well..." Amelia muttered, dipping her head again. She looked back to me, for support, and I reached under the table, resting my hand on her thigh. She nodded slightly at my touch and released a deep breath. Then, she looked back up at her friends.

"I realize that, um, this probably won't come as a surprise to any of you, but I just felt like I should do this the proper way, because, well... well I just thought I should tell you guys that... well that I'm... gay. I like women."

Eleanor let out the loudest roar of laughter, immediately followed by Karmen smacking her, though she was trying just as hard to not burst out laughing. Piper did the most reasonable thing and reached across the table, grabbing Amelia's free hand.

"Ignore those two idiots," Piper stated, gesturing towards Eleanor and Karmen. "Amelia, thank you for trusting us with this part of your life. And yes, maybe it wasn't much of a secret, but it's still a very big deal that you told us, and we will always support and love you, no matter what."

"Yeah!" Ellie 2.0 declared, jumping out of her seat to run over and hug Amelia. "You're the best, Amelia, really. You're the coolest and most amazing person ever!"

"Sorry, I'm sorry," Eleanor choked out. "I just absolutely wasn't expecting that, and you seemed so worried and I just—I'm sorry. I shouldn't have laughed. You have a great amount of courage to tell us, and we still care about you, of course."

"Yes, I'm sorry we're immature," Karmen added. "We aren't belittling your coming out. It's not surprising, but we know it's serious and we're very grateful you trusted us enough to share."

"Thanks," Amelia whispered. "This is such a better experience than coming out to my parents..."

"You came out to those scumbags!?" Eleanor gasped.

"Eleanor, you can't call people's parents scumbags!" Piper scolded.

"But it's true!"

"It really is," Amelia added.

"Wait," Ellie 2.0 stated meekly. "How come Natalie hasn't got anything nice to say about Amelia coming out?"

"Yeah, wait a second," Piper agreed, looking at me, her eyes narrowing.

I glanced at Piper, the thought to react never even have occurred to me. I had already gone through all this with Amelia. I felt like I was just there for moral support, not a reaction. But to Piper and Ellie 2.0, who didn't know I was the first-person Amelia ever came out to, it was weird.

"That's because she already did," Karmen stated with a shrug before I could answer.

"Yeah, Amelia came out to Natalie like... weeks ago," Eleanor added, shrugging as well.

"Wait, but—" Amelia puzzled.

"Guys!" I snapped. "You literally promised you wouldn't say anything and that you'd act surprised!"

"*Umm*, sorry?" Karmen tried.

I spun quickly back to Amelia. "I swear I didn't tell them. Karmen just guessed and I'm bad at lying, and I guess she told Eleanor, but I assure you, I would never betray your trust on something so serious."

Amelia just smiled at me and rolled her eyes in the direction of the others. "I believe you," she answered. "I've known these clowns long enough to know how they are."

"And it's not like it was a big secret," Eleanor stated. "I mean, we've all known for a *long* time."

"Yeah, like a *super* long time," Karmen added.

"I just thought I'd formally tell you all," Amelia answered.

"And this calls for a celebration!" Eleanor exclaimed, reaching across me to give Amelia and high-five. "Congratulations on your queerness!"

"Congratulations!" Ellie 2.0 exclaimed as well. Then she turned to Piper. "We're terribly outnumbered now, huh?"

"Well now, wait just one second," Eleanor declared, grinning impishly. "What's the current update on the whole Veronica situation, Piper?"

Piper flushed deeply. "There is no 'situation.'"

"You sure blush a lot for someone without a 'situation.'"

"We're supposed to be celebrating Amelia," Piper stated. "Let's order celebratory milkshakes."

"We're circling back to this," Eleanor warned, pointing a finger at Piper.

"I think I might get *two* milkshakes," Amelia said, grinning, as she bumped affectionately into my shoulder.

"God, this is the ice-cream parlor all over again," I groaned, though I was teasing, and I smiled largely in response.

That evening, I went back to my apartment. Amelia offered to let me stay with her again, but I needed some alone time to get my head on straight. In just a few days, my parents would be arriving to help me with moveout and last-minute graduation things. I had already texted them and told them the extended family shouldn't come in—that they were limiting seats at the ceremony—but beyond that I hadn't elaborated.

What I really needed to do was figure out what the fuck I wanted to do... but I also kind of just wanted to take a nap and well... watch stupid internet videos until two in the morning. It was fine.

I had two tabs open on my internet browser for job listing, another page opened about jobs you could do with a biology degree, but the page I was on was just relentless memes. I scrolled through until I hit a lesbian centric meme and froze.

Amelia came out. She was out. She came out to me, she came out to her parents, and she came out to her friends. That meant she was certain of her feelings. She was confident enough about her sexuality that she was willing to tell others. So, what was I waiting for? What was holding me back from finally, *finally*, confessing to her that I liked her, that I wanted to be with her?

Of course, that's the kind of realization that I came to at two in the morning, when I was lying awake in bed miles away from the woman I so desperately wanted. It would be reckless to barge over to her apartment then. I had to wait until the next day.

Which was exactly how I came to be at Elk Creek the following day, Friday, throwing open the choir room doors with reckless abandon after school hours. Amelia was inside packing up various items and I, of course, startled her with my abrupt, unannounced entrance.

"We need to talk about some things," I declared forcefully, buzzing with nervous energy.

"You gave me a heart attack," Amelia stated, turning towards me, and shooting me a glare. "What are you doing here, anyway? I thought you said you had to pack?"

"I did and I do," I answered, "but we need to talk."

"You're right," Amelia agreed, nodding. "Here, have a seat. I'll finish this up and then we can talk."

The layout of the choir room had changed since I first arrived at Elk Creek. Before, the center point was the risers with the piano and Amelia's desk to the side. Now though, the risers were tucked away, and rows of chairs filled the floor to allow more comfortable seating for the movies they had been watching. Nervous, I paced towards the piano and ended up sitting on a chair directly next to it, fiddling with my fingers while I waited. I tried to think of what I wanted to say and how I was going to say it, my nerves bubbling even more. Sooner than I was ready, Amelia was done, and she walked towards me, her expression neutral. She sat down on the piano bench, her back to the keys, facing me.

"So... I guess let's talk," Amelia said, breaking the quiet.

"*Umm...* yeah," I answered, but then we just stared at each other in silence. My mind had gone completely blank, and I didn't know what to say. I panicked, but luckily Amelia said something first.

"There's something I've been dying to ask you since we met," Amelia stated.

"What?"

"Why did you agree to hunt down Eleanor and talk to her for Karmen?" Amelia asked. "You just met Karmen, and you had no reason to poke your nose into their business. So, why? Why would you agree to such a thing for a total stranger?"

"Well... I guess a part of me was interested in the whole 'love affair' they kept mentioning," I said. "But I guess... well the real reason was actually because I thought you were super cute and attractive, and I really wanted to get to know you better."

"Really?"

"Yeah, which—wait, actually, that shouldn't even be a surprise to you!" I declared, realizing something as I reflected back. "I *told* you that when you confronted me in my hotel the very next morning!"

Amelia's cheeks colored at my statement. "Yeah, so?" she questioned.

"So!?" I gasped out. "So, you should have known I've had a crush on you since we first met!"

"You... really have a crush on me?" Amelia asked seriously, and you know, I was starting to understand the others' frustration with us. "No, I mean—" she started again, probably noticing the hint of annoyance in my expression. "I just, I thought you said crushes are immature and never lasting."

I sighed lightly and shrugged. "Yeah, well, because they are," I answered. "And yes, I had a crush on you when I first saw you, waiting in line before I knew your name. It was immature because it caused me to do something utterly foolish, which was to chase after Eleanor for Karmen just because I thought it might help me get closer to *you*. But that crush, it changed quickly the second we started to get to know each other, because

I didn't have to daydream about who you were or how you'd act. We were just spending time together and well, I really enjoyed it."

"What are you saying?" Amelia asked genuinely, her eyes locked on mine.

"Amelia Lewis," I stated with a deep breath, "I—" But then I stopped. I was going to say I liked her again, because I did, but that was basically what I told her last time, and a lot of good that did me. Besides, I felt *more* for her. I just wanted to be open and honest with her about how I felt, even if she might not return the feelings.

I let out a chuckle and Amelia looked at me quizzically. "You just make me second guess everything that I do," I said with another laugh. "Look, I just... I don't want you to feel pressured to do or say anything, I just want to be open and honest with you."

"I want that too. There's something I've been fighting and trying to hide from you, but I'm tired of fighting and hiding, and I just..."

Amelia was leaning slightly towards me, as she often did to others when she was attentively listening. I realized that as she was talking, I was leaning forward as well to match her posture. We stared into each other's eyes, just a gaze that was trying to convey the intensity of the words we wanted to confess without actually having to say them. But we needed to. *I* needed to say it.

"Amelia, I—"

"Natalie, I—"

"Oh, sorry, I—"

"Sorry, I didn't—"

We both burst out laughing. "Fuck, we're so bad at this," I choked out, leaning back in my chair, running my fingers through my hair.

"Natalie, I'm in love with you."

What!?

In shock, I jerked, leaning back in my chair too far, promptly falling over backwards, crashing into another chair on my way down. The impact hurt. I landed on my tailbone and hit my shoulder on the other chair as I landed. I sat up slightly, reorienting myself, and groaned.

"My god, Natalie!" Amelia yelped. She dove to her knees, kneeling before me, and reached out to try and help right my position.

I waved my arm slightly, brushing off her concern. "I'm okay."

"Are you sure?" Amelia questioned, leaning closer to me. She gently took hold of the arm I had landed on, pulling me towards her so she could inspect it.

"No, seriously, I'm fine," I said more confidently. "You just... surprised me, is all."

"But... in a good way?"

I nodded. "Of course, in a good way."

I reached towards her, trying to rest my hand on her arm to ground myself before I told her exactly how I felt, but before I could, Amelia practically tackled me, our lips meeting forcefully. I felt the impact, the warmth of her lips, the utter bliss of something I had dreamt of for so long. But I was confused. She... wanted to kiss me? She was maybe probably asexual, and I didn't know what the boundaries of that were, but I kind of thought kissing wouldn't be on the table, and I just—

Suddenly, Amelia pulled away, looking downright confused and terrified. I reached towards her again meekly, just as confused, but she stood and backed away from me. She turned, stepping towards the piano.

"I'm sorry, I didn't know, and I don't want to make things weird between us, I just thought... I mean... I read stuff wrong and I'm sorry. And you know now, so I can't—" Amelia rattled off.

I stood up on shaky legs, the bliss of our kiss now a distant memory as I realized Amelia was freaking out, and quite frankly, so was I.

Finally, Amelia turned around to face me, though she wouldn't look me in the eyes. "You don't feel the same way and I shocked you, I just—"

"What? No!" I declared. "I mean, yes, you did shock me, but not because I don't feel the same way. I just... I didn't think you wanted to kiss me."

Now Amelia was staring at me, equally as confused. "Wha—why? Why wouldn't I want to kiss you?"

"I just, well... I thought you were maybe asexual, and I don't know, sometimes that means no kissing. Which is fine!" I quickly clarified. "I just didn't realize because we never really talked about it, so you just surprised me. But I do! I mean, I want to kiss you, if you want to kiss me."

Amelia cracked a smirk. "You're the loveliest person I've ever met," she whispered. "You're so aware of my comfort and you never want to do anything that I don't want. That's just lovely."

"Well of course. I never want to make you feel uncomfortable."

"And I love that about you," Amelia said, reaching out for me, "but please, Natalie, for the love of god, kiss me."

I didn't need to be told twice. I took two quick steps, reaching Amelia. My left hand slid against her waist, and I tugged gently against her. When she looked up at me almost challengingly, I gently reached up with my right hand and slid it along her neck and jaw, up to her ear. Then, I pulled her head towards mine and kissed her.

Our lips made contact, lightly at first, just trying to align. I pulled her closer, our bodies flush, and I parted my lips slightly to kiss her harder, more fully. Her one hand pulled tight around my back and her other hand found its way to the back of my head. For moments, there was nothing but the soft inviting warmth of her lips and the heat from our bodies being so close.

My heart was pounding. Amelia's fingers on the back of my head were trailing down slightly, touching my neck lightly and sending chills down my spine. A warmth engulfed me, and a need erupted from inside me, a need to be closer, to touch, to taste.

I pulled back from Amelia, only for a second, refilling my lungs with air. As I did, my left hand found its way to the other side of Amelia's head. Before words could be exchanged, I reconnected our lips, this time a bit rougher... a bit needier. In my haste, I knocked myself slightly off balance, stepping forward to catch myself, backing Amelia into the piano bench. I tried to pull back and make sure she was okay, but at the slightest relief of pressure, her arms just tightened around me, and she pulled me back, holding me close.

I decided the piano bench wasn't a problem and the heat in my body was a far more pressing issue. My tongue shot out and ran against Amelia's lips and the moan she released into my mouth had my core shaking. My body pressed against her, backing her up another step. The piano bench was hit again, and Amelia tripped back, but with another step forward I found our balance again.

Our mouths parted momentarily for air, and I waited to see if Amelia would stop us—we were travelling down uncharted territory—but she just turned her head and feverishly reattached our lips. I pushed Amelia again and this time found purchase against the piano. When Amelia's back hit the piano, she gasped slightly, her one arm leaving my back to quickly catch and brace herself. When she did, she unceremoniously slammed her hand down on the piano keys, producing a hideous key smash of sounds that startled us both, breaking our kiss.

Amelia looked down, realizing what had happened, and I burst out laughing, Amelia quickly following.

"*Umm*, sorry?" she muttered sheepishly.

"Do you want to stop?" I asked hesitantly. I knew I didn't, but I wasn't about to push her.

"Why would I want to stop?" she questioned. "Are you... not enjoying...?"

"Of course, I am!" I quickly corrected. "But, I, um... well just a few minutes ago I wasn't even sure you wanted to kiss me, so I just don't know what all you do and don't want to do, and I'm afraid to push you too far."

Amelia bit at her lip. "To be entirely honest, I don't know what all I want either," she confessed. "But how about... I'll tell you if I want to stop, okay?"

"Okay, but are you sure—"

"Trust me, Natalie. If I feel even a little bit uncomfortable, I'll stop you and I know you'll stop because you care about me."

I nodded resolutely. "Okay."

Amelia looked at me expectantly then, and I tugged her back in for another kiss. I deiced to relax and be a bit more daring. Amelia trusted me; she'd stop me if it was too much. So that time, as I kissed her, I also reached down and wrapped my hands around the back of her thighs, right near her butt. Amelia yelped when she felt where my hands went, and I froze, worried I had gone too far, but Amelia just nodded slowly and grasped at my back encouragingly. I lifted her up onto the piano, setting her down on the keys which once again let out a hideous noise. Her legs instinctively spread when I lifted her, and I slowly pressed my body flush against her. When she didn't make a move to stop me, I leaned forward and reattached our lips, pushing her back against the wall of the piano. I couldn't help a grin from spreading across my face when I felt her legs wrap around my lower back, effectively pinning me there.

Even though we weren't aggressively moving, keys on the piano kept going off as we pressed into each other. It was annoying, but neither of us could pry ourselves away to find a better position. I kept my hands on her jaw and neck, to be safe, as I knew she was okay with that, but it was awkward how my arms were hovering and Amelia noticed, breaking our kiss to laugh at me.

"You can touch me, you know," she stated.

"But I—"

"I'll tell you if I want to stop, remember?"

"Okay, okay."

I nodded, gaining more confidence, and gave into the intense urge to feel more of Amelia. I kissed her again, my right hand slowly finding its way down, trailing over her shoulder and down her side to the waist of her pencil skirt which had hiked up to allow her legs to spread. I couldn't see this, as my eyes were shut in pure bliss, but I felt along with my hand.

I didn't want to take things too far, but I did want to feel more. I ran the heel of my palm over her abdomen, feeling her muscles tense at the sudden touch. She was ticklish, I remembered, and smirked, the temptation to break our make out session and start a tickle-war almost too great. I controlled myself though, maintaining a solid pressure against her so she wouldn't jerk away giggling. I pinched at the fabric of her shirt just above the waistband of her skirt, slowly pulling until I felt the fabric loosen. Never releasing her mouth, I felt around the shirt hem and under her blouse until my fingers made contact with smooth, warm skin. I was slowly moving my hand up along her rib cage when I felt a harsh shove to my sternum, knocking me back a step and off of Amelia.

"Shit, I'm so sorry," I stuttered out, my eyes refocusing, and I took a breath. "I didn't—I shouldn't have—I just—"

"No, I..." Amelia muttered. She was shaking her head, her eyes closed. Her hand, which she used to shove me back, was outstretched in the air, shaking.

"A—Amelia?" I questioned. "Did I... did I hurt you? I'm sorry, I—"

"No, no." Finally, Amelia opened her eyes. She reached out then, grabbing my shirt, before she tugged me back in, resting her hands against me, and she seemed to instantly calm down.

I just stood against her, unsure what was happening. My pelvis and lower stomach were against her once more, because she had pulled me close, but I held my arms out to the side in question, not sure if she wanted me to touch her or not.

"It's not that I don't want you close to me," Amelia admitted, pawing at my shirt as she thought. "I just... it got too intense, and I was feeling... I don't—I can't explain it, I—"

"Hey," I whispered softly, reaching down to cup her face in my hands. "You said you'd tell me when you wanted to stop, and you did. You don't owe me anything, not even an explanation. It's perfectly okay."

"Is it though?" Amelia whispered. "I'm not an idiot. I know things were getting kind of heated. Are you okay with that?"

"Okay with what? Okay with getting to make out with you? Yeah, I think I'm okay with that," I laughed.

"No, I mean, are you okay getting all worked up just for me to... stop?"

I bent slightly, tugging at Amelia's jaw until she looked up at me. Then, I softly kissed her forehead. "I'm more than okay with that," I answered.

"I was fully okay with just hugging and cuddling you, no kisses even, so I'm ecstatic right now, Amelia, truly."

"I quite enjoy kissing you too," Amelia answered coyly. "It's the, well, other stuff that I'm not... well I'm not..."

"I know. It's okay. There's nothing wrong with that."

Amelia smiled, lightly pushing me back a step so she could slide down off the piano. Once she was firmly planted on the ground, she tugged her skirt back down to its proper resting place and tucked her shirt back in, smoothing out the wrinkles. I sat back on the nearest chair, rubbing my face, still not entirely convinced I wasn't dreaming.

"Yeah, so, um... to answer you from earlier," I said, looking up at Amelia who was leaning against the piano, "I love you too, Amelia."

A huge smile grew across Amelia's face. "You have no idea how happy I am right now," she declared.

"I think I have a pretty good idea," I answered, mimicking her smile. "We should, um, still talk though... about..."

"About what this means for us," Amelia finished my statement for me.

I nodded. "Look, I would absolutely love to be with you in any way you'll have me. I know that being in a relationship with another woman can have a lot of complications... especially for like, your professional life. I don't want to make anything more difficult for you."

"Oh, Natalie," Amelia said, and there were tears in her eyes. She fell to her knees right in front of me and buried her face into my lap. I stroked Amelia's hair, rubbing circles on her back. I felt her shudder a few times before she moved, looking up at me. "I came out to my parents and friends for a reason," she stated, tears running down her cheeks, but her voice was strong. I reached out and gently wiped a tear off her cheek. "I don't want to hide this part of who I am anymore, no matter what problems I might face. I don't want to miss this... this... what's between us. I don't want to ruin it just because I'm afraid of some difficulties."

"Are you sure?"

"I've never been surer of anything in my life," Amelia declared, reaching out and grabbing the first thing her hands found, which was my shirt, before tugging me closer.

"Then... will you be my girlfriend?" I asked bravely.

Amelia choked against a laugh, a softer sob before full-on laughter erupted from her. "You're such a dork," she said into my lap.

"That doesn't sound like a yes or a no," I stated cheekily.

Amelia sat up on her knees to look me in the eyes. "Yes," she said confidently. "Yes a thousand times over, I will absolutely be your girlfriend, Nats."

I grinned before bending over and giving Amelia a chaste kiss. Amelia smiled back at me when we pulled away before standing and pulling a chair right up against the one I was sitting on. She climbed onto the chair and over, resting her head on my shoulder. We sat like that for a while, in silence, just living in bliss. Eventually though, I broke the silence.

"I guess I should probably tell you... Nicholas knows."

"Knows what?"

"That we have feelings for each other," I explained. "He said he'd be discrete. I trust him. But just, if he says anything, now you know."

"I'll talk to him," Amelia said. "Probably tomorrow at graduation."

"Oh yeah, speaking of, what time is graduation? I'd like to come."

"Six, technically, though teachers have to be there earlier. A bunch of the younger choir students will be there though, so I'm sure you could find them, and they'd point you in the right direction."

"I'll come then. I promised Lizzie I'd help her pack and move tomorrow, but we should be done with plenty of time for me to get over here."

We settled back into comfortable silence; Amelia cuddled against me. It was nice, just the two of us. We'd have to tell the others, and Lizzie, and Nicholas, and... my parents... someday, but it was nice to have it just to ourselves for a little while.

Just before I headed out to leave—to get some rest before helping Lizzie—Amelia stopped me.

"Wait, before you go..." she said. I turned back to her in question, and she grabbed my arm, tugging me closer to her before kissing me. The kiss was quick, but fantastic. "Now go on, get some rest. You're going to be working hard tomorrow!" Amelia stated, pushing me towards the door.

I smiled largely. Right... I could kiss her now. We were... dating! I felt like I was floating the whole way home.

22.

Screwed Over By The System

After helping Lizzie pack up, I headed over to Elk Creek early after Amelia texted me that everyone was there and just hanging out. Also, Amelia cryptically said they had a surprise for me. Being the naïve girl that I was, I thought my surprise might be something nice just because my friends cared about me, but that was dreaming too much.

I met up with everyone in Piper's classroom. The second I walked into the room, I was unceremoniously handed my surprise, which was a screaming baby Isabella. Karmen, who handed her daughter over to me, stated, "Have fun babysitting the kids with Cliff."

"*Umm*, what?" I questioned over the screaming, confused and trying to bounce Isabella.

"All the teachers have to enter in procession at the beginning of the ceremony," Piper explained from where she sat at her desk.

"Yeah, and why hire a babysitter when we have all of *one* significant other that's not a teacher and our college kid friend?"

I located Cliff, the only guy in the room—who was already holding the even smaller baby Katrina. He just shrugged at me in response.

"Haven't you ever heard of the wonders of an at-home babysitter?" I questioned. "Also, take your kid back, Karmen. The ceremony hasn't started yet."

"Sure, the babysitters' names are Cliff and Natalie," Eleanor said coyly.

"Seriously, Karmen," I stated again. "I don't know how to make a kid stop crying! Help me out here!"

Karmen turned, pulling out a pacifier, before sticking it into Isabella's mouth, effectively shutting off her crying. "See? Easy," Karmen declared.

"My rate is twenty-five dollars an hour. I expect a check at the end of the ceremony."

"*Ooo,* what a steal," Amelia teased.

I rolled my eyes. "I hope this entire experience is a disaster, so you never ask me to babysit again."

"Look, if you're living with us this summer, you're going to be babysitting," Eleanor said.

"We're just helping you out, really," Karmen added. "We're letting both you *and* Cliff get real life experience for when you have kids of your own."

"Fine, but seriously, take your kid back until the ceremony starts," I said, handing Isabella back to her mother.

I walked over to Amelia—who was perched atop one of the student desks—and sat beside her, looking around the room. Piper was at her desk gazing over at Katrina in Cliff's arms. Ellie 2.0 leaned her head against Cliff's shoulder, smiling. Below her, Vanessa was standing, her arms up in Ellie 2.0's as she swayed the girl back and forth. Between us, Eleanor was sitting on a desk with Michael in her lap, a toy car occupying his attention. Karmen, with Isabella in her arms, went and sat on the floor in front of Eleanor, and when she did, Vanessa tumbled away from Ellie 2.0 to make silly faces at the baby.

We looked like one, big, happy, extended family. It was crazy to think that only three months ago, I didn't know any of them. How ridiculous it was to think that a last-minute decision to take a vacation by myself had landed me five best friends. Well... make that four best friends and one totally amazing, utterly perfect girlfriend.

I turned to Amelia, and she looked to me, our eyes meeting. She smiled brightly before saying, "Nats and I are going to go hunt down our graduating choir students before the ceremony."

"You best come back here before it starts," Eleanor warned me.

"Yeah, no sneaking off to avoid babysitting responsibilities," Karmen added.

"You guys are awful. There's an entire profession dedicated to this very job, yet you're making *me* watch your kids," I replied jokingly.

"If you're going to be their aunt, you have to spend time with them," Piper stated,

"Their... aunt?" I questioned.

"Metaphorical, obviously," Eleanor said. "Sometimes I wonder if you even actually graduated high school."

"Hey!"

"Michael already calls us all aunts," Ellie 2.0 spoke up. "It only stands to reason that all the kids will want to spend time with their Aunt Natalie too, right?"

"*Aww*, guys!" I cooed. "That's so sweet! I—I don't know what to say."

"Stop being all mushy and go talk to the choir students, so you can get back to your responsibilities," Eleanor declared, waving me out of the room.

Amelia laughed, grabbing my arm, and tugged me out into the hall. The last thing I heard was a slightly quieter Karmen stating, "Do those two seem to be acting a little... strange to anyone else?"

"Sorry you got stuck with babysitting responsibilities," Amelia said as we rounded the corner. "I mean, I'm not really sorry. I think it's kind of funny."

"Yeah, what a wonderful surprise," I mocked. "I do appreciate the kids, I just... I don't know, four seems like a handful, even for Cliff and me."

"I'm sure it'll be fine," Amelia commented. "Anyway, I thought we could go say hi to Shannon, Carlos, and Julia before graduation, if that's alright."

"Sure. I'd like to congratulate them too."

"Exactly, just... first..." Amelia stopped in the middle of the empty hall, glancing to either side of us before she tugged me towards her, kissing me hard. Instinctively, I reached for her arms and pulled her body flush against me, the action causing Amelia to stumble towards me and push me up against the wall.

"I've missed you," Amelia said as she pulled back, grinning.

"I've missed you too," I answered. "Do, um... do the others... know?"

"About us? This?" Amelia asked, gesturing between us. I nodded. "I haven't told them, no."

"Are we going to?"

"Eventually, yes, we kind of have to," Amelia chuckled. "Maybe not tonight though. Tonight is about our seniors, and besides, it's kind of nice having you all to myself without the others poking their noses into our business."

"Agreed."

We got to the choir room where all the seniors had gathered in preparation. The excitement was high and contagious, especially to Amelia. Before I could blink, Amelia ran off to some students, squealing like she was one of them. I spotted Nicholas standing with Shannon and headed over to them.

"Hi, friends," I greeted. "And congrats, Shannon." I reached out and gave Shannon a double high five.

"Thanks, Natalie," Shannon replied with a grin. "You're going to take care of these disasters once I'm gone, right?"

"Of course," I replied, grabbing Nicholas and messing up his hair. "We gotta keep this guy in line, after all."

"Hey, hey, hey!" Nicholas complained. "I have gel in my hair! This is going to take an hour to fix!" I pated down Nicholas' hair, laughing. He huffed at me.

"Ms. Lewis too," Shannon added. "You're going to take good care of her too, right?"

"Most definitely," I answered, beaming.

Suddenly, Amelia jumped up from behind, tacking Shannon in a tight hug. "Congratulations, Shannon!" Amelia exclaimed. She released Shannon, allowing her to spin around and see her captor, and then Shannon promptly grabbed Amelia in another hug.

"I'm going to miss you so much," Shannon stated to her teacher.

"We're still going to see each other next Tuesday for Worlds practice," Amelia laughed. "You can't escape us that easily!"

"I know, but after Worlds I'm going to college in New York..."

"But you're still coming home for winter break, and you'll visit us, right?"

"Well of course."

"Then we can see you over break and hear all about how awesome college is!" Nicholas exclaimed. "And then Natalie won't be so special anymore because she won't be the only college kid crashing our classes."

"I feel like I should be offended by that," I stated.

"We're going to miss you, Shannon, but it's not goodbye forever," Amelia said.

"Gosh, thanks, you guys!" Shannon gasped, smiling.

We weren't allowed to stay too long, as the principal kicked us out so she could rally the seniors. Amelia, Nicholas, and I headed back down the hallway together. We were about to the end of the new choir wing when Nicholas spoke up.

"So... what's the hot take on the current state of your guys' relationship?" he questioned.

"I don't know what you're talking about," I stated, choosing to ignore his nosiness.

"Sure, you do," Nicholas pushed. "Did you two talk about it?"

I looked to Amelia and we nodded. "Yes," we both answered simultaneously.

"And...?"

"We... kissed... once," Amelia said.

"Or twice," I added with a shrug.

"Or thrice," Amelia added with a wink.

"Okay, so y'all made out," Nicholas declared, rolling his eyes. "Glad to know you cowards finally kissed."

"Rude," I stated.

"Anything else?" Nicholas prompted.

"We're dating," Amelia said smoothly, and I felt my heart soar.

"Adorable," Nicholas replied, smiling. "You two make such a cute couple. I love it. Furthermore, I wanted to extend my apology, personally, to Ms. Lewis. If I had known men weren't your type, we would have tried to set you up with some nice ladies, and had I known you had a crush on Natalie, we would have just set you two up."

At that, Amelia blushed. Bashfully, she stuttered out, "Nicholas, I— please—"

"*Ahh*, no, you don't have to say anything," Nicholas said, raising his hand to stop her. "I just expect full details about your adorable relationship moving forward."

"Dude, you're a baby," I mocked.

"You're also still my student," Amelia added cheekily.

"But I'm your friend!" Nicholas pleaded. "Come on, please!? I just want juicy details!"

Amelia and I looked to each other and shrugged. "I don't know..." I stated. "I'd say those details are rated *at least* PG-13. Looks like you'll have to wait another year, bud."

"I utterly despise you two," Nicholas huffed, and Amelia started laughing.

"*Aww*, come on," I said, grinning. "How about you come prove your maturity to us?"

"How?"

"Help me watch two tots and two infants during the graduation ceremony," I stated smugly.

"You want me to babysit?" Nicholas asked incredulously.

"I mean... we don't *have* to tell you about our relationship—"

"Okay, fine! I'll help!"

"That'a boy!"

Graduation went by without a snag. The children were angels, and the students were all excited. After the ceremony, there were lots of hugs and pictures. Nicholas spotted his dad and regretfully said he needed to leave. I looked across the gym and locked eyes with his father. He was intimidating and, well, rude, frankly, but in that moment, he simply nodded his head towards me amicably. Not everything would always work out, but maybe sometimes people just needed someone to stand up for them when no one else would.

Cliff and I passed the kids back to their respective parents. When I brought Katrina over to Piper, she mentioned she had an update on Aniyah.

"I called Aniyah's school yesterday."

"What did they say?" I questioned.

"Well... they mentioned that her father is ill, and her brother had a run in with the law, so she's been staying home to care for her father," Piper explained.

"That's terrible. I should—"

"Mail them a card with your condolences, but mind your own business," Piper suggested for me.

"Piper, Aniyah is sacrificing her education to care for her dad. I can't just send her a card and turn a blind eye!"

"Natalie," Piper warned in her scary teacher—and now mother—voice.

"You just don't understand," I huffed. I turned and stalked off, irritated.

Even though we were all a sort of teacher in our own rights, it was clear Piper didn't understand my feelings for Aniyah. If anyone was going to understand my intense desire to help her, it would be Amelia, who would do anything for her choir students. The bond Amelia had for her students ran deeper than the classroom, whereas Piper's relationships felt a tad more superficial. The bond I had formed with Aniyah ran deeper than the classroom. She didn't deserve to fail her classes just because she had to stay home and take care of her dad. I didn't care what it was going to take, I was going to help her.

I found Amelia just outside of the gym. I must have looked a bit upset, because Amelia stopped me, resting a comforting hand on my arm. "Natalie, are you okay? What's wrong?" she asked.

"It's just... Piper found out that Aniyah couldn't come to lab because she has to stay home and take care of her dad. He got sick and her brother got arrested, so she has to. I want to help her, but Piper keeps telling me to mind my own business." I sighed. "I just... it's not fair that she has to skip school to take care of her dad. She has a bright future ahead of her, but this might compromise her chances."

"What exactly do you want to do that Piper doesn't want you to do?"

"I guess... I should bring her a care package or something, so she knows that I do care and that I'm thinking about her and her family. I want to visit her at home, see if there's anything I can do to help her or her dad out... or her brother even, I don't know. I just want to help, but I can't do that if I can't go visit her and talk to her!"

"And Piper doesn't want you visiting Aniyah?"

"Exactly!" I exclaimed. "I mean, Aniyah doesn't live in the *best* neighborhood, but it's not that bad. I just... I want to help her!"

"We should go visit Aniyah then."

"I just wish Piper could think about it from her perspective, you know, I just—wait, what did you just say?"

"I said, we should go visit Aniyah," Amelia restated.

"Really? But won't Piper be mad if she finds out?"

"Piper's not our mother," Amelia chuckled. "I mean, maybe it's not the safest of neighborhoods, but is there really any public place that's fully safe? I'll go with you, so you don't have to go alone, and we can put together a gift basket tomorrow to bring with us."

"I... would you really do that for me?" I asked in awe.

"Absolutely. Why wouldn't I help you help a girl in need? What's the point in living if you choose to be selfish?"

"God, I love you," I stated, tackling Amelia in a tight hug.

After a moment, Amelia pulled back from me slightly, her one hand still resting on the small of my back. Slowly, she brought up her other hand and tucked a strand of pink hair behind my ear.

"I love you too, Nats. And I love this about you. You have such a big and kind heart." Then, she slowly leaned forward and kissed me, this time softly, full of compassion.

"Well butter my butt and call me a biscuit! What do we have here!?"

Amelia and I jerked apart, only to find Eleanor and Karmen strutting over to us. Vanessa was walking between them, holding each of their hands.

"Hell," Amelia cursed under her breath.

"How long has *this* been going on?" Karmen commented, gesturing between Amelia and me.

"Like... a day," I stated.

"So, it's official then?"

Amelia snaked her arms around my waist and pulled me closer, resting her head on my shoulder. "Yes," she commented, "though we were trying to enjoy it for a bit before we told the rest of you."

"If you were trying to hide it, you shouldn't be macking in the middle of the hall," Eleanor laughed. "*Ooo*, hang on." She released Vanessa's hand and pulled out her phone, making a call. She pulled the phone up to her ear. "Hey, come out the east side door of the gym. Yeah, bring her and Cliff too. Now."

"What are you—" I tried to ask, but Eleanor cut me off, hanging up the phone.

"Cat's out of the bag now. You might as well tell everyone."

"Amelia, Natalie, congrats on your new-found relationship," Karmen said, smiling at us.

"It's about damn time," Eleanor added.

Not a second later, Piper burst through the nearby gym doors carrying Katrina, Ellie 2.0 and Cliff hot on her heels with the other children.

"What's happening?" Piper questioned, looking between the rest of us accusingly.

"We caught them *kissing*!" Karmen exclaimed, pointing at Amelia and me.

"Really?" Piper asked skeptically.

Amelia nodded. "We're dating," she stated, looking over to me. She rolled her eyes. I giggled.

"So much for keeping it a secret, huh?" I laughed.

"*Aww*, you two are so cute!" Ellie 2.0 squealed, grabbing both Amelia and me in a tight hug.

"Hug pile?" Michael asked meekly.

"Heck yeah, little bud!" Eleanor exclaimed. "Hug pile!"

And before we knew it, Amelia and I were at the center of a huge group hug made up of our loving little teacher family.

I ended up at Amelia's that night. We were trying to take things slow, but it was pointless. We were too addicted to cuddling, too used to waking up next to each other. Being apart felt more like torture than anything. So, we just gave in.

As we headed up to her apartment, I talked about some online quizzes I took which were supposed to help me figure out the best career choice for me.

"One of them said humanitarian work," I stated. "The degrees seem to mainly be sociology related, and that's kind of close to biology. Maybe more so psychology, but maybe in another year I could switch my degree to sociology, since I'm stuck going to school for another semester anyway. And I mean, I guess it's pretty interesting. Maybe I could do humanitarian work."

"Beats being a politician, anyway."

"True, I would hate that. Politicians are so full of themselves."

"And lawyers," Amelia added. "Attorneys can be *really* full of themselves. Have you ever talked to a lawyer? They're like, *'Oh my gosh, I went to Harvard, and I graduated top of my class just so I can keep you out of jail for tax evasion.'*"

I laughed at Amelia's weird, snobbish, posh accent. "Lawyers can't all be bad. I mean, look at Veronica, right?"

"I mean, she dumped Piper's case."

"Because she fell in love with Piper and knew it would be a conflict of interest! And she didn't leave Piper hanging, she got one of her colleagues to cover the case."

"You're right. Lawyers aren't all bad," Amelia agreed, unlocking her apartment door. "I mean, when they get all big and fancy and do corrupt things just to get rich people off the hook, that's pretty rotten. But there's got to be tons of lawyers out there with hearts. Like the lawyers that represent the poor and underprivileged."

"You mean, the state assigned lawyers that are underpaid and overworked?" I questioned. "Pretty sure they're just slipping by paycheck to paycheck, trying not to die from the workload."

"Well, I don't know. You said you wanted to help people, so, you could run a soup kitchen, I guess."

"I want to make a big difference in people's lives though."

"They say the fastest way to a man's heart is through his stomach... pretty sure running a soup kitchen would help change lives."

"Yeah, and I'm pretty sure that's not what that saying is referring to," I laughed.

We stepped into Amelia apartment, and she moved forward, dropping her purse off onto a nearby end table. "I didn't know you were a master of the English language," she teased.

I finished kicking the door shut before I reached out and grabbed Amelia's arm, tugging her back towards me. "Hey, enough making fun of me," I said, spinning us so I could pin her against the now closed door. "You know damn well that I'm right."

"*Ehh*, debatable."

I looked at Amelia, just smirking, before bumping my nose against hers. "Did you know, you're really adorable?" I hummed. "Which is annoying, because I'm trying to be the adorable one out of the two of us."

"Are you capable of giving a full complement, or do you always have to make it about yourself?" Amelia scoffed.

"I'm attracted to everything about you," I continued without missing a beat. "Your looks, your personality, your quirks, your laugh... everything."

"Stop talking," Amelia commanded.

"What?" I asked with a slight chuckle.

"Shut up and kiss me already," she declared, practically whining. I couldn't help it; I burst out laughing, and Amelia promptly smacked my upper arm. "Natalie, god, you're impossible," she huffed.

"I'm sorry, I can't help it."

Amelia rolled her eyes before she grabbed my head and tugged me in for a kiss mid-laugh. It took but a second for me to stop laughing and reciprocate her kiss. My hands had just begun to trail up her sides when she pushed me back, only enough to break our kiss.

"Documentary?" she questioned.

"Sure," I agreed.

We watched a documentary about the dairy industry and veganism. The first half was calm, as I was definitely more focused on the beautiful woman curled up against me, but then the documentary started getting really serious and crazy, and by the end Amelia and I were both up and pacing around, ranting about shitty governmental policies.

After we calmed down, we went to bed and cuddled like we always did. This time, the only difference was a chaste goodnight kiss. Then, we settled down, lying on our sides, facing each other. We lied there, looking at each other with lazy smiles, before Amelia nuzzled against my chest.

"I love you, Nats," she murmured.

"I love you too, 'Melia."

Sunday morning was blissful. We had a simple breakfast, didn't do anything fancy, but sitting around in our pajamas with the warm spring sun creeping through Amelia's kitchen window made everything feel calm and euphoric.

Eventually, it was time to get to business. We baked some of Amelia's famously good chocolate chip cookies to bring to Aniyah, then went to the store to grab a few other things. Then, I drove us to Aniyah's house, glad I could remember the way.

As I drove closer and closer to Aniyah's house, I watched Amelia and her reaction to the ever-deteriorating neighborhood. Eventually, I had to ask.

"Look, I don't want to be insulting or something by calling this a ghetto, but—"

"It *is* insulting," Amelia cut in.

"Well, I know, but I don't mean it in an insulting way, you know?"

"It's less about what you mean and more just the connotation behind the origin of the word," Amelia explained. "It's a racially charged word... something used to harm mainly black populations... a demeaning term to describe how they live... a term that was born from racism."

"You're right. I've just... I've been so isolated I don't know what to say. I don't want to be insulting or snobbish or racist, but it's hard because I've never been exposed to this part of life. But, um, I was just wondering... have you ever been on this side of town before?"

Amelia nodded. "A few times, various reasons."

"We have a bit farther to go, want to elaborate?" I prompted.

"Well, we had to go somewhere around here chasing Eleanor down one night," Amelia began. "This was a while ago, but well, she got super drunk and ran off one night after a spat with Karmen. Karmen called us and told us because she was worried about Eleanor, but too gosh darn stubborn to go find Eleanor herself. Anyway, we um... almost got shot at, so I think Piper associates this side of town with danger. But it was solely Eleanor's fault we almost got shot at."

"I—what happened?"

"Eleanor picked a fight with a kid because she's stupid when she's intoxicated," Amelia stated. "I think the boy only asked if she was okay, but she flipped out and started yelling at him. Piper and I found her in the yelling match, tried to break them up... that was when the kid's dad came out of their house with a gun. Piper thought we were goners, but... the guy wouldn't have shot us."

"How can you be so sure?"

"Black men aren't violent *or* stupid," Amelia explained. "He was just using it as an intimidation factor to protect his son, because there are people out that that will and have shot an unarmed, innocent, black kid for no reason. But we were just two white women... Could you imagine if he had pointed the gun at us and we called the police? They would have beat him up and thrown him in prison, if not worse. I didn't feel like we were in danger, I just felt awful because Eleanor was harassing the poor guy's kid. Piper got Eleanor to the car, and I stayed back and apologized. Everything was fine. But Piper lectured me for months afterwards. Piper's smart and well educated, but she only understands racial tension from a strictly textbook standpoint. The real feelings... you have to learn that from experience, I think."

"I guess that makes sense," I replied. "You said you've been here a few times. What else happened?"

"Volunteering, various tasks... picking up trash, gardening, handing out meals on holidays, house visits. Eleanor donates so much of her time, and she got Karmen and me to volunteer too. We owe it to our community since we try so hard with the afterschool program. It helps erase the 'harsh line' between us the more interactions we have with each other."

"Does Piper volunteer with you guys?"

"No... she's... afraid, I think. For some people, it's easy to toss aside an upbringing of racism and fear, for others, it's a bit more difficult. She's trying, I guess, to a certain degree. It's just slow change."

"Is she really trying though if she's not stepping out of her comfort zone to come volunteer with you guys?"

"You have a point. Maybe you could convince her to come."

"I can try."

We pulled up in front of Aniyah's house. Amelia carried our package of various snacks, dry goods, and supplies up to the door and I knocked, waiting patiently. There wasn't an answer for a long time, so I knocked again, and then finally called out, "Aniyah? It's Natalie from Elk Creek. I just wanted to make sure you were okay since you missed the last two labs of the year.”

Finally, I heard footsteps inside and then the door was opened to reveal Aniyah. “Natalie?” she questioned. “Wha—what are you doing here?”

“Hi, Aniyah,” Amelia said, smiling at the girl. Aniyah nodded towards her.

“We were worried about you, so we wanted to check on you and make sure you were okay,” I explained. “We called your school, and they said your dad was sick, so you were staying home to take care of him.”

“We got you a care package too,” Amelia said, presenting the basket.

Aniyah smiled largely, her eyes shining on the verge of tears. She stepped onto the porch and pulled me into a hug. “I can’t believe you’re here,” she said. “I can’t believe you noticed I was gone and that you cared enough to come check up on me and my family.”

“Of course I noticed and of course I care,” I stated. “You’re a great student, a friend, and more importantly, a vet to be.”

Aniyah laughed. “Maybe... or a zookeeper.”

“Regardless, always an animal lover.”

“Would you two like to come inside?” Aniyah asked.

“Sure,” I replied, eager to see if there was any way I could help.

Aniyah led us into her house, telling Amelia to leave the basket on the kitchen table. “I really can’t thank you enough,” Aniyah said again, opening the basket to look through the things we brought.

“We weren’t really sure what kind of things you’d want,” I stated. “If there’s something you need, just let me know. I can go get it for you.”

“I... can’t accept all this...” Aniyah said, frowning.

“Sure you can,” I replied. “Don’t think anything of it.”

Aniyah sniffled and I thought she might start crying. “You just... don’t understand how much this means to me. Things have been so hard since dad got sick. He’s doing really bad and I just...”

“Is there anything we can do to help your dad?” I asked.

“Aniyah shook her head. “No, he... well he needs medicine. We don’t really have insurance though... not *good* insurance anyway, and we don’t have any money because of the last time we had to bail my brother out. And my brother did something stupid to try and get the medicine, and he got caught, so I have to take care of dad. I can’t go to school, because he’s doing so poorly, but I can’t ask you to get the medicine or anything. That’s too much.”

"You have to go to school. You've got finals coming up," I declared. "Maybe we could figure something out, just so you can still finish off the year."

"Thanks, Natalie, but I really don't think—" Aniyah was cut off when an aggressive coughing fit erupted from the other room. Once the coughing and hacking died off, Aniyah called out, "Dad? Are you okay? Dad?" When he didn't respond, Aniyah dashed off to a side room, a look of worry on her face.

I followed after Aniyah, Amelia right behind me. In the other room I saw Aniyah's dad, slouched over in a chair, coherent, but struggling with exhaustion. He was puffy, his legs swollen, which I knew were key signs of heart problems. He was having trouble breathing and looked a sickly color. Aniyah kneeled before him, trying to get him to respond to her. I looked over to Amelia and she looked to me with panic in her eyes. The bottom of my stomach dropped out.

"Aniyah, do you know why he's so sick?" I asked tentatively.

"He was diagnosed with diabetes," Aniyah answered. "We couldn't afford the insulin though. He was watching what he was eating but—"

"Natalie..." Amelia muttered. "He's not okay."

"You're right," I agreed. "We need to take him to the hospital. Now."

"We can't afford an ER visit," Aniyah stated, her voice strained.

"Don't worry about the money," I stated confidently, although *I* was certainly worrying about the money. "We need to get your dad to the hospital, and that's all that matters right now."

"I can't... we'll lose our house," Aniyah choked out as I worked to get her dad standing.

Amelia stepped up beside me to help. "Aniyah, I'll cover the bill," she said. "Don't worry about it."

"But I can't—" Aniyah protested.

"It isn't a weakness admitting you need help," Amelia continued. "Now don't say another word, just accept my gratitude. Help us get your father out to the car."

"Yes, ma'am," Aniyah replied, standing up to help us prop up her dad.

It took all three of us practically carrying the man to get him out to my car. We slid him into the backseat with Aniyah. He was fighting hard to stay conscious, and he was fading fast... scarily fast. Never one to question my judgement, Amelia stayed quiet as I flew down the street, going way over the speed limit, swerving between cars. I didn't know how I felt in that moment. I didn't have time to stop and think about how I felt. All I knew was that there was a man dying in the backseat of my car and I needed to get him to help as soon as possible.

By the time we reached the hospital, Aniyah's dad was basically unresponsive. While Amelia helped Aniyah slide him out of the backseat, I ran into the ER frantically searching for a wheelchair. I alerted the receptionist to our issue and a nurse raced out to the parking lot with me.

"He doesn't seem so well," the nurse observed, pulling him onto the wheelchair. "How long has he been like this?" he asked, wheeling Aniyah's dad towards the building.

"Unresponsive? Since the drive over, maybe fifteen minutes," I answered, racing after the nurse. "Sick in general, it's been like...?"

"Almost a month since he got diagnosed with diabetes," Aniyah answered for me.

"And his insulin?" the nurse questioned.

"We can't afford it," Aniyah replied.

We were met by a doctor and several other nurses inside. They pulled Aniyah's dad inside to a room and took his vitals, hooking him up to a heart monitor. Everything was happening so fast. Amelia, Aniyah, and I were standing awkwardly by his bedside while they asked us a bunch of questions. The doctor told the nurses what tests needed to be run. And then the doctor was gone.

A nurse approached us and said she needed us to fill out some paperwork. Aniyah volunteered for the task and followed the nurse out to the receptionist desk. There weren't any chairs where we were, so Amelia and I just sort of stood next to Aniyah's dad and watched.

After a few moments, Amelia muttered out, "This is worse than Karmen."

"What?"

"I mean, Karmen was in bad shape, and I thought she looked awful, but he... he looks like he's dying, Natalie."

"We're at the hospital now, though, and he's being treated, so he'll be okay," I stated optimistically.

Aniyah returned not long after and she didn't look too well. I asked her how she was doing, and she just shook her head. "This isn't going to be good," she said. "I had to tell them about the state of our family insurance, and I just—"

"Hey, we're not worrying about money right now," I stated seriously. I mean, *I* was, but Aniyah needed to focus on her dad and that was it.

Suddenly, there was an obnoxious beeping and the nurse next to Aniyah's dad jumped, shouting out, "He's flatlining!"

"Oh god!" Aniyah gasped.

I grabbed Aniyah's wrist and pulled the girl back, shoving Amelia back with us so the nurses that were pouring in could get around her dad. Aniyah let out a strangled yelp and I turned her, pulling her close against me so she couldn't watch what was happening. She sobbed against me and shoved her hands over her ears so she couldn't hear either. Amelia and I waited on edge for every countdown and shock they sent though Aniyah's dad, holding our own breaths.

He jolted and his heartbeat returned, the team that had just saved his life sighing in relief. I patted Aniyah and told her it was okay. She pulled back and chanced a look, but it didn't provide her with much relief.

I was maybe thirty minutes later when the entire scene repeated itself: Aniyah's father flatlined, Aniyah panicked, the team came in and managed to save his life, but still, none of us felt relief. After the second time, Aniyah was crying so hysterically she couldn't even stand, and I could barely support her enough to keep her from falling straight on the ground.

"We can't stay back here," Amelia stated to me.

"You're right," I answered, nodding.

I passed Aniyah off to Amelia, who pulled the girl out into the waiting room, and I stayed back to alert the nurses as to where we would be.

Aniyah was inconsolable, not that I was surprised. Her brother was in jail and her father was dying in the other room. I sat awkwardly next to her. Nothing I could offer in terms of comfort would magically fix things, so I had to hope my presence alone was enough.

A few minutes later, a doctor came out to explain to us what was happening. Essentially, Aniyah's father was diabetic and diagnosed at a rather late stage. The lifesaving insulin he needed was too expensive—due to privatization and patent rights and private companies driving up costs for more and more profit—and without it, his body was shutting down and his heart was failing. There wasn't much at that point they could do for him.

I got up to pace around the room. I was... furious... livid. I couldn't believe it had come to something like this. Poor people couldn't afford regular doctor visits, which led to late diagnoses, and then on top of that, drug companies were allowed to jack up the prices of vitally important medicine just because they knew they could make more money, leaving those who couldn't afford it just... screwed! Eventually, Amelia found me, and held my hand, telling me to try and calm down.

"It isn't fair!" I protested.

"I know. I know it's not fair. But please, Natalie, you have to be strong for Aniyah. Now is not the time to fight. Now is the time to be there for her."

"I... I wish I could fix everything so good people wouldn't have to die like this..."

"Please don't beat yourself up over this. We've done all we can."

With our heads down in despair, we headed back towards Aniyah. However, halfway across the waiting room, our path was intersected by a nurse who urgently pulled us aside. She regretfully informed us that Aniyah's dad went into cardiac arrest again, and this time they were unable to resuscitate him. Amelia didn't feel like she could tell Aniyah, and I didn't feel like I could either, so we asked the nurse to tell Aniyah too. We stood by Aniyah's side while the news was delivered, and we were there to hold and support her while she endlessly cried.

The nurse brought us back to Aniyah's dad so that Aniyah could say goodbye to him. She draped herself over him, crying so hard I thought she'd never stop. Amelia pulled me out of the room to let Aniyah stay for a while longer in private.

The nurse who was graciously tending to our case met us in the hallway. She carried a stack of pamphlets in her hands.

"Here are some pamphlets about grief and healing after the loss of a loved one," she said, passing the brochures to me. "There are resources in there to call and websites you can visit for more information and help." The nurse pulled another pamphlet from her pocket. "And here's some information about funerals, taking the next step in the process."

"Oh goodness..." Amelia muttered, taking the funeral pamphlet from the nurse.

"The process usually moves pretty fast. They don't like waiting more than a few days, really," the nurse continued. "I know it's hard, but it'll be such a sigh of relief once it's all said and done."

"A *relief*," I grumbled, still furious. It was an avoidable tragedy. That man didn't have to die. But companies were so greedy, and they cared more about profit than actually saving lives, and—

"Thank you," Amelia answered calmly, interrupting my thoughts.

"You two are just family friends, correct?" the nurse asked, and we both nodded. "Do you know where her mother is?"

"He mother passed a long time ago," I answered.

"She's... an orphan then? Since she's still a minor."

"Yeah, I guess so, unfortunately."

"Then I'm really, *really*, sorry, but I have to call child protective services. It's mandatory, seeing as she currently has no living legal guardians."

"What does that mean?" I snapped.

"They'll likely place her in foster care until they can find a family member that's willing and fit to take her in," the nurse explained calmly. "Otherwise, she'll just stay in foster care until she ages out of the system."

"But, but... she has a life!" I protested. "She has dreams and goals and friends! You can't just uproot her like that!"

"I'm very sorry, ma'am, but I have to contact CPS. Does the receptionist have your phone numbers?"

"Yes," Amelia answered for me, because I was fuming to the point I couldn't talk.

"I suspect you'll take care of her for at least tonight?" the nurse offered.

"Yes, she can stay with us," Amelia replied.

"Okay, well... child services will be contacting you within the next few days to follow up," the nurse said, pausing. "I'm... sorry."

"You're just doing your job, it's okay. We understand," Amelia said.

Once the nurse was gone, Amelia and I went back to check on Aniyah. We found her sitting on the bed beside her father, no longer bawling, but her face was tear stained.

"I don't want to get put in foster care," she stated softly. Evidently, she had overheard our conversation with the nurse.

"We don't want you in foster care either," I said firmly, "but we aren't your legal guardians, so we don't have any say in the matter."

"I... I know..." Aniyah muttered. "Thank you for everything, I, um... well I guess you can drop me back off at my house... while it's still my house, that is."

"Absolutely not," Amelia refused. "You're staying with me until CPS steps in. We'll go back and get your stuff, but we aren't leaving you alone."

"I can't impose myself on you like that."

"You aren't imposing. I'm inviting," Amelia answered strongly.

"Are you sure?" Aniyah sniffled, looking between the two of us.

"We aren't going to let you spend the night alone," I added. "This is a very... unfortunate day. But maybe some sweets and movies will help."

"Thanks," Aniyah whispered.

Amelia left us to finalize some details, already swearing that she would take care of everything. I occupied Aniyah as best I could, keeping her company and trying to keep her mind off negative things. We tried to figure out if Aniyah had any family members that could help with things. She mentioned her uncle, who everyone hated, and her aunt, who never got along with the family and probably wouldn't much care. And then, finally, with dread in our hearts and Aniyah carrying a pain I couldn't even imagine, we left the hospital and headed back to my car.

As we were walking to the car, Amelia's phone rang. Aniyah, who was still softly sobbing, got into the car without a word. I stayed back with Amelia to make sure everything was okay.

"No, really, Eleanor, we can't," Amelia stated. She saw me listening and moved to hold the phone between our ears, so I could hear the other side of the conversation too.

"Karmen and I think it would make for a really good double date though," Eleanor—on the other line—continued.

"Eleanor, we kind of have a situation on our hands," I cut in.

"Oh, hey, Natalie," Eleanor greeted me. "Well, what's going on? Do you guys need help? Because if twice as many hands can fix things twice as fast, we could still possibly catch dinner together."

"We, um, have an orphan sitting in Natalie's car right now," Amelia said, her voice tired.

"What?"

"You know Aniyah from the afterschool program?" I questioned.

"Yeah, of course. She took my physics lab," Eleanor answered. "She's a great girl, very ambitious and driven. Piper said she missed some labs the other day though, which is weird. Is she okay?"

"Her dad just died," I cut in, my voice just as tired as Amelia's.

"I'm sorry, what?"

"Piper found out she missed school because she was home caring for her sick dad, so we brought over a care package today, but her dad was super sick, so we took him to the ER," I explained. "But he didn't make it, and Aniyah's mom died years ago, so now she's an orphan."

"And CPS is going to come take her in the next few days, but she needs a place to stay in the meantime, and we weren't going to just abandon her," Amelia added. "She can stay at my place, but I only have one bedroom, so I have to get home and do some rearranging to figure this situation out."

"We have a spare room," Eleanor meekly said. "I mean, we have the guest bedroom for Natalie, but we have another room. It's technically

Isabella's nursery right now, but there's a twin bed in there and we can just move the crib into our room. Aniyah can stay with us."

"Eleanor, are you sure?" Amelia questioned. "Shouldn't you ask Karmen first?"

"Karmen loves kids. She'll be ecstatic."

"No offense, but teenagers are a bit different than kids," I stated.

"Trust me, it's fine. Karmen knows Aniyah too. We wouldn't be us if we weren't willing to take in younger students in need. Case in point with Natalie."

"I feel like I should be offended by that," I muttered.

"Look, I promise it'll work out. Aniyah can stay with us," Eleanor reiterated.

"Okay," Amelia gave in. "We'll bring her over in a little bit. Thank you."

"No problem. That's what friends are for, right?"

We went back to Aniyah's house so she could collect her few belongings, then we went out to the diner for milkshakes and comfort food.

"How are you doing?" Amelia asked partway through our meal.

"I'm... okay... processing things," Aniyah answered slowly. "It kind of doesn't feel real, almost like he's just away on a trip or something... like he's still going to come home."

"It might feel like that for a long time," Amelia offered. "You can remember him forever, though. You have pictures of him and of course memories of him."

"I know," Aniyah replied. "I just... well there's so much I have to deal with now. Like I need to figure out how to contact my brother, and the funeral, and it's finals week too, and I don't know how..." Aniyah trailed off, fighting hard to keep from crying.

Amelia reached across the table and rested a comforting hand on Aniyah. "Don't you worry about any of that," Amelia stated. "I'll take care of all of it. I'll arrange the funeral and figure out how to contact your brother. You just focus on healing."

"Thank you," Aniyah whispered.

When we finished eating, we took Aniyah to the store to get snacks and more comfort food. Then, before we knew it, I pulled up in front of

Eleanor's and Karmen's new house. I turned off the car and spun to face Aniyah sitting in the back seat.

"Look, you're going to be totally safe and comfortable here with Eleanor and Karmen, but I just want you to know that I'm still here for you. They have my phone number, so I'm always just a phone call away, okay? And I don't know what's going to happen after this, but no matter what, I'll always be just a phone call away."

Aniyah forced out a small smile for me. "You're... too nice," she replied. "And I don't deserve such kindness, but I'll always be grateful. Thank you for helping me when no one else was there for me."

"It's not a problem, really," I answered.

Eleanor greeted us at the door. "Hello again, Aniyah," Eleanor said, stepping aside to let us enter. "Karmen is just finishing up moving some things out of the guest room for you."

"Shame on you for making your girlfriend do all the heavy lifting," I said lightheartedly.

Eleanor looked between Amelia and me, noticing that Amelia was carrying an entire box of stuff, whereas I was only carrying a single grocery bag. "Kind of hypocritical of you to say," she stated. "Besides, the doctor cleared Karmen for lifting up to fifty pounds. She's fine."

"*Umm*, thank you for letting me stay here," Aniyah spoke up.

"It's absolutely no problem at all," Eleanor assured her.

Soon enough, Karmen appeared in the entry hall holding a shrieking Vanessa upside down. "She's upset because I wouldn't let her hit herself in the head with a hammer," Karmen deadpanned, passing the kid off to Eleanor.

"Nessie, you can't hit yourself with a hammer," Eleanor cooed to the sobbing girl, taking her into the other room.

"Sorry about that," Karmen sighed, greeting us. "A piece of the crib fell off when we moved it, so I had to fix it and Vanessa wanted to help, but... she was helping too much."

"I don't want to cause problems," Aniyah stated.

"Oh, no problem at all," Karmen assured the girl. "Honestly, we were planning on moving the crib anyway. We're happy to lend you a room for as long as you need it. Here, I'll show you to your room and give you a little house tour on the way."

Amelia passed the box of Aniyah's things off to Karmen as she headed off with Aniyah. Since I was carrying the groceries, I went off in search of the kitchen, Amelia following me. We found Eleanor in the kitchen with

Vanessa in a highchair, Eleanor working to get her a snack. Vanessa was no longer sobbing, but she still looked rather unhappy.

"The house is very nice, from what I've seen so far," Amelia commented absently.

"Oh, thanks," Eleanor replied. "We can give you a better tour later, but be warned, two toddlers and a baby make for a pretty messy house."

"Sounds like they keep you busy," I stated, dropping the bag of groceries on the kitchen table.

"Yeah, are you sure it's okay if Aniyah stays here?" Amelia questioned.

"I'm positive," Eleanor stated. She walked towards Vanessa with a plate of mac-n-cheese. "You should have seen the way Karmen reacted when I told her. I think if I let her, she'd open our house up as an orphanage..."

"I mean... you could always be foster parents," I offered.

I was kind of joking, based on the situation at hand, but Eleanor looked to me seriously. "We've talked about it before," she said. "We have to finalize our divorces and custody hearings for our own kids first though."

"Of course."

"And actually, speaking of, we could always ask our custody lawyers about Aniyah's case. They might know something," Eleanor said, shrugging. "It sounds like you really care about Aniyah's wellbeing, so it might be nice to stay informed."

"I just want her to be able to finish high school," I muttered. "She has so much potential, and right now, I know she's going to a sub-par school, but she's part of the afterschool program. We could help her apply to colleges and get scholarships. What if she can't find those resources wherever she ends up? Or what if she gets bounced around so much, she stops dreaming and only cares about surviving from day to day? I don't want that for her!"

"Trust me, if anyone has a reason to hate the foster care system, it's me," Eleanor declared. "None of us want that for Aniyah. And I know there might not be anything we can do, but that doesn't mean we can't try."

"Try what?" Karmen questioned, walking into the kitchen. She held a baby monitor in her hand, probably because the other kids were napping.

"I was just thinking we could ask our lawyers about child services and foster care... maybe just to keep an eye on Aniyah's case," Eleanor explained. "I'm not saying we could *do* anything for her, but just to make things less jarring."

"Good idea," Karmen replied. "You know who's a custody lawyer who might be extra interested in helping out one of Piper's star pupils? Veronica. Maybe we should give her a call."

"Now there's an idea," Eleanor replied with a wink.

"Aniyah's doing... about as well as I suspected," Karmen continued. "She's unpacking her things in the guest room and settling in. I left to give her some space and privacy. I told her she could come meet us in the kitchen if she wanted some company or got hungry, but there was no pressure."

I let out a loud sigh. "This whole situation is just so—" I glanced over at Vanessa who was actively fighting her mother, trying to avoid eating— "s-word in adjective form."

Eleanor burst out laughing. "Did you just censor yourself because my daughter's here?"

"The sentiment is appreciated, but let's be honest, she's heard worse from her own mother before," Karmen commented.

"Fine then, this situation is shitty," I restated. "And the week before finals too... there's no way Aniyah's going to be able to pass her exams. She's going to have to retake sophomore year."

"Then she will, and she'll be okay," Amelia said, trying to be comforting. "Aniyah is very smart and driven, you said so yourself. Just because life beat her down a little doesn't mean she isn't going to get back up, dust herself off, and keep moving forward."

"I just... she has so much potential and she's such a good kid. It seems like the whole system's out to get her, and she just can't catch a break. I just want things to be different."

I think Amelia sensed I was getting worked up, because she said, "Hey, why don't we head out? We've done all we can for today and if Aniyah needs us, she'll call, right?"

"Of course," Eleanor confirmed.

"We'll take good care of her, Natalie," Karmen assured me.

"Okay," I gave in.

23.

Realizations And Cheers To The Future

I woke to a persistent buzzing vibration near my head. Stretching out, I realized Amelia was lazily draped across me, asleep, but stirring from the noise. I reached up and found my phone, the source of the vibrating, and realized awkwardly that it was my mother calling me. I slid out from under Amelia an ounce, answering my phone.

"Hey, um, what's up?" I questioned.

"We're almost to your apartment."

Oh shit. It was move out day! And my parents were coming to help me move out! Not only that, but it meant that today was the day I had to confess that I wasn't graduating, and I had to tell them I was moving in with Eleanor and Karmen, two fully grown adults they had never met before. I unceremoniously jumped out of bed, waking Amelia completely, and searched for some clothes to change into.

"Cool, cool," I stated, trying to keep my voice level. "So, I have a lot to catch you up on, but um, I'm over checking out the new place I'm moving into. Where I'm staying over summer. But I should be back soon... like... fifteen minutes."

"Oh, so you *are* staying in the city over summer. Thanks for the heads up," my mother muttered sarcastically.

"I know. I just finalized things, crazy right? Me, always doing everything last minute, who would have thought? Anyway, I'm on my way back. See you soon. Bye." Then I promptly hung up.

When I told my parents I forgot to apply for graduation and therefore was not graduating, my dad was pretty decent about it, but my mom went through the five stages of grief. First was denial: "Oh, stop joking around, Natalie, and help me lift this box." Then anger: "How could you be such a forgetful idiot!?" Next, bargaining: "We can talk to the dean, to the president, surely there's some way to bypass this!" Onto depression: "I've failed you as a mother! It's all my fault that my only child will never amount to anything!" And then finally, acceptance: "You really think it's a good thing? That you'll have another semester to take more classes and explore your options more? And you've researched careers you'd really like? Well alright then, I guess that's the best you can do."

This process took my mother nearly three hours to go through, whereas my dad went, "How'd you manage to mess up that badly?"

And I said, "Because I'm stupid, but I learned from my mistakes and I'm moving forward now."

So, he said, "Alright, good on you," and then we packed up all my things and moved box after box while my mother continued to have a crisis.

The news of my failed graduation created a long distraction, but I knew I was going to have to explain my summer living arrangements soon enough. I was mentally planning on how I was going to do that when the absolutely unexpected happened. I was pushing another cartful of things out to my parents' SUV when I saw Karmen and Eleanor strutting across the parking lot.

"Hey, Short Stack!" Eleanor shouted at me.

"Oh, lord," I muttered under my breath.

"Are those friends of yours?" my mother questioned. "Are they seniors? They seem a little old."

I ignored my mother and ran to intersect them. "What are you guys doing here?" I asked.

"We came to give you a house key," Karmen stated, dropping a key into my hands. "We got a break after proctoring some finals, but we have to stay at school until almost six, so we wanted to make sure you could get into the house."

"Well, are you going to introduce us?" my mother declared behind me.

I turned, stepping to the side so my mom could see Eleanor and Karmen, my dad slowly making his way over to us. "Um, well, mom, this is Karmen and Eleanor. Karmen and Eleanor, meet my mom."

"Nice to meet you ladies," my mom said, nodding.

"It's kind of convenient they showed up, because I'm staying with them this summer," I stated, figuring it was as good a time as ever to break the news.

"Oh, well that's nice. How did you all meet?" my mother then asked.

"Formalities are fun, but we need to finish packing," I declared, trying to pull my mother away.

"Stop being ridiculous!" my mother protested.

"We actually need to get going too," Karmen stated. "It was lovely meeting you though. Hopefully we'll see you again."

"Bye, guys," I muttered.

"Oh, and the babysitter should still be there when you get to the house. Don't worry about her. She'll stay until we get home," Eleanor called.

"So, you *do* know what a babysitter is!" I scoffed.

"A babysitter?" my mother questioned as we parted ways. "Natalie, are those friends of yours from school? Do they have children?"

"Um, well, I mean, they're out of school, they have careers and stuff, and um, yeah, they have kids. But they've got a spare room that they're graciously letting me stay in."

"How did you meet them?"

"At, um... my job!" I declared, relieved I could just tell the truth. "You know, teaching at that high school? I just hit it off with some of the teachers there."

"Oh, well that's nice."

I sighed in relief.

We moved my necessary items into Karmen's and Eleanor's house, my parents surprisingly calm about where I was moving, though my mom was going around their house being pretty nosey. I had been helping my dad with setting some stuff up, but I decided I needed some water, so I went out to the kitchen where I found my mom sitting with Aniyah at the kitchen table. They were chatting a bit, but Aniyah had her nose in a textbook.

"Hey, uh, what's going on in here?" I asked, pulling out a glass.

"I just met Aniyah," my mother said. "Karmen and Eleanor are letting her stay here because her father just died. Isn't that nice?"

"Yeah, it is," I agreed. "How are you doing, Aniyah? Are you... studying?"

"I've decided I want to take my finals," Aniyah stated, glancing up at me. "I don't want to retake sophomore year, if I can avoid it, and I know it's a bad week, but once I get through this week, everything will be better.

Karmen and Eleanor said they could take me into school Thursday and Friday morning so I can take my finals."

"That's nice. Good on you. If you need anything, or ever want some help studying, I've got your back."

"Thanks!"

We left Aniyah and went back to work. My mother questioned me more and more about my life over the past few months, but eventually she got bored of managing my dad and me and went off wandering. My dad and I finished up, then found her out in the living room where she was conversing with the babysitter and looking at some pictures hanging on the walls. My dad headed out to the car, and I went to follow, but my mom pulled me aside in the front entry hall.

"Natalie," she said, "are you aware that these friends of yours are *lovers?*"

I stared dumbly at my mom. "*Umm*, yeah, mom, they're living together and raising their kids, what did you think they were?"

"I just... well I didn't realize it when you first told me, is all," my mother answered.

I just shook my head. "Do you want to grab some dinner before you guys leave town?"

"Sure, dear."

With Aniyah's approval, Amelia did the most cost-efficient things she could. We had her father cremated and Amelia set up a visitation at Eleanor's and Karmen's house for Tuesday evening. Monday night we sat around the kitchen table making plans and I helped Aniyah locate and contact a few family friends. Karmen helped set up an escort so Aniyah's brother could come to the visitation. Then, Tuesday evening, we all dressed in black and sat around the living room listening to stories about Aniyah's kindhearted father.

When the marshals brought Aniyah's brother in, Aniyah ran to him immediately and burst out crying in his arms. He told her he was sorry that he couldn't have been there to help her, and he swore on his life that he was going to be on his best behavior to get out of prison as soon as he could. No matter where she ended up, in foster care, adopted, or on her own, he would find her, and they would never lose contact.

Piper and Ellie 2.0 came to the visitation as well. At one point, Piper pulled me into one of the kids' rooms to talk.

"I owe you an apology," Piper stated.

"For what?" I questioned.

"For telling you to mind your own business," Piper sighed. "If you hadn't ultimately followed your heart, to think, Aniyah would have been all alone when he passed and... god, what a horrid thing. I think maybe if I had supported you right away and not been so adamant you mind your own business, you could have taken him to the hospital sooner, and then maybe—"

"Hey, don't blame yourself," I stated seriously. "What happened, happened, and we're moving forward now."

"I promise, Natalie, that in the future I will support you. Is there any way I could make it up to you for not believing in you sooner?"

"I think we should do something in honor of Aniyah's dad," I commented. "I think it would be really cool if we all spent a day volunteering in Aniyah's neighborhood, helping her community."

"Oh..." Piper muttered, shifting on her feet.

"You said you'd do anything."

"You're right," Piper gave in with a sigh. "It would really mean something to them, right? And they could use the help, surely. I... I'll do it."

"Thanks, Piper," I said, smiling, and I pulled her in for a hug.

Back out in the main room, I mingled for a bit more. The escort took Aniyah's brother away and the family friends slowly left until it was just our normal friend group plus Aniyah... though she was starting to feel more like a part of the group every day.

Eleanor, sitting on the couch, reached over and hit Piper. "Say, how's your situation with Veronica going?" she questioned.

Piper flushed. "There is *still* no situation," she declared.

"You still have her number though, right? Can you call her?"

"Wha—why!?" Piper snapped.

"We want her help with Aniyah's case. We just want to keep on top of things and do the best we can with our current situation."

"I, um... yeah. I can call her."

"Great. If she answers, let me talk to her," Eleanor said.

Amelia ended up spending the night with me at Eleanor's and Karmen's house. She said she didn't want to be left alone after the visitation, and really, Aniyah welcomed the extra company and distraction. Amelia had to proctor finals Wednesday morning, but so did Eleanor and Karmen, so they decided it would be easiest to just all carpool anyway. But that didn't mean they let Amelia off easy though.

"Just remember, we have children in this house, and the walls are thin," Karmen stated with a smirk.

I was sitting on the couch with Amelia, and she turned, pressing her face into my neck. I could feel the heat of her uncomfortableness and I just shook my head.

"We aren't going to do anything," I declared.

"Oh, please. You're two new love birds. I know how it goes," Karmen scoffed.

"Hey, Karm?" Eleanor said, tugging on Karmen's arm. "Leave them alone, alright?"

"What? I can't believe you're being the voice of mature reason here. What's gotten into you?"

"Just... let's go check up on the kids," Eleanor declared, finally pulling Karmen off down the hall.

After a minute, Amelia popped her head up and looked at me. "Are the walls really that thin?" she asked curiously. "Have you heard anything?"

"Anything juicy you mean?" I questioned. "No, just screaming children, mainly."

The following day, I was the adult of the house. Karmen and Eleanor let the babysitter have the day off since I was going to be around all day. I was up at eight when they left, begrudgingly agreeing to watch the kiddos. I spent the morning quizzing Aniyah about history and science while I balanced a baby in my arms, juggling two toddlers that were pulling at my legs while I tried to get some snacks together and entertain them with games.

Aniyah burst out laughing when Michael tugged on my arm, causing me to drop a bowl of applesauce right on Vanessa's head, who promptly started screaming. I groaned, but then I realized Aniyah had *laughed* at me. That was the first time she had laughed since her dad died. I grinned widely and laughed with her.

I dropped Michael off at the table with his snack and left Isabella in her swing to hopefully fall asleep while I took Vanessa back to clean her up. I told Aniyah to call me if anything happened, but she assured me she could handle a couple minutes of babysitting.

I didn't want to give Vanessa a full bath, but her dense curly hair was coated in applesauce, and I couldn't get it out unless I doused her with water, so it seemed like a full bath would just be easier. I had just finished stripping her down when I heard the front door open. Vanessa heard it too, screaming out, "Mommy!" before she took off at a stumbling sprint straight out of the bathroom. I quickly scrambled after her.

"Nessie, what in the world?" Eleanor questioned as the naked, applesauce covered kid threw herself into her mother's legs. Karmen moved and scooped the girl up, looking at her curiously, before glancing at me as I ran down the hall.

"Sorry, sorry," I gasped. "I was trying to clean off the applesauce, but well... she got excited when she heard the door. Why are you guys back so soon, anyway? Did they cancel some finals? Because I find that a little hard to believe."

"We got a call from child protective services," Eleanor stated, concern evident in her voice. "An agent is coming to collect Aniyah in an hour."

"What!?" I gasped. "Why? And they can't! She has finals to take tomorrow!"

"Apparently they located an aunt that's willing to take her, and they'd much rather have Aniyah in the care of a family member than staying with some strangers that aren't officially qualified to be fosters," Eleanor explained as Karmen headed off to get Vanessa cleaned up.

"Did you say an aunt?" Aniyah called from the kitchen. "That's got to be the aunt my dad hated! She was always awful, hated kids, I don't—"

"They can't take her!" I snapped. "She doesn't want to go, she has to finish studying for finals, and they can't take her!"

Another person stepped into the house behind Eleanor, and I turned to find Veronica. surprisingly. "I'm here to hopefully mediate," she stated. "I don't know if there's anything we can do, but..."

"I don't think we really have a say in the matter," Eleanor continued, walking towards the kitchen. We all followed her. "Apparently, her aunt has right to custody, and Aniyah is moving in with her, effective immediately."

"Yes, if this aunt isn't fit to be a legal guardian, they'll review the case in about a month," Veronica added. "Until then though, legally, Aniyah is going to have to stay with this aunt. If she doesn't, or you don't let her, they'll charge Eleanor and Karmen with kidnapping."

"And with our own custody hearings coming up, we can't have that on our records," Eleanor added.

"No, of course not," I agreed. "But there has to be something else we can do!"

"Natalie, I—I don't want to stay with my aunt, please! She makes me uncomfortable!" Aniyah pleaded. "And what if she won't drive me to school to take my finals?"

"We're getting you to school, one way or another, even if I have to physically fight off your aunt to get you there," I huffed.

"Now, let's not be brash," Veronica stated.

I startled slightly at the sound of the doorbell going off.

"Shit, they're early," Eleanor huffed, scurrying off with Veronica to get the door. And I, mad—livid past the point of logic—sprinted after them.

Eleanor opened the front door to reveal a woman, probably a social worker of some kind, and a burly police officer who was escorting her, evidently to make sure things went smoothly.

"Hello," Eleanor greeted them kindly, but I wasn't feeling so nice.

"You can't take her!" I shouted, pushing Eleanor aside and blocking the doorway. "Look, she doesn't like her aunt and she says her aunt is bad news, so she's not going."

"Ma'am, please," the officer stated. "We can do this the easy way, or the hard way, but I'm thinking everyone is going to prefer the easy way."

"Thank you, Carl. It's okay," the woman stated gently. "My name is Sophia Chomsky and I'm the lawyer that has been assigned to Aniyah Smith's case."

"She doesn't need you. She's already got a lawyer," I huffed.

"Hi," Veronica stated, peeking out from around my shoulder. "I'm just... a friend. Though I am a custody lawyer. I've just been advising these ladies. And Natalie, I would *advise* you to step aside and let these people in."

I crossed my arms and stared more challengingly at Sophia.

Sophia nodded. "Natalie was it?" she asked me.

"Yes."

"Hello, Natalie. What seems to be your issues and concerns regarding Aniyah?"

"She doesn't like this aunt that you guys have decided she has to stay with," I huffed. "And look, she just lost her father less than a week ago, plus it's finals week at school, so she's dealing with a lot right now. She doesn't need this added stress on top of it all."

"To the best of our knowledge, Aniyah's aunt is a suitable caregiver, at least temporarily," Sophia explained. "She has children of her own and has never had a run in with child services. She has no felonies or arrests in the last twenty years. Unfortunately, things must move rather quickly for newly orphaned children. If there truly are issues with Aniyah staying with her aunt, we can review those issues in about a month. However, in the meantime, Aniyah needs to be with a guardian."

Veronica rested her hand on my shoulder, but it shrugged it off. "It's only perhaps temporary, Natalie," she stated. "And I can assure you that I will work hard to make sure they're doing what's best for Aniyah."

"Can't you just wait until the freaking weekend once she's done with her finals!?" I shouted.

Sophia frowned slightly. "You seem very concerned with Aniyah's wellbeing and education... may I ask how it is that you know Aniyah?"

"I'm a friend," I stated confidently. "Kind of an older mentor, I guess. She was a student in the biology lab I ran."

"I see," Sophia said, nodding. "Are you the homeowner?"

"No, that would be me," Eleanor stated, poking her head around the door frame. "I own this house with my partner who—" she paused, listening to a wail break out from the backroom— "is tending to one of our unhappy toddlers right now. I apologize. We have a three-month-old, a two-year-old, and a three-year-old."

"Well... the agency has set rules we follow, but I don't see why we couldn't make an exception here," Sophia declared. "Would you mind if I come in and looked around? If I feel your set up is adequate, I'm fine with allowing Aniyah to stay here until Saturday."

"Really?" I questioned, eyes gleaming.

"If I find things suitable," Sophia restated. She turned to Eleanor. "May I ask how you and your partner have come to know Aniyah?"

"Of course," Eleanor replied, stepping aside to let Sophia and the officer into the house. "We're both teachers at Elk Creek. Aniyah attends our afterschool program. We've both taught her."

"Oh, you work at Elk Creek?" Sophia questioned. "I'll still need to run background checks, but I suspect there won't be anything, noting your place of employment. Elk Creek vets its teachers quite thoroughly, as I'm sure you're aware."

"Yes, we're aware."

I followed the case worker around as Eleanor gave her a tour of the house, Veronica following right beside Eleanor. They discussed Eleanor's life in more detail, with mediation via Veronica. Karmen met up with us at one point, carrying a less than happy Isabella with a clean and clothed Venessa trailing close behind. Sophia met all the kids, including Michael, and then she pulled Aniyah aside to talk to her in private—though Veronica went with them.

Afterwards, Veronica requested to speak with Eleanor and Karmen in private. I wanted to ease drop on the conversation, but Sophia kept watching me like a hawk, so I was forced to stay put. When they came back out, they requested conference with Sophia to discuss final details. Finally, with the officer preoccupied, I escaped back into the hall and pressed my ear against the closed door of the room they were in, listening.

"Your house, current living conditions, and set up for Aniyah, as well as your own personal and emotional wellbeing all seem to be great," Sophia began. "Aniyah expressed that she would much prefer to stay here for as long as possible, so I'm willing to allow her to stay here until Saturday." I smiled, squeezing my hands together to keep from making noise. "And personally, if you two are interested, I could work with you to move through the process of becoming foster parents if you would like to house Aniyah here for longer."

"We were loosely debating such things," Eleanor said.

"The process wouldn't interfere with their custody hearings or divorces, correct?" Veronica asked.

"It shouldn't, no. If anything, it could help," Sophia answered. "If a judge knows you've been approved as foster parents, they'll know your home and intentions are in line with proper child-rearing."

"We'll... have to think about it," Karmen replied.

"Of course. Just something to think about if you're interested," Sophia said. "Here's my card if you have any questions. Veronica, if you'd wish to work collaboratively, as you seem to know this group and family well, here's my card also."

"Thank you."

"Unfortunately, because you aren't currently approved for fostering, I'll have to come back Saturday and collect Aniyah. In the meantime, however, I will look further into investigating her aunt and therefore, if she truly is unsuitable, Aniyah won't have to stay there, and we will find other housing. But Aniyah will not be allowed to remain here."

"We understand," Eleanor commented. "Thank you for being flexible with our situation."

"There wouldn't be much point in being a social worker if I couldn't help cater to the happiness of every child I encountered," Sophia replied. "I promise that I'll do my best to put Aniyah in a loving, caring home."

"Thank you," Karmen added.

Sensing the conversation was ending, I moved to step away from the door, but I was too late. Sophia opened the door before I could get away and I fell right to my knees in front of her. She chuckled at me, helping me stand.

"And you, Natalie," Sophia commented. "I applaud you for standing up for Aniyah and fighting for her current situation. If no one fights for the best for these kids... it's easy for them to end up in sub-par homes. Very rarely will an adult come along that is so willing to listen to a child."

"*Umm...* thanks," I muttered.

"Keep doing what you're doing and don't stop fighting for Aniyah," she stated. "I'll do the best I can from my end, but your push back from the other end will always be much appreciated."

"You're the first person to ever compliment my stubbornness," I laughed.

"Lawyers have to be stubborn and unyielding to help their clients. And although you might be a bit brash in your demands, I can tell you pour your heart into every word. That passion is important for us lawyers too."

Huh... how interesting...

Eleanor and Karmen didn't return to work after that, so Piper dropped Amelia off at their house that evening so she could pick up her car again. Karmen invited everyone to stay for dinner and we had a pleasant evening just talking.

"You know, Veronica's a pretty nice person," Eleanor commented flippantly. "She didn't even hesitate to come help when you asked, and she was ready to do literally *anything* to help us."

I glanced to Piper, who was blushing, her head down, ignoring Eleanor.

"She asked about you," Eleanor continued, pointing her fork at Piper. "She misses you."

"I've been busy with finals," Piper finally choked out.

"She really likes kids, you know, and she's *good* with kids. She helped us with Isabella and Nessie while we were getting things situated."

"I invited her to stay for dinner," Karmen added, "but she said she had work she needed to finish up. Such a shame."

"Wow, look at the time," Piper declared. "I think I best get home and relieve the babysitter."

"What babysitter!?" Eleanor barked as Piper quickly darted away from the table. "You mean Ellie 2.0 and Cliff? Who *live* with you!?"

"Bye!" Piper shouted as she slipped out of the house.

After we all laughed, Amelia and I helped clear the table while Eleanor and Karmen started getting the kids ready for bed. Aniyah helped with dishes, then she headed to bed herself, wanting to get as much sleep as she could. Down to just Amelia and me, we stepped out onto the porch to talk for a while longer, where I continued to ramble on about the day's events.

"I just think it was really cool that she was willing to review our situation and change her mind based on what we wanted and what Aniyah wanted," I said. "Sure, they have general protocols for things, but when I put up a fight, she was willing to compromise."

"She sounds like a very good lawyer and a nice person," Amelia commented, "someone who is genuinely happy to be working to make a difference in the lives of struggling kids."

"I know... she's pretty amazing," I said in awe. "She's out there, every day, fighting to give these kids a second, better chance at life. How cool is that?"

"It's pretty amazing."

"You know what else was kind of weird? She said that my stubbornness and passion were two traits that make for a great lawyer. Isn't that crazy?"

"I don't know," Amelia answered with a shrug. "I think you have a lot of qualities that would make for a good lawyer. I've told you that before."

"I guess... but law school sounds really daunting..."

"You could do it. As I say, when there's a will, there's a way."

"Stop sounding like a motivational poster."

That night, I lied in bed, still thinking about what had happened. I was so glad Aniyah was going to get to take her finals, and I hoped she would knock them out of the park. I wanted the world for her, but it wasn't just her. I wanted the world for all my students in the afterschool lab. I wanted the world for all the choir students. I wanted the world for all the kids who were struggling.

I heard muffled giggling through the wall, and I groaned. The walls *were* kind of thin and I was unfortunately right next to Eleanor's and Karmen's bedroom. There was more giggling, but not just innocent giggling, it was flirtatious giggling, pre-amble giggling to a lot of stuff I didn't want to hear.

I debated just plugging my ears and ignoring it—I was the intruder in their house, after all—but as Karmen had said, there were kids in the house! I got out of bed and walked over to the far wall that I shared with their bedroom, ready to knock on the wall, but when I got closer, I realized I could hear, rather clearly, what they were saying. I froze.

"Should we call Veronica and Sophia, ask them about becoming foster parents?" Karmen questioned, her tone clearly more serious than the giggles from just a moment before.

"Do you want to foster kids?" Eleanor asked in return.

"I know how much you hated your time in foster care, with good reason too. So, if we could be the perfect household for a couple of kids, even if it's just for a little while, wouldn't that make such a big difference in their lives?"

Eleanor sighed. "But they'd still be in foster care. They'd either be with us for a little bit before getting transferred to a shitty home, or they'll grow up with us and move out never having had a real family of their own."

"We could be a family for them."

"If you want them to be part of our family, why not just adopt them?"

"Do you want to adopt?" Karmen asked.

"Do you want more kids?" Eleanor countered.

"Yes, if you want more."

"And you'd want to adopt them?"

"You know the doctor said I likely would never be able to have another kid, and I know you have no interest in getting pregnant again. Besides, I know how you feel about the foster care system. There are tons of children that need forever homes. If we're going to have more kids, we should adopt."

"I think that would be nice."

"But then, what about Aniyah?" Karmen questioned. "If we don't get certified to foster, she'll end up with her aunt or dumped into the rest of the system. You know Natalie's right. There's more bad than good out there. I would hate to see Aniyah's potential collapse just because of the way people treat her."

There was a long pause of silence. It was so long, in fact, that I thought they might have slipped into the bathroom, too far away for me to hear. But then, after so long, Eleanor spoke, so quiet I almost didn't catch it: "Let's adopt her."

"What? Adopt Aniyah?" Karmen clarified.

"I mean, obviously it'll be complicated with the hearings, and it'll take time, so likely in the very least Aniyah would have to spend the summer in another home. But she's only, what, sixteen? She's still a minor and she's an orphan. Besides, don't act like you don't love her just as much as Natalie does. I know how close you two got when she took your class."

Another beat passed, but far shorter in comparison. "You're right. I love her too much to see her lost to the system. It would mean so much more to adopt her rather than just foster her. Are you sure though? That's a very serious decision."

"I'm very sure. Are you?"

"Yes."

"I'll make some calls in the morning then. We can work something out, I'm sure."

I stumbled back from the wall, my heart pounding. Would... would they really adopt Aniyah? Would Aniyah be part of our little teacher family... forever?

Thursday I was elated. I felt like I could take on the entire world. That was what social worker Sophia did to me. She made me think anything was possible. The private conversation I had overheard between Karmen and Eleanor made me feel like we had won. It wasn't set in stone though, nothing was. I wasn't going to say anything to Aniyah, just in case. And I knew helping her just meant there were thousands of other kids out there still needing help, but I felt like things were finally looking up and I felt like I was floating.

The afterschool program was over, and I officially no longer had a job at Elk Creek. My termination was partly due to my lack of a degree, but also due to me expressing to the principal that I didn't think teaching was for me. Everyone at Elk Creek was still super nice to me though, and I had five friends willing to break me into the school at all hours of the day (not even counting the choir kids, who I was sure would do the same). I had signed up for some more classes for next semester—a couple sociology classes, a business class, and even a pre-law class, just out of curiosity. I drove Aniyah to school that morning so she could take her finals and then just wasted time until Amelia was done at work.

At Elk Creek, finals were finished for the school year. Amelia was still entering in grades, and I thought Eleanor might also be, so I swung by her room to try and talk to her about the conversation I had overheard. Her classroom door was locked though and the lights out inside, so I figured she had already left, maybe busy meeting with Sophia and Veronica to talk logistics. Either way, I was still ecstatic.

Finally, I got to the choir room and without preamble threw open the doors. I heard Amelia gasp in surprise.

"Can you stop doing that?" she huffed. "One of these days you're going to give me a real heart attack, and then we'll all be sorry!"

"I'm sorry," I stated, "but you should be used to it by now."

"Why so excited?" Amelia questioned, turning to face me as I bounded up to her.

"I'm just—just—so happy!" I squealed. "I'm excited for the classes I'm going to take next semester, and I'm excited about what Sophia did for Aniyah, and I'm excited she's getting to take her finals, and I'm excited that Eleanor and Karmen—oh wait, no, that's a secret, I can't—"

"A secret?" Amelia questioned, looking at me pointedly.

"Yeah, I can't tell you."

"I'm your girlfriend. Spill!"

"Unfair," I declared, fake pouting. "It's a secret about them, not me. I would never withhold personal information from you, but other people are a different story."

"That's because you're such a good person," Amelia declared, grinning.

She stepped towards me, wrapping her arms around me, before she pulled me in for a kiss. Quickly, I was lost in the sensation, only adding to my happy state, and when we pulled apart my head felt fuzzy, and my chest felt warm.

Amelia grinned wider. "So, what was that thing about Eleanor and Karmen?"

I narrowed my eyes at her. "You play dirty," I stated. "But fine. I overheard them talking about something last night."

"Which was...?"

"They were discussing if they wanted to become foster parents, so they could keep Aniyah," I explained. "And they settled on an agreement, I think, but it wasn't what I was expecting."

"Are they going to try and foster her then?"

"No. They're going to try and adopt her."

"What? Really!?" Amelia gasped, leaping into my arms to hug me. "Natalie, do you know how great that would be!?"

"I know, I know, but it's not official yet, so calm down."

"It would be such a great match," Amelia said dreamily.

"I know, and I really hope it works out. I'm just so happy things seem to be working out for Aniyah—as good as they can, I mean. But I just... well I keep thinking about what would have happened to Aniyah if we weren't here for her. And I've been thinking about how it's all worked out because we have Eleanor—who fights so passionately for struggling kids— but how we wouldn't have Eleanor if it wasn't for her grandmother—who stepped in when no one else would and took care of her despite the racism of her socioeconomic status. Like, what would have happened to Eleanor if she had to stay in foster care? I keep thinking about all the kids that are in foster care now, or living with real shit parents, and I just... what could they become if they could escape the system and end up in a loving home?"

"That social worker really inspired you, huh?"

"I just think she's amazing. And I think the work she's doing is amazing too," I confessed. "I wish I could represent all those kids and fight for them the way we're fighting for Aniyah. They all deserve someone to fight for them... each and every one of them."

Amelia smiled kindly at me, reaching out to tuck my hair behind my ear. Then, she rested her hand against my jaw. "Natalie, darling," she said softly, "no one's saying you *can't* do that."

"What do you mean?"

"If you want to help homeless kids find homes... if you want to help orphaned kids find families... if you want to fight for the children forgotten in the world... if you want to unite families that will survive the tests of time... well, you can."

I pushed back from Amelia, just staring into her eyes. She was right. I had always deeply cared for the wellbeing of kids. I shouted horrifically at Nicholas' father because I hated how he treated his son. I felt the need to stand up for all the choir kids because I knew how they were treated back home. I felt the need to protect and help students in the afterschool program, realizing thanks to them and my friends that the world was a messed-up place. There was racism, sexism, homophobia, socioeconomic differences that were all fighting against minority kids. None of those kids deserved that. They didn't set up the society that persecuted them, they were just born into it with no say in the matter, then forgotten and cast aside.

Sophia, the first social worker lawyer I had ever really seen in action, inspired me. At first, I thought she was the enemy, trying to take Aniyah away from us. But when I fought back, she was willing to listen and compromise, because like me, she wanted the best possible situation for Aniyah as well. She lived her daily life fighting to help kids. She was doing what she could to make a difference, to set kids up in better households that could grant them better opportunities. She was making an impact.

Those kids, who were silenced by the lives they were given, needed someone who was willing to help them when no one else would. They needed someone like Amelia, who would listen to them when they felt voiceless. They needed someone like Karmen who would hold their hand and let them know they were valid. They needed someone like Ellie 2.0 who would educate them and give them a voice. They needed someone like Piper who would teach them to be fully good people and make good choices. They needed someone like Eleanor who would fight for them because they deserved better. They needed a social worker with the passion and stubbornness to never give up, even when things seemed impossible.

They needed *me*.

"Amelia," I breathed out heavily. "I know what I want to do with the rest of my life."

The End